GREEN CITY SAVIOR

A GREEN CITY NOVEL

CHRISTEN CIVILETTO

BUFFALO, NY

Christen Civiletto
www.ChristenCiviletto.com
info@christenciviletto.com

Publisher's Note: This is a work of fiction. Names, characters, places, and incidents are a
product of the author's imagination. Locales and public names are sometimes used for
atmospheric purposes. Any resemblance to actual people, living or dead, or to businesses, companies, events, institutions, or locales is completely coincidental.

Scripture taken from Holy Bible, New International Version®, NIV® Copyright © 1973,
1978, 1984, 2011 by Biblica, Inc.® Used by permission. All rights reserved worldwide.

Book Layout ©2013 BookDesignTemplates.com
Book cover design by BespokeBookCovers.com

Ordering Information:
Quantity sales. Special discounts are available on quantity purchases by corporations,
associations, and others. For details, contact the "Special Sales Department" at the address above.

Green City Savior/ Christen Civiletto. -- 1st ed.
ISBN 978-0-9861163-0-8

Praise for Green City Savior

Christians should be at the forefront of preventing and responding to degradation of God's creation. *Green City Savior* reminds us of our Genesis 2:15 role to tend and protect the planet. Thank you, Christen Civiletto, for this timely book on the importance of faithful stewardship.

Nancy Sleeth, author of *Almost Amish* and co-founder of Blessed Earth

Green City Savior is truly an impressive and inspirational book. The book depicts the devastating effects of environmental pollution and how the environment, individuals, and communities were adversely affected. The book tells a fascinating and captivating story of how lives were forever changed because of the misconduct of others. Yet, the book demonstrates how the hand of God can change lives and communities through the efforts of just a few dedicated and determined individuals ... I highly recommend *Green City Savior* as book which you will enjoy reading.

Stephen King, Ph.D., M.Div., M.P.H., Toxicologist & Epidemiologist

Ms. Civiletto paints a vivid picture of a broken city in need of restoration. As she weaves shocking events through her story you may feel the need to do some research of your own. And a few glimpses of corroborating evidence will leave you wondering just how much chilling truth is actually encompassed in this important work of fiction.

Rebekah Ruth, author of *Where the Pink Houses Are*

Green City Savior demonstrates a trilogy of events that could only be orchestrated by our Lord and Savior. God puts in each of us a unique gift of awareness and understanding when "something is just not right." A great story and a great gut check to each of us and our role of awareness in nature and society.

Dr. Shawn Benzinger, Physician/talk show host

To my family – the rich handiwork of God never ceases to amaze me;

To my mom, Judy, and the memory of the late father, Charles, who instilled in me a desire to stand up to wrong things;

To the memory of my Grandma Yola, for her lifelong commitment to good health and wellness;

To the memory of my noni, Josephine, for her unabashed love of Jesus;

and

To the people of Niagara Falls, New York. Our story should be told.

*Yours, Lord, is the greatness and the power
and the glory and the majesty and the splendor,
for everything in heaven and earth is yours.
Yours, Lord, is the kingdom;
you are exalted as head over all.*

1 Chronicles 29:11

Acknowledgements

My family supported this effort, listened to my ideas, and read and re-read my manuscripts for years. Thank you Bill Morris, Julia, Mark, Max, and Luke. I love you all.

Thank you also to my mom and my siblings and their families. You and other family members offered prayer, support, and so much more. I especially thank Antoinette DeMiglio, for speaking the Word over my life; Elio Desiderio for your encouragement and expertise; Cindy Krause, for your keen observation of information relevant to this book; Bob and Marge Houldson for your unwavering support; Jim and Dixie Roberts for your love; and Carmen and Debbie Panaro, for your Bible knowledge. I offer heartfelt thanks to my close friends who cheered me on, or impacted some specific aspect of this book, particularly Karen Orlando, Barbara Luba, Nicole Oursler, Carol Haynes, Alice Whistler (and sisters!), Lisa Wallens, Andrea Segat MacMillian, Jennifer Steinberg, Tracey Axnick, Kristen Adams Smith, Jane and Didier Lasserre, and Robbie Raugh and the rest of our LifeLinks group (especially Beth, Jaimeelynn, Ann, Kim, and Linda).

I greatly appreciate those who read all or portions of this manuscript. You offered helpful suggestions and advice, and gave willingly of your time. Thank you especially to writers Rebekah Ruth, Mary Nero, LoraLee Kodzo, Kathy Ide, Beverly Varnado, Lynn Elibol, Paul Chimera, Chris Morris, and Rebecca Rohan; producer Will Battersby; and readers Robert Strassburg, Art Fromm, and Louis Marcantonio. The members of the Ink & Keys Writer's Group in Buffalo, New York, also offered thoughtful feedback and enthusiastic encouragement—thank you Rebekah Weissert, Lisa Littlewood, Laura Lewis, Kelly Baesen, and Marissa Albrecht. You've all blessed me.

I am grateful for the assistance given by various medical, law enforcement, nuclear, and technical diving experts, including Samuel Morris, Ellen and Garold Morris, as well as a number of other professionals who wish to remain anonymous. Thank you Pastors Daryl Largis, Deone Drake, and Jerry Gillis for solid Biblical teaching. Any errors in this novel are mine, not theirs.

Above all, thank you Almighty God, in whose hand is the life of every creature and the breath of all mankind.

CHAPTER ONE

Dear citizens of Niagara Falls,

You may have known me as Joseph Salvatore Malvisti, business owner, church deacon, family man. A pillar of the city's Italian-American community. I'm "good people," as the locals like to say.

Don't listen to them.

One crisp fall evening in 1946 I made a decision that forever changed the great city of Niagara Falls. It was not a change for the better, as most of you know by now. I would do things differently if I had the chance.

At least, I have to believe I would.

My choice led to devastation and heartache for many. It marred the pristine beauty of the Niagara Frontier and shook my fellow citizens' faith in government.

But that pales in comparison to what it did to my family.

It's probably too late for my redemption, but perhaps not for that of my grandchildren or our legacy. And it's certainly not too late for this city. Niagara Falls is ripe for a rebirth—a return to its former glory and natural beauty. An existence unmarred by toxic defilement or political corruption. Or pride.

You, my friends, have a promising future.

But you need my help.

Enclosed in the accompanying envelope is a memoir, of sorts, that I dictated to a trusted friend. (Weeks of staring at nothing but sterile white sheets and barren hospital walls give a sick man plenty of time to think ... and write.) It's partly my immigration story. An account of how a young Italian man, a boy, really, who arrived in America with nothing but a few childish trinkets in his pocket, built a business that employed and shaped an American city. I reveal some of my deepest hopes, my greatest successes, and my crushing failures.

But it's also the story of Niagara Falls.

Like me, this once-magnificent city soared through the early part of the twentieth century on the wings of industry, only to crash and burn by its end, leaving brokenness in its wake. Corruption has worked its way into the very fiber of this place. It lives as openly as the abject poverty you see on a drive through downtown. The story of my life is bound up in the good and the bad, the right and the wrong, of my adopted hometown.

You are entitled to the truth about what happened to this city and why. I hope that you examine the justifications I offer. Talk about the rationalizations for the choices I made. My desire is that you make better decisions for the future after learning of my mistakes. George Santayana had it right when he said, "Those who cannot remember the past are condemned to repeat it." The past millennium has been marked by astonishing advancements in technology, rivaled only by man's equally stupendous foolishness. Mine included.

Sharing the truth is a start. But this memoir contains something equally important. I aim to inspire you with an innovative idea for the future of Niagara Falls. I've laid the groundwork. I've done what I could. Now it's your turn. Prepare to be renewed, inside and out, my friends. Who says man can't think his way out of despair?

I finished recording this story a few hours ago, knowing the end is near for me. My heart seeks to dwell on eternal things now; I'm done with the hurts and mistakes of this world. But I've asked my friend to make sure the memoir isn't released until both of my adult sons, Joseph Jr. and Salvatore, are dead. You may wonder why I'm waiting until my sons are gone from this earth to make public the truth. I'm not really sure. Guilt certainly plays a part. I failed to provide the guidance required of a father. Since their mistakes are a direct result of mine, I can't live with the thought of helping to send them to prison.

But I also failed to provide the leadership and accountability demanded of a man esteemed in our community.

At least one of those failures is about to change.

CHAPTER TWO

Niagara Falls, New York

D on't go any closer to the water, Harrison James!" The noise of the rushing river snatched away Lydia's words. A few yards away, her six-year-old son stood on top of an old fallen tree, his little hands gripping his fishing rod and his eyes glued to the bobber at the end of his line. Despite her anxiety, she allowed herself a small smile. He'd waited all winter for the chance to catch his first fish.

"Something's gonna bite. I know it." Her first-grader edged toward the shoreline along the trunk worn smooth from years of exposure to the elements. He stopped just shy of where their neighbor's boot-clad foot rested on the dead tree.

"Stay close, boy," Mr. Mahoney growled. His lawn chair rocked unevenly over the top of a thick limb anchored in the mud.

Lydia caught her neighbor's sidelong glance as she and her younger son worked their way down the short embankment behind them. She nodded in response, and then did a double take. Mr. Mahoney held one end of a thin, braided rope. The other end was threaded through Harrison's belt loops and knotted twice around the boy's waist.

The old man leaned forward in his chair. "Your mother will whip my backside if something happens to you."

"Yes, sir."

"This river can sweep you away like that." He snapped his fingers. "You'd be dragged through the rapids and launched right over the American Falls. Got it?"

"Got it." Harrison took another step back, still focused on the bobber. Mr. Mahoney pulled his feet out of the way.

She'd given Harrison the same lecture this morning. Few people had ever gone over those cascades and lived to tell about it.

Lydia's three-year-old yanked on her hand, pulling her through the stick-like brush crowding the foot of the bank.

"Slow down, Trav." She ducked under an oversized, leafless bush. No signs of spring yet.

"I wanna catch a shark." Travis jumped down the last foot to the shore. "C'mon, Mommy."

"Not today." She had to shout above the gusting wind. "When you're a little older, okay?"

"What?"

"When you're older, Trav, like your brother." Raising her voice made it sound harsher than she meant. "This isn't a good place for you to fish."

Lydia wasn't sure Harrison should be fishing here either. In their protected alcove alongside a concrete structure, the water appeared to be no more than a ruffled eddy. But twenty feet beyond where they stood, it became a river on a mission to connect one vast lake to another.

"Not fair!" He stuck out his bottom lip.

"Sorry, love." Lydia thought she heard her cell. Using her knee and elbow to keep Travis close, she pulled it out of her purse. But her ears, aching from the noise of the fluctuating wind and the rapid current, must've tricked her. No missed calls, which meant no potential home buyers or promising listings. She squeezed the slider cell phone closed, shoving it in the front pocket of her purse.

"Need help?" Mr. Mahoney shouted over his shoulder.

"Nope," she yelled back. "Thank you anyway." She shook her head, grinning. For all the fatherly concern he showed her, and even if he had the money to spare, Mr. Mahoney couldn't provide the kind of help she needed.

Together she and Travis picked their way over dead branches and smooth, fist-sized stones to join Harrison and her neighbor at the water's edge. Travis's worn sneakers slipped a few times on the debris strewn all over the narrow beach.

"Hold tight."

Mr. Mahoney's few strands of white hair blew haphazardly around his head. Without his trademark Yankees cap, and in his gray work gear, he looked almost like an extension of the ancient tree beneath him. Secure and enduring; just what she needed in a friend.

"I've got a nibble!" Harrison spread his legs to brace himself. His thin limbs appeared skeletal as the wind pressed his loose jeans against his legs.

Mr. Mahoney sat upright.

"Be careful," Lydia called out. A chilly blast of air rocked her off balance.

"I think it might be a bass!"

Lydia scanned the river, but all she could focus on were the countless whitecaps. She tightened her hold on Travis's hand. "The wind is so strong down here," Lydia shouted to her neighbor.

"And smells bad." Travis wiped his nose on his sleeve.

She looked upwind at the aging row of factories a quarter mile away. Both sides of the river were dotted with red brick smokestacks, their rims smeared black from years of operation. Usually the acrid odor of dead fish and sulfur-like emissions went unnoticed. Everyone in town was used to it. But today it seemed particularly intense, like the river appeared to be.

She wondered if the dozen or so fishermen on the concrete landing had noticed it.

As Harrison played with his catch, Lydia noticed a fit, middle-aged man in a military haircut standing at the edge of the concrete structure, watching. Something about the man drew her attention. He held a book, but no pole.

"I got one! I got one!" Harrison's skinny arms trembled as he yanked the line to set the hook. "C'mon, Mr. Mahoney. I need the bucket!"

"Old folks don't hurry, my boy." Mr. Mahoney stood and grabbed Lydia's free arm for support. "You probably just caught some seaweed anyway."

"Maybe it's a giant shark!" Travis bounced while Lydia held his hand. Each hop wrenched her back.

"Let's see what we've got here." Mr. Mahoney hobbled to Harrison's side. His arthritic fingers covered the boy's small ones on the cork handle. "Stay steady now. Don't jerk the rod."

Together they wound the plastic reel, pulling against the current. Travis inched closer to his brother, but Lydia maintained a firm grip to keep him out of the way.

"There we go. Easy, easy."

Lydia looked on the scene with an ache in her heart. Her father should have been the one to teach Harrison to fish. Or the boys' dad, except that work had been his priority when he was alive. But both men were gone now. Someone must've watched over her when she chose the house next door to Mr. Mahoney.

A dark fish thrashed wildly as it broke the surface. Harrison and Mr. Mahoney flung the agitated creature into a five-gallon container with a few inches of river water in it. It landed belly up, splashing water everywhere. The fish heaved its thick body and thumped dully against the plastic.

"Yes!" Travis yanked his hand out of Lydia's grasp and headed for the pail. Harrison jumped off the dead tree. While Mr. Mahoney unhooked the rope from his belt, the boys bent over the bucket to examine the catch.

Their eyes went wide. Travis looked from his brother to the fish, his small mouth frozen in an O.

"What's wrong?"

No answer. Maybe Travis didn't hear her.

Harrison took a giant step back, nearly tripping on a piece of drift-wood. His face paled. "Mom ... that's not a fish." He grabbed his mother's hand. His body shook.

Lydia looked at Mr. Mahoney. His face was white too. "Get me the lid," he said in his characteristically stern voice.

Harrison rushed to deliver the cover, then sprinted back to Lydia without a glance at the fish, or at his brother still hovering over it.

"What's the problem?" Lydia moved closer, urging Harrison to come along. It couldn't be that bad.

"Come and look." Mr. Mahoney stepped aside.

Even before she reached the pail, the stench of decay assaulted Lydia's nose. The putrid smell triggered memories of her childhood days, living along the banks of the muddy creek just west of Love Canal. One sum-mer her brother caught a bullhead that smelled just like this one. It rest-ed on the creek shoreline and stared at them with dull eyes sunk deep in a misshapen head. A head that sported an unnatural, baseball-sized growth. They caught dozens more like it over the next few summers. Back then sick fish were common. And her brother had been healthy.

The repulsive fish in Mr. Mahoney's pail looked the same, except the growth was bigger. This creature appeared as though a mud pie the size of a dessert plate had been thrown at its head and then fossilized. Dark crags and blistered nodules marked the gross protrusion. Its eyes were virtually eclipsed by it.

Her throat constricted. She couldn't look away.

Travis stood on tiptoe, trying to get a closer look. "It's furry?"

"Just gills and ... a sickness, honey." She couldn't say the word tumor. Too many bad associations. "Let's cross our fingers that it's the only one in this river."

"It's not." Mr. Mahoney pressed the lid into place, thumping it for good measure. "Certainly didn't want this to be Harrison's first experience at catching a fish...."

"Should we put it out of its misery?" Lydia asked, hoping Harrison and Travis couldn't hear her over the river noise.

"No. The DEC might want to measure it. The guys at the fishing club sent a dozen others over to them last fall." He gathered the boys' fishing poles and tackle boxes.

"The Department of Environmental Conservation?" Her eye twitched. "Don't they come around only when there's a problem?"

"Yes, indeed, missy." He picked up the bucket. "You shouldn't be too surprised. Maybe you were too young to remember, but in the '80s, lots of agencies tracked tumors in Great Lakes fish. My buddies and I used to see who could snag the most disgusting one."

"I thought all that dumping around the city was over?" The implications of another potential contamination problem crossed her mind. One more reason people wouldn't want to buy a home here. "Someone's keeping an eye on our area, right?"

"The politicians?" Her neighbor's eyes narrowed. "No. And I'll tell you why—"

Mr. Mahoney was cut off by a shout. The athletic man with the crew cut launched himself over the platform's side railing onto the narrow shore, tossing his book aside mid-leap. He scrambled across the rocky beach toward Lydia.

"Your boy! He's in the water!"

The man raced past her. Lydia spun around and saw that the old tree was partially dislodged from where it had been anchored in the beach. Travis lay on a section several yards from the shoreline, his stomach draped over the trunk. His legs and hips dragged in the water. His little hands held a smooth, short limb in a death grip.

A strangled cry escaped her throat.

One thick branch of the tree remained secured in the muddy shore. But it would work its way loose in no time.

Lydia lurched toward the water, her heart pounding hard. She slipped on the rocks. Her ankle twisted, pain stabbing through her lower leg. Mr. Mahoney reached out to break her fall, but Lydia's momentum knocked him backward into his chair.

She fell into the thigh-deep water. Stiff coontail plants, with their clusters of forked leaves, scratched her hands and wrists. She clawed at the muck and pondweeds to right herself, her leg throbbing in time with her heart.

Lydia lifted her head from the water and spit foul-tasting water from her mouth. Distorted cries of alarm echoed across the river and back. She had to get to her boy. But the algae-covered rocks made it impossible for her to stand, much less move forward.

"I'm coming, Travis!" she shouted over the thunderous river that kept her from her son. She felt helpless, and scenes of another accident flashed through her mind. "Oh, God, no, please, not again."

She crawled to the shore on her hands and knees, hoping the other side of the fallen tree might be shallower or have firmer footholds. When she finally reached more solid ground, her hands were weak from clawing at the slimy mud and her ankle raged with pain. She turned to scan the river. She saw the tree, still barely attached to the shore. But she did not see Travis.

Her stomach heaved. Dark shadows crowded the edge of her vision, threatening to blind her. She staggered forward, prepared to swim downstream and over the Falls.

Before she reached the water's edge, someone thrust Travis into her arms.

Alive.

The man from the platform stood over her, his hair and clothes dripping wet. He panted from the effort of having rescued her son.

Lydia clasped her three-year-old to her chest. The horror of what might have been was too staggering to contemplate. Everything around her blurred.

The stranger grasped her elbow. Her ankle gave way, and she and Travis nearly fell back onto the ground, but he wrapped a sturdy arm around her waist and held her up. People stood nearby, offering to help.

"Rest easy. He's okay." The man's concerned face offered reassurance. "You may want to ice that ankle when you get home. Let me help you get up the bank."

Lydia hugged her toddler's cold, dripping body close. "Oh, Travis. How could I let this happen? I'm so, so sorry. I should never have brought you guys here." She squeezed harder as she made her way up the hill, the man close behind.

"My name's Amos," the tall stranger said.

The preschooler dug his forehead into Lydia's shoulder.

"What were you doing out there, little guy?" Amos touched Travis's matted hair.

Her son's head popped up. "I wanna shark monster like Harry's." A grin spread across his flushed face.

Lydia cringed at her son's naiveté. Suddenly unable to catch her breath, she collapsed onto the grass at the top of the bank. This time, she held tight to her son and didn't let go. She couldn't wait to get home.

Amos squatted and examined Travis's pupils, then both arms and legs. He took off his sweatshirt and put it on the shivering boy. The gesture caught Lydia by surprise. No man had ever helped dress her younger son. She'd been a single parent since before Travis was even born.

The similarities between this situation and the nightmare she'd endured more than three years ago made her sway slightly. Just like today, a stranger had appeared out of nowhere and helped her in a dire situation. As she rested her elbows on her knees, she wondered, how many saviors could one person need in a lifetime?

Amos looked over at her, his eyebrow raised.

"I'm okay."

"You sure?"

"I almost lost my older son when he was about this age," she explained.

Harrison! Her gaze swept the shore, but she saw no sign of him. The safety rope Mr. Mahoney had used lay across a piece of driftwood.

"Harry!"

"Over here!"

Lydia followed the high-pitched voice and spotted movement behind a scraggly bush on the ridge of the riverbank a few yards away. Harrison waved and gave Lydia a thumbs-up. Then he shifted his attention to the pail.

Mr. Mahoney remained on the shore below Lydia and Amos, trembling on the edge of his lawn chair. His ashen face glimmered with sweat.

"Harrison, come sit with your brother." She told Travis to stay put and then limped back down the embankment toward her neighbor. Amos jumped the bank, landing lightly on his feet, and reached him first.

"Are you hurt, sir?"

"Naw, just shaken up."

He carefully flexed Mr. Mahoney's arms and examined his pupils. The old man submitted to the impromptu exam, which surprised Lydia. Conroy Mahoney prided himself on not having seen a doctor in ten years.

Mr. Mahoney turned to her. "You promised me one normal, worry-free day, missy." His gruff voice made his words sound like an accusation. "I don't know if that day will ever come for you. Not in my lifetime, that's for sure."

She slipped to her knees. His words pierced her soul, mostly because they were probably true. She didn't ask for much out of life. A healthy family. Money to pay the bills. Maybe some peace. So far they'd all eluded her. It sickened Lydia to think of her tumultuous life causing him distress.

Mr. Mahoney sat back in the chair, eyes closed. "Those kids are like grandchildren to me," he whispered to the stranger. "No more fishing for us. I'll make 'em some slingshots."

A loud crackling sound captured everyone's attention. Lydia stood and glanced up at the boys. Harrison covered his eyes, but Travis pointed toward the river. The tenuous connection the dead tree had with the beach severed, and the tree floated away. It rocked in the fast current, gaining momentum in the gray-green water. It crashed against boulders and tangled with brushy outcroppings before it disappeared from sight around a bend in the river.

"That'd be something to see going over the Falls, eh?" Mr. Mahoney said, his voice shaky.

"I'm sure. I haven't seen it myself, but I'll bet lots of broken things get swept over that crest." Amos glanced at the mist plume in the distance. "The Canadian side of the Falls will be packed with visitors. Someone's sure to catch it on video."

Mr. Mahoney cocked his head to the side. "You're not from around here, are you?"

"No, sir." He smiled and extended his hand to Mr. Mahoney, his short-sleeved crew-neck shirt revealed tanned skin on muscular arms. "I'm Amos. Been here for just a short while."

"Well, thank you for acting so quickly. You saved a life today."

"Yes," Lydia said, realizing she hadn't properly expressed her appreciation for the valiant rescue. "I can't thank you enough. Thank you for everything."

"Glad to help." Closing his eyes, Amos cupped his hand around the back of Mr. Mahoney's head. His lips moved, but no words came out. He then glanced at the small crowd on the beach. "I need to get going. Take care."

Did he just pray over Mr. Mahoney?

If so, she wondered if her neighbor had noticed. His eyes had widened, but he didn't move away.

Lydia watched for a moment as the brave stranger jogged up the hill toward the platform, stooped to retrieve his book, and headed into Malvisti Park. Clapping could be heard from the handful of remaining anglers.

She leaned heavily on one foot as she made her way back to where Travis and Harrison sat together at the top of the bank. She squatted down to rest her chin on Travis's head. Her ankle hurt like crazy, but at least her sons were safe and sound. "Let's head home, guys."

She stood and took a few steps, but her ankle collapsed again and she fell on her backside.

"Mom, you okay?" Harrison tried to suppress a smile.

"Gimme a minute." She hoisted herself up using the leg of a wooden sign affixed to the concrete platform. She hadn't noticed it earlier. Its sticky texture made her wonder how recently it had been painted. She paused to read the words.

Coming Soon: North America's First Eco-city!

Revolutionary Green Living made possible by Malvisti Industries.

Green living? Made possible by the county's largest landfill owner? What a contradiction in terms.

It must be an early April Fool's Day joke. Around here green innovation meant the delivery of recycling bins. Two sat unused outside the city dump. Besides, she knew the Malvisti name—baseball diamonds and parks all over town were dedicated to one Malvisti or another. The name was synonymous with garbage and wealth.

And, some said, deceit.

Something didn't add up. But she couldn't contemplate that now. She had to get her kids home and her ankle on ice.

The Vallones were done with fishing in the Niagara River. Maybe forever.

CHAPTER THREE

Near Tampa, Florida

Michael Malvisti had never considered his Nissan GT-R cramped until Tyler's oversized frame filled every inch of the passenger seat. Then again, Jillian had been his only rider until now. With her legs crossed—and usually her arms as well—his girlfriend barely made a dent in the leather-and-suede seats. Not so with Big Ty.

His friend took a sip of coffee from his travel mug and leaned over to examine the car's display monitor embedded in the middle of the dash.

He might as well have been in the driver's seat.

"You want to drive?"

"Nah. I don't drive anything I can't afford to fix." Ty reached with his free hand to tap the screen to display the sports car's acceleration g-force. "Nice, man. This ride must've cost you a pretty penny."

"She's well worth it, believe me."

They bumped elbows. Coffee from the travel mug in Tyler's hand splashed across the console and pooled in the folds of the leather gear shift.

"Whoa!" Distracted, Michael missed second and winced when the gears ground. Two retired-golfer types stared at him from the nearby sidewalk. Probably pegged him as a teenager fumbling with his father's latest toy.

"Sorry, man."

"No prob," Michael said, trying to be agreeable. At the next light he wiped down the stick shift with a handkerchief from his suit pocket. Coffee soaked into the JSM monogram, his grandfather's initials.

"My car might not be fixed 'til the end of the week." Tyler took the cloth, cracked open the window, and then wedged the cloth so that it flapped outside.

"Four years of engineering and that's the best you can do?"

"State school. 'Nuff said. I'm not a Malvisti, remember?"

Michael winced.

"So can I catch a ride to work on Monday?"

"Not if you bring coffee again."

"Yeah ... I'll work on that."

Once they were on the move again, Tyler resumed his examination of the in-dash monitor, keeping his body a few inches from Michael's arm. "This thing mapped our route from Gulfport to Tampa. It says we can go another two hundred miles before we run out of gas. Very cool."

"Most cars can do that nowadays."

"Not mine. Dude, my ex would've run this thing to a hundred and ninety nine before she even thought about telling me to put gas in her car." The monitor went blank. "Whoops, I didn't do that, did I?" He put both his hands in the air.

"Relax." Michael reconfigured the screen to show the brake pedal input. "Check this out. This baby tells me everything I need to know. I get constant feedback, customized analysis ...."

"I'm diggin' it. But numbers can complicate things. Sometimes I just want to turn the key, drive fast, and enjoy the ride."

"You know me. I like facts. Accuracy." Michael chuckled. "Too bad Jillian can't give me precise input like this. Why can't she just say she's hungry, happy, miserable, lonely, or whatever? Instead she makes me guess what's going on in her mind and then punishes me for getting it wrong. I can't operate that way."

"I hear ya. But I'll bet she looks great sitting in this seat."

Michael grunted. Her blonde, all-American girl looks were his weakness.

"I want to see her do zero to sixty in three and a half seconds."

"Jillian?"

"No, the car!" Tyler rolled his eyes. "She's one of the fastest rides on the road right now. And we need every one of those horses to get us to work on time. Gun it. It's our big day." Tyler shifted in his seat. "Besides, I've seen Jillian go from zero to sixty in less time than that, and it ain't pretty."

"Too many old people on these streets to be driving anywhere north of fifty." Michael said, laughing outright for the first time that day. He surveyed the gift shops and outdoor restaurants lining the coastal road. "Wait 'till we get closer to Tampa." He checked his watch. They still had a half hour.

Something small and shaggy darted out into the road. Michael's sudden, screeching stop lit up the GT-R's brake monitors.

Tyler's mug spilled coffee all over his lap. "Dude!"

"Some kind of animal came out from between those potted palm trees. I almost hit it." Michael threw the car into park and put on his flashers. The creature could have been a dog, but it had an odd gait. "Let me check it out." Even as he worried over what he'd nearly hit, Michael noted that the car's Brembo brakes lived up to all the hype.

"Before you get out, do you have another one of those stupid hankies?"

"No, sorry." Michael heaved himself out of the low-lying sports car and raced to the front. A light-tan dog with pink bald patches lay on the pavement, just a few feet in front of his bumper. The animal's nails scratched the asphalt as it contorted its body in an effort to regain footing. It gave up and rested on the road, panting heavily. From the looks of it, the dog had long ago lost its back leg.

"Settle down, it's okay." Michael crouched down and let the dog sniff his hand. He was pretty sure he hadn't caused any serious injury; this was just an old, worn-out, crippled mutt.

"Is she okay?" An alarmingly thin man pushed through the potted palms lining the sidewalk and rushed over to the dog. His knees cracked when he lowered himself down to her level.

"I think she's all right, sir."

The old man spoke softly to the dog, stroking her head and belly. "We walk down this street every day. She's never jerked away from me like that." The man's singsong tone suggested an eastern European accent.

"I don't think the car touched her. But she may have fallen when she tried to get out of the way." Michael scooped up her frail form. They moved away from the road and he laid her on the sidewalk. "What's her name?"

"Clary." The man sniffed. "She's all I got left since my wife died a few years ago. I can't imagine losing this old girl, too." The word "losing" came out as "losink."

Michael wasn't sure what he should say. Besides, if he didn't get going soon he'd be late for one of the most important meetings of his legal career.

He stood and studied the old man and his dog. The man's skinny arms poked out from a blue polyester shirt that probably fit him better twenty-five pounds ago. These two were simply surviving until their time came to disappear forever.

"I have bottled water in the car." Michael backed through the palms. "That might perk her up." He popped the trunk and rummaged through racquetball equipment. Behind his golf bag, he found an emergency stash of water.

"Mike," Tyler called from the car window, "we've got to go. I've got prep work to do before the Green City meeting."

"One sec." Michael jogged back to the sidewalk. "Here's a bottle for Clary and one for you. Good luck with everything." He gave the dog a pat on the head and turned to leave.

"What's your name, young man?"

"Michael Malvisti."

Clary's owner narrowed his eyes. "You related to the Malvistis back in Western New York?"

Michael hesitated. He never knew what kind of reaction he would get when he identified himself as a Malvisti. On one of his visits home, a woman had spit on his new Berluti shoes when she discovered his last name. He was almost sure he heard the word *murderer* through her clenched teeth as she thundered off. "Yes, I am."

"Are you Sal Malvisti's son?"

"No, sir." Michael cringed. "Sal is my dad's twin brother."

"Florida's a winter magnet for us Western New Yorkers, but I haven't run across any Malvistis until now. Your family is good people, I've heard."

Michael nodded, relieved.

"Can I buy you a cup of coffee?"

"No, sir, I've got to get to work." Michael backed through the planters to his car. "Thank you anyway." No doubt the man would want to talk about Michael's family. He'd probably need to talk about his dead wife too. Michael could envision that agonizingly uncomfortable conversation stretching until lunchtime. Fortunately, duty called.

"Are you done saving the world?" Tyler asked as Michael jumped into the driver's seat.

"I think so." He gave a perfunctory smile and hoped Tyler wouldn't ask any more questions. Just hearing Uncle Sal's name had irritated him. He didn't feel much like talking.

He activated the GT-R's launch control mode once they reached the outskirts of town. Rear tires spinning, the car rocketed down the road at a heart-stopping speed.

Tyler clutched the passenger grip bar, his head plastered against the rest. "That's all you got?" he shouted above the whine of the twin-turbo engine.

"Not fast enough for you?"

"If I wanted a Sunday drive, I woulda called your mother!"

Michael gunned it. Tyler's stocky frame lurched with each shift of the gears.

"That's what I'm talkin' about!" Tyler whistled. A patch of perspiration soaked the armpits of his blue dress shirt.

Michael slowed when they reached the Sunshine Skyway Bridge. He pretended not to hear Tyler exhale.

Small fishing boats littered the harbor below. Michael's own twenty-nine footer was in its slip down there, ready to be cleaned for what he hoped would be a summer of water sports and good times.

"What was all that about with the dog owner back there?" Tyler asked as he settled back in his seat.

"That old man knows of my family back home."

Tyler scrutinized Michael's face. "Someday, you've gotta fill me in on your folks. After all, you're about to change the face of your hometown as much as your rich family ever did." He laughed quietly.

Michael didn't respond. Beyond the fact that the Malvistis were well known back in Western New York, he didn't know all that much about them himself. His family had always kept him in the dark about the family business. Maybe it was time to find out where—or what—he'd come from. It might clue him in to where he was headed.

Twenty minutes later, they pulled into Michael's reserved spot in his employer's parking deck, attached to a twenty-story futuristic glass-and-steel structure. The name Hessley Development was etched into the buffed steel arch over the entrance. Today's meeting was pivotal to Hessley's latest project, a remarkable development right in Niagara Falls, New York. The place where Michael felt most at home. Nothing about urban living would be the same after their vision took shape. His stomach tightened.

Showtime.

CHAPTER FOUR

Niagara Falls, New York

As Lydia limped toward the parking lot with Mr. Mahoney and her boys, her cell phone chirped. A feeling of dread washed over her. For weeks, she'd been expecting the call that would bring heartbreaking news about her brother. Although Robby's condition appeared stable as of this morning, his cancer seemed to have a mind of its own.

Shivering, she rifled through her purse. "Where's my phone?" She shook the bag's contents onto the dead grass. Crumbs from half-eaten granola bars spilled out with the device.

"There it is, Mommy." Travis popped a chunk of a bar into his mouth and bolted toward Mr. Mahoney. His exuberant laugh rippled across the water. If only she could shrug off the events of the day so quickly.

"Lydia Vallone."

"You need to get home." Her best friend's voice seemed tight.

"Is it Robby?" Lydia nearly shrieked. "What's going on?"

"No, no, no. This has nothing to do with your brother." Dana DuPays's Long Island accent gave her words a sharp edge. "I'm at your house. I came by to show you today's newspaper headline and—"

"Please don't tell me it reads, 'Boy Falls in River, Nearly Plunges over Falls.'"

"No-o-o." Dana hesitated. "Are the boys okay?"

"Yeah, but it's been a horrible day. You know the fishing tree at Malvisti Park?"

"Of course."

"It's no more. Part of it broke away and Travis was almost swept out into the river with it. A complete stranger rescued him. It was terrifying." Lydia wracked her brain trying to remember the man's name.

Dana exhaled. "Sounds like it could've been worse."

"Wow! That sounds like a quote ripped out of one of those self-help books you always read. No matter how much worse it could have gotten, it was still horrible."

"I'm sure."

Lydia swept the scattered contents of her purse into a pile.

"I'll wait for you here. Load the boys and hurry home." Dana clicked off.

"Lydia," Mr. Mahoney called. He jerked his head in the direction of the parking lot.

Lydia lowered the phone and hobbled toward him. Scanning the lot, she noticed an oversized utility van parked a few spaces away from her minivan. Two cameramen stood talking over a tripod positioned between her and her vehicle. Access to Lydia's minivan was blocked by cameras, lights, cords, and stools. Local Channel 2 news stood ready.

Were they there for her? Had one of the fishermen called the news?

One of the cameramen pointed in her direction. Lydia's heart sank. She couldn't handle an interview right now. Her nerves were already frayed from the death watch over her brother. And after today's drama, all she wanted to do was retreat to her house. They'd better not follow her there.

A dark-haired, late-fiftyish woman sat on a stool in front of the news van. She raised a thin arm in the air at Lydia as a makeup artist fluffed and sprayed her hair. Something seemed familiar about the woman's bony frame. Lydia's eyes went wide. "Mr. Mahoney, is that our neighbor?"

"Sure is, missy. Mara Stanton, in the flesh."

Lydia tucked her phone in her jacket pocket, only to withdraw it when she felt a sharp prick. She reached in and produced a broken pondweed stem. A souvenir from a day she'd just as soon forget.

"What's going on, Mom?" Harrison's voice seemed hoarse.

"Some news reporters are here. Maybe to talk to us, I don't know. Don't be afraid. But don't say anything either."

Travis gripped Mr. Mahoney's hand.

"Did we do something wrong?" Harrison stifled a cough with his arm.

"No. I'm sure they're just curious about what happened near the water today. I only hope they don't ask about the guy who saved your brother. I can't remember his name."

"Amos, mommy!" Travis laughed. "Don't you know that?"

"Don't be a smart aleck."

Mr. Mahoney picked up the bucket with his free hand. "You want me to handle Mara for you?"

"Thanks, but no. Might as well get this over with." Lydia headed for her minivan.

Mara slid off the makeup chair and stood. Lydia stared her neighbor in the eye, aware that the camera would record every move, every word, every inch of their filthy clothes and matted hair.

Mara's eyebrow rose as she tracked their progress toward the parking lot. She held a microphone in one hand and smoothed her skirt with the other. As Lydia and the children drew closer, she smiled at the boys. "We heard Travis fell into the water. Is he all right?"

Like she cared. They'd barely exchanged twenty words in the past few years. "We need to get home, Mara. May we pass?"

"We were here for a breaking story on this property, but then we heard on the police scanner about the fishing tree … and your son."

Lydia's lips trembled at the memory of the bare branch bobbing in the river, but she took a deep breath and pulled herself together. "Not today, I'm sorry."

"Please. I need this."

"Need what?" Lydia tried to stay calm. The boys would take their cue from her and she didn't want to upset them. "Never mind. We're coming through. Please excuse us."

Mara planted her feet. "Can you at least tell me about the stranger who saved Travis? Did you get his name?" Her bloodshot eyes bulged; she seemed desperate to get any news, no matter the cost.

"Let us through, Mrs. Stanton." Mr. Mahoney's deep voice jolted Harrison.

She didn't move.

A Channel 4 news van rolled to a stop behind the first truck. The doors flew open and a slight man with thinning red hair jumped out and hurried toward them. Greg Blass looked older in person than he did on television. His crew labored to keep up.

Mara gripped Lydia's arm and leaned closer. "It'll be easier to talk to me than him." She flicked her thumb at the man hustling their way. "He'll ask you on live TV why you weren't there to stop your son's fall. If you'll give me a short statement, I'll block him and you can leave."

"My boys need to get home, I'm sorry." Lydia turned to Harrison. "Follow me." Hand in hand, they skirted Mara's black stool and stepped over a bundle of lighting cords. Mr. Mahoney prodded Travis to follow.

"Hey," Travis called out as he passed by the skinny reporter. "We catched a monster fish." He pointed at the pail in Mr. Mahoney's hand.

Harrison took his brother's arm. "Trav!" he whispered. "Mom said not to say anything." The exertion triggered another cough.

Travis pushed his brother away. "There's a glob on the eye."

Mara tucked the microphone behind her back and leaned over the boy. "Is it one of *those* fish, Conroy?"

"Mrs. Stanton," said Mr. Mahoney, "you are a wonderful neighbor, but you're being a lousy friend right now. We need to get the little ones home. Travis is soaked and Harrison's cough sounds like my hound's baying. Leave us be."

Mara backed off, a look of astonishment on her face.

"We'll talk later," he muttered. "And yes, it was a diseased fish."

She laid her mic on an empty stool and disappeared behind her news truck. Her video crew stared after her. Lydia heard a heavy door being opened and slammed shut.

Greg Blass squatted beside Travis, his combed-over thatch of red hair standing in the wind. "What did you catch today, little fella?" He held the microphone under Travis's chin.

"He's off limits!" Lydia pulled her son forward. She'd never thought of her dying minivan as a refuge, but it sure seemed like one now.

The reporter stood. "Ma'am, what happened out there in the river?"

Mr. Mahoney shifted the pail to his other hand, hopefully out of Greg Blass's sight. "Keep going, boys."

"Can we see the mysterious monster fish?"

"There's nothing to see here. Move along." Mr. Mahoney helped Harrison into the passenger side of Lydia's van while she climbed into the driver's seat.

The reporter moved to Lydia's open door. He thrust the microphone in the van, staring at her with a frightening intensity. "That spot where your son fell in is going to be part of the new eco-city announced today. They're planning to re-build the fishing pier. Do you think it's a safe area for families?"

"Listen, please take that mic out of my face. My son is sick and cold. Don't you people care?" She slammed the door. One normal day. She was overdue.

"I wanna show our monster!" Travis's high-pitched whine shot out from the back of the minivan.

"We need to leave." Harrison cleared his throat. "Mom said."

Lydia barely recognized Harrison's voice. Its flat tone lacked emotion, vitality. She turned the key and willed the engine to turn over. It took two tries before the van came through for them.

Mr. Mahoney wedged the heavy bucket between the second and third seats. "I'll keep the reporters busy long enough to keep them from following you."

Lydia shuddered the whole drive home. The thought of her life being under public scrutiny made her sick. She just wanted to be left alone, to nurse her hurts in private. In her own home.

When she reached her house, the street was quiet. No reporters. No Mara Stanton. Just Dana waving from her new hybrid parked close to Lydia's garage. Lydia breathed a sigh of relief.

❖

Dana opened the dishwasher. "You okay?"

"I feel like I can't do anything right. I can't even keep my kid safe."

Dana chuckled. "Oh, come on. You're a great mom. It can't be easy on your own, but you're doing it. And Travis is fine. Both boys seem to be at peace about things."

"Thank you." Lydia rubbed her forehead, wondering what 'peace' looked like in a child. Travis never stopped moving. "You know, I still can't believe Mara came at us the way she did."

"That's her job, at least for now. She's getting a bit too mature for television news and I heard she's getting ready to wind up her career. I'm sure she was there for a last big story about the riverfront. I can't wait to talk to you about it myself." She closed the dishwasher, turned it on, and then headed out of the kitchen. She stiffened when her gaze reached the window of the adjacent dining room at the front of the house. "Speak of the devil."

Lydia's stomach fell.

"Mara and her husband are out there talking to Mr. Mahoney."

"Is there a camera crew?"

"Nope."

"Anyone else there?"

"Mr. Mahoney's old dog. He's even got a few years on Mara Stanton. How is that animal still breathing?"

Lydia sped to the front door and peered out the side windows. "I've got to say something to her. She won't let this go." She slipped on a jacket and slid her feet into salt-stained shoveling boots. She shouted to the boys that she'd be outside.

Dana followed Lydia out the front door. "I've gotta see this. You've never confronted anyone in all the years I've known you."

"She's messing with my children."

"I've got your back." Dana shut the door behind her.

Lydia marched down her driveway, feeling no pain in her ankle now. "Mara, I need to talk to you."

"Sure."

Lydia crossed her arms. "You scared my boys with all your cameras and questions." Her voice shook.

"Look, we were there for a different story, and then someone told us about what happened to Travis. A child falling into the river is pretty newsworthy. And when you resisted, I backed off ... until I saw that jerk Greg Blass. He provokes people into saying things they regret later. I didn't want that to happen to you."

Lydia hesitated.

"I've seen him do it for years."

Maybe she should give Mara the benefit of the doubt. "Listen, I don't want anything about me and my boys made public."

"I understand. I'm sorry."

"Promise me you won't corner me like that again."

"I won't." Mara looked up and down the street and took a step closer. "I can't make the same promise about Channel 4. I heard there's something on that property they're going after. They may have thought Travis' incident had some connection. Personally, I think that's ridiculous."

Mr. Mahoney looked at Mara from under his overgrown eyebrows. "Are they sniffing around for something in particular?"

She glanced at her husband before responding. "Maybe. You guys were fishing on riverfront land once owned by the Malvisti family. I'm not sure who owns it now, but does anyone remember hearing rumors that it was being sold to an out-of-state developer?"

Lydia vaguely recalled a series of investigative articles about the properties. The write-ups cited environmental studies. She hadn't paid much attention.

"Well, someone bought it."

"That hardly seems worthy of an investigation." Lydia didn't understand the connection.

"But the folks at Channel 4 think so." Mara continued. "They believe there's something wrong with that property. One of the station's new reporters has been sticking her nose in places I would never venture into."

Dana sucked in a sharp breath, but said nothing.

"I heard that area's contaminated with chemicals." Jeff Stanton darted a nervous peek at his wife. "A buddy at work's brother-in-law is a surveyor. He saw some deformed deer over there. There might've been radiation or something."

"Don't be stupid." Mara wagged a thin finger in her husband's face. "You shouldn't say things like that out loud. The government tested the property. It's fine."

Jeff backed up a step, nearly tripping on a briefcase set on the ground. "Someone else saw a two-headed snake."

"Just stop." Mara's eyes turned hard.

"There's no need to get upset." Dana stared pointedly at Jeff. "There's no more contamination there than anywhere else in this state. We used to hear the same stuff on the middle school bus. Nothing more than urban legends. None of it's true."

Jeff folded his arms. "There must be something to all those rumors. That property was on the market for a long time."

"Our politicians probably made a pile of money in that sale somehow." Mr. Mahoney harrumphed. "At our expense, of course. Crooked, every one of them!"

The dog lifted his nose to sniff the wind. Dark clouds coming from the direction of the river threatened rain.

"Even Monk smells something fishy." He nudged the hound with his work boot.

"At least there's some positive news." Dana directed her next comment to Lydia. "I've been trying to talk to you about the article I read in today's paper. The new buyer of all that Malvisti property is launching an incredible development project. It'll incorporate Malvisti Park into the design, right where you were fishing today."

"Why would I care about some office buildings?" And why would her son falling in the river have any connection to it?

"Oh, it's much bigger than a few buildings." Dana smiled. "If the buzz today around our real estate office is right, we're about to experience something that few of us have ever encountered in Niagara Falls."

"Low taxes?" Jeff moved back to his original spot next to his wife. "The sun?"

"Honest politicians?" Mr. Mahoney turned his head and spat on the grass behind Monk.

"No." Dana's blue-gray eyes sparkled. "Something much bigger. Niagara Falls is about to know *prosperity*."

"I think she's right." Mara reached in the briefcase and pulled out a letter-sized folder. "Here's the front page from today's *Western New York Courier*." She handed it to Lydia.

Lydia forced herself to concentrate as she read it.

Hessley Development, a Florida-based commercial developer, announced to-day that it will move forward with a landmark eco-city in Niagara Falls, New York.

Cascata Verde, a self-sustaining, mixed-use development, will be a 750-acre, $10 billion project, situated on rehabilitated brownfields and reclaimed landfill sites near the Niagara River. It is expected to include 15 million square feet of residential, retail, and office space, as well as hotels, restaurants, civic buildings and a high-end day care. An organic vineyard is expected to yield a crop in two to three years.

Hessley representative Suzanna Frederick said the revolutionary community will be powered by wind, solar, and biofuel technology and will support 25,000 people. Groundbreaking for the "Green City," as Hessley employees have dubbed the development, begins this fall.

Dana grabbed the paper from Lydia and held it high. "Niagara Falls will no longer be a depressed, welfare-dependent city. We'll have jobs. And money. But I'm most excited about the fact that our backward region will join the green revolution taking place everywhere else in the world." Dana lowered the paper and her voice. "Do you realize this development could be the first step in getting this area back in tune with nature?"

Mara half-smiled. "It's about time this city got something right."

Gossip about proposed shopping centers, theme parks, and golf courses had flooded this area for as long as Lydia could remember. None of the rumors ever materialized. Why would this so-called Green City be any different?

Mr. Mahoney grimaced. "I still think the politicians are up to something."

"Have faith, Conroy." Mara's head tilted.

"Until its pearly gates open for business, I don't believe for a minute that the project will be built here." His flushed face conveyed strong conviction.

"Why do you say that?" Dana's brows drew together.

"Because nothing can save this godforsaken corner of New York State." Mr. Mahoney gripped his cane in trembling hands. "I've been a resident of this county for more than seventy years. For decades, we've been fed one line of hogwash after another about this or that project. Very few provided real jobs. Or real income. Our politicians always find ways to screw it all up." His cane sank deeper into the saturated ground.

"He has a point." Lydia felt like a protective daughter. "Remember the hole they dug downtown a few years back for an interactive Revolutionary War museum?"

"That 'war pit' is still there," Mr. Mahoney growled. "A gaping testament to our politicians' ineptitude. One of the Malvistis was behind that one, I'm sure of it."

A dark look flickered across Mara's face at the mention of the prominent local family.

"I think the project fell apart when the money ran out." Lydia took back the newspaper. "That happens every time something promising comes along. I'm not going to get worked up over this article."

Dana's eyes bore into Lydia. Surprised at the intensity of her gaze, Lydia couldn't think of anything she'd said that would've offended her friend.

"Let's think positive." Mara placed a bony hand on her hip. "I'm sure they wouldn't have announced it in the paper if it wasn't going to happen."

"Spoken like a true journalist." Mr. Mahoney chuckled.

"Thanks." Mara winked at him. "Maybe I'm naive, but we're overdue for a miracle here."

A car in need of a new muffler slowed as it approached the house and pulled into the driveway. Lydia's babysitter, Angie, emerged, holding a newspaper to her chest. The headline screamed, "Our Savior Has Come!" Underneath, in a slightly smaller typeface, it read, "Cascata Verde: A Reality."

Travis's high-pitched scream tore their attention from the headlines to the open front door. "Mommy! Harry sick!"

Lydia took off for the house, but her weak ankle caused her to trip on the driveway. She ripped off the salt-encrusted boots and flung them into the bushes.

Dana jumped over her and reached the door first. "Oh, no!"

"What is it?" As she stepped over the threshold, Lydia saw Harrison lying on his side, his nostrils flaring as he tried to catch his breath. His face was gray. The fear radiating from his eyes mirrored her own.

Jeff gripped his cell phone. "I'll call 911."

Angie laid both hands over Harrison's contracting ribs. His chest rose and fell rapidly. She prayed aloud.

"Hold him while I get his medicine," Lydia yelled over her shoulder as she dashed into the adjacent dining room, her socks sliding on the wood floor.

Travis, kneeling at his brother's head, sniffed and wiped his nose on his sleeve. "I not do it."

Travis' distress tore at Lydia's heart. She rummaged through a cabinet, immediately spying the case she needed.

"No, you did the right thing and got help." Dana tousled the preschooler's hair. "You're a brave kid. Let's just think good thoughts about your brother."

If only good wishes were enough. If that were true, her brother wouldn't be dying right now. Her dad would still be with them. And the boys might still have a living father.

Travis's chin trembled.

Mara put her arms around his shoulders. "Let's go with Miss Dana and wait for the ambulance outside, okay? That's an important job."

Travis kept looking back at his brother as the two women led him out. When a siren screamed in the distance, tears erupted.

Lydia raced back to the tiny foyer and slid to a stop beside Harrison. Her fingers flew as she assembled the nebulizer machine, filled it with medicine, and plugged it in.

Jeff lifted Harrison's limp hand and massaged each finger. "His nails are blue!"

"C'mon, love." She forced the mouthpiece to his darkened lips, encouraging him to inhale the lifesaving vapor. "You can do it."

The seconds ticked by, punctuated by an occasional "Thank you, God" from Angie, who kept her hands around Harrison's ribs as she mouthed constant prayers.

What is she thanking God for? Lydia's stomach clenched.

Color slowly returned to Harrison's face.

Lydia kissed her son's forehead. She crouched low to study his chest, looking for signs that air was getting where it needed to go.

A half-formed thought gripped Lydia as she continued administering the medicine. "It's unfair," she choked out.

"What is?" Angie kept her eyes on Harrison.

"My dad didn't deserve to die of cancer. You knew that, and you only met him in his last weeks of life."

"He was a great person."

"So were my aunts, uncles, and cousins. Good people. They didn't deserve what happened to them."

Angie looked up. Compassion showed in her eyes.

"And my brother shouldn't be battling it at thirty, either. And ..." She sat up and gestured at Harrison's thin body. "This is just wrong!"

Angie stood. She placed a hand on Lydia's shoulder.

Lydia's shaky voice became a tormented whisper. *"Why is my family dying?"*

CHAPTER FIVE

Tampa, Florida

Michael took a shallow breath, and then another, hoping his irregular breathing wouldn't disturb the stillness of the packed conference room. No one had so much as coughed since Hessley Development's CEO marched through the glass doors a few minutes ago. Rebecca Waters's presence commanded the attention of all thirty people seated at the massive marble table.

She set her laptop on the table and opened it.

A well-dressed man with salt-and-pepper hair leaned over the side of his wheelchair and pulled out her chair. That must be Hessley's new outside lawyer. Michael suspected that the high-priced attorney would participate in all future project meetings. More legal involvement meant a longer, more expensive project. But it was a necessary evil to keep everything on track.

Michael allowed his eyes to dart to the opposite side of the table. Tyler's thick fingers curled tightly around a stainless steel coffee mug. Its bright green-and-ocean-blue Hessley logo stood out like a beacon, as if to remind each employee who put food on their table. The man on Tyler's right sat ramrod straight, his hands poised over a razor-thin laptop.

Michael hoped the combined decades of experience in design, engineering, architecture, urban planning, and the law represented in this room would result in a positive report today. Green city builders didn't come any better than these.

39

Rebecca sat. "Good morning, team."

"Good morning," the team exhaled in unison.

"Thanks to your hard work, North America's first large-scale, self-sustaining community, one capable of producing its own power and food and recycling its own waste, is now a reality. I am proud to announce that our landmark eco-city project in Niagara Falls, New York, is on course. Hessley Development is setting the pace for a radical change in the way human beings live. Our creation is one planet living in action."

Scattered applause broke out across the room. Michael clapped, although he was interested more in Rebecca's enthusiastic demeanor than her words. Offering praise to others was not something his boss did often.

Rebecca waited for the room to quiet. "Cascata Verde's design has drawn accolades from everyone. This morning, bioremediation giant Pavati Biotecnologia signed a fifty-year lease with us."

The room exploded with cheers.

"Well done." The distinguished lawyer next to her flushed with enthusiasm. "Plenty of clean-up opportunities for Pavati in Niagara Falls, that's for sure."

"Thank you, Raul." The corners of Rebecca's mouth turned upward, though the smile never reached her eyes. Michael scaled back his assessment. They had caught her in a momentary high.

"So, let's roll up our sleeves and get to business." Rebecca grabbed the projector remote and pressed a button. A row of diamond bracelets slid down her wrist, casting citrine reflections across the whiteboard behind her. "I called today's meeting to gauge our progress and adjust the agenda to accommodate the next phase of the project. Until now, the legal, design, architectural, environmental, agricultural, power generation, and business teams have been working independently from one master plan. Today, we converge our efforts."

She tapped a few keys on her laptop. Artist's renderings of the project appeared on the whiteboard. The drawings revealed a hemisphere-shaped urban landscape. The straight edge of the half-sphere ran parallel to a wide river. Three round towers, two with solar panels on top, were grouped at the waterfront. Smaller round buildings cascaded in a stepped arrangement below the three towers. Their green living roofs offered a natural contrast with the blue shimmer radiating from the state-of-the-art skin wrapping the buildings. The towers harmonized beautifully with the riverscape in the background. Further south along the waterfront, a swath of majestic, two-hundred-foot-tall wind turbines fanned out across the riverbank. The artist even included acres of vineyards, just outside the grassy wind turbine safety zone. Smaller wind machines, mostly for temperature control purposes, would be erected within the vineyards themselves. Perfection.

Michael's heart soared every time he saw the presentation. Hessley had reinvented the urban community to enhance the quality of human life. At the same time their innovations minimized mankind's environmental impact. Together they had created something of value, something lasting. His grandfather would've been proud.

He noticed that some modifications had been made to the drawings. Micro wind turbines, roughly the size of a small child, had been added to the roofs of both residential and commercial structures. He wondered whether wind-power technology was ready for such a large-scale installation. He didn't think so.

Squinting, he searched for other changes. He scanned the tree-lined streets radiating out from the tower cluster. Nothing new there. Each main street served as a district boundary for residential, retail, or entertainment purposes. Ample green spaces stood out between the districts, and every sector emptied into a single expansive green space, dotted with trails and recreational facilities.

He suppressed a smile. Cascata Verde had the potential to shake up the design world from one end of the planet to the other.

"We are justifiably proud." Rebecca gestured toward the whiteboard. "But we have set the bar high. We are setting an example of stewardship for the Earth's sake that will eventually foster social change. The world's eyes are on us from this point on."

"Amen," Raul mouthed.

Michael blinked. Their corporate mission was beginning to sound like a new religion. A green theology of sorts.

His boss's manicured fingers pressed against the table. She studied the faces on each side of the table, as if trying to assess each person's level of commitment. Rebecca Waters had staked her reputation on the groundbreaking eco-city. Nothing short of an act of God would stand in the way of its successful completion.

"Today I want each of you to summarize your department's area of innovation, provide an update, and outline your group's major objectives for the next three months."

Michael shifted in his seat. He hoped against hope that she would start at the far end of the table. But he couldn't predict anything having to do with Rebecca with certainty today.

"Michael." Rebecca's wry smile set his bones twitching, although he couldn't pinpoint why. "I think it's appropriate that we start with you." She turned to the group. "Michael's family sold Hessley Development much of the property that forms this community. They also donated Malvisti Park to the Green City project." Her light green eyes, pale as aquamarine, shone. Was it gratitude?

Michael hoped his coworkers wouldn't break out into another round of applause. Instead, they gazed at him with open curiosity. The details surrounding the property sale and donation had been kept under wraps for years. Even he wasn't sure about the specifics, which wasn't all that surprising since his father shared little with him about anything.

He raised the microphone attached to the table and plunged in. "My group handles all real estate-related legal matters for Cascata Verde. We work with a team of local lawyers, and our job is to secure the appropriate permits, address zoning matters, obtain ZIP code authorization, and the like. We get waivers where needed and handle preliminary districting issues for portions of the Green City complex. Most of that work is complete. Over the next three months, our group will finalize some remaining residential zoning problems and smooth out title discrepancies with the Malvisti Park sector. We do not expect any delays."

Rebecca addressed the group. "Michael has one more area of responsibility. His will be the face of all the goodwill associated with the Malvisti name. If a challenge of any type arises in Niagara Falls, we send the hometown boy with the philanthropic family to address it. Understood?"

Everyone responded affirmatively.

The appointment was news to Michael. A burning sensation rose from under his collar. Despite what the old man had said this morning, he wasn't sure there was any goodwill left in the Malvisti name.

Tyler gave him a rueful smile.

The group focused on solar power went next, followed by the head viticulturist, a grape specialist brought in from the Western New York area. Rebecca asked a handful of questions about air flow, water drainage, and soil quality for the prized vineyards. All accounts were concise and upbeat, and revealed a well-managed but massive project.

Michael needed to stretch. To pace. To get out from under the surreptitious glances of his colleagues.

After two hours, Rebecca called a fifteen-minute break. She swept out of the heavy glass doors and walked to a waiting elevator. No one moved until they heard the ping of the elevator doors signaling her departure. Then cell phones sprang into operation. People left their seats and leaned against the window ledge, gawking at the yachts moored in the bay. Nearly everyone refilled their coffee mugs.

"I think she's happy," one of the outside attorneys said. "And that makes me happy."

Rich is more like it.

Michael wandered to the window. Tampa Bay was dotted with colorful spinnakers that vibrated wildly as sailboats steered toward the open ocean. He wondered if he'd have time to get out on the water this summer. Or to do anything fun, for that matter.

He worked his way around a small group of lawyers to swipe an onion bagel from the marble-and-wood-inlaid sideboard. At the coffee station, Tyler's athletic body was rigid as he mechanically poured a cup of coffee, then added sugar and milk. Ty avoided eye contact with Michael as he walked back to his seat.

Michael sent a text. *Wassup?*

His friend shook his head slightly, furrowing his brow at the glass doors.

Michael wasn't sure what he meant, but left him alone.

Everyone was seated by the fourteen-minute mark. Thirty seconds later, Rebecca strode into the room, her expensive perfume preceding her.

Raul pulled out her chair again, studying her appreciatively. Michael could see where a man would find her attractive. Rebecca's deep auburn hair was cut into a severe angle, framing a regal, pretty face. Above her high cheekbones were eyes that radiated intelligence and a quick wit. She spoke four languages, earned advanced degrees in architecture and design, and oversaw the construction of a green kibbutz in the Israeli desert. Not to mention two award-winning smart buildings in Europe.

But she also had a legendary ruthlessness.

Michael wondered if Raul knew that Rebecca had designed the Italian marble table at which they all sat, then required a guarantee from the manufacturer's owner that it be delivered undamaged. The table arrived with a small crack. By collecting on the pledge, Rebecca acquired a villa on the shores of Lake Como, Italy. Rumor had it that the quiet sobbing of the owner's wife as they turned over the villa keys had not caused Rebecca a moment's guilt. Ironically, the media exposure over the villa incident led to Hessley connecting with Cascata Verde's new anchor tenant. Rebecca was lucky that way.

Lucky or not, Michael wasn't sure she was human. Her employees had never met a family member, let alone a friend.

Good luck, buddy.

"Any questions before we get back to it?" Rebecca's curt tone indicated that she would prefer to press on.

"Yes," said a woman at the far end of the table.

A look of annoyance flickered across Rebecca's face.

Michael stole a quick glance at the speaker, Suzanna Frederick. Her thick braid fell to the middle of her back, and her ankle-length skirt billowed over her chair, presenting a stark contrast to Rebecca's tailored appearance.

"Could you highlight the changes that have been made to the master plan? I see some things that I didn't know had been included."

"Certainly." Rebecca's irritated tone belied her positive response. "The changes do not impact the overall footprint of the project, but merely add details that will enable us to better connect with Western New Yorkers."

Rebecca paused as people turned their attention back to the drawings. "European squares generally center around a church or cathedral. Using that as inspiration, we've designed a small, picturesque building that looks like a church in the main piazza. It sits at the terminus of several streets. Western New York has a population strongly influenced by certain ethnic backgrounds, including German, Polish, Irish, and Italian."

"That's why there are so many great restaurants in the Falls," Raul noted.

Rebecca ignored the interruption. "We believe the church will resonate with the locals. Plus, our demographic studies reveal that the residents consider themselves somewhat religious, even though most don't attend church regularly. The building won't function as an actual church, but will be aesthetically pleasing and contribute to the overall community feeling."

Grandpa Joe would've been in an uproar had he been alive. To him, missing weekly mass wasn't an option.

Rebecca pressed a key on her laptop. An artist's rendering of a compact stone-and-cedar church appeared on the screen. The structure featured a modest honey-colored wooden spire, with two miniature versions of it just below and on either side. Square, stained-glass windows appeared at random intervals throughout the front and sides of the structure, giving it a modern edge. The charming, well-proportioned building brought the intersection to life.

"We'll spend the money on the outside, but the inside will be relatively plain."

"The church could be used as a voting site," Suzanna suggested. "Maybe for town hall meetings."

"Indeed." Rebecca clicked, closing the drawing. "And any national candidate serious about the environment will make a speech in Cascata Verde. Since you brought it up, Suzanna, make sure we have a large flag and an official-looking podium in that church."

"The community can use the piazza to handle the overflow from meetings at the church," another woman suggested.

Raul laughed. "I went to law school in that area. Some years, there's maybe two to three weeks of warm weather in which to use the square. And for one of those weeks it will rain, maybe even snow." He used his hands to shift his legs in the titanium chair frame. "We'd be better off building a massive fireplace in that church."

Quiet laughter spread across the table, especially from the veteran travelers to Niagara County.

"That's enough, folks." Rebecca stiffened. Her agenda was in danger of getting hijacked by free-flowing ideas.

Michael recognized a glimpse of the familiar Rebecca. At least he knew that territory.

She placed her hand on the attorney's shoulder. "You may be on to something, counselor." She looked across the room at a wall-mounted gas fireplace. "Let's include a circular stone hearth in that church entrance that incorporates the newest-generation, EPA-certified wood-burning fireplace. After all, we are all about the unconventional, aren't we?"

The lawyer sat up a bit taller. A few employees made notes.

Michael checked his watch; it was nearly past lunch. He wanted to return to his office and get back to work. He wondered if Tyler felt the same. But when Michael looked at him, Ty was distracted by the phone in his hand. His face was drained of color, but otherwise expressionless. Ty knew that Rebecca would fire him on the spot if she knew he was texting during a meeting, didn't he?

Her gaze fixed on his face. "Your turn, Mr. Morales."

Ty cleared his throat, set down his phone, and addressed the others. "I'm the project manager for the environmental engineering group. We've completed the initial testing and finished our reports to various agencies. We'll continue to ensure regulatory compliance once construction begins."

Tyler looked at Rebecca. She gave him a barely perceptible nod, her business smile firmly in place.

The summary was short. Very unlike Ty.

"Thank you, Mr. Morales. You may be excused."

Michael froze. Rebecca once fired her right-hand woman in the middle of a meeting like that. In fact, she'd used that very same phrase.

Tyler gathered his phone and laptop. He kept his eyes glued to the floor, despite the fact that every eye in the room was fixed on his back. He walked deliberately out the glass doors.

Michael switched his gaze to Rebecca, hoping to gather some evidence that his departure was prearranged, and that he didn't just watch his best friend get fired. Rebecca pecked at her laptop. Her face revealed nothing.

After an uncomfortable silence, she looked up abruptly. "Suzanna, you're next."

The true Rebecca Waters definitely hadn't disappeared after all.

CHAPTER SIX

Michael halfheartedly poked at the day-old vegetarian loaf in the refrigerator. Normally he could force down Jillian's leftovers. Occasionally he even liked them. But tonight not even a black bean burger smothered with ketchup held appeal.

He rummaged through the near-empty pantry and found a protein bar and a can of mandarin oranges. Not much of a dinner. But his stomach rumbled. So he grabbed the can and rinsed off the pop-top lid.

Michael stepped out onto his second-floor balcony, relaxing his shoulders as he settled himself into a sturdy wooden deck chair. The moist, unrelenting breeze coming off Tampa Bay caused a long row of stately palms to bend over in the wind. Boats rocked in the choppy water as they steered toward the community's private dock.

His neighbor, Paulie, saluted him from the fly bridge of his thirty-five footer. The middle-aged bachelor spent most days relaxing on his yacht, *Singhull*. There were no women on board to complicate matters. Lucky man.

Michael heard the garage door open just as he was about to snap open the can of oranges. He tilted his head back, steeling his defenses. Criticism was just around the corner.

Jillian barely glanced at him through the screen door of the balcony. "I didn't think you'd be home this early."

Michael rotated his chair to see her better. Her straight blonde hair was drawn back in a perfect ponytail. Hostility radiated from her eyes. She threw her purse on the counter and began flipping through the day's mail.

Michael pulled the lid off his oranges and stared at them. His hunger had given way to anxiety. More and more, they spent their nights at odds. About everything.

"So, how was your day?" Michael stood. The can slipped through his fingers, dropping noisily on the balcony's tile floor. Syrupy juice dribbled out as the can rolled away. Deal with one problem at a time.

Jillian tore open a letter. "Not great. Practice was cut short because Coach came down with the flu. We couldn't get a full session in, and our next game is Sunday."

"Sorry to hear that." Michael squatted to examine the mess. He debated whether to go inside and get a paper towel or simply kick the oranges off the deck.

Jillian jerked her head up, her silky ponytail swinging. "I can see you've got other things on your mind." She wiggled her keys in the air. "I'm going to squeeze in a Pilates class tonight. And I'll be leaving early tomorrow morning to go over a routine with one of the girls." As she strutted away, he remembered the strikingly attractive pro cheerleader who'd stolen his heart a year ago. Now, he saw only a woman for whom nothing he did was good enough. He slid open the screen door. He'd clean up the mess the right way.

Michael heard the garage open and the roar of the Charger as she peeled off.

If only every night went as smoothly.

Michael did have a lot on his mind. The ever-growing Cascata Verde project would transform the look and feel of his hometown, hopefully in better ways than his family's imprint had. He needed to talk to Ty about the latest developments. But why hadn't Ty responded to a single text or call all weekend?

He'd have to swing by Tyler's apartment in the morning.

As he mopped up the tile, Michael caught the mandarin orange can rolling back and forth in the breeze. Some dinner. A sudden yearning for Grandma Ziatta's chicken cacciatore rose up in him. He longed to take a hunk of her crusty Italian bread and soak up the imported olive oil at the bottom of the salad bowl. For dessert, her famous *cucidati* cookies, filled with fresh figs and topped with a white, sugary glaze and colored sprinkles. His stomach growled even louder.

Something in him missed not just Grandma Ziatta's cooking, but also the predictability of his grandparents' traditions. Grandma had Grandpa's food on the table at 5:30 sharp every night. And they always ate together. Jillian would've choked if Michael suggested she make him dinner, let alone sit with him while he ate it.

On his way back to the kitchen, Michael cupped his hands to prevent the soaked paper towels from dripping all over the manual for his new dive computer. The booklet sparked a moment's interest. Maybe it would help him take his mind off Jillian. And his empty stomach. If he spent enough time studying this spring and summer, he should be able to finish his mixed-gas diving certification by fall.

But five minutes later, Michael couldn't stand it any longer. He picked up his phone.

"Hello?" Grandma Ziatta's caregiver's upbeat voice was a refreshing change from his girlfriend's sharp tone.

"Hi, Lucy. Is she still up?"

"Let me put her on, dear." He heard some fumbling over the phone before his grandmother's heavily accented voice came on the line. She sounded weaker than just a few days ago.

"How are you, Grandma?" Michael said loudly. He hadn't seen her in so long, he'd almost forgotten what she looked like.

"I'm-a cold up here, but never mind that," she said. "I want to tell you something." He detected a note of impatience in her scratchy voice. "I *need* to tell you something."

Michael grinned at the way she added an "a" to every third word or so. *Mind* became *mind-a*, and *need* became *need-a*. "What's that?"

"Your grandfather was a good man."

"I know. I admired him a lot."

"He loved America. And he worked hard to put food on the table. He did things the right way." She paused to take several shallow breaths. "You be like-a him," she said with finality.

Michael could picture her brushing her rough hands together as if getting rid of bread crumbs. He smiled. "He was a good man because he had a good woman behind him, Grandma."

The line went dead. He held the silent phone to his ear, not ready to break the tenuous connection to his grandparents' house in Niagara Falls, the warm and welcoming place he'd known for most of his childhood. He considered it home.

He wondered if Grandma Ziatta knew what she was saying. Grandpa Joe built a business from nothing. As their bank account grew, they invested in Niagara Falls more than anyone else.

But Grandpa as a patriot? A man who *loved* America?

Michael searched his memories for any evidence about his grandfather that would suggest patriotism beyond the norm. Did he serve in the military? Michael wasn't sure. He remembered his grandfather mentioning someone nicknamed "The General." But no one in the family had ever met a general. Michael wasn't even sure the guy was real.

Then again, he was uncertain about a lot of things when it came to his grandparents. Why did they leave Italy? And why did they settle in Niagara Falls? How had Grandpa Joe created such a profitable business in a declining city? Would Hessley's Green City ever be that successful?

He'd been so wrapped up in trying to navigate through his own young adult life that he never thought to ask these questions of his grandparents. His knowledge of his extended family was built on the shadows of vague memories. With his grandfather gone, and his grandmother not far behind, time was running out. He needed to learn more.

He resolved to start with his father. At least they would finally have something to discuss with each other.

❖

The next morning, Michael knocked on Ty's apartment door twice before ringing the doorbell. He pressed his ear to the door and tried the handle.

The door pushed open easily. Tyler never left the door unlocked.

His military training took over. Michael picked up a branch from below a nearby crepe myrtle.

He knocked again, and then flung the door open all the way, pressing himself against the doorframe. He peered into the hallway, recoiling when a rank odor reached his nose.

When his eyes adjusted to the darkness, he saw Tyler's bulky form lying across a garment bag and briefcase on the hallway floor.

"Ty!"

His friend didn't respond.

Michael scanned the living room for an intruder. Not seeing one, he raced over to Ty and rolled him face up, searching for signs of breath. He felt a slow and steady pulse coursing through Ty's carotid artery. "You okay, man?"

Ty covered his eyes against the morning sunlight. "Yeah. I think so."

"What happened?" Michael looked around the room. The usual assortment of dirty socks, pizza boxes, and empty Coke cans littered the floor. Car magazines and bills covered the coffee table. Nothing out of the ordinary.

"Been a long coupla days." Ty rubbed his bristled face with both hands.

"Yeah?"

"Head's killin' me."

Michael helped him stand up.

"Can you give me a lift to work?" Ty pawed at the hallway wall, steadying himself. "I was gonna call a cab. My piece of crap car is still in the shop."

"You sure you didn't get hit by a truck?" Ty's bloodshot eyes were puffy. It looked as though he hadn't shaved in days, a sight Michael had never witnessed in years of hanging out. Despite what his apartment looked like, Ty was a clean-cut kind of guy when it came to his appearance.

"Dunno." He rocked on his heels before Michael anchored him. "Feels like it."

Michael's skepticism heightened. Ty's state went beyond a lack of sleep. "I'll buy you a cup of coffee on the way. You obviously need it."

"Sounds good. Let me take a quick shower and I'll be ready to roll." Ty yawned, then shuffled down the hall to the bathroom.

Michael shut the front door, staring after his friend.

❖

While Michael drove, Ty squinted his eyes as he looked idly out the car window, as if the bright sunshine was too much for him. He yawned every few minutes.

"So," Michael said, "I'm guessing you didn't get fired."

Tyler squeezed his forehead with both hands. "This stays between you and me, okay?

"Understood."

"I'm not a hundred percent sure what's going on. But during the Green City meeting last week, Rebecca sent me two texts spelling out exactly what I was to report. Which is what I did. Then she wrote that I was supposed to go home and pack, and be at the airport by six thirty. A car service was waiting for me outside the Hessley building."

"Where'd you go?"

"Buffalo. I met with some people from Tomeo Environmental. For years, they did the independent environmental testing for Malvisti Park. Now they're doing the same for the entire Cascata Verde project."

"Never heard of 'em."

"They've been around since the '80s, long before Hessley bought the land. Several people at Tomeo looked a lot like you." Tyler grinned. "You know, slicked-back dark hair, brown eyes. Kept saying things like 'fuhget-aboud-it' and 'bada-bing.' Their heavy colognes almost did me in."

"You know, not all Italians are related."

"Whatever." Ty took a sip of coffee and placed it back in the holder between them. "Anyway, we worked hard in a freezing trailer, ate a lot of macaroni, and then they brought out some Sambuca to toast the project ... maybe that was the problem."

"But what exactly were you doing there?"

Ty blew out a breath. "So much, man. We spent two days in the on-site lab looking at raw sampling data from the site. We made hundreds of adjustments to prior reports, filled out some new reports, and submitted everything to EPA and a few state agencies. It was a blur. A cold blur."

Michael looked sharply at Ty. "I just looked over the Master Plan. Those reports should have been finalized months ago."

"Yeah, but they needed revisions. And someone from Hessley had to sign off on the final submission. Me, apparently."

"Did you collect any new soil or water samples?"

"Oh, no. I would've been there for weeks. No thank you. Not in that cold. Tomeo did the first round of chemical and radiological testing long before the land sale was completed. There were some problems, but the site was remediated and cleared before the deal closed. You wouldn't believe how many corrective-measures studies were done there. Tomeo did a second round *after* the remediation was complete, and those are the results we worked on all weekend."

"How's the site look?" A sense of unease came over Michael. Sampling was always a dicey process in Niagara Falls.

"It's clean." Ty reclined his seat and appeared to close his eyes.

Clean. Michael repeated the word, wondering where they'd be if the results weren't good.

Tyler abruptly sat up. He pointed to the roadside. "Isn't that the old guy and the dog with no legs you met last week?"

Michael switched his gaze to where Ty indicated. "Yep, it is. And Clary's only missing one leg." Michael rolled back the sunroof and shot his hand out the top.

Clary's owner noticed the slowing sports car before seeing Michael at the wheel. A look of recognition transformed his face and he waved back using a folded newspaper. The elderly man was wearing the same blue polyester shirt that he had on when Michael first met him.

"Mr. Malvisti, how are you?" he shouted. Clary perked up, looking around expectantly.

Michael lowered the passenger's side window. "Doing well, thank you." He turned to Tyler and waited until the window had closed again. "I really wish he wouldn't call me that. Mr. Malvisti is my dad."

"It makes you sound old," Ty agreed as he shifted his huge frame to pull out his phone. "And intimidating."

"You know, that seat will remember your favorite settings."

"Someday soon, when you're tired of this ride, I'm buying it off you. Look at this –I just got a text that I'm getting a raise *and* a mid-year bonus. Heck, Hessley must be doing even better than we thought."

"Good for you," Michael said. "You deserve it. I knew you weren't as dumb as you looked."

"Don't be so sure."

Privately, Michael wished that Tyler would take Jillian instead of the car. Michael could feel it. Things were coming to a head in their relationship.

He sensed a rough road ahead.

CHAPTER SEVEN

December 22, 2003

I was nearly fourteen when I realized that God had forgotten Italy. I should have kept this revelation to myself. It required action once I put it into words. Instead I blurted it out to my parents during their afternoon *riposo*, their daily rest from work. My mother made the sign of the cross as she half-fell, half-sagged across our sheet-covered loveseat in the parlor—the one reserved for company (mainly, Father Marciano).

My father slid to his knees in front of her.

I shifted my feet, eyes glued to the puff of white flour hanging above my mother in the still, dead air. I wasn't going to take it back. I wouldn't even explain my pronouncement unless they asked.

They didn't. Or couldn't, in my mother's case. She was out cold. My father patted her rough hands until her eyes fluttered open, his thin mouth set in a grim line.

He agreed with me. I was sure of it.

We made our home in Torre Annunziata, a small city in the province of Naples located in the region of Campania, Italy. We didn't own property. We didn't farm land. My parents worked at the "white art." Pasta-making had long been the economic engine of this seaport town. It probably still is.

My father's mother rented us two rooms in her flat. Our family's apartment building stood at the end of a row of light-colored, low-rise

59

structures, blocks away from the rocky shore of the Gulf of Naples. It sounds idyllic except that we lived under the southern shadow of Monte Vesuvio. It loomed larger over our lives than even Noni's formidable presence.

Today, experts call our volcano the "most dangerous in the world."

Back then, we already knew. The Mountain, as locals called the volcano, destroyed our city in 79 AD and again in 1631. If I remember my history, it also erupted in 1794 and 1906. The city was covered in ash during those smaller eruptions, but it survived. For generations, the Torresi people linked significant events with the volcano's active cycles. Someone might say, "Such-and-such factory was established during the year of the eruption." That would be 1906, when sea level lowered slightly and the Mountain erupted days later.

I hated being at the mercy of something outside my control.

My birthday, July 5, 1913, fell on one of those milestone days. It marked the start of the Mountain's thirty-one-year period of ash and lava outpourings. Superstitious midwives were split as to whether the events surrounding my arrival were an auspicious start to a boy's life. Nevertheless, the wrinkled women, eternally clad in their black mourning clothes, took all necessary precautions, including warding off the evil spirits with a corno, or horn.

I don't think their ministrations worked.

Famines, war, Mussolini, earthquakes, volcanoes. Conditions overall were desperate in Italy in the 1920s. My mother used to curse the Fascists, muttering to Saint So-and-so that the devils, as she called the Party members, were stealing our freedoms one by one. My father would hush her, nervously parting the heavy, floor-length curtains at the front of our apartment. He'd steal a quick glance before jerking them shut. It's a good thing he never heard Noni talk about Il Duce and the Party. She couldn't read, but she knew enough to be repulsed by the propaganda that served as my school textbooks.

I learned a few other things from her. Like how to curse like the fearsome harbormaster down at the port, even before I entered the second level. She also taught me to hide my dismay over rising to the ranks of avanguardista, an after-school Fascist youth movement I was "encouraged" by my teachers to attend.

Just as the Mountain's silhouette formed the backdrop for our city, fear was the canvas upon which even the most innocuous of my childhood experiences were drawn. I had heard about strikes that scourged the city. I became convinced that these strikes, whatever they were, would claim my parents when they left for work. Great sobs (mixed with more than a few curses) racked my body for a full half hour after my parents left each day. Noni would yank my arm and haul me to the back room, where she would hand me a broom. *"Abbastanza!"* Enough! As I grew older, special police bands formed throughout the region, adding to my anxiety.

How could any thinking person not agree that God had forgotten us? He had forgotten me.

By fifteen, I wanted something better. The neighbors below us had cousins who'd moved to America. No one had heard from them yet, but I was sure they were happier and richer than they had been in our afflicted land. I saw an opportunity to create my circumstances, not be defined by them. I told my dumbfounded parents that I had discovered a new place to put my faith. America—the land of unlimited opportunity and plentiful food—became my new god; prosperity and prominence became the saints I worshipped.

And, oh, my friends, I was a willing acolyte.

CHAPTER EIGHT

One Year Later
Niagara Falls, New York

Dana balanced a high-school yearbook on one knee, turning pages between strokes of toenail polish. She stopped on a page. "Now, that's a laugh."

"What is?" Lydia paused, her mascara brush held suspended in mid-air. She looked at Dana through the reflection in her oversized bathroom mirror.

"You were voted 'most carefree' in high school."

"Why's that a laugh?"

Dana flipped the book around. "See this dark-haired, athletic girl with a twinkle in her eye?" In the half-page photograph, Lydia's arm draped the stocky form of a baby-faced boy. The caption identified him as Christopher Magnano, the "most carefree" male student.

Lydia rolled her eyes. "You making fun of my fitted purple jacket with the ruffled waist?"

"No."

"My big hair?"

"No."

"Then what?" Lydia zipped her makeup bag and leaned close to the mirror to examine the results. Passable. Everyone else at the reunion would probably be just as pale after another long, ugly winter.

"Most carefree?" Dana set the yearbook aside and bent over to check her nails. "I think you deserve the 'most changed' vote tonight."

Lydia turned toward her. "Yikes. That was harsh."

She continued to study her hands. "Just an observation. You're always worried."

"Look, a lot of bad stuff has happened. I can't just snap out of it. I'm always thinking about my brother, and whether his cancer's spread, and I've got a lot of anxiety about Harrison's health. I mean, we've been to the ER a half-dozen times this year and no one really knows what wrong." Lydia returned to her reflection. "I'm doing the best I can."

"Hey, I'm sorry." Dana's lips twisted, almost wistfully. "I didn't mean that the way it sounded."

"I hope not. No offense, but I worry about you sometimes."

"Why? Because I speak the truth?"

"No, because you look at things so dispassionately." She stretched a strand of hair through the straightener. The heat kicked on.

"What are you talking about?"

"Here's an example. Our real estate clients are always talking about why they're moving: divorce, loss of a job, a promotion. Some families need a bigger house because a parent is sick or a twenty-something moved back home. Radical life changes. And many of them aren't good. We both know too many of our clients are hurting."

Dana stood. A flush of red had spread upwards from her neck. "What are you getting at?"

"Their distress doesn't seem to bother you. 'People just need to rise above that emotional drama and push themselves to a better self.' Isn't that what you always say?"

Dana studied the floor.

Lydia released another lock of straightened hair. "I can't do that. Those stories affect me. They prove that life is hard. Some days, it's unbearable."

Dana took a breath as if to speak.

"Wait." Lydia held up her elbow, still holding the straightener. "Despite the claims of those cliché-ridden books you've given me over the years, things don't always turn out all right."

"But those challenges will help them open their eyes to better themselves. To continue on their individual paths to knowledge."

"Never mind. I don't want to argue. Let me finish my hair, and then we can leave and get this reunion over and done." Lydia leaned over and hugged her friend. Dana stiffened and pulled away.

"You know I'm not a hugger." She bent over to check her toes again. "Look, I know you've been through a lot. But it's chipped away at the fun, crazy girl you used to be. You hardly ever leave your house anymore except for work. Or to see Robby."

"We had zero worries back then. Now I wake up every day in fear of what's coming next. That's why it's better to stay home—less likely a disaster could take what little I have left."

"We were young, I'll give you that. But we still had huge concerns, even by adult standards."

"True." Lydia gazed at her picture in the yearbook. "Maybe you're right. I do look sort of happy in that pic."

"I remember the day they took this shot." Dana grinned. "You'd just convinced Mr. Columbo not to punish anyone for going to Malvisti Park on senior skip day. You were the most lighthearted person I'd ever met. I think that's why we became friends. We were opposites. You were fun; I'm mean and rude."

"That's not true! You're blunt, take-charge … but never rude." Lydia teased the crown of her hair to give it volume. "To be honest, I can't wait to get this reunion over."

"Didn't you learn anything from those books I loaned you? You are affected only by your thoughts. Choose to be positive and that will become your reality." Dana ran her fingers through her blunt-cut hair to bring out the platinum-blonde highlights. The edges just brushed the knot of her black halter top, showing off the two-carat diamond earrings she'd popped into her earlobes. "I'm looking forward to it."

"Well, I'm dreading it." Lydia stood in front of the mirror, a round brush dangling from her hand. "I mean, how many other single moms will be there? How many others will be sleep-deprived because they're worried sick about their children? Or devastated over a dying brother? Or wondering when the next house sale will come along ...." Her breath caught in a hiccup. She squeezed her eyes shut. "I don't want to see regular people with normal families. I want to be normal."

Dana shrugged. "It is what it is."

"I hate that saying." Lydia whirled around. "It's trite and it's hurtful."

"But on some level it's true. You can't change facts. I didn't expect to go to my twenty-year high school reunion without a husband or kids. You can't make things what they aren't. But you can work to make them what you want them to be."

"If that were true, then I'd have a living, healthy and complete family. And I'd be rich. Rich enough to move my little house to an untouched island where no one is sick or dying. And where there's no slush or snow."

Dana grinned. "I know you're not talkin' about Niagara Falls."

CHAPTER NINE

Lydia leaned closer to Dana across the pub table and tipped her head toward the four men slouched against the bar. "They look so different from twenty years ago. I can't pinpoint it, but I think it's something about their eyes."

Dana shrugged. "All I see is less hair and bigger stomachs."

"Do I look that much older? Tell me the truth." Lydia tried to suppress the smirk trying to break out across her face.

"You don't look a day over twenty-five."

"Maybe you need to take a closer look."

"No need. I see you nearly every day. Sometimes twice a ..." Dana's voice trailed off.

Lydia followed her friend's stare; she saw a broad-shouldered man with a sizable stomach, standing at the end of the bar and stuffing his face with chicken wings. "Who's that?"

"Worst-date-of-my-life John. Don't you remember? He's the one who took me to that cast party where I ended up with alcohol poisoning."

"And Chris and I took you to the hospital to get your stomach pumped. That was a nightmare."

"No kidding. I wonder if he still thinks he's God's gift to womankind."

"Sometimes I wonder how we survived those years." Lydia gazed at all the clusters of people talking, catching up. She and Dana had done the rounds already, talking to everyone they cared to, and ended up sitting alone in a booth. She tapped her foot to Heavy D on the overhead speaker. Some things hadn't changed in twenty years.

"I should've looked at that yearbook with you," Lydia said. "I'm so bad with names."

Three women dressed in sweaters and jeans paraded toward the ladies' room, joking with one another. Lydia had no trouble identifying these women on sight. They'd been the popular girls at school. And they still attracted attention from every male in the room. Lydia waved and smiled as they passed their table. They waved back. Now that she thought about it, their class had been close in a way that transcended cliques and people groups. Football standouts, flute players, or druggies all got along well enough. It probably had something to do with bonding over the multiple traumas they'd collectively experienced as children. Love Canal sprang to her mind. How many of these people had to move because of that man-made disaster?

Lydia returned to sipping her pop.

Snippets of conversation from the adjacent booth drifted into her ears. Someone mentioned Cascata Verde.

"Now my cousin in San Jose will stop making fun of us," a woman said. "We'll finally be a city that sets trends instead of trailing ten or fifteen years behind them."

"I heard that each house will have a rooftop garden that doubles as a rainwater harvester. I hope it works for snow!"

Lydia discreetly glanced at the occupants of the next table. She recognized the class salutatorian, Gary, now a skinny, balding man. The pregnant woman beside him appeared to be his wife. Across from them sat a couple Lydia didn't recognize. Both had red faces, as if they'd gotten either too much sun or too much booze.

"The new anchor tenant is an Italian company and they've already started accepting resumes," said Gary. "They're doing cutting-edge research on the bioremediation of radionuclides. I've waited a long time to be able to use my engineering degree and actually get paid for it."

The red-faced man laughed. "A radionuclide?"

Gary straightened. "It's an isotope that emits radiation as it decays. That's why this bioremediation company is perfect for this area. Their technology uses altered bacteria to clean up radioactive material in the soil. Or even water."

"They should start in my backyard," said the woman. "I think it glows at night." Everyone chuckled.

"That's nothing." A short, bearded man walked up to the table. Tim … what was it, Toscana? Lydia had had a crush on him in school, but he'd never shown any interest in her. "Nobody can beat the bonfires in my backyard. Without gas or any accelerant, they go a good twenty, thirty feet in the air. It's my dirt, man. Something's there."

"Party at your place." The woman with the flushed face announced. "We'll be there 'bout 11, pyro-boy."

Lydia couldn't help but laugh.

Dana tapped her chin with an orange-polished nail. "I've been thinking."

Better than eavesdropping, Lydia figured.

"I wonder if this eco-city might be a huge opportunity for us. They're starting to build the condos and single-family residences. When those go up for sale, they're going to need a couple of competent local real estate professionals, don't you think?"

"Did you have someone in mind?"

Dana's face lit up. "I think we should contact the developer and offer to help sell all those green homes."

"There's no way Lakeside Realty could take on a project that big." Their disorganized boss could barely manage the trickle of homes he brokered in a given year.

Dana grinned. "I didn't say anything about Lakeside. Just us."

"You're not suggesting we quit our jobs?" Her voice rose slightly.

Dana seized Lydia's hand. "Calm down, girl."

Lydia's throat constricted. "I can barely afford to put food on the table and pay my mortgage. And you want me to gamble on something that's never been tried anywhere else? That may work for you, but I've got the boys to worry about."

Dana shook her head. "You are so pessimistic. Mr. Mahoney's bad energy is rubbing off on you."

"I ... I don't know. I don't like risk. And I don't want to get my hopes up for nothing."

"I understand." Dana adjusted her necklace. "But sometimes you've got to take a leap of faith. I know we can present the developer with an offer he can't refuse."

"Like what? Send the mafia to deliver a biodegradable proposal?"

Dana cocked her head. "Not a bad idea." Her eyes twinkled for a moment. "But seriously. We can offer them a team approach to selling those homes. You and I would head the team, and we could hire an assistant or two. As the partners, one or both of us would be available for all showings. We could cover that office seven days a week."

Lydia crossed her arms over her abdomen. "You know change gives me *agita.*"

Dana rolled her eyes. "Working for Lakeside upsets your stomach too. But I have confidence in this. I believe in us. Maybe we could even work out a deal where we could live in on-site apartments while the homes are being constructed. That'll save us money and allow us to walk to work every day. We'd reduce our gas use. You wouldn't have to put so many miles on your dying minivan. We could even drive to our showings in a golf cart."

"It's March and it's still freezing outside. Probably snowing right now. Then what?"

"We'll use a truck with a snow plow, fully equipped with warmed seats and hot chocolate dispensers."

"Clever. Love the chocolate part."

"Look, that developer is going to need agents with a solid reputation if they expect to sell this radical vision here. Western New Yorkers are skeptical about anything new. But since we know the locals, they'll trust us. Look at the referrals we could get just from our acquaintances here." Dana swept the room with her arm. "We'd be an enormous asset to Hessley."

Lydia gazed absentmindedly at her classmates while considering Dana's proposal. It would be exciting to see Western New York rise up from the wreckage of joblessness and decline. And even more exciting to play a part in making that happen. But she couldn't afford to take chances. "I'll think about it."

"Think hard. We can be a part of harmonizing this area back to nature."

"Dana DuPays and Lydia Vallone! What are you guys talking about so seriously over here?" A heavyset man sat next to Lydia. He set his water down, winked at Dana, and gave Lydia an affectionate hug.

"Chris Magnano, how in the heck are you?" Lydia asked. "We were just looking at our yearbook picture together."

"I'm just fine. But I didn't expect to see you here, Dana. Someone told me you moved away. To Long Island or something."

"I did, but I came back a few years ago." Dana shrugged. "You know, family ties and all that."

Lydia knew she would offer no other details. Few people were allowed beyond that hard-as-nails exterior.

"Me too," Chris said. "I worked in San Diego for a few years, but I missed home. I wanted genuine Buffalo wings and Italian bread. And real people. We're a different breed here." He held up his water as if saluting the guys at the bar.

"I hear you," Dana said lightly. "When I lived in Nashville before Long Island, they put seeds on a loaf of Wonder bread and called it *Eye-talian*. I couldn't stand it."

Chris laughed heartily, then shifted his attention to Lydia. "Are you still that same carefree girl I knew so long ago?"

"Hardly." She studied his round face for a moment, feeling a catch in her throat. They had been close in high school. But a lot had happened in twenty years. She gave Chris a wan smile. "Are you still the carefree boy I knew so long ago?"

His eyes darkened, and he played with the condensation on his glass. "Not so much."

Apparently life had been difficult for them all.

Jackie Panetta, their former class president, called for everyone's attention from the far end of the room. The people at her table tapped glasses with forks. It took a few seconds for the buzz of conversations to end.

"Thank you for coming," Jackie said loud enough to be heard in all corners of the bar. "It's been great seeing everyone again. Many thanks to the reunion committee for all of their hard work. Before we get back to reconnecting, I think it's appropriate that we acknowledge our classmates who have passed on. I'd like to read their names aloud and then have a moment of silence.

"Karen Reinherd," she began. The outgoing cheerleader had died of a rare leukemia shortly after they graduated.

"Tommy Richards." Lydia didn't know the star quarterback had died. Judging from the expressions of disbelief around the room, not many others knew either.

"Reesa Murphy." Lydia looked at Dana, who shrugged.

"Kristina Tullo." Gasps came from all over the room.

"Stephanie Stopawicz."

More gasps.

"Jason Babcock." The people at the next table raised their eyebrows at one another.

"Sarah Stillman." Jackie's chin quivered and tears spilled down her face. Jackie and Sarah had been like sisters. She took a breath and continued reading from the list. "Sammy Weilecz. Robert James."

"This is sickening," Lydia choked out.

"Brittany Borden. And Mark Gutierrez." Jackie closed her eyes. "Please, let's have a moment of silence."

The group stayed quiet for several minutes. Lydia hadn't expected to have lost this many classmates. Not this soon, anyway.

Jackie cleared her throat and everyone looked up. "These classmates have left behind seventeen children. The Reunion Committee established a scholarship trust fund for them at Niagara Regional Bank. Please consider contributing financially. I hope you all have a fantastic night." She smiled weakly. "Let's enjoy each other's company while we still can."

Tentative applause accompanied the end of her speech. Conversations picked up where they'd left off, and the silence for the dead was soon replaced by the banter of the living.

Lydia's mind veered off in another direction. She had no idea what would happen to her children if she couldn't take care of them. Dana might agree to take on the responsibility. She couldn't have children of her own—yet another fallout from Love Canal—but she didn't seem to have any desire for them. She'd called children "monsters" for so long that Lydia believed she meant it. And Lydia's mom probably wouldn't be up for it either. Robby's illness seems to have sapped the life from her.

"It's so sad, all those kids who've lost parents." Dana's voice sounded hollow. "I'm definitely going to contribute to that fund."

Lydia wished she could do the same. But she didn't have a dime to spare. Perhaps, if this business proposition of Dana's panned out, she'd have a little breathing room for a change.

"So, what are you doing now?" Dana asked Chris.

His head swiveled from Lydia to Dana. "I'm a technical writer for a California company that lets me work from home."

"You were always good at technical things," Lydia said. "You're very logical."

"This guy? Logical?" John-the-ex-date dropped into the chair beside Dana. His broad shoulders pressed against hers.

She took a sip of her drink, her body rigid. "John," she said without turning her head. "How are you?"

"Better than I deserve." He nodded a hello to Lydia, then turned to Chris. "I saw some articles in an underground city newspaper that were authored by a C. T. Magnano. Is that you, man?"

"Yeah." Chris' ears turned red. "I do some freelance work on the side. I did a series on environmental issues."

John nodded curtly. "I've seen your articles all over the web. Impressive."

"I don't know about that, but the subject is important to me."

"Why, Chris?" Lydia felt certain there was a story behind the stories.

"Because, as we just heard, we've got a lot of sickness around here." He paused, as if uncertain whether he should continue. "Niagara County residents have very high rates for thyroid disease. We've got more cancers, especially prostate, lung, breast, colorectal, and bladder. Our leukemia rates are off the charts. And those are just the more common types of cancer. The county has just started tracking the so-called rare cancers that have been striking here regularly."

Lydia felt a familiar pang in her stomach. Her father's cancer was so rare, specialists told her it would be statistically impossible for anyone else in the city to receive the same diagnosis that year. But since his death, she'd heard about a dozen others who'd succumbed to the same disease. Most of them had been diagnosed around the same time as her dad.

Toxic talk had always been part of life in Western New York. They'd grown up with factories all across the city. But Lydia had never thought about how the chemicals made or used by those factories might be affecting the families who lived here.

"It's also important to me because of Love Canal. Just after I was born, my parents had to move a few blocks west because of all the contamination over there. I read that officials drew an arbitrary line around the toxic area and declared that everyone outside it was safe. How could my parents have thought that toxins wouldn't touch us once we jumped to the other side of the fence?"

"Geez, Chris." John huffed out a breath. "Moving a few blocks away was about as effective as putting a no trespassing sign on top of the dirt. You know as well as I do that chemicals move."

Lydia squeezed her eyes to prevent tears from spilling over. Maybe that's why she'd lost so many family members.

"We were a Love Canal family too." John's voice had quieted. "To this day, my mother feels guilty for keeping us there so long." He looked at his watch and grimaced. His knee bounced, causing the bench to shake.

"Now that I'm older, I wonder why the adults weren't more afraid to live here." Lydia pressed her hands together. "Why didn't they flee this cesspool sooner? And why didn't they go farther away after being forced out of a toxic area as big as Love Canal?"

John studied Lydia's face. "Maybe they were just busy with life. Busy raising kids. Surviving. It happens."

"Sure." Chris added. "And don't forget, air pollution and illegal dumping were regular occurrences when we were young."

"They knew so little then, but they knew enough." John said hoarsely.

Lydia raised her eyebrows.

Dana sighed loudly. Lydia imagined Dana wanted to change the subject. They had never talked about the region's pollution problems, not even when Dana was told she probably couldn't have children because of her past exposure.

"Do you remember seeing small fires in the fields near the river?" John stilled his leg. "And lawns that spontaneously burst into flames?"

"Yeah, all the time. How about those corroded 55-gallon drums lying around everywhere?" Chris shook his head. "No one said anything about them. Nobody seemed alarmed. There was no news coverage, no investigative articles or Internet videos. That's why I write about it when I can."

"Well, we should've known that wasn't normal." John folded his hands. His knuckles turned white. "The politicians knew. Of that I am very, very sure."

Chris tapped his water glass. "Until I moved to San Diego, I used to think all cities had dirty, sprawling factories spewing brown-tinged smoke. Dilapidated buildings with tiny broken windows, surrounded by rusted equipment. It never occurred to me that other cities didn't smell like sulfur."

"What do you think, Dana?" John twisted in his seat to look at her.

"That everyone was aware of the risk and stayed." She lowered her eyes. "It's time to release all of that negative energy and move forward, guys. That's why the new eco-city is so important. It's our triumph over all those terrible things that immobilized our region and kept us down for too long."

The men looked skeptical. Chris hung his head, his full lips pressed together until they'd lost color.

"It's not that simple." Chris looked up and stared at her long enough for her to do the same. "The contamination problem was, and is, worse than people know. Just look at places like Bloody Run. That creek overflowed every time it rained. It left deadly waste along the creek bank. I'm sure it's still there."

"Why didn't I ever hear about that?" Lydia asked.

"Most people haven't." Chris replied. "Look, for years, local factories met a huge portion of the national demand for pesticides and bleaches. Chemical companies drove our economy back then."

"I hadn't realized this area played such a big role in the chemical industry. Probably the military, too." She felt clueless. "And wastes from those industries are still buried around here? How is that something you just 'let go.' Dana?"

"You don't." Chris interrupted. "And that's what makes me nervous about Cascata Verde."

"What?" Lydia's eyes went wide. "It's supposed to be our city's savior! Don't you believe that?" She looked at Dana for confirmation. Dana's eyes had turned a steely blue. The atmosphere around the table had changed.

John stood. "Sorry to interrupt this thrilling conversation, but I have to leave. First I'd like to borrow Dana for a minute." He flashed a hopeful look at her.

Dana grabbed her purse and jacket. Lydia wondered why she was so eager to go with John when she hadn't said too much to him. Maybe she just wanted to get out of talking about this depressing topic.

"John," Lydia tugged on his sleeve as he stood at the head of the table. "Before you go, I'm curious about something. Why were you following those environmental articles Chris wrote?"

"I'm a viticulturist. Since soil conditions impact my grapes, I make it my business to know what's in the ground." John started to lead Dana by the elbow to the back of the bar.

"Wow." Still watching John and Dana, Chris rubbed his hands behind his shaved head and exhaled. "And here I thought my readers were just a bunch of tree-huggers."

Halfway to the back of the bar, John turned and met Chris' eyes. Although John's face was hard to read, Lydia was sure something unspoken had passed between them.

She waited until John and Dana were out of earshot. "What just happened there?"

Chris didn't respond. He seemed confused.

"C'mon Chris, fill me in!"

"I think he's trying to tell me something."

Lydia clutched Chris's arm, startling him. "Chris, maybe someone should investigate Cascata Verde? Do you know any of the reporters at the *Courier?*"

He looked around apprehensively. "You need to keep your voice down. I've been warned to lay low when it comes to environmental issues around here."

Her heart lurched. That sounded like all the more reason to look into it. "Well?"

"But just between you and me, I'm on it. There's a lot of rumors about the green city property. And I'll keep on it as long as I'm able to wield a pen."

At least someone with half a brain was doing something. Lydia took a deep breath.

"If you'd like to know what's going on, I'll keep you posted."

"Please do."

"I'll stay in touch." He hugged her and left.

Dana returned to the table. Her cheeks flamed, but her eyes had warmed back to a crystal clear blue. "I'm ready to go."

Lydia jumped up and threw on her jacket. She waited until they were slogging through slush in the parking lot to ask about John. "Well?" They made a beeline towards Dana's car at the far end of the lot.

"Miracles never cease," Dana said with a hint of sarcasm. "He actually apologized for contributing to my near-death experience that night at the cast party."

"Really?" Lydia wondered what John was after.

"He even asked me to forgive him." Dana gave a nervous laugh. "He told me that he's not the selfish person he was all those years ago."

"Oh? What else did he say?"

Dana's eyes crinkled at the corners. She stopped outside her car. Freezing rain bounced off the sleek sides of the hybrid. "He said he came to the reunion for two reasons, and the first was to say those words to me."

"What was the other reason?"

"I don't know!" She ran her fingers through her short hair. "I was so shocked that I was reason number one, I forgot to ask."

❖

Exhausted, Lydia arrived home, paid Angie for babysitting, and went to bed. No doubt the boys would be up early.

She dreamed that the sound of lapping water awoke her. She opened her eyes and, in the pitch black of her room, saw luminous droplets rolling down the bedroom walls. More beads of the radiant water materialized on the ceiling. Soon, sheets of shimmering liquid cascaded down the walls, pooling into translucent blue-tinged puddles on the floor. She sprang out of bed, yanked off the sheets, and feverishly tried to soak up the water.

But no matter what she did, she could not stem the flow.

The shrill sound of the house phone jolted her awake. Her heart pounded in her chest. Somehow, even in her confused and shaken state, Lydia knew that Robby was in trouble.

CHAPTER TEN

December 23, 2003

Friends ... I can call you that now, can't I? After all, I'm opening up my life for examination, shining a light on some of the darkest corners of my soul. It's easier to expose those secrets when there's some form of familiarity between us.

Bear with me. Men weren't taught to share feelings in my day.

I count my arrival in Niagara Falls on July 4, 1928, as the day I knew my dreams were not big enough. It was an awakening of sorts. (I declared it my new birthday, in fact. The old one had too many bad associations.) You see, my immigration story didn't really start until *after* I arrived in America.

Don't get me wrong. The journey here was fascinating, especially for a teenager who had never gone anywhere outside Torre Annunziata. I left Italian soil on April 13, 1928, on the *SS Conte Grande's* maiden voyage for the Genoa-Naples-New York passenger service. My pockets were stuffed with a couple dollars and a few childish possessions. I had promised to write my parents and send money; Noni had pressed a glass brooch into my hand after roughly patting my cheek and kissing me good-bye. I passed the time on the ship talking with people who told me about their vocations as printers, stonemasons, or bakers. Our discussions forced me to think about my skills before arriving at the immigration station in New York City. I had to come up with something to put my hands to or they might turn me back.

I would do anything to avoid that fate.

After we arrived, I spent a few months working in a choking Pennsylvania coal mine hundreds of feet below the Earth's surface. A few miners—who wouldn't be alive if it weren't for my actions—convinced me that I had what it took to be somebody. Maybe even a leader of men. But coal mining was like being at the mercy of Vesuvio. Men died or were hurt all the time. I needed more control over my environment; I wanted too much to be my own man.

A group of us miners heard about jobs in the expanding power industry in Niagara Falls. Power, whatever that entailed, sounded good. I was hooked. Especially when I got wind of the number of straight-off-the-boat girls who had settled in the city's Little Italy. My plan was simple: obtain a good-paying job, an Italian wife, a little house, and, eventually, a large family. The American Dream.

But my real transformation as an American took place the day I first laid my eyes on Niagara Falls.

On that July afternoon, I got off a train and walked into a crowd later estimated at more than 100,000 people. Niagara buzzed with enthusiasm. Every intersection, every building, every resident of this city was *alive*. Her power enterprise had opened the eyes of the world to unimaginable potential in manufacturing, tourism, and invention. Anything was possible in this city! People drove cars, bought radios, and went to the movies every weekend. They owned toasters and vacuum cleaners. Citizens worked at jobs with livable wages. And the food? No rations here. I had tumbled into a world of consumerism that I could never adequately describe in a letter to my parents.

As I neared the famous Falls, and as tiny droplets of water stained my coat, the vibration of the more than five billion gallons of water per hour that thundered over the crest made my heart rate rocket. The deep reverberations that shook my insides hit a little too close to home—Vesuvio sometimes rumbled like this. Despite the feelings of helplessness that threatened, I moved closer to the crest of the American Falls.

My ears dulled in the unrelenting roar. Mist pricked my eyes and neck until I was forced to use my hat as a shield. I could hardly see more than a few feet in either direction.

My first encounter with the mighty Niagara Falls left me feeling small and hollow, but somehow full of expectation, too. All that rushing water seemed to have purpose, like it was doing something that mattered.

From under my hat, I peered through the spray and the throng of tourists, looking for a place to catch my breath. A black iron railing materialized. It ran parallel to the American Falls on my left, curved in front of me, and continued to my right along the rim of the Niagara Gorge, a steep-walled chasm below the Falls. My shoulders relaxed when I gripped its solid form. An anchor, perhaps my first since leaving Italy a few months before.

Someone bumped me from behind. "*Mi scusi.*" A short man tipped his soggy fedora as he passed. He hustled along the wet barrier fence, paying no attention whatsoever to the Falls.

More people pressed in around me, forcing me to hug the railing. I inched along with care, the mist tapering the farther I moved from the brink of the Falls. A sudden gust of wind swept the thinning vapor in another direction. I stopped in my tracks, staring in awe at the sweeping panorama of sky, water, and layered rock.

Below the Falls, the turbulent lower Niagara River dissected the deep gorge shared by the United States and Canada. As I gazed at it, I noticed thousands of people scurrying away from the spectacular cascades behind me, excitement rippling through the crowds.

"He's alive!" A boy in a felt cap gestured toward the shoreline below. Men flocked to my railing. Women clutched small children, keeping them at a safe distance from the edge, but appearing curious nonetheless. I looked over the railing, but saw only scattered groups of people working their way along the steep gorge trails leading to the water.

Tourists? I didn't think so. They would have been running the other way, towards the cascades.

Curiosity seized me. I joined a line of enthusiastic youths stumbling down one of the treacherous gorge paths. Whistles, yells, and repeated hurrahs punctuated the steady rumble of the Falls, which was by now far behind us.

"There he is!" A young woman in our group blew a kiss at a powerfully built man standing in the center of a crowd. Water rolled off his wavy dark hair and dripped down his torso. Men in rolled-up sleeves, some standing in the shallows of the swirling river, hung a towel around the muscular man's shoulders. His barrel-shaped chest puffed up in pride with each new "attaboy" from the group standing protectively around him. Smiling, he basked in the cheers ricocheting around the great chasm, especially from the Canadian side of the gorge.

I grasped the shoulder of the boy below me. "Who is it?"

He turned and stared as if I had missed the second coming of Christ. "It's Jean Lussier, Mac. Where you been hidin'? He just shot over the Horseshoe Falls in a rubber ball—the Maid of the Mist crew towed him to shore!"

Jean Lussier? Never heard of him. All I knew was that the front of the muscular man's tank suit was made from fabric bearing the image of America's flag. I swallowed. He might just be the embodiment of the perfect American male: strong, proud, and fearless. And here I had been cowed by the mere tremor of the Falls.

Our small group safely reached the river's edge. The man of the hour stood hatless and smiling, sporting a triumphant bruise over his right eye. He waved to the adoring crowd, lifting his hands high to acknowledge the spectators along the lip of the gorge. His erect bearing made him appear taller than his medium-sized frame.

I pressed closer, snapping a twig beneath my feet. The man who had stared down the Horseshoe Falls fixed his defiant eyes on me. Young and ego-driven, I took his probing stare as a challenge. It might seem silly to some, but I imagined that he had passed on to me the mantle of great daring and courage.

He looked away only after someone handed him a cigar. Applause erupted as he clenched it between his teeth and grinned. (No wonder locals had dubbed him Smiling Jean.) Newspaper men asked him if he'd broken any bones. An admirer wanted to know if he had been scared. His every response elicited excited chatter. Somewhere up above, a band struck up a new jazz chorus.

My transformation took root then and there. Before, I had only wanted the opportunity to create my circumstances, the chance to be my own man. A productive worker, husband, and father. Now I wanted to have influence over others. I wanted to embody everything great and strong about America. Someday the crowds would be shouting for me.

And, eventually, I wanted something more. My contribution to this magnificent city would last. She lacked the culture and sense of ancient history that we took for granted in Italy. I could improve this already grand city, not just for myself, but for all citizens. I would be this city's hero.

Lussier went on to sell pieces of his famous rubber ball to tourists, resorting to bits of rubber from a tire store when his ball ran dry. I lost respect for him then. His attempt to get rich at the expense of others made him no more than a swindler. He did nothing to improve anything for anyone but himself. Lussier was a one-off novelty.

My desires ran deeper.

I spent the next seven decades seeking and winning admiration from the citizens of Niagara Falls. Some say I got rich off her. That I exploited her natural resources. Sickened her people. Perhaps so. But I also gave back. I employed people. I built things for this city. I gave her a spectacle of parks, buildings, and amenities that no one had ever before provided.

Now I wonder ... was I really any different from Mr. Lussier?

CHAPTER ELEVEN

Buffalo, New York

"I brought you dinner."

Lydia jolted awake and found Dana standing over her in the hospital's isolation room. "I must've fallen asleep."

"That's what happens when you sit here for a week, for hours on end." Dana peeled off her heavy coat, sending wafts of the crisp outside air into the stale room. "I brought pork roast and potatoes, but they wouldn't let me bring it up here. You'd think workers in a religious hospital would be a little happier around Eastertime."

"Thanks." Lydia stretched. No doubt the rhythmic hiss of Robby's breathing equipment had lulled her to sleep. She went to her brother's side and stared at the needles sending IV drips into Robby's hand.

"How is he?"

"Very weak. They're giving him a transfusion. We'll see if his numbers improve, but his weeklong slide just keeps on going."

"I can't stand seeing him like this." Dana turned away. "He should be playing hockey and running from hordes of women instead of ... this." She waved her hand vaguely toward the tangle of equipment.

The electronic pump drip counter clicked. The metrical sounds of equipment had stopped annoying her long ago. Now they signified that Robby was still with them.

"So," Lydia said, grateful for Dana's distraction, "Tell me about the pitch to Hessley's CEO. How'd it go? Where'd you do it?"

"At Hessley's home office, which, by the way, is fabulous. Rebecca Waters designed and decorated the whole building. The conference room next to her office had a gorgeous view of Tampa Bay."

"Did you see palm trees?"

"Oh, yes. All along the marina. Breathtaking."

"I'll bet." Lydia sighed. She looked outside at the dismal grayness of the early spring sky. The region might not shake this shroud of oppressive clouds for a few weeks more.

"When I landed in Buffalo this morning, I saw a gun-metal gray cloudy landscape stretching from ground to sky. No horizon whatsoever. Made me wonder why we live here."

She asked herself that all the time.

Lydia wished she'd been able to go with Dana to Hessley's Florida headquarters. But too little money, too many responsibilities, and too much uncertainty with Robby's condition added up to plenty of reasons not to. "Well, what happened in the meeting?"

Dana removed her long leather gloves and hung them neatly over the chair. "First of all, they're pretty far along with this green city development. It's a good thing we didn't wait even a day."

"I'm glad you pushed us."

"I described our current sales volume, which was not that impressive when compared to real estate in Florida. Or anywhere, really. Then I talked a bit about my entrepreneurial ambitions." Dana raised a perfectly waxed eyebrow. "Rebecca Waters and I aren't so different."

"How so?"

"She's a professional, single woman. Respect is important to her. She started her own development firm after having had success in other fields."

"Anything else?"

"Yes, actually." Dana rested her eyes on Robby. "We both have a fundamental respect for the Earth. Nothing religious, mind you. Neither of us can understand how human beings, especially those Bible-thumpers, believe they are superior to other living things. That people are entitled to more than their fair share of limited resources. It makes no sense."

"You sound like two peas in a pod."

"Totally. And we both hate air conditioning. More importantly, I think we both recognize that our responsibility is to this planet. We each must use the talents we have to bring people in harmony with nature."

Lydia wasn't sure what to say. The eco-city was a business proposition. Money was at its root, pure and simple. "You presented our PowerPoint proposal?"

"Yep. That went over well. I discussed our marketing strategy. I told her we envision potential residents buying into a way of life, an Earth-centered philosophy, and not just a neighborhood or a floor plan. She seemed impressed."

"Good. Then at least some of our preparation time was well spent." Although they had never discussed earth-people-harmony, whatever that entailed, they had worked hard running the numbers and marketing aspects of the proposal. Lydia was surprised that their nighttime brainstorming session had resulted in anything productive. Harrison and Travis each had a fever. While she and Dana worked, Harrison lay quietly on the couch, watching a fishing show. But Travis was hyper, demanding water, then ice cream, more clothing, then less clothing. And, of course, her mother called a few times with updates on Robby. After tucking the boys into bed, she and Dana had worked until after eleven.

"I also presented our ideas for marketing the property regionally. I suggested that Hessley advertise through websites and e-zines oriented toward environmentally and spiritually conscious individuals. I encouraged her to attract up-and-coming artists who could form an arts enclave within Cascata Verde. Hessley could promote creativity by building homes with natural-light studios to encourage expression and thought."

"I love those ideas." Lydia sat up, her eyebrows raised.

"We discussed the division of labor between them and us."

"Are we close to any type of understanding?" Lydia slid to the end of her chair.

"I think so. We drafted an independent contractor arrangement. We sell exclusively for Hessley, and they use us exclusively for all residential sales. Commission is a set five percent, which you and I will split. Our main responsibilities are to be accessible, available, knowledgeable, and enthusiastic about the eco-city."

"We can do that." She'd force herself to act hopeful and excited, even if it meant faking it until she made it.

"Hessley will provide business cards, signage, office supplies ... and guess what else?"

"An office?"

"That's already included. We also get free access to the new Falls-themed spa that's going in at the site."

"A spa? I don't have time to run to the bathroom, let alone hang out in a spa."

"You'll make time. And there's more."

"Let me guess, an organic chef will come to my house and prepare breakfast, lunch, dinner, and snacks?"

"Nope, although that sounds good." Dana laughed. "We get a car to share."

"I don't believe it."

"And not just any car. A luxury hybrid, to use when we're on the property or when we're driving around town on real-estate business. It's just temporary, though. The eco-city will be mostly car-free sometime after people start moving in."

"It'll be the most expensive vehicle I've ever driven." Lydia's brow wrinkled. "What if I scratch it or plow into a snowdrift?"

Dana shook her head. "Why is disaster always the first thing that enters your mind?"

"That's all I know, I think."

"Look, it's important that we look like hip professionals," Dana said, looking pointedly at Lydia's zip-up hoodie.

"What are you saying?" Lydia looked down at her sweats. "They match, kinda."

"You'll need a new wardrobe."

"I'm not going to have to wear hemp pants and organic cotton blouses, am I?"

"That's exactly what I mean."

Lydia wasn't sure whether Dana was serious, but she could see that her friend had a point. "You did a great job, my friend."

Robby stirred, and Lydia checked on him. His hand twitched. His eyes blinked in his comatose state. Was he uncomfortable? Lydia pulled a chair close and sat down. What was he feeling? What did she need to do? A sense of powerlessness engulfed her. They'd been rehashing this scene ever since the reunion a week ago.

"How are the boys doing?" Dana asked quietly.

"Travis is back to his energetic self. Harrison has his ever-present, low-grade fever." Lydia kept her eyes trained on Robby's hand. His fingers were blue, much like Harrison's last spring after his asthma attack landed him in the hospital. She still hadn't paid off half the bills from this year's ER visits.

"Harrison looked so small and fragile lying on the couch the other night."

"The doctor says he's within expected growth ranges, but ..." Lydia pursed her lips. The blue fingers set her to thinking. *Robby is dying. And Harrison doesn't look right either.* She blinked, erasing a half-formed thought from her brain.

Lydia jumped when Maria, the nurse, stepped in the room. "Ladies, you should be wearing masks and a covering. Robby's white blood cell count is off and he can't be exposed to any germs." Maria grabbed a mask from a mounted wall dispenser. She pinched the nose clip to secure it against her face.

"Oh, I forgot!" Lydia handed Dana a mask from a dispenser in the back of the room, then slipped on her own. "He's too young to be going through this nightmare of chemo, recovery, and more chemo."

"This is our fifth patient under thirty to reach a critical point this month," Maria said. "Two children down the hall are going through the same thing."

Lydia swallowed. Angie had long ago mentioned high rates of respiratory illnesses in children around here. So had Chris Magnano. "I learned last week that eleven people from my high school class have died, mostly from rare cancers. Eleven."

"That seems statistically impossible. You're so young." Disbelief registered on the nurse's face. "Where'd you go to school?"

Lydia told her.

She nodded, a knowing look flashing across her face. "Most of the young people I've cared for were from that area. Something's not right over there. Too many tumors, lumps ... odd things." Maria gently pulled a blanket closer to Robby's chin and read his vital signs. "I'll be back in a few." She hurried out the door.

Dana put up her hands, her palms facing Lydia. "I know what you're going to say. But contamination is everywhere, and we'd need to move far away to escape it. I'm not willing to do that, especially with this fantastic opportunity that's opening up for us." She took out her phone from her oversized bag and checked for messages.

"Dana, I'm sorry if—"

"Hold that thought!" Dana stood and led Lydia into the hallway. They pulled down their masks. "Let's talk out here. I just got a text from Rebecca Waters." She squinted at the screen. "She's asking if we can do a conference call at ten tomorrow morning. Yes! She needs an hour."

"Sounds like we're a go," Lydia said. She glanced at the heavy clouds darkening the window at the end of the hall. She had to switch gears. Focus on her livelihood. With just a handful of house sales this year, and little money in her savings, the only other option would mean moving in with her mom. The four of them would suffer in her 900 square foot home.

"Ready to take a leap of faith?"

"Yeah. I'm ready … ready for a new vocabulary, new sustainable materials …" And new concerns. But she didn't want to appear negative. "A self-sufficient life." Lydia poked her head inside the isolation room door. Robby was a shadow of his former active self. She looked back at Dana, her voice strong. "Definitely ready."

Dana looked like she wanted to hug her, but she clutched her purse instead. "I'm excited."

"Me too." Lydia wondered whether their friendship could withstand the deluge of activity and change. She certainly hoped so. "This must be what it feels like to jump over the Falls without a barrel."

"Hey, the last guy who tried it survived."

Maria returned with Robby's oncologist. Lydia stepped away from the doorway. They entered Robby's room without a glance at the women. Lydia dashed to the room window, partially obscured by thin blinds. She watched the doctor make some notes.

They emerged, his face dark.

He put his arm around Lydia's shoulder. "Robby is very close to the end. I'm sorry, Lydia. It's time to talk about some options."

Lydia grabbed the doctor's arm as alarms suddenly rang from Robby's room. Maria rushed in with the doctor and Lydia close on her heels. At least two monitors flashed and beeped. She couldn't believe it. Flat lines. No life.

Lydia's vision darkened and her knees buckled. Her once- thriving family continued to be decimated, person by person.

It wasn't fair.

Dana caught her from behind. She heard great, shuddering sobs. She couldn't tell if they were Dana's or her own.

CHAPTER TWELVE

December 24, 2003

I was hungry back then.

The Great Depression showed only slight signs of receding in Niagara Falls in the late 1930s. Banks, restaurants, and factories folded under its impact.

And so did people.

My banker and his family were by now regulars at the Pine Avenue soup kitchen. Hundreds lined up behind them, even on days when inhaling the sub-zero air could sear a person's lungs. The hungry masses, bundled in long woolen coats, bowler hats, and scarves, were our neighbors and fellow parishioners. Our milkman.

I was starving, too. But my cravings were not so easily addressed because I wasn't hungry in the physical sense—my stomach was full. Our pantry was stocked. It was my spirit that ached and gnawed. Hankered for sustenance. It never felt satisfied.

One frigid late afternoon in January 1938, I thought I had found the cure for my discontent. I took my family to stand vigil at the rim of the Niagara Gorge, just past the American and Canadian Falls. Come to think of it, we stood at the same location where I had witnessed Jean Lussier's exultant step ashore ten years before. I stood shoulder to shoulder with thousands of others. Only this time, I was a *resident*. A genuine Western New Yorker, complete with frozen feet and numb fingertips.

An international crowd had assembled to await the demise of our beloved Honeymoon Bridge. Ice had laid siege to the magnificent steel arch structure. It was only a matter of time before that iconic symbol of Niagara Falls came down.

Two days before, a sudden winter gale on Lake Erie had pushed ice along the upper river until it plunged over the Falls. A colossal jam developed. The towering, mud-streaked ice pile inched north and began its two-day assault against the bridge. Soon, nearly thirty feet of frozen water encased its downstream trusses. That kind of pressure could reshape steel, maybe even the Falls themselves. Everyone knew the bridge footings wouldn't hold.

So we waited. More people arrived. The Canadian side held a capacity crowd.

Within an hour, the support bracings warped. My boys said it looked like soft licorice. The bridge groaned. Ice snapped from somewhere under the trusses. A piercing crack, followed by a crunching sound, cut the air. My sons pressed closer to me and my wife.

"How are you t-t-today, Mr. Malvisti?" A man's tremulous voice jolted me from behind.

I turned, slightly unnerved by the intrusion. The voice belonged to a man from my church parish, with prominent cheekbones and a threadbare coat. His hollow-cheeked wife shivered next to him.

"Well, my friend." My mind grasped for his name as we shook hands.

"How l-l-long do you think she'll hang on?" The man nodded toward the doomed structure. Deep lines crisscrossed his forehead. More than the bridge was on his mind.

"I think—"

Another crack. This time the ground rumbled. A section of the snow-covered roadway closest to the American border dropped into a U-shape beneath the bridge. Splintering sounds ricocheted across the gorge.

"Papa, did you see that?" Salvatore's voice rose. Sporadic pops and crackles from deep-surface fissures gave the frozen river a sinister, life-like quality. The boys would not soon forget this day.

"Not too long now, men." I smiled reassuringly.

A wrenching sound drew everyone's attention to the center of the span. Seconds later, a scraping noise was heard, and a series of loud snaps pierced the dull roar of the Falls. The spectators' cries from Canada could be heard clear across the icy border. A man carrying a movie camera crossed the ice below us, heading for the bridge. Another daredevil. Maybe even Lussier.

I gave it another half-hour.

"C-c-can I have a moment in private, s-s-sir?"

Sensing desperation, I nodded. The man stepped back several feet. Spectators filled the gap between us and our families.

"I d-d-don't want to intrude on your t-time, Mr. Malvisti." He winced. The man slowed his speech, lowering his voice to a whisper. "I have some land, sir. It's all we have." His breath formed white clouds as he looked down at his feet.

"What of it?" I had an idea of where this was going but wanted him to spit it out himself.

"Name a p-p-price and it's y-y-yours. I know you ... you'll take care of us. It's just me and the missus."

A gunshot sound reverberated off the gorge walls. Grating noises rattled my nerves. The buckled road section draped even more.

My wife turned to catch my eye through a space between frozen spectators. She motioned for us to return to the railing.

I placed my hand on the man's back, but nearly recoiled in shock. His ribs protruded through his thin coat. "Come see me Monday night. My home."

He nodded. His shoulders slumped as he exhaled, louder this time.

We ducked around a family clinging together, whether for warmth or in fear I didn't know. We reached the railing in time to join our families and watch the center span fall and collapse on top of the ice. Puffs of smoke or ice rose in an even row and then dissipated in the wind. The ice had pushed the bridge clear off its footings.

At first, the body of the span remained relatively intact. But after a few minutes, it yawed precariously downstream, where rivulets of water flowed more freely through the thinner ice. Spear-sized splinters poked up from what used to be the wooden roadway. A roller coaster of horrors. Men trekked over the ice to investigate.

My sons talked to each other in the excited half-sentences that only twins could understand. Police and latecomers scurried every which way across the snowy landscape. Somewhere behind us, I heard a woman crying as a man led her away.

My throat tightened as a sense of unease within me grew. The bridge had been solid, expertly engineered and crafted by man. How could it be lying at a twisted angle on the ragged ice below? What was happening in the world? Were we doomed too? I understand why that woman had cried. Our trusted institutions—whether banks, bridges, or bonds—had failed us. We needed security. Something, or someone, we could trust.

The thought of owning land, secure and solid, unmovable, seemed right. So I ran with it.

Monday came. Instead of the starving parishioner, my banker's wife showed up unannounced at the house. She offered to sell me a small piece of property. On the night of the bridge disaster, her husband had jumped to his death from the twentieth story of the United Office Building, another human-designed architectural wonder overlooking the Falls. He had left her to provide for seven children.

Like the bridge, this intelligent, hardworking man had been swept off his foundation. I tried hard to not picture him twisted and broken on the sidewalk, but the image was seared in my brain as definitively as that of the lost bridge.

I agreed to purchase the woman's property.

Around six o'clock, the emaciated man from church showed up with the deed to a fine parcel of land. (I had made some inquiries and toured the riverfront acreage earlier that day. The flat property boasted a view of the mist plume from the Falls a few miles downstream. I liked it immediately.) Pasquale was his name. I told him we'd work something out. My wife and I had saved up some cash. Plus, I had my Noni's Italian brooch. She had no idea of its value, I'd wager.

That night, the events of the week seized hold of my mind. I couldn't sleep. A volcano could bury ancient cities. A windstorm could wreck a bridge within hours. A bad economy could crush the human spirit. They all had one thing in common. The things built by man were vulnerable. The work of humans is temporary, maybe even fleeting.

I became convinced that land offered the strongest sense of permanence. Ownership of something so solid, so ... *not* man-made ... proved I belonged. And was there to stay.

Somehow, and I don't fully understand it, the acquisition of land quieted the gnawing hunger in my spirit.

The next year, I bought two tracts of farmland from a man who was too tired to work it anymore. The bank was breathing down his neck. His pregnant wife found more security in having some cash. I got a bargain. Soon I owned a contiguous swath of untapped land along the upper Niagara River, and other large parcels throughout the Niagara Frontier. We planted orchards on some of the inland properties. Others we let sit. I relished my right to use my property in any way I saw fit.

As my land holdings increased, so did my expanding version of the American Dream.

Our status in the community changed. Meals at restaurants in Little Italy were served *gratis*. Residents regularly left baked bread, cookies, and fresh vegetables on our porch. Businessmen sought out my opinion. Farmers sought out my money.

I had respect.

Some say I took advantage of families in distress. I don't look at it that way. Just before the Honeymoon Bridge disaster, President Roosevelt had spoken in Niagara Falls about his Work Progress Administration initiatives. Our local WPA projects were part of his New Deal promise to Americans. He put unemployed citizens to work in return for financial assistance. I offered people my own version of a new deal: I bartered property for money. It gave debt relief to some, and to others a chance to continue farming the property they could no longer afford. Residents lived without the constant specter of financial ruin. I offered life, liberty, and the opportunity to pursue happiness.

Eventually, I had the power to influence people and control my surroundings. My power continued to expand, as did my appetite for it: more land, more wealth, more power. Above all, I craved the respect that came from being able to leverage my considerable assets.

Now, as I lie here all these years later in my gloomy hospital room, I realize a sad truth. I'm hungry again.

Only this time, the gnawing has nothing to do with property, wealth, or power.

It's a soul hunger. A spiritual longing.

It probably was back then too.

CHAPTER THIRTEEN

Niagara Falls, New York

L ydia dashed into the restaurant, nearly colliding with a landscaping crew waiting to pay at the crowded register. The owner's celebrated ciabatta bread drew patrons from throughout the county. Pictures all over the wall showed everyone from politicians to construction workers enjoying the pressed panini, with their thick slices of fresh mozzarella, and ripe tomatoes and basil soaked in imported, extra-virgin olive oil.

Lydia stood on her tiptoes and scanned the packed room. *Please still be here.* Relieved, Lydia spotted Angie reading a newspaper at a table against the back wall.

"Sorry for being late." Lydia peeled off her wet jacket and slid her purse under the chair.

"No problem." Angie hugged her. "I don't volunteer until three."

"I ran by Niagara Regional on my way here." She sat on the bench opposite Angie and took a breath. "They have a fund for the children of our deceased high school classmates, and I wanted to donate. But I forgot how crowded this place always is. I had to park way down the street."

"I still can't stop thinking about Robby, Lyd. He was such a great guy."

"Thank you." Lydia smoothed her wavy hair, which had frizzed in the sleet. She tucked a stray piece behind her ear. "And thanks again for all your extra help with the kids these past few weeks. You've been a life-saver." Lydia's eyes blurred. She yanked a stack of napkins from the table dispenser.

"Oh, Lydia." Angie reached for Lydia's hand.

"I'm just a mess." She dabbed under her eyes. "I'm so sorry."

"No problem," Angie said. "Let me pray for you." Angie bent her head and prayed for healing and peace for Lydia. Before she closed her eyes, Lydia noticed customers at a nearby table cast curious glances their way.

"Thank you," Lydia said when Angie finished. "People always say I'm in their prayers, but no one has actually prayed with me. I feel a little better already."

A raspy-voiced waitress greeted them. Lydia recognized her as a longtime friend of her mom's. She took their order without writing anything down and then turned to Lydia. "How's your mom?"

"Devastated. Withdrawn. Thanks for visiting with her last week."

She nodded and then moved to the next table.

"Sadie's worked in this restaurant for over thirty-five years," Lydia said. "Nice lady."

Angie unfolded her napkin and laid it on her lap. "So, what did you want to talk to me about?"

"I've been thinking about a few things lately. Most of my relatives have died of cancer. And at my high school reunion last month, I learned that several of my classmates have died of cancer or some other rare disease. It made me think about something you told me after Harrison had that asthma attack a year ago." Lydia refreshed her cell screen. "Wow, I can't believe that was a year ago."

"I can't remember. What'd I say?"

"You mentioned that our area has high rates of asthma and other diseases. I've heard that from a few others since." Lydia sipped her water. "I want to learn more. Your husband's almost done with medical school, right?"

"Yes."

"And you volunteer with County Hospice. So, you must know a lot between you, right? Can you guys help get me get started?"

"I'm no expert, Lyd, but I'd be happy to help you figure things out."

"It just seems like everyone I know is sick or dying. There's been too much loss. Family, friends, clients, you name it. Something's not right. And now there's my brother." Lydia wiped under her eyes again. She didn't dare validate her worst fears by adding Harrison to that list.

"What do you want to know, specifically? Some of this information might be available online through the state health records."

"I'd like the facts about our cancer rates around here. I want to know what chemicals are buried in our county, and where they are now. And I want to know what type of environmental testing has been done at Cascata Verde."

"That's quite a list."

"I know." Lydia exhaled loudly. "I started poking around on the Internet. I even read my friend Chris Magnano's articles on the area. Too bad I didn't take chemistry or physics in college. I'm overwhelmed with the science ...the ... everything."

Angie leaned forward. "I try to take things a step at a time. The problems in this area didn't happen overnight ... although, there are some exceptions to what I just said." Angie paused again and looked sideways at a picture mounted on the nearby wall. "I mean, there were some specific decisions that sent us down a bad road. But—"

"How do you stay calm all the time, Angie? You're always serene, that's the best word for you. Don't you ever just lose it? Do you do yoga or something?"

"Trust me, I've had a lifetime of struggling with some pretty dark things." Angie bit her lip. She looked as though she wanted to say more.

"I don't believe that. You are so sweet and giving."

"Listen, I know you came here for some environmental information. And I'm happy to talk about that with you. But I think I should tell you a little story about me. I'm not proud of some of my decisions, but it all ties together with your questions, I promise."

Lydia had assumed her sitter's life was typical, uneventful even, compared to the heartache and disappointment that plagued her own. Angie volunteered with hospice, and was married to a great guy who just entered medical school. She had a son in college, and took care of the boys whenever Lydia needed her.

Angie sipped on her pop. Her eyes darted to a table in the opposite corner of the restaurant. "I grew up several miles from Malvisti Park, off the lower Niagara River. Out by your mom, as a matter of fact." She lowered her voice and looked back at Lydia. "We were close to a large tract of land that was used as a dumping ground for toxic chemicals and radioactive wastes."

"Who dumped there?"

"The federal government. Private companies." Angie's almond-shaped eyes darkened. "The workers there had no idea they were handling toxic waste. Very little of the material was disposed of properly. So, as a result, contaminants soaked into the soil, seeped into groundwater, and were tracked all over the county by snow plows, sanitation trucks, industrial vehicles, animals, and people."

"That's insane."

Sadie delivered their food. After thanking her and waiting for her to leave, Angie continued. "Did you know that the remnants of World War Two's Manhattan Project are still buried right here in Western New York?"

"I vaguely recall hearing something about an atomic bomb. But I never gave it much thought." Lydia added the war project to her list of things to check out.

"Throughout the 1980s, a silo on the Manhattan Project site leaked radon. Radon is a radioactive gas that's linked to breast cancer. We lived downwind of that silo."

"Wow." Lydia kept her eyes on Angie as she took a bite of her sandwich.

"Seven women on our street got breast cancer or leukemia. They all died in their thirties or forties. My mother died of breast cancer when she was only thirty-five."

Lydia swallowed. "I'm so sorry."

"I was devastated. I had no one to guide me through my teens. I was clueless about everything, from make-up to clothes ... to boys."

"I can't imagine being without a mom at that age. That's terrible."

"I tried to fill the emptiness in my heart with a bunch of things. I went after guys and partied endlessly. I made sure I was distracted or disoriented every waking moment." Angie's eyes brimmed with tears.

"What about your dad?" Lydia stuck a fry in her mouth.

"He was too busy drinking himself into a stupor to parent me. He needed to carry on because other people depended on him. But he couldn't get beyond his own pain."

Angie went to take a bite of her panini, but paused. "My wild streak ended when I got pregnant."

Lydia stopped chewing. They'd been friends for a few years, and she never knew the turmoil that Angie had experienced. Was she so lost in her own misery that others didn't matter? Guilt crept into her heart.

"No guy wanted to be with a girl who was pregnant, and I had no money to buy my own drugs or alcohol. I lost my fast-food job. Most of my friends. It was the lowest point in my life." She took a bite.

"So Andre isn't Thaddeus's father?" Lydia asked gently.

"No. That crazy boy is long gone. Last I heard, he was in prison somewhere on the West Coast."

"So what did you do?"

"I floundered around for a while. Then I remembered the nice hospice volunteer who helped care for my mom when she was dying. I found her, and she gave me some hope and much-needed advice."

"Ironic." Lydia dabbed her eyes with a napkin. "You and I met the same way. We would've never met had my dad not gotten sick. I miss him so much."

"I forgot about that."

"So, did the hospice lady help you out? With money or support for the baby, I mean?" Lydia knew she was crossing a line by asking about those issues, but she couldn't help it. She needed to hear a story of survival.

"No. But she told me some things that changed my thinking. She said that people will always disappoint us. They'll betray us. They'll leave. They'll die. But God never disappoints us. He loves us unconditionally."

Lydia's desperate thoughts froze. God? She pulled back a bit. She didn't like where this was going.

"I couldn't have said that about any other person in my life. Not even my mom, and she *really* loved me. She was such a good person."

"But God disappointed you, too, didn't He?" There was no easy way to say what she meant. "I mean, your mom still died."

"God never promised that people we love wouldn't die. He promises that He is sufficient to sustain us through it."

Lydia let that sink in. She could use some sustaining, especially on the financial side.

"I finally understood that the hole in my heart could only be filled by God. Nothing else could ever fill that void. Not boys, drugs, alcohol, not even a child." She paused. "For a time, some of those things made me feel better. Or at least dulled the pain a bit. But the relief never lasted. When the boy left, or I sobered up, I was even emptier than before. I knew I couldn't continue that cycle." Angie finished her toasted sandwich, chewing slowly.

"I can't imagine how you felt." Lydia wondered if God provided Angie with a place to live, money to survive. Those were some of the worries that plagued her days and nights. She didn't think God was that involved in people's lives, or that he cared what happened on a day-today basis. The God she'd always heard about was remote. Someone to be feared.

Angie set down her napkin on her empty plate. "I started reading the Bible and began to see that God has a plan for me. For all of us. His plan is to bring imperfect, disappointing people *and* things, back in relationship with Him, through the perfection of Christ. It's a plan to fill us up and satisfy that thirst we all have. I've accepted His plan for my life. I try to surrender to Him my fears, worries, desires, thoughts, and actions. And He has been faithful, even when I wrestle with those dark things. The peace you asked about? It comes from the knowledge that God is sovereign; that He's in control."

Lydia wiped her mouth. A million objections sprang to mind. "How could a God who's in control allow so much to go wrong around here? Or anywhere in the world? Everywhere I look people I know are suffering. And some of them are innocent people, like your mom. And children." *Like Harrison?*

"Here's where my story ties in with your original question. As you look into the environmental issues and learn this area's history, I think you'll see that much of the suffering is the result of man's bad choices. Not punishment from God."

Lydia definitely didn't like where this was going. It sounded too much like wishful thinking.

Angie lowered her voice to a whisper. "People made the choice to contaminate this land, Lydia. People dumped wastes, polluted the air, and poisoned the water. Then lied about those actions when the justification seemed right. The consequences of those choices—sickness, disease, deception, mistrust—have caused the devastation you asked about. Not God."

"I've never thought about all the suffering being the result of people's decisions. I guess it's no different than when my children suffer consequences as a result of their own bad choices. I give them that lecture all the time." Lydia relaxed her shoulders. "Why are we whispering?'

"Turn around and look at the table in the back corner."

Lydia did. She saw a woman and three men seated there. The tallest man, in his well-cut dark suit, matching light blue tie and handkerchief, and thick mustache, dominated the conversation. He seemed familiar. Lydia turned back to Angie and cocked her eyebrow.

"Now look at the pictures on the wall next to us."

Lydia glanced at the black-and-white photographs nailed to every available space on the wall. The one closest to her showed a tall, mustachioed man in a dark suit with a handkerchief in the pocket, shaking hands with men who had corporate names on their hardhats. Another showed that same man standing at a podium between the former governor of New York and the parks commissioner. She zeroed in on still another photo that showed the same figure in a suit and hardhat, smiling as he lifted the first shovelful of dirt over his shoulder. In the background, two young boys stood clapping, hardhats nearly covering their faces. Lydia wondered if the man in the picture was those boys' father.

She took a closer look at the gentleman at the corner table. He looked exactly like an older version of the man in the pictures.

She looked at Angie for confirmation.

Her friend nodded curtly. "He's a bad, bad person. One of our longest-serving city council members ... and an industry owner."

Lydia resisted the urge to peek at him again.

"After my mom died," Angie said, "I needed to know what killed her. As I researched our environmental history, I learned the truth."

"What did you learn?" Lydia held her breath.

"Cancer didn't kill my mother. Evil choices did."

Lydia sat back. She knew that there was much more to the story, and that somehow the politician in the corner was a part of it. Concepts flitted in and out of her mind, but she lacked the ability or the knowledge to connect them.

While she processed what she'd just heard, Sadie deposited their lunch bill in the middle of the table. Then the aging waitress lowered herself to eye level, expertly balancing a tray of food in her right hand. "I've caught a word or two of your conversation, girls. Here's what I think. It's time for people to take authority over this land in the name of God," she whispered. "He's at work here, girls. We're being prepared for a spiritual renovation, a reawakening." She smiled at Lydia, straightened, and delivered food to the high-powered patrons at the corner table. Snippets of an animated conversation about the organic vineyard at Cascata Verde carried across the room.

"A reawakening, huh?" Lydia cocked her head, hoping that Sadie wouldn't hear her next words. "Where are people getting this? My neighbor Mara thinks we're overdue for some miracle. And I think Dana is convinced that the eco-city is the dawning of the Age of Aquarius. In fact, we're working on a deal to sell real estate there."

"Ha." Angie dug through her shoulder bag for her wallet. "Hey, maybe something is coming down the pike. I heard that a church near Cascata Verde prays for the community's workers every week, right near the old fishing tree at Malvisti Park."

"You mean the former fishing tree." Lydia sat back in her chair and folded her arms.

"Ooh." Angie chewed her lip. "Forgot about that. Sorry."

The man at the corner table stood to offer a toast, drawing all eyes in the restaurant to him. The others seated at his table raised their glasses.

"Gentlemen ... and lady." The politician inclined his head toward the striking, auburn-haired woman on his right. "To prosperity and abundant grapes for the Niagara Frontier!"

"*Cin cin,*" they replied, clinking glasses.

Many of the restaurant-goers clapped, smiling broadly. Some held up their own glasses and repeated the traditional Italian toast. Others shouted, "*Salute.*" It seemed that although no one was quite sure what had just transpired, something exceptional had happened.

But when Lydia looked back at her friend, she was startled by the look of revulsion that had transformed Angie's face.

CHAPTER FOURTEEN

Niagara Falls, New York

M ichael hadn't felt this happy in years. He'd spent all morning with Grandma Ziatta, and, despite the fact that she called him Joe, his father's name, she seemed very with it. Lucy said she hadn't shown that much energy in months. And now, at the green city, virtually the entire city of Niagara Falls had shown up to celebrate Cascata Verde's ceremonial ground-breaking. Months of frenzied preparations had ended last night around midnight, when Hessley's planning team decided to cordon off safety zones to keep people off the bulldozers. The site would revert to a construction zone within hours of the last celebratory shovelful of dirt.

He had to admit, the hard work of planning had paid off. Stroller-pushing parents crowded the makeshift walkways as residents greeted one another. Children ducked under and around the orange protective ropes. He spotted more than a few people stretched out under Malvisti Park's mature trees, whose leaves had just started to turn red or yellow. Picture perfect. He even looked forward to relaxing with Jillian after the ceremony; their relationship seemed more solid now that both of them had committed to spending more time together.

He wondered if scenes like today resembled the old days Grandpa Joe talked about--when neighbors walked up and down the streets of downtown Niagara Falls after dinner and people actually knew one another.

Too bad his father wouldn't allow himself to share in the excitement of the moment.

"Keep up, boy," Joe Malvisti, Jr. growled over his shoulder. His father marched toward the restricted VIP areas, close on the heels of Uncle Sal. "This thing needs to start on time."

The Hessley employees-only section offered refuge from the pre-ceremony pandemonium. As he headed that way, Michael unbuttoned his suit and extended his hand to the dozens of well-wishers who slowed their progress. Faces became a single, colorful blur.

"Master Michael." A very elderly woman reached up from her wheel-chair and pinched his cheek. "I remember you as a child, holding hands with your Grandpa Joe at this park. Good man, God rest his soul."

He embraced her, wishing with all his might that his grandfather were here to witness the historic occasion. Grandpa Joe had never heard of an eco-city, Michael guessed, but he would've been impressed with the innovations in engineering.

"Mr. Malvisti!" A young female voice rang out.

The three men bearing that name turned in her direction.

The woman flashed her Channel 4 press credentials and elbowed her way through the crowd. She held a wireless microphone flat against her chest. "May I ask a question, councilman?" Her hopeful smile seemed genuine, even as she struggled to catch her breath.

"Absolutely, young lady."

A cameraman caught up and rolled tape.

"We've been waiting all summer for this event. How do you feel now that the ceremony is finally here?" She flipped her mic toward Uncle Sal, who was resplendent in a dark tailored suit with a handkerchief in the pocket, just like Grandpa Joe had always worn.

"Fantastic!" Sal's eyes drifted to a package tucked under her arm. "This is a dream come true for all of us. We've waited a long time, but it has been well worth the effort and planning."

"How so?" Her smile seemed too bright.

Unease crept over Michael. These were softball questions. Reporters weren't this friendly unless there was a reason.

"This Green City will broaden our county tax base. It will fuel a new and prosperous beginning for Niagara Falls."

"Well said, sir," she gushed.

More reporters and camera crews surrounded his uncle, forcing Michael back a few feet. His father frowned in Sal's direction, then rotated on his heel and pressed on toward the dignitaries' platform. The press didn't need Joe Malvisti, Jr. Uncle Sal could always be counted on to provide an attention-getting sound bite.

"One more question, Councilman Malvisti?"

The smile had disappeared from her eyes. Michael swallowed. They were about to find out the reason behind the pleasant demeanor.

"Go ahead, sweetheart."

"Why do the people who live near Malvisti Park have higher rates of virtually every type of cancer than the rest of Niagara County?" She thrust the microphone close to his lips.

Sal's eyes flickered. Michael could see his jaw working, even from his vantage point outside the first ring of reporters. He stepped back even further as noisy clicks from dozens of cameras exploded in his ear.

As she waited for a response, Michael noticed a stocky man behind her wearing a baseball cap pulled low over his face. Had she had brought along protection?

"Young lady." Sal's mirthless laugh chilled Michael. "The area in and around Malvisti Park has long been the seat of this county's chemical and manufacturing industrial base. Niagara Falls was built upon these heavy industries, a fact that you obviously are too young to remember. These businesses probably employed your grandfather or your great-grandfather." Sal paused to take a breath, seeming to grow taller.

A middle-aged man in the crowd hollered. "That's right, Councilman!"

"Those hardworking men were able to provide for their families at a time when to do so meant something." Sal raised his fist in the air. "They would be proud to know that this area has today been transformed for a new and higher purpose."

The reporter drew a bound stack of documents out from under her arm.

But Sal didn't seem to notice. He had hit his stride, speaking directly to his wider audience. "It's time to move forward and celebrate the promise and anticipated prosperity of Cascata Verde!"

Uncertain applause filled the circle of spectators and media. Only one person cheered outright. Mayor O'Donahue placed his hand on Uncle Sal's shoulder, as if standing in solidarity with the defender of all things industrial.

Sal nodded at his only vocal supporter. Together, they turned away and walked along the path to the VIP section. The crowd thinned, although the oversized man still hovered near the young woman.

Michael eyed the reporter's thick set of papers. Yellow sticky notes, some with arrows, stuck out everywhere. Anxiety started in his stomach and spread until the hair on his arms stood on end. He braced himself. She wasn't done.

"Councilman," the reporter spoke directly into the microphone. Passersby stopped, shushing one another. "Industrial pockets exist all over the region, and we've just found some reports that suggest that none of those pockets have rates as high as those in the neighborhoods or schools right around Malvisti Park. Experts suspect toxic contamination. How do you respond?"

He turned to face her. "I don't know where you are getting your statistics, young lady, but I suggest you check your facts." Sal's grave expression telegraphed a warning. "This is a misguided attempt to keep Western New Yorkers down. We're all tired of hearing recycled stories about contamination and high rates of cancer. We have finally achieved something great and lasting here. Look around you." Sal brushed away the growing cluster of microphones surrounding him and the mayor. He mopped sweat from his forehead with a handkerchief, ignoring the shouted questions from other reporters.

Michael's head swam. Where was this information coming from? What if rumors tainted Cascata Verde? What if the media ignored today's historic event and focused instead on the possible presence of chemicals? Years of hard work would be wasted. This region's only opportunity for growth and long-term survival would be lost ... then again, his worry might be misplaced. Around here, it wouldn't be the first time that jaw dropping revelations had been met with a collective yawn. The journalist's questions would just as likely be forgotten by lunchtime.

Through a break in the crowd, Michael thought he saw the huge man grasp the reporter's elbow. Startled, she drew back, retreating to her cameraman's side. She whispered something to him, and the technician trained his video on the stranger's now-retreating back. Something seemed familiar about the large man's swagger as he plowed through the crowd.

Michael tightened his fists. No one should scare a woman like that. He traced a course through the cordoned-off construction zone that would intersect with the stranger's path. His all-access official badge would come in handy. He started in that direction.

"C'mon back here, luv." Suzanna Frederick clutched Michael's arm from behind, redirecting him toward the VIP area. She raised her brow when their eyes met. "You look irritated. Everything okay?"

He decided against mentioning the man, although he checked his projected pathway again. No sign of the stranger. Or of the female reporter who had been just a few yards away.

He reluctantly joined Suzanna as they walked to the Hessley VIP area. "Did you see what just happened with my uncle Sal and the media?" He peeled off his overcoat.

"No, but tell me about it later. I only want to hear good news today." She untied the belt of her oversized crocheted sweater. "I'll never get the weather in Western New York. Yesterday it was fifty-eight and today it's seventy-eight."

"It's probably our Indian summer," Michael replied absently. He glanced over his shoulder once more. He didn't see anything out of the ordinary, including the man.

"That sounds decidedly non-PC."

"What, Indian summer?" Michael chuckled. "It's a mild, sunny break in the fall chill that doesn't last more than a few days."

"Never heard of it." Suzanna shielded her eyes from the sun. "The crowd is growing by the second." She pointed beyond the line of benches Hessley had provided for the residents. "Look at all the blankets spread out on the grass beyond the folding chairs. Everyone in town is here to support this venture."

His gaze swept even farther, to the area where a high school band performed. At first, he only saw parents and students clapping energetically, encouraging the young players. But then a circle of kneeling teens with arms linked caught his attention. They seemed to be praying. Seeing the group of young people made Michael's mouth go dry. If the reporter had her facts right, the health of many of these young adults could be impacted. The clamorous music added to Michael's agitation.

Mayor O'Donahue clapped a hand on each of their shoulders. "Top of the mornin' to ya!"

"Good morning, luv!" Suzanna's enthusiasm restored some of Michael's good humor.

"We're ready. You folks should join the Hessley team in your special area. We've got some water waitin' on ya."

"Correction." Rebecca emerged from the crowd. "Michael, your seat is over there." He followed her extended finger to the dignitaries' platform. An empty chair filled the gap between his father and uncle.

A green ribbon hung off the back of the seat. Matching ribbons tumbled off ceremonial shovels neatly lined up against the platform. Michael's name appeared on one of them. His heart sank.

"I'd prefer to sit—"

"Your uncle insisted." Rebecca put on her eco-friendly wooden sunglasses. "Plus, having two generations of Malvisti men here conveys a sense of community and continuity about the project. I like that. Consider yourselves one of the "closed loop" designs that characterize our smart buildings."

"I'm not a project." He kept his tone light. "And I'm definitely not a politician. Just let me—"

"Seriously, Michael." Her voice turned sober. "You are the face of all the Malvisti good will. Be proud of the legacy you've inherited. Build on it."

His stomach recoiled. From what little he knew about Uncle Sal, he wasn't sure he wanted to be associated with his family's brand of good deeds.

Before he could object further, Rebecca's attention shifted to the arrival of the governor of New York. It was no use. He walked over to the empty seat, on the way admiring the neat line of wind turbines positioned upriver. The Hessley public relations team had spent two hours yesterday siting the podium so that turbines framed the camera shot. Today, the vanes turned placidly, each turbine on its own rotation schedule, as if they had always been a fixed part of the landscape.

Michael's father's eyes barely registered Michael's presence as he took his seat. Judging by his dad's demeanor, the man would be gone within five minutes of today's closing remarks. It was the Joe Malvisti way. Close down, contribute little. No wonder that, with his grandmother sick and his dad's first wife long dead, the men in his family had slowly, yet undeniably, drifted apart.

He looked from his dad to his uncle. Their physical similarities as fraternal twins had become more pronounced with age. Although Uncle

Sal still wore a mustache, and his dad did not, they had the same thick, gray-streaked hair. Both bore a masculine, authoritative nose. Uncle Sal's son, Danny, exhibited a striking resemblance to both men, but, at least the last time Michael had seen him, his cousin's bulk had become his most pronounced attribute. Michael was different. With his mother's northern-Italian fair skin and hazel green eyes, he stood apart from them and their obvious Italian heritage.

He spotted Jillian's silky blonde locks in the crowd. She stood on her toes, following the actions of the governor. She waved whenever the popular leader's gaze swept in her direction. Since when did she care about politics?

"Fellow citizens," the governor began. "This is truly a momentous day." The crowd jumped to its feet. "Not only for Western New York, but for every city that has made the decision to put aside the old ways and attempt something new. Something magnificent and responsible. Something that could change the world forever!" Thunderous applause threatened to drown out his next words.

Jillian cheered wildly. Funny, for a year she'd never shown any real interest in the project. He had been surprised—but happy—that she'd agreed to come up for the groundbreaking ceremony.

"Cascata Verde is a new beginning for Western New York," the governor continued. "Growth, prosperity, success, and clean, environmentally responsible living are the new buzzwords by which the Niagara Frontier will be known."

At this, people chanted, "Prosperity, prosperity, prosperity!" Someone started the wave, and it rippled back and forth across the audience for thirty seconds or more.

Conflicting emotions welled up in Michael. The reporter's supposed facts weighed on him. But taking part in this historic event felt pretty good. Many people had expressed to him their excitement over job possibilities or new opportunities. For once, something good was happening to Niagara Falls. Cascata Verde was not just an innovative development project. It represented a fresh start—a second chance that would transform his hometown for the better.

"I want to say a few words before I turn over the microphone to Rebecca Waters, President and CEO of Hessley Development," the governor announced. More shouts from the residents. "She had the foresight to see the potential here on the banks of the glorious Niagara River. She had the guts and the know-how to make it happen. We are incredibly grateful to her." The governor beamed at Rebecca and then stepped away from the bamboo podium.

Rebecca lowered the microphone and removed her sunglasses. "I'm thrilled to be a part of this historic day." She seemed perfectly at ease before the capacity crowd. "Our thanks to all of you. You've provided much of the manpower, machinery, and technical ability to get this project off the ground. The labor force in the Buffalo-Niagara region is incredibly skilled. Your talents and training will become more apparent as buildings, parks, homes, and other structures continue to take shape."

Spontaneous applause broke out. The mayor wiped his eyes, gathering his wife's hand in his own.

Michael felt a part of something enduring and significant. Once again, he wished Grandpa Joe was still alive. Even though he'd probably never heard of green buildings, the eco-city concept and its community feel would have pleased him.

"Today we are here to break ground for Cascata Verde's first and tallest office tower. The tower will be occupied by Pavati Biotecnologia, an Italian company."

Gleeful shouts escaped from a group of young adults about a hundred yards to Michael's right. They waved oversized signs with their résumés printed in an extra-large font.

"Some of you may not know what Pavati Biotecnologia actually does." Rebecca grinned. "Except, of course, the résumé-wielding group in the back."

Laughter and shouts of encouragement filled the makeshift arena.

"Pavati Biotecnologia," she explained, "is a diversified service provider in the area of bioremediation. Scientists in this field use microorganisms, like bacteria, to reduce, eliminate, contain, or transform certain contaminants. These contaminants include toxic chemicals, radioactive isotopes, or heavy-metal industrial waste. Those toxic materials are found in soils, sediments, water, or air. My friends, Pavati performs these miracles on a large scale. As we speak, it is building diversion and filter installations to connect the Niagara River with its facility operations. That river water will continue to be purified and improved over time. We are moving toward healing and harmony with the Earth."

Murmuring spread throughout the audience. He suspected that Rebecca's new-age lingo didn't sit well with this traditional crowd.

Rebecca pressed on. "On behalf of Pavati Biotecnologia, I want to share that its representatives appreciated the warm welcome from all of you." She gestured to a row of suited individuals at the front of the audience.

The Pavati executives stood and bowed gracefully.

"The Pavati firm is headquartered in Milan, Italy, just south of Lake Como. Lake Como is Niagara Falls's sister city. Our family ties run even deeper now." Whistles could be heard over the excitement.

A male reporter stood and cupped his hand over his mouth.

His uncle tensed. The media was not his ally today.

"What's next, Ms. Waters?"

"In the following months, we plan to pour foundations and frame homes in the residential districts. We'll start the community church and other buildings in the commercial district. Our vineyard's grape stock is undergoing grafting as we speak. We're on time, within budget, and very pleased with the progress so far." She motioned toward the wind turbines behind her, their dazzling presence needing no further comment.

Michael stole a glance at his father. The old man's attention was far from them. Maybe he was thinking about Michael's mom, who had injured her hand and couldn't make the trip from Florida. Then again, his dad was never one for public scenes of any type.

"The Honorable Mayor O'Donahue will officiate over the actual groundbreaking. *Per Fortuna ha continuata!* To continued good fortune!"

Mayor O'Donahue summoned ten people to the edge of the blue ceremonial carpet. Michael, the other Malvisti men, the governor, Rebecca, and area politicians joined him in readying their chrome shovels. They posed for pictures. A drumroll sounded. Together, at the mayor's signal, they struck the earth and flung their payload into a small pile in front of the crowd.

Shouts and shrill whistles punctuated the fervent applause. People waved their arms in approval. The ceremony ended with a stirring rendition of "The Star-Spangled Banner."

Michael heard his father draw a deep breath. He looked over in time to see him button his coat and pull out rental car keys.

"Dad, can you wait to meet my girlfriend?" Finally. Michael pointed toward the spectator seats. "She's making her way over here."

He checked his watch. "Make it quick."

"Why the hurry, Joe?" Uncle Sal leaned across Michael.

His father stiffened. The brothers had barely spoken today, except to greet each other with a handshake. Michael didn't know if they had ever been close.

"Here she is." Michael stepped aside to make room. "Dad, Uncle Sal, this is my girlfriend, Jillian Smith."

His father looked mildly surprised at the beauty before him. His mouth turned up in one corner.

"We didn't think you had it in you, eh, Joe?" Sal kissed her hand. "Ms. Smith, with your California good looks, and obvious superior taste, what are you doing with our boy?"

"I've been wondering the same." Jillian's response lacked any touch of irony.

Laughing outright, Sal put his hand on the small of her back and steered her toward the podium. "Have you met the Honorable Flynn O'Donahue or our esteemed governor?"

They disappeared from sight. Her delighted laughter rang out over the commotion of the dispersing crowd.

Michael ground his teeth. Aside from flying in from Florida with him, and until today, she had shown zero interest in anything he'd accomplished during this project.

"That's a dangerous one, son," his father said. "Like your enemies, keep her close. See you soon." He shuffled away. No doubt Joe would be on the next plane back to Florida.

Michael felt torn about what to do next. He needed to keep tabs on two people, his girlfriend and the husky stranger. He couldn't deny that the man gave off bad vibes. And he didn't want anything to mar this momentous day. Michael's hand went to his waistband, where his pistol used to be. That is, before Jillian pitched a fit about it and he'd reluctantly sold it.

He set off in the direction where he'd last seen the man, certain the guy was up to no good.

CHAPTER FIFTEEN

A sturdy man wearing an orange T-shirt and khaki shorts stopped Michael as he crossed the grounds in pursuit of the stranger. He extended his hand. "Chris Magnano."

"Nice to meet you, sir." Firm shake; tired eyes. Michael judged him to be in his late forties.

"I live around here. Can I ask you a few questions now that the groundbreaking is over?"

"Sure." Michael glanced around, anxious to track down the man who'd startled the reporter. Michael was certain the man wasn't here for the ceremony. But Rebecca had impressed on him that meeting residents was an important part of cultivating good will. "What's on your mind?"

"I know this is a day for celebration and all that, but as an environmentalist I have some real concerns about Cascata Verde"

"The environment?" Michael couldn't hide his surprise. "Our eco-city is the most advanced development project of its kind. Once complete, we will generate our own power, raise our own fish, lettuces, tomatoes, and much more using aquaponics. We'll even recycle our waste." He could go on and on, but slowed as he thought about the female reporter.

"I understand all that, sir, but—"

"And we've diverted a substantial portion of construction waste to promote recycling and reduce landfill materials. As an environmentalist, this should be a thrilling day for you." Michael worked to keep his tone pleasant.

"My concern relates to what lies beneath this complex, sir."

Michael's pulse quickened. This was Ty's territory. "I'm a commercial real estate attorney, not a scientist. I'm not sure if I'm the person to help you there."

"Are you familiar with Tomeo Environmental?" Mr. Magnano pulled a piece of paper from his back pocket.

"I know it provided independent environmental testing for Malvisti Park, and now provides consulting for Hessley." He thought back to last year's conversation with Ty.

"Yes." The resident pointed to the sheet. "And since the early '80s *only* Tomeo Environmental has tested at Malvisti Park. And *only* Tomeo has provided the raw data that underlies required EPA reports and other state and federal mandatory reporting."

"Okay, so what's your concern, Mr. Magnano?"

"I think we should know more about this company. It's had an important role here, but seems to operate in the shadows."

Michael tried to keep his face impassive. "What makes you say that?"

"It's right here." He held the paper out, but all Michael could see were blanks. "I looked it up on the Internet. It's registered as a Delaware Corporation licensed to do business in New York. It has an agent for the service of legal papers, like it's supposed to, but I couldn't find an actual business office."

"I'm not sure what you're getting at."

"Something's not right, Mr. Malvisti. You seem like someone who shoots straight. Am I right?" He narrowed his eyes at Michael.

Sal Malvisti's booming voice could be heard somewhere behind them. A silvery laugh followed.

"Of course." A lump formed in Michael's throat. This line of questioning was too close on the heels of the young reporter's questions. "Look, Hessley has a stellar reputation and would have relied on a reputable contractor for environmental testing. We've sampled the area ourselves too." He didn't add that Tomeo had actually obtained the samples.

Chris studied him for a moment. "I appreciate that reassurance. Maybe I'm a conspiracy theorist at heart and read a little too much into it. Thanks for your time today, sir."

"It's understandable. This project is a really big deal." Michael took out his business card and handed it to Chris. "Let me know if you have any more questions."

"Great." Chris shoved the card deep into his shorts pocket.

"And call me Michael. Otherwise, things could get mixed up around here." He would never be comfortable as Mr. Malvisti.

They shook hands. Chris lingered for a moment. Michael could tell that the local man had something else on his mind.

Suzanna's husky voice broke in. "Michael, can you do us a favor?"

Michael excused himself from Chris, who thanked him again and left.

"Rebecca and I are going to try to catch an earlier flight back to Tampa. Will you drive us to the airport?"

"Sure." He dug around in his overcoat pocket for his cell. He looked at it and bit his lip. No texts from Jillian. Then again, he hadn't expected any. She seemed to get along fine without him.

Suzanna put her arm across his shoulders and shook him playfully. "What's wrong with you, luv? Snap out of it!" Her oversized butterfly rings and turquoise bracelets scratched his neck as she gave him a squeeze.

"I had no idea I was going to have to participate in the ceremony." He shook his head. "I'm not comfortable being in the news with my family."

"Man, get over it. Everyone looked terrific. It's been a perfect day. Now, let's go. I really, really need to get home."

❖

Michael unloaded Suzanna's and Rebecca's heavy bags at the terminal curb. "A minute, Rebecca?"

"Go." She checked her watch. Suzanna stepped out of earshot.

"I had a Falls resident ask me questions about Tomeo." He searched his boss's face for a reaction. None.

She motioned impatiently for him to elaborate.

"He asked me if Tomeo's legitimate. He said it doesn't have a physical address." Michael stepped up onto the curb. "How should I respond to such questions in the future?"

"That's simple." She looked at him like he'd lost his mind. "Tomeo has a long track record of reliability at the site. It handles testing, remediation, and reporting. It's always on time."

"But do we have any reason to be concerned about this company?" Michael instantly regretted asking the question. Rebecca didn't like to be second-guessed. Then again, she hadn't exactly answered his real question.

She narrowed her eyes at him and drew back. "There's no problem with Tomeo or the remediation it did at this site. I can assure you that possible or likely contaminants fall within acceptable ranges. I've no reason to suspect a problem." Her brow furrowed. "Did this person mention anything else?"

"No."

Rebecca shouldered her carry-on. "Then don't worry about it." She caught up to Suzanna and they left.

Through the airport's glass windows Michael saw dozens of camera-toting journalists checking bags to go home, their presence a subtle reminder of the significance of North America's first eco-city.

He thought so much about Rebecca's words that he couldn't recall actually getting on the New York State Thruway to return to Cascata Verde. What were "likely" or "possible" contaminants? What about the unlikely or "not possible" contaminants? Shouldn't someone test for those too?

More importantly, besides Chris Magnano and a lone reporter, did anyone actually care?

❖

By the time Michael returned to Cascata Verde, it had gone back to being a fully operational construction zone. A fleet of equipment and innumerable orange stakes stood where a sizeable crowd had celebrated just over two hours ago. Even the wind had changed direction and cooled.

Michael parked in the lot closest to the river and got out to walk. He searched for the old fishing tree, his familiar landmark. It wasn't there. He hoped it hadn't fallen victim to the Pavati filter installations.

So much had changed in Malvisti Park since his childhood. The skinny saplings he and his cousin Danny had helped to plant had grown into tall, yellow-leafed oak trees. He wondered why Sal's son hadn't made it to the ceremony. Truthfully, even though they hadn't seen each other in years, he was relieved not to have to deal with his hot-tempered cousin.

The setting sun ignited the river, creating orange flickers of light. The river breathed potential. One or two people's concerns would not be enough to squelch the opportunity surrounding this place.

He climbed onto an old concrete structure near the water. Floating branches, sticks, and construction debris whisked by him, heading downstream toward the Falls. He was able to make out jagged boulders just below the surface. The river ably hid her rocks.

Michael glanced at his watch. He and Jillian still had time before their evening flight back to Florida. He jogged over to the construction trailer to see whether anyone was still there. A note taped to the door in Jillian's neat handwriting told him she was at Galvecchio's. With Uncle Sal. "Why am I not surprised?"

He sighed.

"Mr. Malvisti?" an unsteady female voice startled him. The sound came from the direction of a parked backhoe.

"Yes?" Michael scanned the vehicle. Its yellow paint reflected the sun's fading rays, providing an extra measure of light. "Who's calling me?"

"I've heard that you're not like them." She let out a whimper. "Is it true?" Muffled sobs from under the far side of the truck followed.

"Not like *who*, miss?" His mind shot back to Chris Magnano's comment. *Not like the rest of the Malvistis?* His stomach clenched.

The woman began to cry. The sound of something clanging against the backhoe added to his unease.

"Are you hurt?" His pulse roared in his ears. "Can I help you?"

"No. And don't you dare come near me," she rasped. "I shouldn't be talking to you."

Michael squatted. He peered under the vehicle, hoping to see her. A movement behind the truck's oversized rear tire caught his eye. A woman's thin, bare leg was still visible in the declining light.

"I need something to cover myself."

Michael whisked off his overcoat. On impulse, he stuffed some bills into the pocket, carefully rolling the coat into a thick wad. He flung it over the cab of the backhoe. Two bare legs scurried toward the rumpled pile. Dark mud stains streaked the right one.

"Let me help you."

"No! Stay over there."

"What's happened?"

She let out a sob. "I ... was told that I need to quit my job and disappear or ..." Short, gasping breaths prevented her from finishing her sentence.

"Slow down and take a deep breath, ma'am." He looked over his shoulder. The site appeared empty. "Or what?"

"Keep your voice down," she hissed.

"What did someone threaten to do?" he whispered.

"They said they'll go to my family's home."

"And do what?"

Her anguished wail communicated fear and pain. "Hurt my parents. And my sister."

"You sound hurt. Let me take you to the hospital. The police can come and talk with you there."

"No, no, no. Those thugs said if I told anyone I could kiss my family good-bye!" The sobbing intensified. "They attacked me. My clothes are … shredded."

He couldn't leave this terrified woman alone and hurt at a construction site. "What can I do? Just name it, anything you need."

"You've done all you can for me." Her voice deepened. "Leave me alone."

The sun sank in a hurry. Security lights attached to the construction trailer flicked on.

"Miss, please let me help you." He didn't dare approach her in the dark. She'd been traumatized enough.

"No." Her voice flattened.

"Why not?"

"Don't you know?" A bitter laugh followed.

"I must be missing something." Anxiety over the woman's situation gave way to confusion.

"You're the one who needs help now, Michael Malvisti."

CHAPTER SIXTEEN

Michael stood just inside the entrance of Galvecchio's. Uncle Sal held court at the oblong table in the middle of the darkened room. Extra chairs spun off like satellites from its corners.

Cheers for Cascata Verde rang out like a child's game.

Wedged between Uncle Sal and Mayor O'Donahue, Jillian shimmered in a silver cocktail dress. Michael didn't recognize any of the others, except the mayor's wife, whose scoop-necked blouse revealed a flush of red spreading upward from her neck. Jillian's familiar manner with married men often had that effect on their wives.

Two waiters delivered antipasti trays to the table. A man Michael recognized as Galvecchio's owner filled empty wine glasses from a crystal decanter.

The party had just gotten started.

The mayor's wife elbowed her husband and pointed in Michael's direction. The table quieted. Patrons throughout the restaurant stared at him.

"Michael!" Uncle Sal saluted him with his wine glass. "Come join us."

Normalcy returned to the restaurant.

He and his uncle had barely spoken at the groundbreaking ceremony earlier. Why was he being so friendly now? Must have been the house red.

"No, thanks." Michael took a few steps closer. "Jillian and I have a flight back to Tampa soon. We've got to go now, unfortunately."

His girlfriend wrapped her fingers around Uncle Sal's arm. A ring he didn't recognize reflected light from a candle on the table. "I changed my reservation. I didn't think you'd mind." She made no move to get up.

"Go on," Sal encouraged her. "Tell him about our plans."

Her white teeth flashed. "You neglected to take me on the *Maid of the Mist*, so Uncle Sal reserved the entire boat for a trip tomorrow. After that, Flynn is taking us up in a hot air balloon to see the Falls." Still holding Uncle Sal's arm, she tipped her head back and grabbed hold of the mayor's shirt collar with her free hand. "I am so looking forward to that, Mr. Mayor."

Her boldness unnerved Michael. She'd held him spellbound once too.

"It's not often we have a celebrity cheerleader with us." The mayor pressed his lips to the underside of her forearm. He squeezed his eyes shut, allowing his mouth to hover over her thin wrist.

Mrs. Mayor threw her napkin across her bread plate and scurried toward the restroom.

"I have a meeting tomorrow." Michael shifted. He dug his thumb into the ring of keys in his hand. "I need to head back tonight."

"Meet you at home then." She twinkled her fingers in dismissal.

Mayor O'Donahue jumped to fill the wine glass she held in the air. Someone toasted the Green City, and the partygoers returned to their celebration.

Anger roiled his insides. Sure, Jillian's shameless flirtation irritated him. But more than simple feminine manipulation was at hand here. Michael was learning that, like Uncle Sal, Jillian calculated her every move. Those two were cut from the same cloth.

Tonight's words from the desperate woman echoed in his mind. Was this why he needed help now?

"Jillian." He kept his tone reasonable. "Can I talk to you alone?"

She sipped her wine, engrossed in conversation with Uncle Sal. But Michael knew she'd heard him.

"I need a minute with you." He waited a few seconds, then turned and headed toward the door, convinced that an unholy alliance had been forged.

A thick-set, exhausted-looking man in the booth closest to the door cleared his throat. Michael recognized him as the environmentalist from earlier in the day. When Michael passed, Magnano took a last sip of his drink and slid out from his seat. Then he casually followed Michael outside.

The injured woman's words continued to trouble his mind. Did he need help *now*?

Michael gauged the distance to his rental to be about seventy yards. The inky night provided sufficient cover for whatever was about to transpire. Knowing he could take the bulky guy in a fight, he decided to let this situation play out.

Michael wound through the double-parked cars just outside the restaurant door. He jogged across the road and stepped over a concrete barrier into the municipal lot. Five rows to go.

The heavier man kept pace. Michael looked over his shoulder, gauging him to be about two car lengths behind. A horn honked from an unseen car. Michael sped up.

"Trust me and don't talk." The environmentalist labored to breathe. "Your uncle's driver does double duty."

Uncle Sal had a driver?

Puzzled, Michael slowed. The rental waited two rows away.

Chris dashed around a small truck on Michael's left. He cut in front of the vehicle, then turned left to jog alongside Michael's rental. He tossed a white bag next to the driver's side wheel and kept moving.

Michael simulated a fumble with his keys, dropping them near the tire. As he bent over, he snatched up the crumpled item. A nearly weightless doughnut bag.

"Use a trash can!" Michael snapped at the man.

Chris chuckled before disappearing into an unlighted corner of the packed lot.

With a tap on the remote, the car door clicked open and Michael slid in behind the wheel. He had prosecuted war criminals, secured multi-billion-dollar real estate deals, and even trained with the Marines' Special Forces. Now he was picking up trash in a dark parking lot.

He wondered whether there was anything inside. If so, it didn't weigh much. Maybe it was a piece of paper with Chris's phone number so Michael could respond to the man's earlier questions. Whatever the reason, he'd have to look at it later or risk missing his flight. He shoved the bag into his briefcase, looked around for any suspicious activity besides his own, and pulled out of the lot.

As his adrenaline ebbed, his thoughts returned to the hurt woman at the construction site. Had she gotten to safety? What was it she tried to warn him about?

❖

Forty-five minutes later, Michael sat in a secluded seat in the airport's main terminal. Best to inspect Magnano's bag before going through security. Continuing the pretense of preparing to enjoy his doughnut was borderline ridiculous, but he unrolled the bag as if he knew what was within.

He peered inside and found two white napkins. He pulled them out and pretended to wipe his mouth. Peanut crumbs coated the bottom of the bag. Half buried in the morsels he saw a photograph. He reached in and pulled it out, then held the picture up to the light, squinting to make out the details.

When he recognized the image, his heart threatened to explode. Tears sprang to his eyes. What he'd thought was just a fabled family story, changed and embellished over the years, was brought to life in front of his eyes.

At least in black and white.

CHAPTER SEVENTEEN

Near Tampa, Florida

Michael had forgotten about Apollo Beach's towering smokestacks until he turned off Highway 41 toward the coastal town. Side by side, all along the community's Florida gulf shoreline, the vents belched plumes of harmless water vapor from the nearby power plant. The industrial scene seemed out of place against the tropical backdrop.

He closed his window. Tampa Bay was known to emit a sulphur-like smell at low tide, and he sure could smell it now. No wonder his parents moved here. A familiar landscape. Recognizable odors. No doubt this town reminded them of the life they had left behind in gritty, industry-driven Niagara Falls.

Michael pulled up to the wrought-iron gate of their sprawling Mediterranean-style house. Vines covered the yellowing stucco walls. Tangles choked the plentiful mangrove trees.

Michael hadn't been here in over a year. The house held no great memories for him, and nothing about it felt like home. Home was Niagara Falls.

He parked and grabbed his legal pad, Chris's doughnut bag, and a loaf of Italian bread he'd brought from a bakery in the Falls and frozen for his mom.

His mother stood in the arched doorway with her arm bound in a sling. "Thanks for the bread!" She reached out with her good arm to hug him even before he reached the top marble step. "Dad forgot to get some when he was there for the groundbreaking."

"You're lucky." He kissed her cheek. "I had to give two others away on the plane to avoid a riot. How's your wrist?"

"Hurts. I'm sorry I couldn't be there for your big day."

"That's okay. This project will be around for a long, long time."

"Your dad and I were just talking about him meeting Jillian in Buffalo." Her eyes darted to the GT-R. "Did you bring her along?"

"No, she's still up there." He shrugged. "Sightseeing."

His mom furrowed her brow, but didn't ask any questions. "Your dad is having a glass of wine out on the terrace. I'll be right out with those fava beans you like." She disappeared into the kitchen.

Michael's stomach growled as he made his way through the spacious house to the stone patio. They'd added a stainless steel outdoor kitchen, stocked bar, and a dining table for twelve. Expensive amenities for guests and family members who would never come. Tall palms and shorter scrub trees blocked any views of neighbors.

"Evening." His father stood slowly from his chair and shook hands with Michael. He tightened his bulky sweater around him, lowering himself with some difficulty.

"Everything OK there?" Michael gestured toward his father's knees. He set down the pad and bag next to his chair.

"Bit of arthritis, that's all."

"Since when do you have that?" He shrugged off his tie and sat across from his father. Lights along the saltwater canal winked. Only the occasional boat motoring inland broke the hum of cicadas.

"The past few years, I guess. Nothing to worry about." Joe rubbed his legs and then his fingers. The older man's eyes glassed over, but his speech seemed clear.

Michael assessed his father's mood. Contemplative, maybe on the quiet side. Typical. "How was the rest of your trip in the Falls?"

"I spent some time with your grandmother, and she mentioned a young man that had been to see her, which I assumed was you, but other than that I couldn't wait to get home." He gulped his wine.

"How come?" Michael wondered if Uncle Sal had something to do with his father's desire to leave.

"It's no longer familiar to me. Everything looks different, smells different." He paused for a moment. A plane passed overhead. "That's quite a boss you have."

"Are you referring to Jillian or Rebecca?" Michael asked, only half kidding.

"I mean Rebecca." He finished his glass. "She's a stunning and accomplished woman."

"She is sharp," Michael agreed.

"Jillian is ... beautiful." His dad studied him. Something like pity clouded his eyes. "So, you wanted to talk to me about something?"

"Yeah. Been thinking about a few things lately." Michael decided to plunge right in. "I'd like to learn more about our family."

"What about it?" Joe's voice lacked emotion.

"The business, the people." Michael shrugged. "Everything."

"Why?" Joe stood and shuffled over to a wine refrigerator nestled below a granite counter. He pulled out two bottles before deciding on a Chianti Classico, which he opened with great effort. He shook his hand out, wincing once or twice.

"Because I know very little about our family. I don't know who we are or where we came from. There's a lot of blanks. We used to have close cousins, aunts, and uncles. Where'd everyone go?"

"Some died." His father pulled out a second glass. "Some moved out West."

This was going nowhere fast. Frustration set in. "Can you give me a few details about Malvisti Industries? I mean, how large is it? Is it one company or several?"

"Your grandfather started a business. It was successful. Sal and I took it over. What more do you need to know?" He poured a full glass of wine, sniffing the glass before swirling it around and tasting its contents. Michael caught a whiff of the strong, aromatic flavors from several feet away.

"Okay, can you tell me more about Grandpa Joe?"

"I just did."

"I mean, what was he like as a young guy?" Michael relaxed his shoulders; this might take a while. "Was he a good father to you?"

His dad looked down into his glass, staring blankly at the dark, robust wine. "My father was easy to understand." He made a weak effort to swat away a mosquito, but missed. "He was an immigrant who worked hard. He put food on the table and a roof over our heads. That was success for fathers of that generation. I don't know much more about him as a person."

Surprised at his father's candor, Michael pressed on. "Why did he come to America?"

"Same reasons as everyone else. Conditions were desperate in Italy." Joe sank into his chair. "He watched his own parents struggle."

"So he came here and started a landfill business." Michael switched to leading questions, hoping for more specifics.

"Nope. First he went to Pennsylvania to work in the coal mines."

"That's news to me."

"Just for a few months. He never talked about those days. I knew from my own research that there was an explosion in a soft coal pit. A few hundred men died that day."

"And then how did he end up in the Falls?"

"He probably followed the crowd. Niagara Falls became a boomtown because of the power industry. Lots of young men made their way there."

"What else do you know?"

"Not much. He got on his feet working for a gypsum company. Eventually he worked his way to a supervisor position. At night, he worked as a factory laborer." Joe stretched his leg, flexing his foot back and forth. "I think he used to deliver the evening newspaper in between his jobs. It was just him, Grandma, and whoever they sent money to back home, so they were able to eventually save a little money. They bought some land."

"I never knew all that."

"Like I said, that's about all I know."

Michael considered his next question. This conversation was the longest they'd ever had, longer even than the lecture in which his father had tried to talk him out of joining the Marines. Today, he just might get some answers.

"What did he do with the land?"

"He planted fruit orchards. Your grandmother loved that. She canned and gave away food all the time."

"I didn't know Grandpa and Grandma were farmers."

"They weren't, really. They occasionally worked some of the land, but mostly my father hired workers. Many of them were the same farmers who had originally owned the land." Joe yawned. "He was a businessman, through and through."

"What did they do after farming?" Michael wished for the millionth time that he could talk to Grandpa Joe about these matters. Talking to his father was like pulling teeth.

"You know the rest."

His mother set an antipasti tray on the table between them. "Michael Malvisti! Please tell me that you didn't have doughnuts for dinner on the way out here!" She pointed to the crumpled bag on the floor.

"Don't worry. Someone gave me that bag. And it contains something cool that I want to show Dad."

"What is it?" His dad hated surprises.

Michael picked up the bag and unrolled it. He chuckled to himself thinking about the covert manner in which he'd acquired its contents. He pulled out the picture and held it out to his father.

Joe's fingers trembled as he grasped the black-and-white photo.

"It's Grandpa Joe." Michael watched for a reaction. "He's sitting with a huge group of men. Some of them are in uniform."

"Carmella, turn on another light out here." He grimaced. "And bring me my glasses, will you?"

She did as he asked, just as she always did, and then leaned over her husband's shoulder. Her eyes narrowed. "The civilians are dressed so sharp. Forties, you think?"

Michael leaned forward and took a closer look. Men with slicked dark hair and tailored striped suits sat stone-faced. A few sported mustaches. All the men were clean-cut and dignified. The old picture couldn't hide the confidence that radiated from this impressive gathering.

"It looks like a formal event." She commented on the u-shaped table and fine tableware. Then she pointed out the massive crystal chandelier and suggested that they were at a country club or dining hall.

His father kept his thoughts to himself. He grunted once or twice as he studied the expressions of those seated around the table.

Several minutes ticked by.

"My father's sitting with Sammy Carlosi, Vito Facchione, and Tony … what's his name?" Joe looked into the distance, trying to recall. "Camelli. There's Monte, Chuckie Romo." Joe swore under his breath. "Most of these guys are dead now. Maybe all of 'em."

"I remember the names." Carmella smiled half-heartedly. "Your father's business friends."

Joe snorted. "More like disciplinarians, when necessary. This guy,"— he pointed to a stern-faced man sitting rigidly near Michael's grandfather—"used to cuff me in the head just in case I thought about doing anything wrong."

"I've heard those names all of my childhood." Michael thought for a moment. "Grandpa used to meet them at the downtown coffee shop."

"Bunch of miserable old jokers," Joe's voice was quiet, almost angry. "I could never figure out what they talked about every day."

"I can tell you." Michael grinned at the memory. "Wakes and funerals. Someone always brought along a newspaper so they could read the obituaries. They paid their respects to every person they knew, or who might be related to someone they knew."

"Humph." His father was beginning to sound just like them.

"He took me to a viewing once, you know."

Joe raised an eyebrow slightly. He reached for his wine.

"It was loud. People talked a lot about the 'old days,' but all I could think about was the dead body in the room."

"What old days?" Joe asked, suddenly curious.

"The days when Niagara Falls was a growing city. They told me that cars were not allowed on Main Street, and that people walked everywhere they needed to go. I had this vision of smiling women dressed in high heels and 1940s-style pinned-up hair, parading children down bustling streets."

"You were hearing about how the greatest generation lived during and after the war," Carmella offered.

A bullfrog bellowed from the banks of the canal, drawing Joe's attention.

"I'm guessing this was long before more than half the population of Niagara Falls fled?" Michael knew the question would irk his father.

But Joe showed no emotion. "Things change," he said, not taking his eyes from the dark expanse of the waterway.

The photo confirmed his father's words. Those old men at the coffee shop were once sober-minded business leaders. World War Two weighed on them, changed them. It was evident in their countenance, in the orderly way they were standing. No one tried to outshine another.

"Who are the other civilians?"

"Industrial leaders around town."

Michael leaned closer to his father, studying the faces of the men entrusted with the city's commercial and industrial foundation. Their expressions telegraphed a belief that they could do anything, anywhere they wanted.

"And this man?" Michael pointed to a burly, uniformed soldier. "It's General Leslie Groves, right?" He knew the answer, but wanted to hear the confirmation from his father.

"Yes. It looks like a number of aides are with him."

"How did Grandpa become acquainted with the general?"

"I don't know." Joe's face paled.

"Where are they?" Michael shifted. Grandpa Joe had mentioned the General several times over the years, but, until a few days ago, Michael never knew if the stories were real. "What's going on in this picture? Why were they gathered like this?"

"I don't know, Michael." Joe tossed the photo on the table between them. "Stop playing the lawyer with me."

Carmella stepped back. She shook her head at Michael, as if urging him not to agitate his father.

But Michael couldn't stop. For too long, he'd been wondering about the family. Wondering about a lot of things. The reporter's questions during the groundbreaking had only sparked his interest even more. Plus, he couldn't shake the feeling that the reporter and the woman hurt at the construction site were one and the same. Too many unknowns for his comfort.

"I'm part of this family, aren't I?" He looked apologetically at his mom. He picked up the picture and studied his grandfather's face. "I want to understand the business, and what we're about."

"Just be thankful for the opportunities our business has given you. You've had a good life, gotten the best education. How do you think you were able to go to that pricey law school of yours?"

Michael's head snapped up. "I was able to go to that law school as a result of eight years of service to my country." He shoved the picture back into the waxy bag. He'd rarely asked for anything from his family, a fact that his father had never recognized. Neither had his father ever acknowledged Michael's military service.

"Come on, boy. You've benefitted from the business in many ways, don't deny that."

"True. But I've also worked my tail off to be where I am now." Michael thought about leaving. He didn't need this. But they were getting somewhere, for once. "I just want to understand where our family fits into the big picture. I thought I could start with you."

Joe picked up his wine, and seeing that it was empty, set it back on the armchair table. He closed his eyes. When he opened them, he looked directly at Michael. "Understand this," he said, his voice low and firm. "We put people to work, provided needed services, paid our taxes, and improved that city. That's all you need to know about the family business."

The cicadas momentarily stopped their sing-song cry.

Michael hated being shut down. "Would Uncle Sal tell me more?"

"Michael." Joe stood unsteadily and pressed his finger into Michael's chest. "Do not talk to Sal. Not about anything, especially Malvisti Industries."

His father's hand shook. He used the arms of his chair to lower himself back into the ornate outdoor seat.

"Your dad is upset." Carmella placed her good hand on Joe's shoulder. "Why don't you men talk about something else." She bent to his ear and whispered something. He nodded and she left quickly.

"We've been talking about all the wrong things for too long now." Michael towered over his father's once robust frame. "I've never questioned you, Dad. But now I need some answers."

"I'm done talking about this subject." He took a deep breath and coughed. "Go home and forget this foolishness."

Carmella returned with a small container of pills and a glass of water. Joe emptied the pills into his hand and swallowed them noisily. He downed the glass, then returned it to his wife. "Let sleeping dogs lie, Michael."

Ignorance wasn't possible anymore. There were too many holes in the Malvisti family story. Nothing seemed to add up. Why were they so wealthy? Why had they kept him in the dark about the business?

Michael clasped his father's shoulder and left, clutching the doughnut bag under his arm. Answers weren't going to come out of this industrial beach city.

But today's conversation was a start, at least.

And it only whetted his appetite for more.

❖

Even from the boat dock, Michael could identify the unmistakable aroma of steak wafting up from his galley. Probably his neighbor. "That you, Paulie?"

"It's me, sweetie." Jillian's blond head emerged from below. Her week in Niagara Falls must have agreed with her. She fairly glowed from head to toe.

He hopped on board, more surprised than angry. "What's going on here?"

"I'm so sorry." She flashed him a coy smile. "I messed up bigtime, didn't I?"

"Yeah." Vanilla fragrance overpowered the grilled meat. He forced himself not to say more until she offered something in the way of an explanation.

Instead, she moved into his arms. "I really missed you. That'll never happen again. Promise."

He closed his eyes, trying to remind himself why he was mad at her. "But what *did* happen?" He held tight, stroking the back of her head. "Why did you stay up there so long?"

She moved her mouth close to his ear. "I just got carried away with all the excitement over the Green City. I wanted to see the whole town. You didn't show me *anything* besides Cascata Verde, you know."

He pulled away, his arms still encircling her waist. "But you don't even know my Uncle Sal, Jill. Where'd you stay? Why haven't you called?" He dropped his arms. "I don't get it."

She took him by the hand to the top of the galley ladder. "Let's talk about it after we eat. Food's getting cold. And I've got some surprises for you."

He jumped down the last two rungs.

"Sit over there and relax."

He propped himself up on his elbows on some pillows she'd arranged. Through the cabin windows he could see the first pinks and oranges of the Florida sunset. The streaked clouds emanated soft color.

She handed him a plastic wine goblet and set a tray of cheese and crackers on the table next to him.

This was the Jillian with whom he had first fallen in love. The Jillian that would try anything, even if it involved buying and grilling meat. The woman that wanted to hear what he had to say. The woman whose attention was hard to resist.

He took a sip of wine. And then another.

CHAPTER EIGHTEEN

December 25, 2003

By 1944, I could buy just about anything.

Anything, that is, except peace.

That year, Monte Vesuvio's latest spasmodic period of upheaval came to a violent end. The Mountain covered my Italian hometown in a foot of ash. After years of working in the dust- and flour-filled pasta factories, my parents' lungs had simply had enough.

At least they died together.

My son, Joe Jr., once asked whether I felt guilty about leaving my parents to die in Italy. I didn't. Even when money became no object for me and I offered to pay their way, my parents still wouldn't come visit me. They were too afraid of the boat, too old for the transatlantic journey. They argued that Noni, who was close to death herself, couldn't be left alone, and that she would never leave her beloved Italy. And on and on. The fact is, they were stubborn.

I sent money. God only knows if any made it into my parents' hands. Letters from home were sparse. And when they arrived, they were short and contained just the facts. Some letters bore the censor's stamp, others contained entire sentences crossed through with heavy black ink. My Noni would have rebelled against the Regime, had she known what I learned after I left. She would've cursed them all, never caring about the threat of arrest.

149

Vesuvio defined my birth, and, in some ways, my first death. Once my family was gone forever, neither The Mountain nor the Fascists would ever again have the power to affect me.

Torre Annunziata for me has been silent ever since.

❖

I continued to prosper. Land, power, and wealth became my security. I needed more of them, just to ensure that I could continue to control my surroundings. They, in turn, guaranteed respect. I had become something of a land baron in my new hometown of Niagara Falls. The hunger within me abated ... for a time.

As I wrote before, I dreamed big dreams on my way to America. And even bigger ones once I got here. But even I could not have imagined the heights to which I would rise. Garbage came into my life. And with it, opportunity.

"The formula is simple," I told my wife one evening as she stood at the stove, stirring sauce. "People create human waste. Chemical and manufacturing plants generate industrial waste. All of the waste needs to go somewhere."

"But why are these ... industries coming to Niagara Falls?" My wife struggled to find the words in Italian. We'd never heard of chemical factories back in Italy.

"The Falls make all this happen. We offer cheap power and easy access for moving goods around. Manufacturers like it here." I watched as the wheels turned in my wife's mind. "More jobs mean even more people. So where do you think all of the garbage goes?"

"The street!" She waved a fist above her head. Like me, she remembered how Italian factories used to pile garbage in the alleyways. City officials wouldn't remove it until the citizens went on strike, thrusting their collective fists in the air.

"I plan to use some of our land to bury waste."

She tasted her sauce. "Go on."

"I don't care if the land borders the river or is smack dab in the middle of a farming community." I shrugged. "There is a need and we will meet it."

She kissed her fingers, blessing the enterprise. Then she added a pinch of sugar to the pot.

My instincts were not wrong. Our unused land—combined with a relatively complacent population that didn't ask too many questions—offered a perfect love match for the growing waste problem associated with an expanding population and factory operations. Industry in Niagara Falls had exploded. Chemicals, especially pesticides, had become essential to everyday living. The need for waste disposal had skyrocketed.

The government further spurred the waste industry when it converted our city's chemical and manufacturing facilities to wartime production. Niagara Falls became instrumental in the process of making uranium ore useful. The more the factories grew, the more people were needed for jobs, and the more my business flourished.

I started to bury a lot of garbage. Some of it was just your average run-of-the-mill municipal waste. But a lot of the waste I started to truck out of Niagara Falls' factories contained a variety of new and ultra-hazardous chemicals. I buried those, too, and made a fortune. Eventually, I buried even worse things alongside those chemicals.

But I don't want to get too far ahead of myself. During those heady early days, all of my property, including the portions abutting rivers, creeks, and farmland, were put to productive use. I owned the land, and I had the right to do with it whatever I wanted.

I knew my rights, yes. And I exercised them.

And I used my power to pursue whatever opportunities and ideas seemed right to me. I enabled businesses to operate. I employed residents, neighbors, my friends' sons, and their friends too. I paid my taxes. I donated money. Through all of this, I became as essential to the local economy as the Falls themselves.

But something FDR said began to work on me: *Men, possessed of such great power, carry likewise a great responsibility.*

Maybe the Bible says something along those lines too. Either way, I didn't focus on the responsibility portion of the equation. And even if I had, how could I have known that justice and responsibility went hand-in-hand?

Maybe that's where my life got off-course.

Looking back on that time during the war, I realize that justice required more of me. More questions. More accountability. More truth. I didn't *do justice* to my sons or employees. I didn't serve the highest interests of the charitable, business, or military relationships in which I took part. This is painful to admit. But on my watch, things had become horribly corrupted. Defiled, even. And the impact fell most heavily on the people who lived and worked in this city. My friends, our neighbors, and even our milkman.

Lord in heaven, I was about to see them suffer.

There would be no peace on my mountain. Or in my heart.

CHAPTER NINETEEN

Niagara Falls, New York

"We've got the go ahead?" Lydia stopped chewing the cap of her new Cascata Verde pen. "We can officially sell houses?"

"Yes!" Dana twirled her office chair and threw her own pen in the air. "Cascata Verde homes and condos are now ready for pre-construction purchase! I arranged for a temp this week. We should have tons of calls after the brokers' open house this afternoon."

Lydia tilted her head. Dana had not discussed hiring help with her. "Are you sure hiring someone's okay with Hessley?"

"Oh yes," She circled the chair again. "Rebecca was fine with it, as long as the temp only answers the phones. Hessley is sending two corporate employees to help us today."

"Where was I when you talked to her?"

"You had to take Harrison to the doctor for the umpteenth time." She sighed. "Then your sitter couldn't take the boys, which was just as well because your van was down. Sound familiar?"

Lydia remembered. Until today, she'd missed every milestone for the Green City, including the groundbreaking, because Harrison's asthma had flared up. Or because he'd spike a fever and she couldn't leave him. She stuck the pen back in her mouth.

Was it too much to ask for one easy month? Just thirty days during which no one got sick, or a bill collector didn't call?

153

Or her boys didn't need her to be mother *and* father?

❖

Lydia had three rooms to check over before the start of the open house. She stole a glance out of an upstairs bedroom window. Nearly two hundred people milled about in the frigid February air, many of them stomping their feet in an apparent effort to keep warm. "Dana, come over here, right away!"

"What is it?" she said, irritably. Dana's hair had frizzed from her inspection of the steam shower. The stress of the day was starting to show.

"Look." Lydia pointed to an area of the construction site that had been roped off to restrict access. The framed building that would eventually be the Suspension Spa and Wellness Center held the attention of the crowd.

Dana gasped. "So many people came!"

"This idea is going to fly!" Today's turnout provided the confirmation Lydia had needed. After years of planning, and months of construction and hand-wringing, it had come down to this: a packed model open house. In the middle of winter, no less. Financial peace was just around the corner.

"I had no doubt." Dana wiped a smudge from the window. "Our city was known as the Honeymoon Capital of the World and Cataract City. But this eco-city concept will change everything. It's redefined us. This new way to live has come to stay."

"I hope you're right." She ran a cloth over a bamboo night stand.

"And why not? People are basically good and they gravitate towards things in harmony with the Earth."

"Are you being serious?" Lydia balled up the dust rags in her hand. "I would never say people are good. I mean, I care about people. But you don't have to teach five-year-old boys to lie. They just know."

"I don't expect you to understand." Dana smoothed her hair in a mirror. "You're a pessimist at heart. Mr. Mahoney's rubbed off on you."

Lydia didn't think so, but the words hurt nonetheless. She pasted on a smile, eager to show off the most modern and greatest model home in North America.

For the next four hours, Lydia led successive tours through the spectacular show home. The visitors expected to see the high-end appliances, multiple accesses for natural light, and the expansive views of the river. But they didn't expect the extras. She proudly highlighted the passive solar heating systems and low-VOC construction materials. She reveled in the oohs and ahhs escaping from the visitors, many of whom were educated about the latest in green technology. Some brokers were taken with the environmentally friendly trim and shelving, low-emitting paint, or innovative flooring. Hessley had even thought of light pollution reduction to improve nighttime visibility. Others seemed impressed by the simple lines of the home.

And then there was the group of brokers blessing each room of the model ... she wasn't sure what to think about them.

By the end of the day, her repeated use of Hessley's mantra left an indelible mark in her brain: "sustainable development meets the needs of the present without compromising the ability of future generations to meet their own needs." To her, the definition had another meaning: sustenance for the present needs of her family. Her heart swelled. She had a new lease on life after today.

"Ms. Vallone, I have some questions." An expensively perfumed older woman placed her hand gently on Lydia's arm. She introduced herself as Violet, a broker from New York City.

"How can I help you?" Lydia sneezed.

"My goodness." She reached into her oversized leather bag and handed Lydia a fragrant tissue. "The homes are beautiful and well-designed. I love the plans for bicycle storage racks throughout the community, as well as the miles of parks and trails."

"Me too." Lydia wiped her nose. "Those are some of my favorite features."

"But I'd like to know about the environmental assessments that have been done on this property. Are you familiar with any of those?"

Her heart sank. "What exactly are you looking for, ma'am?" She wiped her nose again, which gave her a moment to think. This day was about a fresh start for the community. And for her. The past had no place here.

"I'd like to know about all testing and clean up measures taken here." The woman pulled out her smart phone. She appeared to consult a list. "I know that a development of any size would have different types of environmental testing. There would be Phase I and II assessments. I'd like to see those, for a start."

"I'm not sure about the specifics of the testing, but I'll look into it." Lydia scanned the area for one of the Hessley staff members to rescue her. No luck.

"Here's my contact information." Violet produced an engraved card holder from her bag. "Would it be possible to hear from you soon?"

"Sure." Lydia smiled uncertainly. She sneezed again.

More toxic talk. She dreaded telling Dana about the request.

❖

Lydia thrummed her paper note pad. She hadn't had a chance to discuss Violet's request with Dana before the conference call with Rebecca Waters at headquarters.

"We've had a successful open house, from start to finish." Dana spoke directly into the speakerphone. "Your design team, Ms. Waters, produced a finished product unlike anything ever before seen in this slightly-behind-the-times area."

"Let's get down to specifics." Rebecca's clipped tone suggested that she was in a hurry. "And, by the way, one of our commercial real estate attorneys just joined us here. He doesn't work with residential sales, but keeps tabs on anything real estate-related. His name is Michael Malvisti."

"Hello Ms. Vallone, Ms. DuPays."

Dana responded. But Lydia's thoughts galloped in another direction, distracting her. This attorney shared a surname with the infamous local family. They had to be related.

Dana kicked her in the ankle. She refocused.

"So, how many brokers came through?" Rebecca Waters asked.

Dana reviewed her laptop screen. "Two hundred and four. They came from as far away as Toronto, Canada, and New York City. One broker even showed up from Miami."

"What feedback did they offer?"

Dana nodded at Lydia to take over.

"The responses were overwhelmingly positive, Ms. Waters and ... Mr. Malvisti. Agents liked the natural elements in the kitchen. The master bathroom's glass and steel rain shower elicited all kinds of favorable comments." Lydia scanned her scribbled notes. "Everyone liked the generous room sizes, and agreed that the homes were priced right. The brokers from Toronto were especially impressed that we kept costs relatively low. Then again, they're used to a pricier real estate market."

"Agreed," Dana chimed in. "I heard much the same."

"On the negative side," Lydia continued, "one broker felt that the low-VOC paints were less vibrant. Another felt that the sidewalks should be wider to allow for both biking and walking." Lydia flipped to a second page. "A third asked that we speed up our construction schedule, although I don't think that's a negative comment, exactly."

"Did anyone have specific buyers in mind?" The masculine voice this time. He seemed friendly enough, especially for a lawyer.

"Yes." Dana spread out dozens of business cards. "We have at least seventy-eight very likely buyers, based on broker feedback. Some of those buyers are employed by Pavati Biotecnologia. Most will purchase a home sight unseen. The remaining brokers anticipate a strong interest from their clients. We'll hear from a few this week, I think."

"Any unusual questions, requests, or observations?" Rebecca Waters asked. Typing could be heard through the speaker device.

"No, not a one," Dana replied, shrugging.

Lydia needed to speak up. Perhaps not about the prayer group, but she should definitely mention Violet. She avoided Dana's gaze. "I did have one out-of-the-ordinary request. I haven't yet had a chance to discuss it with the others, though."

Dana looked at her sharply.

"What is it?" The attorney, this time.

Lydia's palms started to sweat. She didn't expect to have to address Hessley's CEO and one of its lawyers at the same time. Let alone one with the last name of Malvisti. "A broker, a woman named Violet, asked me about environmental studies for the property." Lydia ignored Dana's icy stare and plunged ahead. "She wants copies of any existing Phase I and II environmental assessment reports. And a few other things."

Lydia mouthed an apology. Dana's face turned white with anger. Lydia could only imagine Dana's response to a report about the religious people. She would need to keep that information to herself for now.

"What did you tell her?" The CEO spoke rapidly. Furious clicks could be heard.

"Only that I would check into it and get back to her."

"Remind her that Cascata Verde is built near the site of a closed landfill." Rebecca paused, as if choosing her words carefully. "Several chemical plants operated nearby. Most of our properties were brownfields when we acquired them. Any contaminated parcels have been cleaned up or covered with a site barrier. Also, to prevent any future human or animal contact with chemicals in the ground, a two-foot layer of soil covers large areas of the site where residential, commercial, and park space is underway or planned. We've taken every remedial measure. The site is safe for humans, plants, and animals alike."

"Will do."

"Ladies, we do not release the actual assessments or evaluations because they represent only a picture of the site at a point in time. Work at the site is ongoing, especially during the construction phases. The various types of barriers we use, for example, are not reflected in the reports that she seeks. The reports would be misleading."

"Thank you." Lydia scribbled down some of Rebecca's wording. "I'll follow up with a telephone call to her tomorrow morning."

The lawyer's voice came over the speaker. "Let me give you Tyler Morales' telephone number, Ms. Vallone. He's our go-to guy for environmental matters relating to Cascata Verde. You can call him anytime."

"Thank you." Lydia blew on her damp palms so she could properly hold the pen. She recorded Morales' number and felt reassured by the attorney's offer to make him available. She planned to talk to Morales first to better understand the site history. When the call ended, she breathed a sigh of relief; it wasn't as bad as she anticipated.

Quiet descended for the first time that day.

Lydia relaxed her shoulders as she loaded her papers into her briefcase. Bone weariness had set in. Her cheeks hurt from smiling.

"How do you think it went?" Dana avoided looking at Lydia while she straightened her own papers.

"Fantastic." Lydia shrugged into her coat. "We're going to sell a lot of houses. And make a ton of money." She grabbed the last of her information sheets and filed them in the coffee-colored credenza behind her desk. "How can I complain?"

"Oh, I don't know, you'll find some way to make money generation hazardous to your health." Dana set her hands on her hips.

"You're not funny."

"Let me see ... the dollar bills are laced with drugs. The fifties are contaminated with penicillin-resistant germs." There was no mirth in her comments.

"I didn't have a choice. Rebecca asked me the question, and I answered truthfully."

"Guess not."

"Do you think I made that up? I don't even know the first thing about Phase I or II environmental statements. Or assessments. Whatever."

"It just surprised me, that's all. Violet asked a highly unusual question for a broker. I'm thinking she's a plant from some domestic eco-terrorism group." Dana picked up her office phone. "I may contact the FBI and see if we can learn anything about her."

"Are you serious?" Lydia stopped packing. "Now who's the killjoy? Me or you?"

"Lydia, I'm just kidding!" She put the phone back on the cradle. "You had to disclose the question to Rebecca. And, to be honest, that woman asked me the same thing and I pretended not to hear her. Several people were speaking to me at once and I could get away with ignoring her. She must've sought you out."

"Thanks for the heads up." Dana's confession took her off guard. "Listen, I need to run to pick up the kids. I'll call you tonight. Do you want to come over for dinner? It's taco night."

Dana looked as if she considered the invitation for a moment.

"My mom and Angie are coming over too."

"Oh." Dana picked up a stack of papers. Her mouth hardened. "No, I'm going to stay around here and prepare e-files for these potential buyers. You're killing trees with your paper notes. I'll call you later."

Lydia lugged her bulky briefcase to her minivan. She had been averaging a mere one house a month with Lakeside. Now, the expected commissions from dozens of homes would bring in more money than she'd ever made, even after she split everything with Dana. She might even buy a new car. Life seemed to be on the upswing, at least financially.

"Why don't you let me help you with that, Carefree Girl." Chris Magnano pushed himself up from leaning on her van.

Lydia dropped her briefcase. "You scared the daylights out of me!"

She gave him an awkward hug, then bent over to pick up her case. "You've lost so much weight that I didn't recognize you. You look great."

"Thanks. You're looking pretty good yourself."

"What are you doing here? How did you get past security?" She took in his tan flannel-lined Carhartt work jacket, baseball hat, and paint-splattered carpenter jeans. He fit in with every other worker at the site.

"I came with an agent I know, and then busied myself with shoveling the paths around the model home." He indicated the concrete sidewalk. "Looks great, don't you think?"

"Never better. But you didn't sneak into a secure construction site to play in the snow. What's up?"

"Drive me to my car outside the South entrance." Chris walked around to the passenger's side, and opened the door. "I'll tell you on the way."

"I'm not used to having an adult passenger." Lydia gestured toward the front seat piled high with sneakers, race cars, and last week's mail. "Sorry. Kids, you know?" She tossed a hardened peanut butter sandwich under her seat.

"I wish I knew. I'll just sit back here with the booster seats and ... hey, look at this, it's GI Joe!" Chris good-naturedly set the action figure on his lap. "We're all set."

After the van warmed up and the windows cleared, Lydia maneuvered through the security checkpoint and waved to the guard on duty, Officer Biondi. "Okay, now talk."

"I brought you some doughnuts, that's all." He tossed a crumpled bag on the pile next to her.

"What kind?"

"The ones that show a large anomaly buried about a thousand yards from here." He leaned forward. "Right in the middle of Malvisti Park."

"An anomaly?"

"Yes, something unusual or unexpected in an area that's being studied."

"Forget doughnuts, what are you talking about?" She took her foot off the pedal.

"There's an electric imaging study in this bag. Essentially, scientists mapped what's under Malvisti Park. The map shows a large metallic object buried deep in the earth."

She felt blood drain from her face. "What is it?"

"Dunno." Chris scanned the icy street. Flurries bounced off the windshield like summer sandflies. He unstrapped and leaned forward. "But it's a sphere about 40 feet in diameter. Pull over here."

Chris had parked on a plowed section of the shoulder of the road leading to Cascata Verde's southernmost entrance. Her head spinning, she slid to a stop behind his compact car and put the minivan in park.

"Wow." She slid the papers out, trying to make sense of the scan. "Where'd you get this stuff?"

"A concerned group of private citizens. They're gathering information and trying to nail down some facts."

"Is one of them named Violet?" Lydia's inner alarms sounded. Dana's mock conspiracy theory suddenly didn't sound so far-fetched.

"I've heard that one of them might be an employee of someone connected with Cascata Verde." All traces of good humor were gone from Chris' voice now.

"Why are you giving this to me?" Lydia checked her rearview mirror. The windows had fogged over. "You told me to lay low, remember?"

"Yes, and you should keep doing that for now. But you're on the inside. I'm sure you come across all kinds of property-related information. And I know that if there's something out there, you'd want to know about it. Am I right?"

"That's true ... I think. But I need something solid, not rumors. I can't lose this job. I've got a lot on the line right now. Things are just starting to pick up for me."

"That's exactly what I'm banking on. Facts. I trust nothing else. I want you to look at the scan, and see if anything comes across your desk that could possibly relate to this object. We need to know more about it."

Lydia swallowed. "Okay, but understand that I *really* need my job and I won't lie to Hessley. Rebecca Waters took a gamble on me and Dana. She's the best thing to come in to my life in a long time."

"Understood." He looked wistful as he retrieved keys from his pocket. By this time, sizeable snowflakes had accumulated on the wipers. "I don't expect you to lie. I do expect, knowing you as I do, that you will do the right thing. You're one of the good ones, Lyd." With that, Chris left the minivan and jogged to his own car. He pulled out without turning on his headlights.

Lydia's eyes rested on the rearview mirror. Surely the security cameras had caught Chris's coming and going. Officer Biondi had already seen her with a man in the van. She swept the bag containing the report out of sight. It joined three similar ones containing stiff, half-eaten bagels coated in frozen cream cheese.

Tension seized her shoulders. What would she do if something odd came to her attention? Would she alert Chris? Or would she notify her employer and trust Hessley to fix it? Maybe she could probe the environmental guy about the study. Tyler Morales? She hoped he already knew about it.

One thing she would definitely not do is tell Dana about the doughnut bag surprise. Or the prayer group. At least until she knew more. Those omissions, lies really, would be the first in twenty-five plus years of friendship. But it was justified. Things between them had already become strained over Lydia's negativity.

For now, her job was to sell houses. Not to ensure the safety of a city.

Or pray over it, either.

CHAPTER TWENTY

Northern Florida

Michael surveyed the two-story dive shop from the driver's seat of the GT-R. He checked his course paperwork again.

"Seriously, is this *it?*" Ty opened the passenger door and stepped out.

White paint flaked off the sides of the building. Two sagging, aqua-trimmed additions jutted out like afterthoughts from both sides of the ramshackle main structure.

Only the oversized red and white Diver Down flag hinted at life within.

"My cave diving instructor works out of this shop." Michael put away his confirmation and got out. "He's supposed to be one of the best. Guys swear by him."

"I hope this guy's legit." Tyler stretched. He hobbled a few steps, groaning as he stood erect.

Michael chuckled. "What's the matter with you?"

"My battered legs won't let me do three hours of driving anymore."

"When did you get so old, Ty?" He pressed a button on his key fob.

"My divorce did it to me."

"No, *you* did it to you." Michael unloaded a bag from the trunk. "Sign up for some recreational diving before you leave. You'll love it." He hefted it to his shoulder. "Maybe it'll get you back in the game."

"Thanks, but no." Ty reached the building first and waved Michael in. "I want to start the environmental assessments for Hessley's new Florida property. That'll take up most of my time 'till I come back for you on Friday."

"Suit yourself."

A desiccated palm tree grew forlornly at the entrance. "Mikey, they can't even keep a tough plant like the saw palmetto alive. I'm worried for you, bro."

"Relax."

A bald man slapped the reservations counter and pointed at Michael. "Your instructor will be here in a few minutes, sir. Let's get you checked in for your lodging." Expensive sunglasses sat perched on his deeply tanned head. He took Michael's credit card and handed him a clipboard loaded with paperwork before turning to Ty.

"How 'bout you, sir?"

"No thanks." He stepped back. "I'm just a bubble watcher."

Michael flipped through the pages, scratched his name across the bottom, and then handed the man his completed forms. "I hope I survive. After the legal releases I just signed, I think you own my house now. Maybe even my first-born son."

"Lawyers." Ty smirked. "Can't stand 'em."

"The equipment you sent ahead arrived just this morning, Mr. Malvisti. Hang on a minute and I'll get it." He removed the set of keys from around his neck. "Diving conditions are perfect. Should be a great week."

"Thank you, sir," Michael said. "I've been looking forward to this for a long time."

The men walked back to the car. Heat shimmered off the vehicle and a layer of fine dust clung to its frame.

A dilapidated cargo van barreled into the parking lot, coming to a sloppy diagonal stop just a dozen feet from the GT-R. The van's engine protested noisily long after the driver had cut it off. The owner clapped a ragged cowboy hat on his head as he finished the last twangy line of a country song before opening the door.

Both men stared at the newcomer.

"Mike." Ty kept his voice low. "I think that's your instructor."

Michael studied the van. Dive equipment hung neatly on the inside. Beneath the worn hat, the man's weathered face confirmed a life spent under the Florida sun. Ty was right.

"Howdy, fellas!" The energetic, wiry man hopped down from the van's running board. He wore stringy cut-offs and work boots with no socks. Thirty-five, forty years old? Michael couldn't tell.

"Bubba Triffin," the man said in a thick North Florida accent, sticking his hand out to Michael. "But everyone calls me Albert."

"Michael Malvisti." Chances are, this guy had never heard of his family.

"Ho, ho, you're my man this week. I've heard all about you from a former student. He says you're smart. I like smart. We're gon' learn a lot." He flashed a toothy smile at Michael. "You up for it?"

"I am." Michael warmed up to the cowboy.

"How about your friend here, Mr. Malvisti." He sized up Ty, who towered over him. "He comin' to watch?"

"No, sir. He's dropping me off and heading out on business," Michael said, introducing them.

"You two fellas get situated while I check in with the desk. Nice meetin' y'all." Albert got back into the truck, whistling something that Michael didn't recognize. It took a few tries for the van to start, but it roared to life after he pumped the gas a few times. Albert pulled into a dusty corner of the parking lot, leaving a mix of exhaust and gas to sully the still air.

Ty coughed. "I almost don't know what to think, man." He gestured toward the dozens of off-color bumper stickers on the rear doors about cave divers and women. "You sure you're gonna be okay?"

"Hope so." Michael walked back to the GT-R. A new layer of dust blanketed the body and hood. "I need a Bubba van for these trips." He wiped off the sideview mirror. "She's a city girl."

"Another few days out here and supercar here is gonna melt."

"Yeah." Michael squinted at the sky. "I'm glad you're taking her. She prefers shaded parking decks, maybe even an underground ramp."

"And what time does she get fed and diapered?" Ty kept a straight face.

"I keep her nearly full, all the time." Michael cracked a smile. "Make sure you use high octane gas. I left you money in the sunglasses compartment."

"Is this ride like walking a puppy in the park?" Tyler asked. "Will girls flock to gawk over her?"

"Stay away from the kind of girl this car attracts." Michael turned away.

"Alrighty then." Ty whistled. "I'm not quite ready for that scene anyway."

"No, not until you clean your apartment. Why don't you hire someone to come in every week?"

"Because that costs money, bro. The divorce was brutal. You'd be surprised at the amount of money I live on, even with that sweet raise last year. It was just enough to cover repairs if I ding your car. I wasn't born a Malvisti, ya know."

Michael paused. "Hey, you know how you keep asking me about my family?"

"What family?" Ty grinned. "I believe that's your usual response."

"Funny. Listen, I'm trying to learn more about our history. For the business. Maybe you could help me. You've got the technical background I need and you know I trust you like a brother."

"What do you want to know?"

"Everything." Michael shouldered his bag. "What's the scope of the Malvisti waste business? Why did my family make a killing in a business that doesn't seem particularly lucrative? I've got questions across the board."

"Why do you care about all this?" Tyler took off his sunglasses and wiped them with the underside of his shirt. "It's in the past."

"Whatever my grandfather did, it's lasted. And it's made lots of money. With Hessley's Green City, we're about to reinvent innovation. I want to build on my grandfather's success, and not make the mistakes my uncle or father did, you know?"

Ty raised his eyebrow. "Gimme a week." He held out his hand for the keys. "I'll do some research on my downtime. Maybe talk to a few people. Confidentially, of course."

Michael scoffed. "There's nothing hush-hush about my family name. You understand that, right?"

"Give me a little credit. I won't disclose any specifics." Tyler climbed into the driver's seat. "Anyway, Hessley's already gotten a few calls this month about Cascata Verde that Rebecca wants me to handle. It'll give me the perfect cover."

"Do it, then." A white cloud sailed over them, giving both humans and vehicles a reprieve from the sun. Michael hoped he wasn't disrespecting Grandpa Joe by digging into the family's background. For too long, Michael had filled in the blanks about his family out of admiration for his grandfather. But sometimes he assumed wrong. It didn't give him much to go on for the future.

"You look anxious." Tyler started the engine. He revved it a few times. "I can handle this."

Michael took off his shades. He looked Ty square in the eye. "Just be careful. I've been warned about something bad coming my way."

"Trouble for you is trouble for me, bro. You sure 'bout this?"

"Not really." Michael tapped the window frame. "But do it anyway. There are some things a man's just gotta know."

CHAPTER TWENTY-ONE

Niagara Falls, New York

The lump in Lydia's throat expanded.

She rested her hands in her lap and squared her shoulders. She drew in air, squeezing her eyes shut. Lydia tried to conjure up a vision of an ideal vacation spot at the ocean. Or anywhere, except Niagara Falls.

It was no use. Her eyes darted underneath her lids. She jumped from her seat. "The book you loaned me recommends this centering thing." She walked over to Dana's desk and stood with her hands on her hips.

Dana reluctantly pulled away from the computer. "And?"

"It doesn't work."

"What's the matter with you today?" Dana's tone stayed even. She returned to the screen.

"I don't know." Lydia closed her eyes to avoid seeing the batch of documents on her office desk. Red "sign here" stickers poked out from both sides of dozens of home purchase contracts. "Lots to do."

"I know. I've got the same amount of work."

"Does your throat feel tight? Is your heart racing?" Lydia pressed her eyes, trying to avoid smearing her eye make-up with the tears that threatened. "I have all these weird symptoms. Like I can't sleep, but I'm exhausted."

"Yeah?"

"Plus, the sheer number of calls over the Point-Of-No-Return Miracle has been ridiculous, don't you think?" Lydia tapped a pen against her leg.

"Well, it's not every day that a construction crew rescues a bunch of teens from going over the Falls. Luck and a rope. Pretty sensational."

"Still." Lydia laid a hand over her heart, alarmed by the violent thumping. "There's been a call every five minutes. People think Cascata Verde has something to do with it. Like this place is special."

Dana pointed at the floor in front of her desk. "Come here for a sec."

"What are you going to do to me?" Lydia moved toward her.

"Stand here." Dana removed the pen from Lydia's hand. "Take a deep and slow breath."

"Okaaay."

Dana placed her hands on Lydia's shoulders. "Breathe in and say 'let,' then blow out your breath and say 'go.'

"I feel kinda stupid."

"Just try it."

She complied, but felt no different even after five breaths.

Dana removed her hands. "Try this. Bend at the waist." She demonstrated.

"What if someone walks in and sees my backside?"

"Relax your upper body." Dana's limp arms swung gently. "Just hang there for a few moments. Shake your arms loose."

"Blood is rushing to my head."

"Just let your tensions flow out of you towards the floor." Dana reached over and ran her hands down Lydia's arms. "Now inhale and slowly rise to a standing position. Picture yourself breathing in positive energy."

"The blood is flowing, that's for sure."

"Feel better?"

"I guess." Lydia stood and shrugged. "I have a bit more energy than I did a few minutes ago."

"Take a walk around the property. Go by the vineyard. They're expecting an early bud break this year. Maybe there's already something to see. Imagine that with each breath, each step, you're gathering your scattered thoughts and energy back to your inner self." Dana thumped her chest. "That's your calm center. Let's see how you feel when you return."

"Fine. I'll try it."

"Too bad Suspension Spa isn't open yet." Dana went back to tapping on her keyboard. "A few hours in there and you'd be a new woman."

"When have you ever known me to have a few hours that I could sit in a spa? I'm racing from the moment I awake. I shower, throw on clothes, and make at least two different breakfasts—"

"You're getting unclear." Dana saved her document and turned to Lydia. "You'll throw yourself off-balance after that litany. Remember, you are seeking a state of clarity and peace. You're centering yourself."

"Oh ... But then I race home from work to cook dinner, shop, do laundry, take kids to lessons, bathe them, get them in bed ... at which time I run around the house picking up, washing clothes, sorting bills and school papers."

"Hire someone to help. You can afford that now, or at least as soon as we get some closing checks in a few weeks." Dana opened an email. "Relax. Get centered."

"I just hope that while I'm running all over the house I get some exercise—"

Dana rolled her head back. "You chose to have two kids, Lydia."

Stung, Lydia grabbed her sneakers and shoved her feet inside. "I didn't exactly choose to be a single parent! I think a walk is a good idea. Text me if that Ty Morales from Hessley calls." Lydia clamped on a hard hat on her way out.

Breathe and walk. Calm center...

Lydia set out opposite the vineyard. Being alone out near the grapes and the turbines was the last thing she wanted.

Walk and breathe. One block. Two blocks.

A surge of pride in Cascata Verde's progress improved her mood. Once the snow from the day of the brokers' open house had melted, construction activity had surged. Almost ninety-five percent of the residential units were scheduled to close over the next few weeks. She waved to a few of the painters that she recognized.

She walked briskly down a main avenue towards the central piazza. Park benches arranged in comfortable patterns throughout the common area beckoned to her. Further down, new blacktop trails crisscrossed the semi-wooded Malvisti Park, all meeting in the center near a tranquil fountain. Already, even in the early spring weather, workers on break seemed to be enjoying the spruced-up park.

Her heartbeat evened out as she kept walking. For the moment, all seemed right in the world.

The nearly-complete church rose up before her. Its fieldstone facade glinted blue and brown hues, depending on the way the sun struck it. The open copper, wood, and stone spires bespoke strength. She could tell its roots dug deep.

Everything fit.

How unlike her own weak, crumbling self. She couldn't even manage to look put-together on the outside, let alone keep the inside from caving in. She had to see the rest of the structure. Maybe, like her, the church's interior was still a work in progress.

Lydia looked both ways for cars and stepped into the road. Halfway across, a windswept trail of black smoke against the city's skyline caught her attention. She held her breath as she followed its trajectory back to the source. Flames shot from the back of one of the wind turbines along the river. She uttered a cry. How could a turbine catch fire?

She hurried up the church steps to get a better view. Chunks of burning debris fell straight downward from the structure, causing a second smoky plume. The fire arced a hundred and fifty feet in the air. Sirens raced into Cascata Verde from opposite entrances of the development.

The door to the church flung open. A fully-suited fireman carrying a mountain bike burst across the threshold. "Pardon me, ma'am." The man raced down the stairs, mounted the bike and took off unsteadily in the direction of the fire. He shed some tools at the intersection.

"Don't just stand there gawking at the man, get in." Dana pulled a golf cart close. "First responders are already there. Your purse is in the back."

"Nice timing." Lydia looked around for the fireman, but saw only workers pouring out into the street.

"That thing doesn't look too stable from here." Dana pulled onto a road that curved near the mile-long wind farm complex.

"One blade looks like it's beginning to melt. Look how close it is to the next one!" Lydia steadied herself and stood up in the cart. "This is surreal. The fire is literally in the air. Did you know turbines could burn?"

"No." Dana frowned. "There's got to be a good explanation for this. Our green technology is safe, and people need to believe that it's safe. It's our future."

Lydia sank deeper into the sustainable fabric-covered seat. "I'm sorry if I was short with you earlier. I'm very, very tired." She kept the hostility out of her tone.

"It's all right." Dana pulled over for another emergency responder. She looked over her shoulder at Lydia. "It takes time for each of us to create our own reality, our own path."

"My entire walk to the church at the piazza was devoted to thoughts other than worries over the boys, finances, sickness, or bad news."

"Keep meditating—" She jerked the cart back onto the road and floored the gas pedal.

Lydia gripped the grab handle.

"… and think good thoughts about those grapevines near the turbines. I hope there's not too much damage to the vineyards."

Emergency vehicles clogged the approach to the wind farm's safety perimeter. Firemen had already uncoiled hoses from the trucks, although they hadn't yet turned them on. Dana lurched to a stop on the roadside. They got out and joined a growing crowd of Hessley contractors and lab technicians from the vineyard. Everyone seemed visibly shaken by the blazing mid-air spectacle.

"Start with the leader line!" A bulky fireman directed the crew. "Ladder's up next."

"*Water it down, boys. Out.*" The order came over someone's walkie-talkie.

"Don't tell me!" A woman clapped her hand over her mouth.

"They're going to spray the turbine!" Another voice shouted.

Lydia tried to gauge the height of the machine against the distance between it and them. She was thankful for her hardhat. "Are we safe here?"

"Probably, but be prepared to get wet."

The monster-sized hoses came to life. A separate group of firefighters started in on the ground fire emanating from a debris pile.

Anxious chatter rippled across the crowd. People backed away from the gate to the safety enclosure. An earsplitting grinding noise startled everyone. The turbine's mammoth metal post tilted away from them. It teetered before toppling into the river. Columns of steam sizzled high into the air. Metal scraped against rock as the strong current took hold, causing goosebumps to prick Lydia's arm. The top portion of the turbine's post disappeared in the water.

Firemen turned off the hoses, staring at the stump where the turbine had been mounted. The crowd fell silent.

Only Lydia's cell phone disturbed the stunned stillness. She squelched the sound, hoping Tyler Morales wasn't the caller on the other end of the line. She'd hate to be the one to break the news to headquarters that Cascata Verde had just lost turbine No. 6.

"Oh shoot." Dana ran her hands through her short hair. "I forgot to tell you that Angie called my cell on my way to get you. She couldn't get through to you."

Lydia glared at her friend. "I never heard it ring." She punched the send button.

Angie picked up and spoke rapidly. "Don't panic, but I can't get Harrison's nebulizer to work. Not enough mist is coming out." Harrison coughed weakly in the background. "He's having a bit of difficulty breathing. Just a little, so don't speed on the way home."

"I'm on my way." She returned to the cart, and grabbed her purse and keys from the back. "Call 911 if it gets worse. I'll be right there." She didn't bother to say goodbye to Dana. Still clutching her cell phone and wearing her hard hat, she bit her lip as she forced people to move aside so that she could get to the office to pick up her van.

Officer Biondi shook his head as he waved her through the security checkpoint a few minutes later. Someday he might not be so forgiving about her speeding. At the entrance to the neighborhood, she barreled through a corner church parking lot to bypass a stopped school bus, all the while rehearsing an explanation in case the police pulled her over.

The sign in front of the community church caught her eye.

"Can't Sleep???? Don't count sheep – talk to the Shepherd."

"That's me. No sleep." She spoke the words aloud. Just thinking about her anxiety-filled nights gave her the jitters.

A black SUV raced from the direction of the bus across the opposite end of the parking lot. Even through the vehicle's tinted windows, Lydia could see that the church sign had drawn the driver's attention too. The SUV closed the distance between them in seconds. She veered, clipping the vehicle's front quarter panel with her rear bumper. Rattled, she skidded to a stop, slammed the car into park, and jumped out. Her purse fell from the minivan, depositing its contents all over the blacktop parking lot. *What more could go wrong?*

The passenger seat window of the SUV rolled down, revealing a distinguished, but flustered, older man. He made no move to get out.

"Oh," Lydia squinted. She'd seen that thick, well-groomed mustache before.

"Yes. Hello." The man breathed heavily. "The incident is our fault. Let's take care of this between us, shall we?" He fished around in his inner suit pocket, pulling out something that barely fit into his huge fist. She could have sworn that he was looking for a gun had he not been driving an expensive vehicle and, for all appearances, looked like a respected and familiar-looking member of the community.

"My kid is sick and I can't wait for the police to arrive." She moved closer to the open window, concerned about his struggle to catch his breath. "Are you okay?" Her voice sounded like a young girl's.

"This should take care of the matter, miss." He thrust a thick wad of money into her hand. The hundred dollar bill on the outside caught her by surprise. She held the heavy bundle, staring at her hand for a moment. The entire minivan wasn't worth this amount of cash.

"I can't take ..."

"Keep it. I've got a rather urgent situation to handle myself." His breath suddenly ragged, he peeked out the front window in the direction of Cascata Verde, where the smoke trail streaked across the entire horizon. The SUV tore out of the parking lot before she could return the wad of bills.

"But I can't!" She sucked in her breath. Recognition dawned. She had just come face-to-face with the well-dressed man from the restaurant. The same man depicted in the pictures on the wall next to Angie. The man whose family had something to do with the death of Angie's mom. And who knew who else. Forget her peaceful center; a new feeling swelled in her chest.

Anger.

"I won't take your money, Councilman Malvisti!"

CHAPTER TWENTY-TWO

December 26, 2003

My story only gets harder to tell. It's one thing to admit to being a go-getter, hungry for land, success, or recognition. Everyone experiences those desires at some point in life, right?

I'm no exception.

But it's quite another to explain why I made the far-reaching decisions that impacted you, the residents of Niagara Falls. Read what I offer on these clean white pages before you judge me. You might have done the same had you been me.

On a chilly day in the fall of 1946, I found myself standing next to the man who some credit with saving the world. At the time, I didn't know General Leslie Groves that well. But I knew enough about him to be fascinated and somewhat awed. He spearheaded the Manhattan Project, which led to the development of the atomic bomb. Every American citizen owed him a debt of gratitude for his extraordinary service and perseverance. The man was a hero.

His intensity had not diminished since the first time we met, during the war. At that time, I was simply one minor cog in the wheel of a military machine that was working overtime to develop and deliver an atomic bomb.

I couldn't have joined the service if I tried. I was needed at home, running my waste disposal business to serve the war effort. It was my right and my duty. No one for hundreds of miles could handle the same volume of toxic radiological by-products of the nuclear era.

The responsibility fell to me.

I was proud of my country and wanted to work hard for her, for my family, and for my God. America, after all, had fulfilled her promise to me. And then some. I was convinced my role would assume a deeper significance in the war's aftermath.

But on that chilly fall day, General Leslie Groves's face was impossible to read. I had hoped he would at least be impressed with the powerful, fast-moving river dominating the landscape before us, but he said nothing.

We were standing at the edge of the Escarpment, a vertical ridge of land rising 250 feet above the lower Niagara River. Our unique vantage point allowed us to see the river on the final leg of its thirty-six-mile eventful journey from Lake Erie to Lake Ontario, the smallest of the Great Lakes. At this juncture, it passed through the end of the steep, tree-lined Niagara Gorge and evened out as it snaked toward the lake.

The surge of movement and energy was unmistakable. Like us, full of purpose; forever advancing. I realize now that the river continually worked to cleanse itself, repeatedly washing away the defilement that was my business.

Still, the General remained silent.

An aide who had been hovering a short distance behind us produced two cigars. We smoked companionably. I craned my neck to catch a glimpse of Lake Ontario, hazy and undefined on the horizon. Behind us, occasional laughter and clinking champagne glasses could be heard from the country club dining hall. Some of the event guests had spilled out onto the club's patio to take in the spectacular view. They kept a respectful distance from us, huddling in groups of two and three. The extraordinary issues of the day were on everyone's lips.

"We appreciate your continued service to our country, Joe," the General said at last, clapping his worn hand across my shoulders. His rumbling voice sounded grave, as if he were trying to convey a deeper, unstated meaning.

I acknowledged the statement with a brief nod, but stared straight ahead, as did he. Words failed me.

The aide piped up. "This delivery is special. A unique disposal project. I know we can count on you." His steaming breath mixed with the General's cigar smoke and hung in the crisp evening air. The tang of wet, decaying leaves permeated the space around us. The heady smells were almost overpowering. It would take two or three thunderstorms rolling in from the lake to shake the stubborn leaves loose, and usher in the bleak and seemingly unending winter that defines Western New York.

Tonight, everything was magnified.

"I'm here to do whatever is needed, sir." I turned to meet the eyes of the man I so greatly admired. I took in his burly, uniformed frame and his rows of colored ribbons. The General's thick hair curled slightly on top, making the silvery gray strands sprinkled throughout even more noticeable.

I shivered as a gust of wind blew in from the lake. Foaming whitecaps appeared on the river, vanishing as quickly as they appeared, like fireflies on a hot summer night. Another uncommonly cold winter had been predicted. I didn't doubt it. The General appeared unaffected by the chill, or the view. His focus was on weightier matters, I was sure.

I turned to the aide. "When can I expect the delivery?" I immediately regretted asking. I knew from past experience that the General and his entourage would supply me with details on a need-to-know basis, and not a word more.

"Before the first snowfall. You can expect a convoy of wide trucks. There may also be an armed escort." The aide lowered his voice, taking an almost imperceptible step closer. "Don't draw attention to it. You will be given particulars in case anyone asks. We'll be in touch by messenger the day before." His clipped tone left no doubt that the conversation was over.

The General took a last look at the vista before us. I wished that he would notice the layers of rock on the Canadian side of the gorge, still visible in the fading light. The sight set my heart soaring. I wondered whether he had taken the time to see the Falls. The forces that had wrought this landscape far surpassed even his ability to build, destroy, or reshape entire cities.

I was about to tell him that this scene was the legacy of glacial melt waters. The ice sheet that covered this part of North America more than 18,000 years ago had scoured out large basins as it marched stoically southward. Enormous quantities of water spilled into these basins as the sheets retreated. One such spillway—the original site of Niagara Falls—occurred at the rise where we now stood. Over the past 12,000 years or so, the Falls had fitfully etched their way upstream and through the stratified rock to its present location, our great city of Niagara Falls.

I didn't say a word, though. I had been struck silent by humility as I began to comprehend the power of God versus that of man. The hand of the Almighty crafts beauty. Man doesn't always have that luxury. Especially not now, when the balance of world power hung precipitously in the hands of a few. Our actions were necessary for the war effort, I reminded myself. And though nothing beautiful could result, the interests of our country—of humanity itself—must prevail.

We walked back to the club and rejoined the others in a celebratory banquet. There was much to commemorate. The bomb had worked. Man proved unequivocally that he could harness nature. But on that day, neither the general nor I fully understood that the fallout had only just begun for this ancient and magnificent environment.

But God understood the danger. He knew the consequences. He left us with few choices.

Why didn't He stop me?

CHAPTER TWENTY-THREE

Northern Florida

Michael ran his fingertips over the GT-R's hood. Wincing at the burn of hot carbon fiber on dry flesh, he shook out his hand, then used his shirt to wipe away a fingerprint from the driver's side door. He'd missed the car this week almost more than he missed Jillian.

"I had my doubts about your survival, bro." Ty cut the engine and leaned out of the open window. "Did you get your certification?"

"Oh, yeah. Albert's great. One of the best instructors I've had." Truth be told, he'd learned more here than in all his years of diving.

"Anyone drown?"

"Close." Michael let out a derisive laugh and scooped up his dive equipment. "We had some re-breathers in front of us and they kicked up a cloud of silt, choking the caves. Bunch of amateurs. We had zero visibility for a few minutes. I swam right into the cave wall while doing a lost-line drill."

"Really?" Ty raised his eyebrows. "Sounds like a rookie mistake."

"Maybe. But when your mask and regulator get knocked off, you start thinking that know-nothings should be barred from being down there."

"So how'd you breathe?"

"Luck, pure and simple." Michael stepped back and scrutinized the rest of the car. No dings. Nothing amiss. "I inserted my secondary regulator, then located my mask on the back of my head. A diver's got to stay calm and not panic."

"That's cool."

"How'd your week go?" Michael opened the driver's side door.

Ty grimaced as he extracted his bulk from the seat. He stretched, dangling the keys high in the air above his head. Almost out of Michael's reach. "We bonded. I want her."

Michael snatched the keys from his hand. "I meant, how'd work go?"

"Been a busy week." Ty shifted his gaze somewhere beyond Michael, his lips pressed together in a line. "And I ... learned a few things, ya know?"

"No, I don't." Michael raised an eyebrow at him. "What's up?"

"Let's get in the car first." He nodded toward the keys in Michael's hand. "I assume you're doing the driving back to Tampa."

"No, you take the wheel." He tossed the ring back. "My balance is off. Too much water in my ears."

Once they were settled, Tyler got right to the point. "I did a little research this week on your family's business."

"You look concerned. Good news, bad news, what?"

"Hard to say. Your family owned a whole lotta landfills in Niagara County, I can tell you that." The car roared to life.

"I knew there were a few." Michael tugged the seat belt across his lap. He felt out of place on this side of the console in his own car. Then again, he had the same feeling as a supposed member of the Malvisti family.

"And there's a lot of interesting stuff buried in that city."

Michael looked away, steeling himself for his friend's next words. He could tell by Ty's failure to get to the point that it wasn't anything good. "What's there and how much?"

"I know you're a facts man, but we need to back up and start from the beginning. I think the back-story is what you're really after." He pulled out of the dusty lot.

Michael put on his sunglasses. "Lay it on me."

"Think World War Two."

"Okay. What about it?"

"From your history books, you may remember that General Leslie Groves was tasked with the job of 'understanding and harnessing the power of the atom.' That's a quote from an Internet article I found."

Michael's stomach pitched. He hadn't told his friend about the black-and-white picture featuring his grandfather and General Groves. Maybe it was just a coincidence. "You have to back up that far?"

"Yes, it's important. Stay with me here. You probably know that General Groves was put in charge of the Manhattan Project. That Project was an effort by the US, the UK, and Canada to develop the first nuclear weapons for use in World War Two. The General's team of scientists and military leaders tapped into production facilities across the nation in a massive, secret effort to enrich uranium and plutonium." Ty took his eyes off the road to glance at Michael. "With me so far?"

"Yeah. My father alluded to some of those details. Many of those production facilities were in Niagara County, right?"

"Yep." Ty took a deep breath before continuing. "The production of nuclear weapons requires a continuous source of refined or enriched uranium. So several Niagara County chemical and metallurgical manufacturers converted their factories to handle various steps in the enrichment process."

"What does this have to do with my family?" An uneasy feeling arose in his gut.

"Those transformed facilities needed to dispose of some pretty hot waste. Lots of it. Otherwise, the whole process would've ground to a halt. It could have jeopardized the Manhattan Project and Niagara County's role in it." Ty stole another glance. "Your grandfather was able to accommodate them."

So Tyler's mentioning the general in the same breath as Grandpa Joe was no coincidence. For the second time in a week, Michael had trouble catching his breath. And this time there was no extra air tank to rescue him. He cracked the window and sucked in the warm air to steady himself before speaking. "But ... our business is *garbage*."

"Dude, do you get what I'm saying?" Tyler pulled onto the highway, shifting expertly. "Grandpa Joe buried all that radioactive and chemical *garbage*."

Michael balled his hands into fists. Sweating, he crouched forward in his seat, searching his mind for facts about his family that should have clued him in to their real business. Was this "The General" his grandfather had mentioned? If so, no one in the family ever seemed bothered or curious about their relationship. Maybe Grandma Ziatta would remember something. Although she couldn't remember what she had for breakfast, she was still able to recall events that occurred long ago.

He angled his head, causing water to shift somewhere deep within his right ear. "So the nation needed Joseph Malvisti and he delivered? Is that what you're saying?" His voice echoed across his head, ricocheting bad news from one side to the other.

"Yeah, man." Ty focused on the road. "I take it you had no idea?"

Michael snorted. Before today, he had never had a single negative thought about Grandpa Joe. Now, doubts crept into his mind, challenging some of his long-held assumptions about his family. Since he had modeled his life after his grandfather's values, what kind of man did that make *him*?

His mind teemed with questions. But one stood out above all others. "Just how much was he able to accommodate?"

"Between 1945 and '46 alone, he buried more than twenty thousand tons of radioactive and toxic waste generated by local factories—and some others across the nation."

Land and money. A grim joining of mutual interests. No wonder the Malvistis were so rich. "What about the usable stuff he didn't bury? The refined uranium?"

"Most of it was used in the war effort. Like the bombs that were used to destroy Hiroshima and Nagasaki. That's what forced the unconditional surrender of Japan in 1945, you know. So don't be so hard on those guys. They helped save the world."

He ignored Ty's last comment, keeping his focus on the near-empty highway in front of them. A nauseous feeling had formed in his stomach. His family had entwined themselves in more than just routine waste disposal. How could he have been so naïve? "And what was my family's involvement after 1945?"

"That's where things get hazy." Tyler took a sip from a water bottle that had been wedged in the console. "After the war ended, Niagara County continued to have some relationship with America's defense programs. Weapons-related activities were ongoing near the Malvisti landfill sites, but I don't know anything more specific."

"C'mon, Ty. Are you saying that my family could have been involved in secret government programs? Are you kidding?"

"Hey, don't get aggravated with me." Ty cranked the air conditioner. "Just reporting what I found."

"I'm not." He loosened his seat belt, hoping to squelch the rising panic inside his chest. "I'm just trying to comprehend the fact that my family might be in the toxic trafficking business."

"Let's keep digging and see."

"Bad pun." Michael allowed himself a smile. "Did you learn anything about the landfill underneath Malvisti Park?"

"Nothing other than what we already knew. It was contaminated in the past. But Tomeo Environmental tested it, remediated, and tested again. I've seen the reports. It's all good."

"You just told me that tons of toxic and radioactive material got moved around the county. The landfill under Cascata Verde was in operation back then. I think it was closed in the '80s. Tomeo's sure that everything's fine?"

"If there was a problem, it would've come up in the site assessments."

Michael removed his shades. He poked his water-logged ears to clear them. "Did I tell you that someone at the groundbreaking questioned whether Tomeo's legit?"

"No." Tyler's voice rose slightly. "What did they say?"

"That the business doesn't have a physical address."

"Dude, I've been there, remember? Rebecca sent me two years ago."

Michael raised his eyebrow. "But you only got as far as the on-site mobile lab, right? You never went to an actual office."

"Oh yeah, you're right. Sorry, that whole trip was a blur."

What an understatement. "You were so out of it when I found you that I think something more happened on that trip. Maybe they drugged you or something."

"Hope not."

And if that's true, then what kind of people worked for Tomeo?

Michael's cell phone jolted him. He pulled it out and grunted. "My dad." He punched the screen.

"I just hung up with Grandma Ziatta's nurse." Joe coughed twice before continuing. "Grandma died about an hour ago."

Another blow to the gut. He was not prepared for the news, especially delivered by his emotionally detached father. "She's gone?" He felt a pang of guilt for not calling her yesterday, and even worse for not being there when she passed on. "What happened?"

"She was in her nineties. It was her time." Another set of hacking coughs. "I'm flying out tomorrow morning to begin making arrangements. Why don't you shoot up tomorrow night? I'll send a car to the airport for you."

"No need. I'll meet you there." Still clutching his phone, Michael tipped his head against the headrest and looked upward. He didn't want tears to spill over in front of Ty. "Dad ... I'm sorry you lost your mother."

"Sorry, too, son." He hung up before Michael could say good-bye. So much for a father-son connection. At the moment, he missed his big-hearted, loving grandfather all the more—at least the man he thought he knew.

"Well, that's the end of an era."

"Sorry to hear the news, Mikey."

"Thanks."

"What was she like?" Ty turned down the fan.

"She was a no-nonsense lady. A force of nature. She canned, sewed, grew vegetables...." Michael fiddled with his phone. A smile played across his trembling lips. "And, man, could she cook! Nobody does Italian like my grandma. I always put on a few pounds when I'm home."

"Sounds kinda like Jillian." Ty chuckled.

Michael laughed outright. "Grandma was a good woman. No doubt she earned a spot up in heaven just for putting up with my father and uncle all these years."

"Are you heading up to the Falls, then?"

"Yeah." He swept his thumb across his cell. "And I want to stop by Tomeo on the way from the airport to her house."

"I'll try to get you directions." Ty lowered the air-conditioning fan even further. "And Mike ..."

"Yeah?"

"Don't tell Rebecca that you're following up on Tomeo, okay?"

"Your turn to give me some credit." He clicked on the airline's website. "Besides, I'm getting good at undercover work."

Ty gave him a quizzical look, but he ignored it, switching his attention to his smartphone and speaking to the airline representative. "Round-trip flight from Tampa to Buffalo for tonight."

"Tonight?" Ty accelerated. "What's the hurry?"

"The race is on, my friend."

"For?"

"Facts. If I can beat Uncle Sal and my dad to the family homestead, my grandparents' old house will be full of 'em."

He'd need to rely on his wits ... and maybe a bit of luck. This week's dive training had been good preparation for surviving more than just caves.

CHAPTER TWENTY-FOUR

Niagara Falls, New York

Lydia urged her friend to continue up the incline of Cascata Verde's main road. "Trust me. You're going to love the way the church looks now." Its graceful curves cleared her mind and brought a smile to her face every time she saw it.

Dana grimaced. "There's dozens of outstanding buildings in this community. The spa is a marvel of modern architecture. Pavati Plaza is magnificent. I mean, no one has ever seen cascaded towers that resemble the Falls!" She threw her hands heavenward. "But you go on and on about this church. I don't get it."

"You'll see." Lydia could see her breath in the chilly March air. "I'll be quick. I just want to drop off something for the needy." She patted the jacket pocket where she'd stuffed the bulging envelope from last week's run-in with Councilman Malvisti.

"Technically, doesn't the *needy* include you?"

"Yeah, well ..." Lydia sped up her pace. There was no easy answer to that question. Sure, she needed the money until their closing checks started arriving. The winter weather had wreaked havoc on the missing paint spots dotting her minivan. She could practically see the rust developing already. But the whole incident with the councilman forcing his money upon her just felt wrong. She didn't want any part of it, needy or not.

The sun moved past its high point. The temperature climbed noticeably after they rounded a corner. Lydia removed her jacket, looking up in time to see the church's cedar spires and shingled roofline set sharply against the crystal-clear blue sky. The coarse wood and stone components still fit together just right. The symmetry of this house of worship might be the closest she would ever come to feeling whole.

Dana drew a sharp breath. "Okay, okay. I'll admit, it's pretty. Have you talked to anyone on the inside?"

"No, and not for a lack of trying. Other than that fireman who bolted out of here during the turbine fire last week, I haven't seen a soul go in or out."

The women marched up a short set of rough-hewn steps that led to a spacious fieldstone terrace. Arched red-hued doors warmed the outdoor gathering space, creating a comfortable place for visitors to congregate. Lydia waved to the landscapers planting burning-bush shrubs along the front wall. A perfect spot for wedding pictures.

Lydia hesitated. "Should we knock?"

"Nah. It's a church. It's supposed to be open to people."

She tested the iron handle. It gave way under the slightest pressure.

Lydia pulled the door open just wide enough for both women to slip in. A dull pounding echoed across the bare sanctuary. Between blows, a deep, masculine voice could be heard singing along with a radio. The vocals came to an abrupt stop after something clattered to the floor.

"Hello?" Lydia stopped in the foyer beside a massive, circular fireplace hearth.

"Wow, Lyd." Dana ran her fingers along the hearth's smooth stones. "This is a really cool design element. It has Rebecca Waters written all over it."

A rugged man appeared in a doorway at the far end of the building. He squeezed his left thumb while making his way over to them.

Lydia knew that confident gait. His broad shoulders curved in a way she had seen before. Her heart nearly stopped as he drew closer. The question was, would her son's rescuer recognize her?

"I'm Amos." He let go of his thumb and offered his hand. "One of the pastors here. Can I help you?"

"Lydia." She paused after she grasped his hand, wondering whether her name would ring a bell. It didn't seem to. "And this is Dana. We work for Hessley in the real estate office."

Dana nodded, but kept her hands at her sides.

Lydia stifled a sob, nearly overcome at the sight of the courageous man who two years ago had saved her family from certain devastation.

"Are you always this choked up about your job?" He smiled.

She put her hand to her mouth. "Sorry."

Amos's eyes widened. Recognition dawned. "You're Travis's mom! Lydia Vallone, right?"

"Yes."

"How is that little guy?"

"He's doing great. Gave up fishing ... and took up the slingshot. A healthy and alive five-year-old." Lydia used her jacket to wipe the tears that trickled down her face. "Thanks to you."

Dana smacked Lydia's arm. "So he's the handsome hero, eh?"

"Dana! He's a priest, for goodness sake. Don't say that!" Lydia felt herself blush. That didn't come out right.

"Actually, I'm not a priest," he said good-naturedly. "I'm a military chaplain, and I just started preaching here at this nondenominational church."

"Where'd you come here from?" Lydia took in the deep wrinkles that framed his kind eyes. This man had saved her son. She wanted to memorize every detail of his face.

"I was last stationed in Italy. I moved here two years ago after I retired from the Navy."

"Why?" the women asked in unison.

"It's a long story, and someday I'll tell you. But maybe it had something to do with little Travis." Dimples appeared when he smiled.

Lydia stepped back. *Could it have?* She crushed her jacket to her heart.

"We didn't know this building would function as a real church." Dana glanced towards the front of the room. "What do you have in mind for this place?"

"Rebecca Waters has given me wide latitude. My plan is to lay a solid, Biblical foundation for this congregation. A living, breathing reflection of God's love."

Although Lydia wasn't sure what he meant, she could tell he believed every word. He certainly had been like a god to her and her family.

"Anyone join yet?" Dana seemed skeptical.

"A handful of construction workers showed up a few weeks ago. Each week they bring along a few other workers from the site."

Dana looked at her watch. Lydia knew she wanted to leave, but she was curious as to whether Angie went to this type of church. "What does a nondenominational church believe?"

"We follow Jesus, pure and simple." He gestured broadly around the sanctuary. "It's a Bible-based teaching church. Come visit sometime. Our Easter service is next week."

"Are you one of those crazy born-again types?" Dana spiraled her finger next to her head.

He chuckled. "Why does believing what it says in the Bible make me crazy?"

"Sorry." Dana shrugged. "But some of those people are just weird."

"Ooh! Your thumb is bleeding." Lydia backed up. Blood rimmed his nail and dribbled down his palm. Small flecks of red stained the wood floor around his steel-toed boots. "It might need a stitch or two."

The chaplain pulled a rag from his back pocket. "Just a nick. Nothing to lose sleep over."

Lydia forced a laugh. She'd have to be *getting* sleep in order to lose it.

He folded the dingy cloth in half and applied pressure. Obviously this guy wasn't too hung up on germs. Lydia cringed. "We have a first-aid kit at the real estate office. It has *sterile* Band-Aids."

"No, thanks." Amos grinned. "I have a few more scraps of cloth in the back."

Dana retied her jacket around her waist. "We need to run." She walked through the foyer to the entrance door and waited. Her long nails tapped against the door handle.

"It was nice to have met you both. Rest in the Lord, Ms. Vallone. He alone will make you dwell in safety."

His words reminded her of the church sign that had caught her attention just before her collision with Councilman Malvisti. *Can't sleep? Don't count sheep—talk to the Shepherd.* She wasn't sure how to respond. "Thank you" was all she could manage. As she caught up to Dana at the door, the packet she'd shoved in her pocket earlier flapped against her thigh.

"Oh! I almost forgot." Lydia turned to face Amos. "We came by because I have something to donate." She pulled the thick envelope out of her jacket pocket. The hundred dollar bill that poked out from the opening would sure buy a lot of groceries. But dealing with Sal Malvisti had left a bad taste in her mouth.

"Thank you." He weighed the package in his uninjured hand. "We'll put it to good use."

"Someday, when you tell me the story of how you ended up here, I'll tell you the story behind the wad of money in that envelope."

"That's a deal. I hope you'll visit soon."

Lydia smiled weakly and they hustled out the door. She hadn't been to church in years. Besides throwing up a quick prayer or two for her brother, or talking with Angie that one time, she hadn't thought of God in a long while. Maybe that was why He continued to punish her family with sickness. And sadness.

The thought struck her nearly breathless.

❖

"Why haven't you said anything about Pastor Amos or the church?" Lydia hustled to keep pace with Dana.

"There's nothing to say." She lifted her shoulders. "I'm not comfortable in churches. I'm especially not at ease with preachers." She pointed at Lydia's feet. "Your laces came undone."

Lydia stopped to re-tie her shoe. "He seems nice, though, don't you think?"

"I don't want to talk about chaplains. Or churches. Or God." Dana folded her arms. "I don't even want to be around people who talk about those things."

"Got it." Lydia pulled on her laces.

"Oh, my!" Dana clutched Lydia's shoulder. "Look at the Pavati Tower complex!" She pointed toward the riverside business plaza.

Lydia stood, then froze.

The tallest Tower emitted a turquoise-tinged glow. The hazy light appeared to flow in ribbons. It folded gently downward, illuminating the shorter buildings below it. Soon, they too were bathed in the soft radiance.

"What's happening?" Dana voice held a reverence. She searched inside her jacket pocket for her cell. "Whatever it is, it's absolutely amazing. I hope I can get it on video. I mean, how would you ever explain this to someone?" She recorded the strange sight by holding the phone high over her head.

The blue-green hue seemed too vivid to be real. Lydia had never seen anything to rival it. Not even the azure Caribbean seas of her honeymoon had captivated her attention like these colors did.

Landscapers gathered on the sidewalk. Some removed their hats. A few yards away, a painter sank to his knees and crossed himself. A look of annoyance clouded Dana's face.

"Maybe it's reflecting the sun," Lydia offered.

"Could be, ma'am." A man in paint-stained white overalls joined them. "Those eco-skins nowadays are amazin'."

"I think it's more than that." Dana shivered.

After a few seconds, the glimmer faded. But the buildings, especially the tallest tower, seemed wrapped in a vibrant afterglow. Windows on the building stood out in sharp relief. Lydia almost didn't trust her eyes. Had she imagined that the green roofs on the lower plaza buildings seemed unnaturally lush?

They all looked at one other, not saying anything. Hundreds of people on this street had witnessed the event. They all appeared as dumbfounded as Lydia felt.

"That's the positive energy I want to tap into, Lydia. I knew it existed." Dana wrapped her hands around her cell phone and pressed it to her forehead. "That essence filled my crown chakra with light."

"What are you talking about? You're freaking me out."

"The feeling I just had—that's how religion should make you feel. Angie can have her God. You can have your charming little church. But nothing compares to this kind of experience."

Lydia studied her friend. "What exactly did you feel?"

"Connectedness. A universal consciousness. Peace." Dana bowed her head and wiped a tear from the corner of her eye. "That's the real thing right there. This community will provide a way for people to be in unity with the Earth." When she looked up, a faraway expression had transformed her face. She looked ten years younger. "I can't wait to talk about it with Rebecca Waters. She'll understand the significance of this."

Lydia felt nothing beyond confusion. Then again, the past few years had left her emotionally and physically wrung out. Maybe there was no room inside her for good feelings of any kind. And she obviously lacked a chakra, whatever that was.

❖

All of the office phone lines flashed at once. Word of the unusual occurrence had spread like wildfire. While Lydia cleared the calls, Dana listened to the messages. She announced that local TV stations were en route, the mayor would arrive in minutes, and Hessley's corporate office needed an immediate update.

The paint-splattered worker popped his head into the office door. "Any official word? I still think it's the buildin' wrap. High tech, you know."

Lydia jumped at the intrusion. "Nothing yet. But a Hessley PR rep will be here in a few hours. Maybe we'll know more by then."

"Something's changed in the community." Dana stretched her hands over her blonde head. She waved them back and forth like a rock groupie. "Can't you feel it? I can almost *see* a difference."

"I'm just baffled." Lydia shook her head. She walked over to the back office windows and looked across the community. Workers flooded the streets. Several people had climbed to the top of the nearly complete Suspension Spa, probably for a better view. "I don't know what to think."

"You'll learn. Keep on your path." Dana answered a call, but then cleared the lines for a second time. "Let's head over to the plaza. I want to see the Pavati towers up close." She hurried to the door. "Come on, Lyd."

"Are we making too much of this?" Lydia stepped into the sunshine, close on Dana's heels. "It was probably just a weather event, or mist from the Falls that drifted upstream. Maybe that painter's right and it has to do with the materials used on the skin of the building? Don't they absorb or reflect light for heating and air conditioning systems?"

"They do, but I don't think that's what happened just now." Dana hugged herself. "This phenomenon is life-changing. You watch."

"Watch what? What do you think happened here?"

"Just wait. You'll feel it."

The women joined dozens, possibly hundreds, of workers making their way to Pavati Plaza. Officer Biondi shouted for them to wait for him to catch up. When Lydia turned, she saw him rush toward them, looking as dazed as the rest of the onlookers. Sweat dribbled down his temples. His uniform hat had gone missing.

"They can't find an explanation. I'm going crazy here, answering questions left and right. I've got nothin'." The normally composed security officer clicked off his radio. "I called in some local police back-up, but I'm not sure what they're going to do beyond gape at these buildings like we all are."

"We may have more company soon." Dana pulled her phone out of her jacket.

Lydia cut her hand between Dana's eyes and the cell. "C'mon, Dana. We've still got houses to sell and work for today."

Biondi tapped Dana's shoulder. "Cancel any showings today, girls. We're restricting access to the property. Hessley's orders."

"Do we really need to take such drastic action?"

"Pictures surfaced on the 'Net about fifteen minutes ago." He pocketed his radio. "This is big, Miss Vallone. Big."

Dana traced her thumb across the screen. "I took some video. Give me a sec and we can check it out."

A blurry image appeared in which Pavati Tower bobbed wildly. Distorted streaks of green and blue dominated the picture.

"I was shaking. Sorry."

The security officer huddled close. The image stabilized, changing in a way that left Lydia nearly breathless. Every nuance of color seemed visible on the screen. Then she saw a movement in the image that they must have missed live.

"Did you see that?" Dana replayed the video.

"Give me that!" Officer Biondi snatched the phone and tapped the screen. He watched the short video again. "Impossible! Buildings don't do that."

Dana's smug smile shocked Lydia. "It's proof."

Biondi's eyes widened. "Are we talkin' a crime here or what?"

Lydia wasn't sure where this was going, but she knew something New-Agey was about to come out of Dana's mouth.

"Cascata Verde's been built over an energy portal, Officer." Dana wrenched her cell phone out of the officer's hand. "Something amazing happened today. It's a confirmation for all of us."

"Of what?" Lydia's skepticism grew. What had happened to her intelligent and logical friend?

"Haven't you figured it out yet, Lyd?" Dana clasped Lydia's elbow. Her eyes glittered with an intensity Lydia hadn't seen in a long time.

She drew back. "What are you talking about?"

Dana spun Lydia around to face Pavati Plaza.

Biondi held his breath as he followed the direction of Dana's eyes. He pressed the call button on his radio.

"Cascata Verde is going to rescue us, people."

"What?" Lydia narrowed her eyes at her friend.

A serene look softened Dana's face. Her blue eyes seemed crystal clear. "My friends, Niagara Falls's savior has come."

A whoop could be heard over the radio.

"This has been a long time in coming. It's our destiny, our time," she added.

To Lydia's amazement, her normally stoic and rational friend began to cry through her smile. Deep heaving sobs of ... happiness?

CHAPTER TWENTY-FIVE

Tampa, Florida

A capacity crowd filled Michael's flight to Buffalo. Passengers vied for limited overhead storage space. Grimaces marred tired faces on both sides of the aisle. A teenager let loose a string of obscenities after a heavyset woman stepped on his foot. Even the normally unflappable flight attendants, Tracey and Nicolette, seemed flustered. Lips tight, they used as few words as possible to urge fliers to ready themselves for takeoff.

He braced himself for an unpleasant trip.

Belt secure, he prayed for a brisk tailwind. Thankfully, his seatmate had already buried himself in the *Tampa Bay Times.* Michael was in no mood to work at a conversation. Besides, he had too many things to think about before landing in Buffalo. What could he contribute to Grandma Ziatta's funeral? Could he find Tomeo's office? Could he get to his grandparents' house before his father arrived? At least he had until tomorrow to make arrangements for Jillian's flight. To his surprise, she'd insisted on flying in for Grandma Ziatta's wake after cheerleading tryouts ended that weekend.

"Ladies and gentlemen," a voice boomed over the speakers two hours later. "Captain Duke Bauer here. We're approaching the Buffalo-Niagara International airport, folks, but they've got us in a holding pattern. We're going to make a wide right over the Falls." Several passengers snickered at the reference to the Buffalo Bills' low point in the annals of football history. The missed field goal that cost the Bills a long-awaited Super Bowl victory was only one misfortune in a string of hard-luck stories out of the region. "Be sure to look for the Cascata Verde project taking shape below us. It's a stunner."

Michael strained his neck to see out the opposite window. Passengers on that side of the row crowded the glass, making it impossible to see anything from his side.

"Oh!" An older female passenger pressed her nose to the window with a view. "There's a green building shaped like Niagara Falls!"

The man next to her pushed the woman back against the headrest. "That building's blue! You don't know what you're talking about."

"You're color blind, George." She waved her hand in a dismissive gesture.

Murmuring erupted from the passengers closest to the couple. Michael thought he heard a young woman say the building seemed to pulse.

He gave up trying to get a glimpse and shut his eyes for the landing. This day needed to end. And soon. He'd run the gamut of emotions in the span of a few hours. Elation over his diving certification. Distress over the most likely source of Malvisti wealth. Grief over the loss of Grandma Ziatta. Sadness had won the day.

The plane glided to a smooth stop. Passengers emptied the overhead compartments, taking care to avoid injuring those seated below. A tiny, wrinkled brown woman gazed up at Michael. "Did you enjoy that spectacle down below?" Her eyes held the joy of a sweet memory.

"I couldn't see anything from this side."

"That's a pity." She looked heavenward. "I hope I live long enough to see the miracle that the Green City performs for our lost town."

He went along with her good humor. "Me too, ma'am."

Passengers joked with one another as they disembarked. The teenage boy carried the heavyset woman's bag to the jetway. Nicolette handed out bottled water and exchanged pleasant comments with passengers as they deplaned. The mood on board the plane had lightened significantly.

Perplexed, Michael stayed in his seat and activated his phone.

Fourteen text messages rolled in, one after the other. All from Rebecca. Hopefully these texts had nothing to do with him and Ty poking around about Tomeo. He called her right away.

She picked up after the first ring.

"It's Michael. I just landed."

"Good. Drive to Cascata Verde. There's a curious situation there. Some type of light reflected off Pavati Plaza a few hours ago. The highest tower supposedly still has a slight shimmer. I saw pictures on the Internet earlier, and security office sent some strange images."

"Was it blue or green light?" Michael asked quietly, only now understanding the couple's debate on the plane. He stood and followed the old woman as they shuffled forward.

"I'm not sure how to describe it, actually." Rebecca paused. "It's ... unusual."

"There must be some plausible explanation. Our architects are just beginning to understand the light and shadow effects on those new building facades, especially this thin-film integrated photovoltaic technology. Maybe that explains it?" Michael caught curious glimpses from nearby passengers.

"I thought of that, but why haven't we seen it before today?"

"Good question." He lowered his voice even more. "Maybe it's a hoax?"

"I don't think so." The sound of sharp nails on a keyboard reached his ears. "We've had zero threats on the property."

"What do you want me to do first?"

"Reps from Tomeo are already there. Make them conduct every test they can. Our building design team is getting on a plane first thing in the morning. Also, go ahead and talk to our on-site real estate agents. They saw everything. Let's conference later tonight."

"No problem." Michael hung up, grabbed his carry-on, and headed up the aisle. He thanked Nicolette for the free water as he exited the plane.

There had to be a logical reason for the light. The outer envelope of the buildings at Pavati Plaza consisted of a system of photovoltaic components built into the façade. The solar technology simultaneously generated power and protected the inside spaces, but he didn't think it would give off light energy.

As he rolled his small suitcase through the terminal, another thought crossed his mind. Could Hessley's PR department have engineered a gimmick? He didn't think Rebecca would ever authorize such a scam. On the other hand, she was so consumed with Cascata Verde that she didn't even acknowledge his grandmother's death and the reason for his visit in the first place. His mind teemed with possibilities, none of them good.

❖

"Lot of action here tonight, sir." Officer Rubino searched Michael's backseat and then confirmed out loud the license plate and color of the vehicle, speaking into his walkie-talkie. A voice crackled back, authorizing the entry. He handed Michael an all-access parking pass to Cascata Verde. "Security's in overdrive. Puttin' in some long hours."

"Are you staffed okay?" It had taken Michael twenty minutes to reach the gated entrance. Virtually every car ahead of him had been turned away.

"Yes, thank you, sir."

"Do you have enough food to get you through your shift?"

"Yessir. Got a stash of mints and candy." The officer leaned down close to the driver's side window. "On Ms. Waters's orders, we're not allowing access to any members of the press or public. Between you and me, I think we've got ourselves a situation here, sir."

"How so?"

"When I made my patrol two hours ago, I noticed a maple tree that had been planted in front of Pavati Plaza. I was lookin' at it because it seemed taller than when it was planted a few weeks back. I did another round a half hour ago. I'll be darned if that tree isn't taller and healthier looking than earlier today!"

The security officer's deep-set eyes appeared clear. Both pupils seemed normal. No odor of alcohol underlay his minty breath. Still … this was crazy talk.

"And wait till you see the vineyard! Bud break doesn't start for another month or two, but those flowers look ready to bust open!"

"I'm sure there's an explanation, Rubino. We'll get the right people here to figure it all out."

"Do you think it's radioactive, sir?"

"Radioactive?" Hysteria had taken hold. "No, nothing like that is happening."

He took it slow into the community. The residential sectors stood empty, but in the business district, throngs of people, mostly contractors and their workers, stood around in Pavati Plaza.

A construction supervisor approached the driver's side window. "No explaining it, Mr. Malvisti. We've given everything a look-see and nothing's turned up. Your environmental crew is out walking the property now. Tomeo's got gamma detectors, PIDs, and a bunch of other field devices, but they said nothing's wrong."

"Tell me what you saw."

"I wasn't actually here, but you can still see a slight afterglow, for lack of a better word." The contractor gestured toward the tallest of the Pavati towers.

Michael looked, rubbed his eyes, and looked again. "Subtle, but something's there all right."

He parked and stopped a few others on the street. Person after person described similar details. Michael gave up scribbling notes.

After an hour, the Tomeo employees still had nothing to report except that air sampling canisters had been placed around the community. Those results would take a week, at least.

"Mr. Malvisti." A platinum blonde in business attire appeared out of the crowd. A white-pink lotus pendant fairly glowed from around her neck. Rebecca, he remembered, had a similar piece of jewelry.

"Dana DuPays, one of your real estate agents. We've met over the phone."

"How are you, Dana?"

"Fantastic, actually. My partner couldn't be here, but I wanted to check in with you."

"What do you think we have here?"

"I've got a video to show you." She held up her smartphone. "We should probably look at it back at the office. Rebecca Waters seems anxious for a report. She's been in regular contact with me and every other Hessley employee on duty tonight."

Michael read between the lines. Rebecca was driving everyone crazy.

They skirted small groups of people huddled together along the street. Random bits of conversation reached his ears.

"... an angel image appeared on the smallest tower."

"... I saw a flying dove, I swear."

Michael thought back to college psychology 101. He'd learned names for this type of mass hysteria. Conversion disorder?

Dana set the phone on her desk when they arrived at the real estate office. "Touch here when you're ready."

Michael pressed the screen. "I can't see much." He looked at her. "It's a blur."

"Just wait, it'll clear up." A smile spread across her face.

The image focused. Waves of light appeared to roll down the smooth façade of the buildings.

"Don't you see it?" Dana tapped his arm.

"See what?"

"It's an image of Niagara Falls. See the separations? This portion of the water represents the divide between the American Falls and the Horseshoe Falls." She shifted the phone a bit. "There's the Bridal Veil Falls, too."

He could see where the waves *could* be interpreted that way.

"And did you see the hint of a rainbow in the background?"

He looked closer. "I'm not sure ... possibly." A few flecks of color caught his eye.

"It's Gaia." Dana folded her arms.

"As in, *Mother Earth?*"

"Yes, absolutely. Gaia has poured out her energy, wisdom, and power on Cascata Verde. We're on the verge of a transformation that will spread far and wide, Mr. Malvisti."

He wasn't sure whether she was joking. But he was saved from having to respond when Rebecca used FaceTime to call him. He tapped a button. Her back rigid, she sat perched on the seat of her office chair. Smeared eye makeup shadowed her normally flawless face. Exhaustion had set in. Only Michael could appreciate the significance of seeing Rebecca in a slightly-less-than-perfect state.

It humanized her somehow.

"What's your assessment?" Rebecca spat out the question.

"No explanation whatsoever." He shrugged. "Nothing seems amiss physically. According to Tomeo, all field environmental tests are coming back clear, and there's been no light activity other than a slight greenish afterglow."

"Anything else?"

"Ms. DuPays thinks that her cell phone video shows some more detail." Michael tried to keep the skepticism out of his voice.

"Play it for me." She rose out of her chair as she watched, hands braced against the desk. "I see buildings radiating light, just like the Internet clips. Is there something else?"

"The video seems to show aqua-colored water coming off the Pavati Tower in great waves. I think it depicts Niagara Falls."

"Forward it to my phone," Rebecca said irritably.

Dana tapped her phone. "This might sound a little strange, but I believe that living organisms interact with their inorganic surroundings on Earth. Maybe that's what's happening here. Complex systems are working together to sustain the conditions that nourish life. To bring harmony. Cascata Verde is a picture of that harmony and that's what makes it so special."

What was this woman talking about? Michael looked for a strong negative reaction from Rebecca. Seeing none, he wondered where his boss stood on this issue.

"That might be true, Dana. But I've got reporters, spiritualists, politicians, and eco-skin architects and engineers contacting me left and right. They either want explanations or have all the answers."

Now that he thought about it, he wasn't sure what he believed, either.

"I'm planning to issue a statement that, while we appreciated the beautiful sight, there's nothing more to report and we'll continue as before with the knowledge that something harmonious and peaceful occurred here today."

Dana nodded in agreement.

"Tie it in with the beauty of this location and the goals of the Green City." Michael ran his hand through his hair. "I would add that some things just can't be explained."

"Keep Cascata Verde closed except for construction and work crews, but resume the previously scheduled home showings." She looked pointedly at Dana. "We have our first wave of residents arriving in a few days. Until then, this site remains closed to the public. I don't want random people wandering around the property."

"You got it."

Michael laid his coat across his arm. "I'll be in contact with you both tomorrow morning."

"One more thing." Rebecca's eyes softened. "I'm sorry to hear about your grandmother. She was a fine lady. A world-class cook, and an expert at *scopa*."

"Thank you."

She clicked off before he could respond further. A long-ago memory surfaced of him and Danny sitting in front of a fireplace while their grandmother taught them the traditional Italian game of cards.

How did Rebecca know that about Grandma Ziatta, anyway?

Michael sprinted back to his car. He left the community with more questions than answers. More speculation than facts. His mind felt ready to explode. And, as much as it threatened to short-circuit his tired brain, he needed to be the first to get to his grandparents' house.

Pavati Plaza wasn't the only problem that needed solving tonight.

CHAPTER TWENTY-SIX

Niagara Falls, New York

Michael cringed at the streaks marring the stucco exterior of his grandparents' Tudor-style home. Mildew. The result of neglect. Even in the crisp darkness he could see rotted beams and flaked paint on the window trim encasing the lead windows. The Florida dive shop was in better condition than his grandparents' once-stately mansion.

Then again, no one had really lived here for the past eight or nine years.

He jammed an oversized key in the iron lock and turned it to the left. It took a few shoulder thrusts to open the heavy door, but once inside he was rewarded by the faint, but familiar, aroma of sautéed peppers and onions. Love, food, and comfort were ingrained in the walls and fabric of this home. How he missed the security and warmth of this place.

The loss of his last grandparent left a gaping hole inside him.

Michael switched on a light and ducked into the family room. Memories washed over him. The great hearth crackling after his grandfather used an iron poker to stoke the fire. The scent of Christmas pines mingling with the savory smells of roasted sausage. Grandfather Joe calling for a round of toasts with *"facciamo un brindisi,"* and then *"salute!"* He'd always give Michael a sip or two of spumante, or sparkling wine. The pain of Grandma Ziatta's death was made more acute by these memories. The family in his mind's eye no longer existed, at least not after today.

Out of habit, he sat on the plastic-covered couch to check his boots for mud or dirt. Next to him, clusters of picture frames and kitschy religious relics adorned the end tables. He moved in for a closer look and scoffed. The photos portrayed a loving, tightly-knit family. The Malvisti family today hardly resembled the images displayed here. He moved on.

Upstairs, the hall light barely penetrated the darkness. Musty air filled his lungs. Floorboards creaked under his weight as he hurried to a back bedroom where he remembered an antique wardrobe filled with papers.

Inside the piece, he found such a large jumble of pictures, receipts, and cards, that he had to smile. Grandma Ziatta had saved everything. There was no order to her treasures, although she had written in her loopy handwriting the dates and names for each of the pictures: "Netta and Italo, Wasaga Beach, 1946." Or, "Maria and Joey, Jr. 1964."

That one caught his interest.

Before tonight, Michael had seen only a few pictures of Maria, his dad's first wife. In each of those, this tiny, dark-haired woman wore her childlessness like a shroud, with shame and desperation wrapped tightly inside. Maria died of heartache, according to Grandma Ziatta, although his grandmother's tone suggested that Maria had somehow brought that disgrace on herself.

But this particular picture of his father and Maria showed something different. The young couple leaned against a blue convertible Mustang. Someone had snapped them laughing. Eyes twinkling, his dad held the keys just out of Maria's reach. His other arm was wrapped around her slim, bare shoulders. Here was solid proof that his dad was once capable of feeling joy. Too bad all those good emotions had disappeared by the time Michael arrived.

Michael put the album away. He didn't want to intrude on his dad's other life, the one the old man kept sealed away.

He riffled through another drawer, making piles of birthday cards and school programs from his and Danny's elementary days. Even after a half hour, he had yet to run across a scrap of information about the family business. He considered leaving until he spotted three photo albums lining the bottom of the drawer. He'd hit the mother lode. Inside, neatly clipped newspaper articles told the story of his family and a company dedicated to community service. He hadn't known that Grandma was Niagara Falls's Volunteer of the Year in 1954. Another picture featured a youthful Grandpa Joe accepting an award, with two nearly-identical looking young men at his side. It had to be Uncle Sal and Dad.

Finally. Details of a family he didn't know, but of which he was a small part. These albums might fill in some of the blanks. He put away the piles on the floor, scooped up the books, and hurried out of the room. An eerie quiet cloaked this house. Pressed on his chest. He couldn't wait to get out of there. It just didn't feel right without his grandparents.

Cool air greeted him at the bottom of the steps. He set the albums down on a hallway table before stopping at the kitchen, Grandma Ziatta's domain. He half expected to see her at the stove, stirring sauce in her flowered apron, and wondering aloud why he hadn't taken the time to see her all week.

The odor of stale cigarette smoke greeted him instead.

He froze.

In the dim light from the living room, he perceived the presence of someone's massive bulk in front of the stove.

Had Magnano tracked him here? Was this the danger the scared woman at the construction site had warned him about?

Michael saw a quick movement. Then heard a click.

Adrenaline coursed through his body, allowing him to assess the situation in a hurry. There was only one response. Michael leaned back and used a side kick to take out the man's thigh.

The intruder grunted, reacting sluggishly as he hunched over to protect his hulking body. A heavy object bounced to the floor. Michael moved in, elbowing the man in the solar plexus, then a rib, and finally rotating him into a choke hold. He used a foot to kick away the object.

"What are you doin', Mikey!" Danny's raspy voice grated on Michael. But he squeezed tighter, using one hand to switch on the stove light. His cousin's bloated face contorted in pain. Thick, too-long dark hair curled out from under his hat. Danny looked ten years older than Michael.

"You're lucky I didn't kill you!" Michael loosed his hold. "You saw the car in the driveway and you stood completely still in the shadows, saying nothing?" Michael wanted to kick him all over again. Instead he pushed him toward the middle of the kitchen. "That's just stupid."

Danny coughed, hugging his upper ribs. A new Doxa dive watch flashed in the dim appliance light.

Showy. Nothing's changed.

"My dad said I might find you poking 'round the place."

Michael ignored the comment. "Why are you here?"

"I'm here all the time." Danny rubbed his chest. "Remember, I'm the one who visited Grandma at the nursing home, handled the house?"

"You've done a crappy job."

"Shut up." Danny leaned over, struggling to catch his breath. "The better question is, what are *you* doing here?"

"None of your business."

Michael swept the floor with his foot until he found the object that had fallen. A six-inch blade. He picked it up and tossed it on the table. "What's with the knife? You knew it was me."

"What's with those photo albums?" Danny jerked his chin toward the hallway table, still massaging his chest.

"I'm looking at them." Michael turned to leave. Cousins or not, they had nothing to say to each other. It had always been that way with them. At least, ever since Michael's family had picked up and moved to Florida.

"I'm outta here." Danny spat into the sink. "My dad said we'll finalize funeral arrangements when your father gets here. Until then, stay away from this place."

From the front doorway, Michael kept an eye on Danny until he disappeared into an unlit section of trees. A truck rumbled to life. They had grown into two very different men, bound only by a grandfather they both revered.

"Hey, Mikey," Danny shouted from somewhere in the dark. "We had a good time with your girl after the groundbreaking." The truck roared down the driveway, lights flicking on after it met the main road.

Was that what Jillian had been up to? The thought of Danny within two feet of her filled him with anger. His pulse quickened. Then rage took over. Michael jumped in his car and sped backward down the dark, curved driveway.

He slammed his brakes where the blacktop met the road. He squeezed his eyes shut, clutching the steering wheel for support. *You've grown. You're the logical Malvisti, the one who's learned to solve problems responsibly.* Michael released his grip on the wheel, resting his head on his knuckles. In the past, they'd have wrestled until someone broke the other's arm or dislocated an elbow. Paybacks always hurt. But they were no longer ten year olds, competing for the approval of the older Malvisti men.

He took a deep breath.

❖

Two days later, Mother Nature, or whoever was in charge, unleashed a fitting tribute to his grandmother in the form of a torrential rainstorm. It pleased him that so many of Michael's grandparents' friends, at least those still living, had ventured out to pay their respects. Their walkers thudded dully on the mauve funeral parlor rug. With Grandma Ziatta's death, there was just a handful of the city's old guard left now.

Jillian stood next to Michael at the end of the family's receiving line, a feminine finish to a line of gruff Malvisti men.

"This wake has been more bearable than I thought," he whispered to her.

"Yeah?"

"I've heard so many stories about my grandparents. I've filled in some parts of their lives that I've wondered about for a long time."

"That's cool." Jillian scanned the line of mourners with no more than a passing interest.

"Grandma Ziatta volunteered for fifty years at a local food pantry." He thanked a well-wisher and turned back to Jillian. "A few of the people she helped came to express their gratitude. Can you believe that?"

"Will this last much longer?" She stretched her arms in front of her.

"Jillian, c'mon." Michael felt his face heat up.

"Sorry." She shifted. "These heels hurt. You try standing in them for two hours."

As time wore on, people gathered in the upright wooden chairs in the center of the room. He listened as they caught up on news about mutual friends or commiserated about aches and pains. He heard a lot of talk about the old days. Forget social media—this was how his grandfather, and many others of his generation, stayed connected. Face to face.

A priest performed a short service at the end of the visiting hours. Uncle Sal thanked the wake-goers on behalf of the family. A somber note descended, punctuated by the driving rain that could be heard on the roof. Visitors filtered out into the downpour.

"I hear you were at the house the other night." Uncle Sal placed his hand firmly on Michael's shoulder. "What were you looking for?"

"Nothing. Why?" Michael stepped back. Those oversized hands were made to intimidate.

Sal drew back his lips, pretending to smile. "There's nothing there for you. Your father and I will get things straightened out, and we'll let you know when we're done."

"Are you telling me to stay out of the house?"

"Yes." His eyes bore into Michael's. "And stay out of our business. It doesn't concern you."

"Lots of things concern me." Michael stared back, unfazed by his uncle's tone.

"Like what?"

Michael took the bait. "What kind of waste did we really bury around this town?"

"Butt out, or you'll wish you had come to your senses sooner, my boy."

Sal turned toward Jillian. He kissed her on both cheeks. They talked quietly, and then Uncle Sal strode out the door, not even pausing to say good-bye to Danny or Michael's dad.

What had just happened?

Danny sized up Michael, smirked as his eyes settled on Jillian, and then followed his father into the damp night. Michael clenched his fists. They would have it out soon, he knew.

"I told you not to ask him about the business." Joe shrugged into his trench coat. "That's for the good of all of us, including you. Do you understand?"

"Then answer some questions for me." Michael stepped close to his father. "By your own admission, the family business affects me."

"Always the lawyer, aren't you?" Joe fished around in his suit pocket.

His mom materialized beside him. She handed his father a small open box.

"What's done is done. Move on." Joe turned his head to the side and discreetly dropped a pill into his mouth.

"Move on?" Michael re-buttoned his suit jacket. "Is that what you did when you fled to your gated community in Florida?" He signaled to Jillian it was time to leave.

"Look at me!" his father hissed. "The stakes are much higher than you understand. You'll put us all in jeopardy. Let Sal handle things and don't question it."

A cynical laugh escaped Michael's lips. He knew his tone was borderline disrespectful, but he couldn't help it. Something was so wrong in this family. "Maybe that's been the problem all along. Uncle Sal and his way of handling things."

Joe glared at his son. Then he turned to Carmella and nodded curtly.

Perhaps his dad was right about one thing. It was time to move on. Even now, surrounded by his family's secretive, shut-down ways, by his grandmother's pictures and mementos, and by the stink of funeral flowers, he longed to return to his modern house. To his forthright, rational way of thinking. To his innovative eco-city. Things made sense in that world.

At least, they did until recently.

But he was fooling himself to think that his family's past was unimportant. His grandfather's notions of respect, power, and financial security didn't seem to translate in today's world. Yet, unless he better understood their past, the consequences of his family's shadowy history would bind him for the rest of his life. How could he know what kind of people they were? How could he better himself or his life without knowing what had failed?

The foundation felt too shaky for this Green City builder.

CHAPTER TWENTY-SEVEN

December 27, 2003

I spent the early 1960s in a mental murkiness.

My condition had nothing to do with the hallucinogenic drugs that had clouded the lives of many people. (Or livelihoods—I purposefully left the drug trafficking and loan shark business to my friends in the local families). My mind instead was absorbed with the business of managing my ever-expanding version of the American Dream.

My secondary responsibilities (or so I had convinced myself) as husband, father, church deacon, and burgeoning philanthropist, further complicated my harried life. Today many people experience anxiety or stress and get help. But in my day, the nights and days of every self-made man were shadowed by unrelenting pressure. It came with the job. We dealt with it.

My position required me to be one step ahead of my friends and two steps ahead of my enemies. (Very often, I wasn't sure who was friend or foe.) I routinely dealt with contractors, politicians, road haulers, foremen, and leaders in our region's heavy industries, some of whom I called friends. I made critical decisions with little information to guide me. I didn't always have the time or the wisdom to link my actions with their long-term consequences. Not as a businessman. Nor as a parent.

I most certainly didn't have time to discern truth.

The commotion of life must have obscured my vision. How else can I explain the evidence—obvious in hindsight—that I missed? Like me, Niagara Falls had been swallowed up in a gray fog. The physical proof could be seen everywhere. A tangible, toxic miasma hovered over our city. The darkest smog could be traced to the factories along Chemical Row. When operating at full capacity, my friends' industrial operations could dim the already limited sunlight that fell upon Western New York.

Nobody could escape the effects. Grit lined children's nasal passages and irritated our throats. The pollution corroded roofs and paint, and sometimes left the inside of our windowsills peppered with telltale black dust. A writer once described our city as "an open vent placed squarely atop the pit of hell, complete with sulphur-like fumes and brown-tinged smoke."

Pathetic.

But all "normal."

Ours was an industrial town. This is what the ideas of great inventors looked like once the four walls of a factory were built and the operation was running. These factories drove our economy. They represented advancement. Gritty, stinking progress. And more and more toxic traffic for me.

But a memory from that decade still haunts me. Looking back, I squandered a major opportunity to gain clarity, to piece together the links between our industrial activities and the physical health of our city. One exceptionally warm fall night, I stood with my wife and sons in an unlit, open-air sports arena to inaugurate my latest gift to the citizens of Niagara Falls: a brand-new baseball stadium. One that could (and, shortly, would) be lit up at night. At least baseball's Golden Age had not bypassed Niagara Falls.

Like the audience, I was weary of waiting on our mayor, a florid man famous for stretching political dinners into the late evening. He was almost an hour behind tonight. Thankfully, a distraction presented itself: A full moon had risen, captivating the residents packed into their stadium seats. Brilliant radiance washed over their upturned faces. An otherworldly quiet descended over the audience, spreading calm where before there had been restlessness.

My wife nudged me and then lifted her chin toward a spectacle closer to earth. A shapeless mass of grayish-white pollution spewed from the uneven row of smokestacks that framed the venue. It had sneaked up on us, quietly filling the horizon and then drifting skyward. I removed my bifocals. I didn't need them. The rim of the darkened stadium railing stood out in sharp relief against the pale haze.

The enormous cloud drifted skyward. Just when I thought it would eclipse the moon, ghostly beams penetrated through gaps in the hazy mass. The mystical effect inside the stadium held us spellbound. Something pure had breached our toxic air. Too bad we couldn't have called it understanding.

I shivered, anxious to get on with the purpose for our being there.

Even at this late hour, my people, my friends and supporters, had shown up in force. I narrowed my eyes at some commotion around the entrance to the field. After I replaced my glasses, I saw that the mayor and his entourage had arrived. It was time to start the celebration.

I had chosen to christen the stadium from the grassy expanse between first base and right field. I motioned for my sons, Sal and Joe Jr., to gather closer. I tightened my two-handed hold on the red switch bar. The boys each grabbed a wrist.

We waited for the signal.

"Three, two, one ..." Spectators led the ear-piercing countdown.

I sucked in my breath. The possibility of operation failure hadn't entered my mind until now.

Together we yanked the metal lever.

Air exploded out of my lungs as twenty-six towering metal grids came to life. Fluorescent rays flooded the state-of-the-art sports facility. They illumined the toxic cloud shrouding the stadium. Soft beams bounced back to the field. The result provided a surreal experience, much like the moonlit spectacle a few minutes before. Oohs and aahs erupted from the crowded seats. I took it as a good omen. Man, aided by technology, could produce miracles too.

"Let there be light," I shouted. It seemed apropos.

The crowd roared. The shrieks of young players sitting along the dugouts stabbed my ears. For some of them, a future in sports would be earned on this diamond. My intervention and our money breathed new life into this, by now, floundering city.

"Malvisti! Malvisti!" Citizens chanted my name until the mayor took over the microphone.

The city deserved night baseball, and I had delivered it. It had taken one year to successfully convince financiers around the country to back a minor-league organization. Joseph S. Malvisti Stadium would serve the new ballclub and the nearby schools well.

Today, I was the man.

As so often happened at public displays like this one, my thoughts wandered to that other so-called champion, Jean Lussier. I'd heard that he was working at one of the defense factories just yards behind the stadium. What had he ever given this city except daredevil folklore? I had contributed something of worth. Something that would help people enjoy their brief, over-worked lives in this industrial city of cities.

I wondered if he was in the audience that night.

The mayor shook my hand and then grabbed me in an emphatic embrace. I recoiled from the whiskey on his breath. He let the applause peter out and then raised the microphone. "Ladies and gentlemen." He extended his hand toward me, my wife, and our boys. "Joseph and Annunziata Malvisti's generosity knows no bounds."

Someone whistled. Raucous cheering followed. It took a full minute for order to return.

"Folks, we are blessed to have the most modern baseball field in the United States!" Members of the audience clapped loudly in acknowledgment, hopefully ignoring the fact that the mayor slurred through the pronunciation of "states." He described my humble beginnings. He summarized my financial giving and volunteer work. He numbered the people employed by Malvisti Industries and highlighted our role in the local economy.

Tears traced my wife's chin. Sal bent to hug her, stiff in his new suit but plainly exhilarated by the attention. But where was Joe, Jr.? He'd been there just a minute before. I hoped he'd left merely to baptize the men's lavatory.

The formal dedication ended. Sparkling wine awaited us in the upstairs announcers' booth.

"You did it, Joe. Congratulations." My friend Vito shook my hand, his voice somber. "Catch up with me when you can. I wanted to stay for the party, but I've got to get home." He lowered his bloodshot eyes.

"Everything okay?"

"Eh. Not really." The balding man cleared his throat. "Rosalie is sick. Real sick."

My stomach dropped. I loved Vito like a brother. "What is it?"

"Lung cancer." His mouth drooped into a sad smile. He affectionately punched Sal in the shoulder and left.

That night marked the first time I remember hearing about that insidious disease.

I looked at the pollution still circling the stadium and wondered briefly whether there was an association. A glimmer of truth attempted to pierce my addle-brained state of mind, but I closed it down. Fast.

The crowd poured out onto the field. Supporters needed my attention. My focus shifted to the pressing matter of my offering to the city. I didn't even think to look for Joe, Jr.

How had I not made the connection? Back then, regular people knew little about the dangers of factory emissions. But I had a front-row seat as an industry insider. I knew all about operating in the shadowy business of waste disposal, including our uninformed handling of the toxins left behind by those smokestacks. I saw workmen develop respiratory problems and odd skin conditions. Many of them died at a young age.

Patterns of information and concepts in our industry should have sparked more awareness in my mind, but I never saw it. I didn't want to see it.

And I wish I had never heard of cancer, either.

It claimed Rosalie that summer, and Vito a few years later. Three more close friends died in the next few years. Certain cancer rates in Niagara Falls soon surpassed every other city in New York State. Maybe even the United States. It's enough to make a man sick. And wonder. How far-reaching was this disease? Did man himself bring about this sickness? Was this God's way of punishing us for trying to know what He knows?

I'll soon be its next victim. And most certainly not its last.

I had personally seen to that.

In the decades that followed the stadium experience, I started to put the facts together. My role in the defilement of Niagara Falls became crystal clear.

Now, as a nearly dead man coming out of a century of innovation, I know even more. Someone has shone the light of understanding in my mind.

It wasn't just the physical evidence that should've clued us in to the fact that we had defiled this city; my aching conscience also bears witness. God Himself had seen to that.

CHAPTER TWENTY-EIGHT

Niagara Falls, New York

L ydia's facial nerves twitched. The unfamiliar sensation distracted her, forcing her to hang up and try Tyler Morales's number again. Today, her jumbled mind could only handle one thing at a time.

If she was confused, she could only imagine what was happening at Hessley's headquarters 1,500 miles away. For weeks, the Pavati Towers "miracle" had turned their office and lives upside-down. She and Dana, as well as Hessley itself, had been deluged with calls from paranormal researchers, potential buyers, and environmentalists of every stripe. And that was on top of the arrival of the first wave of residents.

The media attention also, unfortunately, spurred an explosion of postings on a protest website attacking Hessley and Malvisti Industries. Someone posted pictures of blue-tinged chemicals that were supposedly visible in the puddles of Malvisti Park. Rumors about deformed animals resurfaced. Talk of radioactivity went viral. The site had registered four thousand hits that morning; the number grew by the hour.

Tyler Morales picked up on the first ring.

"It's me again, Tyler." They'd talked on the phone so many times over the past three weeks that she was sure he was sick of her. "Did you see what surfaced online today?"

"Yes, I did. We've been monitoring the site off and on." The Hessley engineer sighed into the phone. "Look, these eco-extremists are fringe members of society. No one listens to them. We're going to ignore it for now."

"What about concerns from ... regular people?" She thought about Violet, the real estate broker. And Angie. Chris Magnano. Even Dana's ex-date, John, the grape-grower. They didn't seem crazy. Who wouldn't be concerned about mutant snakes? Radioactive turtle shells? Or even rainbow colors in puddles?

At least Mr. Mahoney hadn't mentioned finding any more fish plagued by tumors. Her face tightened as she recalled that awful day two years ago.

"Things should die down soon. It'll be a mere blip on the radar screen, trust me." Tyler cleared his throat. "In my experience, if regular people get worked up at all, it doesn't last too long. They have lives to live. Mouths to feed. Home values to preserve."

She swallowed. His words hit a nerve. As mad as she'd been after Harrison caught the sick fish, hadn't she stayed quiet ever since?

"We'll get to the bottom of things, but, in the meantime, ignore these scare tactics. I'll recommend that Hessley host a town-hall meeting if public concern grows." Tyler kept his voice light. "Fair enough?"

"Sounds good." If Hessley's environmental engineer wasn't worried, then she would try not to be either.

But he didn't know about the resistivity scan Chris had given her a few months ago, which, in all the home closing excitement, had largely slipped her mind. And what about the supposed high rates of disease around Cascata Verde? What about her family and all the sicknesses they'd experienced? Worries buried in the back of her mind re-emerged. The time seemed right to ask a few questions and maybe mention the scan. The office was empty, for once.

"You there?" Tyler paused.

"Yes. Sorry."

"Keep a positive outlook." Tyler thanked someone in the back-ground. "And be alert. Monitor the local papers. You never know who's going to start asking questions. I'll notify security to be on the lookout for trespassers."

"Tyler?" Lydia looked around once more to make sure Dana hadn't returned. "I have one more question."

"Shoot."

"The website talks about *legacy* waste." She swallowed. "That's old contamination, from what I read. Material that was buried long ago." She knew she was taking a chance by sounding disloyal. But she had no choice. Her peace of mind was at stake. "Since Malvisti Industries is the former owner of some of Cascata Verde's property, are we at all concerned about the old stuff?"

"Not at all." Tyler reassured her. "We have plenty of studies to confirm that the landfill was properly repurposed into Malvisti Park, and that the brownfields around it were completely remediated."

Dana burst into the office, her eyes an electric blue-gray. "Guess what!"

Lydia motioned for her to be quiet, pointing to the phone. The resistivity scan would have to wait. "Thanks, Tyler. I'll look forward to speaking with you soon." She hung up and stared at Dana's mussed hair. The amulet around her neck twisted backward. She didn't even seem to care that her free-trade organic cotton blouse had come untucked.

"Bald eagles have been spotted near the river!" Dana grabbed her canvas shoes from a spot near the door. "Let's take the cart and drive over there. People are gathering to see them."

"I've seen eagles before." She sized up her friend. They had a ton of work to do. It wasn't like Dana to put business aside for something frivolous.

"But these birds are special. They used to live around here, but disappeared years ago. Don't you remember Starlite from when we were teens?" Dana waited for a response. "Well?"

"No." Lydia wracked her brain. Nothing about birds rang a bell.

"Naturalists are all excited about it. Someone thought they saw an eaglet." Dana dropped into her ergonomic chair and swiveled toward Lydia. "Change is afoot!" She slipped out of heels and into her new vegan walking shoes.

Lydia waved contracts in the air. "I think I'll stay put."

"There's something very special going on here, Lydia. I can feel it. The positive energy emanates off every building, every home." She fixed her necklace, patting it in place. "The new residents have noticed it too. It's as if humans and nature are connected, being renewed."

"You've talked to the residents about positive energy?" Lydia blinked twice. "We've got to be careful, Dana. Remember, there's no official position from Hessley on the Pavati Towers so-called miracle. And who knows who's doing the asking? We might have people fishing for information to post online."

"No, no. Don't worry. I always steer the conversation toward positive things when a resident raises environmental questions or concerns. It works every time." Dana darted out of her chair and skipped to the door.

"I've got to get some things done before I can leave." Lydia reached for a folder covered in sticky notes. "Go on without me."

She didn't feel right and had no desire to be out in the rain. Nor did she want to hear any more about healing circles or electromagnetic energy sources pulsing from beneath the Plaza. Lately, Dana felt positive energy on every corner. She obsessed about cosmic cleanings. Her friend was going too far.

Dana opened the door, but didn't leave. "Did you know that azaleas have bloomed at the plaza complex?"

"And?"

"They usually don't grow here. The grounds crew planted a few as an experiment. And, hello! It's April, so the fact that *anything* is blooming is a big deal."

"Global warming?" Lydia *had* noticed the azaleas. Another curiosity, nothing more.

Her eye spasmed. It was time to seek out another opinion about all this stuff. Mr. Mahoney would surely have something to say. But she had another person in mind who might do more than blame the politicians. Someone who might also pray for her.

❖

"There's been a lot of talk about signs and healing, Pastor." Lydia settled herself on the edge of the church foyer's stone hearth. Pastor Amos dragged over a chair. "Some say there's a powerful positive energy portal under Cascata Verde."

"So I've heard." The fair-haired pastor flipped the seat backward to sit facing her around the curve of the hearth.

"Others say the Pavati Towers Miracle is a manifestation of paranormal activity." Lydia rubbed her right eye. "Officer Rubino at the security gate swears it's radiological. Maybe it does have something to do with contamination? What do you think?"

"I can't give you an answer." His brow wrinkled. "About a dozen church members have asked me about these issues, and I'll tell you what I told them. I think it's probably best to focus on the matters over which you can exert some control."

"Like what?"

"Like how you respond to these rumors, especially the unexplainable things." Amos steepled his hands together on the chair back.

"What do you suggest?"

"It all depends on the perspective with which you view the world."

"Sounds wishy-washy, if you ask me." Lydia rubbed her right ear. It felt hot, but not to the touch.

"Maybe." He studied her face. "But everyone has a worldview, Lydia. It determines how we interpret things. It might even determine how we treat other people, who or what we worship, or even how we view the environment."

The turn in the conversation caught her by surprise. For weeks, she hadn't discussed much beyond real estate, breathing techniques, rumors of toxins, or childhood sicknesses. All very specific situations. "How so? Can you give me an example?"

Amos's eyes lit up. "This subject has been on my heart for months. Let's go big picture for a minute. Some view nature from a people-centered perspective. They believe that resources exist solely for the benefit of mankind ... that man is infinitely more important than the rest of Creation."

"Like man can take whatever he wants or needs?"

"Exactly." He held his forefinger in the air. "But other people view mankind as simply a part of nature, sharing the same limited resources. They argue that humans should reduce their consumption and exploit the environment as little as possible. People, animals, plants ... we're all in this together. We're all equal."

"That makes sense, doesn't it?" She thought about the Green City. Everything from the materials used to the decisions made were tested against a framework of sustainability. Rebecca and Dana took that role seriously. "Isn't that what God would want?"

"Perhaps."

Lydia sat back against the stone alongside the fireplace. "I don't understand. We should limit our impact, right?"

"Sure, but not every living thing was created in God's image, right? People were."

"I not sure I'm following you. If God created every living thing, then doesn't He exist in all living things?"

"That works as long as we don't begin to worship the *created* things instead of the Creator. Look, some people take that view to another level. They see the natural world as having a form of spirituality itself. They revere Mother Nature, or even the Earth, as a living organism."

Lydia thought for a moment. Hadn't Dana just mentioned something like that? "It's god-like, but not God."

"Exactly. Here's another view. God tasked man, the pinnacle of all His Creation and possessing the capacity for moral accountability, with the great responsibility to care for the Earth. As believers, since our obedience is required, we love the things God loves. His Creation." Amos paused. "So we use the resources we need, but also protect the things that God loves."

"I don't think many people think about the environment in terms of obedience or morality." She could tell Amos did.

"You're probably right." He lifted his hands. "So depending on your view, you might respond differently to the issues you raised when you walked in here. But here's the bottom line. If we believe that God is in charge, we should act like it. We don't need to fret, or cower under the sheets until there's an explanation."

"So, as a chaplain, what do *you* do with all this craziness around here?"

"Again, I try to keep my focus on what I *can* do. For example, I can control how I treat the environment. How I do my job. How I confront things that are wrong. Since the Word of God is my guide, I try to do those things in a way that is consistent with the Bible. That means that I should never be complacent, but allow my life to be ruled truth, transparency, humility, and gratitude."

"My head is starting to hurt." She felt her forehead involuntarily, confirming a suspected fever. "You know, I believe in God. I just need to look at my children to know there's a creator of some type. But He's not in charge of my day-to-day life. Heck, I'm not even in charge of what happens on a daily basis in my life! There's been so much sickness, stress … death." Her voice hitched when her brother's sweet face came to mind. "And I can't find any explanations for the odd events happening right outside my office door. It's unnerving, but I'll try what you've suggested. Focus on the things I can control."

"That's a good start. And God does care about your everyday life, Lydia. Let's pray He sustains you, day-by-day."

She repeated the phrase, trying to puzzle out whether God was really in control or what His purpose might be. Maybe she should talk to Angie next.

"You can stop by any time with questions. I've got a couple books that you might like, too."

Hopefully they weren't more self-help books, like the ones Dana usually gave her. Lydia looked inside toward the sanctuary. This time there were seats. "How are things going here? More people showing up?"

"Yes, thanks for asking. We're up to about a hundred, including around twenty electricians who have formed a Bible study. The congregation is equal parts workers and the first wave of residents."

"That's wonderful." She rooted through her purse for some eye drops. What was wrong with her right eye? It wouldn't close properly. "You've worked hard for that success."

"It's not because of me. And definitely not as a result of my guitar playing. God has a plan for me, and for this community."

"Now you sound like Dana. Only her plan revolves around Mother Nature, not God."

"He has a plan for you, too, Lydia."

"Simple as that, huh?" Lydia got up from her perch on the hearth. Unsteady for a moment, she returned to her seat on the fireplace edge.

"You okay?"

"My ear is bothering me." She felt behind her ear and around the side of her head. Pain stabbed wherever she touched. "I feel off-kilter."

He went to a first-aid box mounted on the wall. "I've got some pain reliever in here. And some sterile rags." Amos turned to her, smiling. "Would either of those help?"

"Hope so." Laughing, Lydia pulled a stainless steel water bottle out of her purse, a gift from Dana. She threw back the pills, still contemplating Amos's words about God having a plan for her.

"We've gotcha covered, body and soul." Amos smiled as he returned to his seat. "If you believe in God, Lydia, then I encourage you to find out what that requires of you. Take it to the next level."

She nodded.

"Oh, Lydia!" Amos got up and stepped around his chair. He cupped her chin and turned her face to the overhead light. "Your eye is drooping. Can you close it?"

"I ... I don't think so." She squeezed her eyes tight, but the entire right side of her face felt sluggish. Her right ear started to hum. She pressed it and shook her head. It grew louder. And hotter, unless she just imagined the burning sensation enveloping the side of her head. "What's happening to me?"

Amos helped her up. "Let's get you checked out."

Suddenly, her right eye wouldn't blink at all. She couldn't smile properly either. She had no control over her own face. Was this a stroke? Lydia held her hand over her racing heart. Her breath came in shallow wisps.

If she couldn't do something as simple as close her eye or smile, how in the world could she protect her children?

CHAPTER TWENTY-NINE

L ydia lay in bed, trembling. Her dream had cast her on a narrow road alongside a sparkling blue-green lake. The marine landscape stretched away from her for miles. She couldn't see any end to it. Through her peripheral vision she detected movement. Massive concentric circles of water rippled far off in the distance, as if something very large was about to surface in the pristine water. But the smell of the shimmering liquid pulled her attention away from the oddity. Sharp and sweet. She could almost taste it. She inhaled deeply, lifting her arms high. Waves lapped at her toes.

Out of nowhere, a gentle waterfall cascaded over her shoulders. The sparkling lake was more refreshing than any creek she had played in as a child. She felt whole, revived.

Vital.

Until the phone jolted her awake. It happened every time.

She jerked herself to her elbows. A rush of worries came flooding in, as if waiting for her to gain full awareness before they pounced. Topping the list was her Bell's Palsy diagnosis. The paralysis of her facial muscles would be temporary, the doctor had said. Lydia wondered whether temporary meant days, weeks, or months. Seven days had already dragged by.

"'ello." The working half of her mouth tried to compensate for the dead side. She pulled off the eye patch and clenched her cheek muscles in an attempt to blink. No luck.

"You sound bad." Dana took a sip of something, swallowing loudly. "Face still frozen?"

"Yeah." She reached for her eye drops. "Hang on, let me juice my eye." The word *juice* came out so slurred, she doubted Dana would understand it.

"Listen, I need you here as fast as possible. Urgent meeting with Hessley. Michael Malvisti and a bunch of other lawyers are going to participate in the call."

"Is 'der a problem?" She sat up at the involvement of lawyers, especially the one with the last name of Malvisti. Liquid ran down her face. Instinctively, her left hand felt around her cheek.

"Nothing that can't be addressed quickly. More contamination rumors surfaced online and Hessley's decided to respond at a town hall meeting. Time to set the record straight and get past all this stupidity." Through the phone, Lydia heard Dana's car beep as if the keys had been left in the ignition. "Just get here as soon as you can."

The good feelings from her dream had ebbed away when the phone rang. Now a sense of dread flowed upward from the pit of her stomach. One peaceful day. *Why was that so elusive?*

❖

As she backed out the driveway a half-hour later, Lydia saw two figures in her rearview mirror. She hit the brakes, surprised to see Mr. Mahoney's stooped form in the road. Mara was bent over next to him, stroking Monk's head.

She was about to honk when she saw Angie waving her hands wildly from the front doorway. Her sitter jumped the last two porch steps and jogged shoeless over to Lydia's car window.

"I forgot to tell you something."

"What?" Lydia shifted into park.

"I feel the need to tell my mother's cancer story on a green movement website."

Lydia's body aches worsened. "The anti-Hessley site?"

"Yes. But don't worry, it's not directed toward Hessley. It's more of a compilation of environmental wrongs committed against our region."

Lydia gripped the steering wheel. "Only you can decide how to handle your story, Ang."

"But are you okay with that? I think it's important for me to participate."

"Sure." Lydia chewed on her numb cheek. "Just be careful. There might be some extremists involved with that site." Her half-paralyzed tongue slurred all the s's.

Angie raised an eyebrow. "I'm sorry, but I can't really understand you."

Lydia gave Angie a thumbs-up.

"Okay, as long as you're sure." Angie smiled and then leaned in to hug her. She trotted back to the house, waving before shutting the door.

Lydia turned her head to back out. Mr. Mahoney and Mara had moved out of the way. She rolled to a stop beside them and leaned out the window, but didn't say anything. Better to let others do the talking.

"Hey!" Mara smiled. "We were just talking about Dana's appearance this morning on the *Western New York Morning Show*." Her eyes widened as she caught Lydia's eye patch. "What happened to your face?"

"Temporary paralysis." Lydia knew what she was trying to say, but she couldn't imagine anyone being able to make out those words.

"Huh?"

Lydia shifted back into park. "What appearance?" She worked hard at enunciating so she'd be understood.

"Didn't you know? She went on TV to talk about the Pavati Towers Miracle."

Lydia winced. Dana hadn't told her, nor had she asked Lydia to come along. Probably because her drooping face would've scared people. Viewers might've blamed Cascata Verde for her condition. Lydia motioned for Mara to continue.

"She said the Green City is our region's destiny. The miracle was a cosmic confirmation. The morning hosts were quite excited." Mara turned to Mr. Mahoney. "Right, Conroy?"

"I guess." He coughed and then spit on the road.

"A lady did a live tarot-card reading." Mara patted Lydia's shoulder. "Sorry you missed it. Very interesting. Good things are coming our way."

"Eh." Mr. Mahoney used his walker to draw closer to the car. "Tarot cards. A glowing building. Eagles. All gimmicks. Some politico probably ginned this up to create a buzz." He rested his elbows on the metal device. Frayed duct tape secured its handles. Monk limped along next to him and then collapsed noisily on the asphalt.

"Let it go, Conroy." Mara flicked her eyes toward the end of the street. She chewed her nail. "Even if it's a publicity stunt, we all need something to hold on to. Look at how our outlook in this area has changed for the better since we learned about the miracles at the Green City. People actually want to live in Niagara Falls now. And we don't have to pay them to move here."

Lydia winced again. The city had resorted to paying off college loan debt for recent graduates who agreed to move downtown. Population numbers meant everything when it came to federal aid.

"And what are healing circles, anyway?" Mr. Mahoney stood straighter and crossed his arms. "Sounds like a bunch of hooey."

"Healing circles?" Lydia repeated, leaning farther out the driver's side window.

"Dana's interview," the old man answered. "I'm surprised you didn't know. You two oughta get on the same page." Mr. Mahoney used his foot to nudge Monk in the belly. He nearly lost his balance, quickly grip-ping the walker's front bar. "You alive, buddy?"

"I thought she handled the last caller rather well." Mara kept her gaze on Lydia's good eye.

"The one asking about the Green City's two-headed snakes?" Mr. Mahoney lowered his gravelly voice. "It was probably your husband, Mara."

Anger stripped her face of color. "Better not have been him. He knows better than to bring that up again."

Mr. Mahoney shrugged. "There are a lot of people raising questions these days. Could've been anybody." His voice trailed off.

Lydia eyed Mr. Mahoney carefully. Now that she could see more of him, he seemed thinner than last week. Less invincible. "You okay?" She nodded toward his leg.

"'Course I am, Ms. Captain Hook." He slapped his thigh and chuckled. Monk's ear jerked. "Just kiddin' ya. Got a pain in my leg today. Humor takes my mind off of it."

"Want me to take you to the doctor?"

"Nah. You take care of yourself, missy." His bushy eyebrows knit to-gether. "I can drive just fine ... if I decide to go anywhere."

She relaxed slightly. Mr. Mahoney's indignant tone made him sound more like himself. She couldn't bear to think of anything happening to him.

"By the way, I've been doing some woodworking. Just finished two fine slingshots for my boys. I'll bring 'em over soon and set up some tar-gets for them to practice."

She nodded, cringing at the thought of Travis with a weapon of any type.

"One more thing, Lydia." Mara bent lower. "I'm putting my house on the market. Are you still handling residential home sales?"

Lydia shook her head. "I can refer you to someone. Time frame?"

"Right away." Lydia detected a note of desperation in her neighbor's tone. "I've already started getting rid of everything I don't need."

Mr. Mahoney's eyebrows melded together. "Where will you go?"

"Probably out west."

"Hold on to that snow blower for me, will ya?" He hooked Monk's leash around the walker and shuffled back toward his own house.

Lydia assured Mara that she would call her soon. She resisted the urge to ask whether Jeff would be joining her in the move. Mara probably wouldn't have understood her anyway.

As she drove away, her worries mounted. Her body had let her down. What if her face never returned to normal? What if Harrison's ever-present cough turned into something more serious? And what if Cascata Verde was *actually* contaminated? For the past few weeks she had paid her bills on time. The boys had new sneakers with proper foot support. She could think about getting a new car. But if something happened to the Green City, their newfound security could disappear overnight.

Her face tightened, pressuring her ringing ear even more.

Was there anything over which she had some measure of influence? What was it Pastor Amos had said? She had control only over how she responded to things? That she had to trust God for the rest?

She searched her options. So little was dependent on her words or actions.

Dana texted. *Conf call 5 mins!*

She pressed the gas pedal and flew out of the neighborhood, still thinking about what she could control.

An idea popped into her head. The town-hall style community meeting might be a good start for a new way of approaching problems. She could do her best today to help prepare others for it ... despite her misgivings about the involvement of a Malvisti.

Everyone knew that family name. 'Malvisti' was prominently displayed on the newly renovated shopping plaza downtown. The older

Malvisti, the one who'd died some years back, had reportedly been involved in all kinds of questionable business activities. And Sal Malvisti had been a political fixture since before she was born. But in all fairness, the only thing she knew about Michael Malvisti was that he was Hessley's main real estate lawyer. And he'd been pleasant enough in the limited interaction she'd had with him.

Maybe she could give him the benefit of the doubt. It was possible that he was different from the rest of his family.

Another idea dawned. She could turn over the resistivity study to Tyler Morales. No one other than Tyler would need to know it came from her. It was one small piece of information, and then her duty would be done.

That made three responses within her control.

She felt better already, even if she still couldn't blink her own eye closed.

❖

The conference call was already in full swing by the time Lydia arrived at the real estate office. She took a steadying breath and set down her briefcase.

Dana frowned at her and muted the phone. "I told them you were in the office already." She took her finger off the button.

Lydia slid into the chair on the opposite side of Dana's desk. She'd driven as fast as she could, but heightened security at the Green City's entry gates had resulted in more questions and longer lines. The Pavati Miracle had its downside, too.

"So. We've got less than three weeks, folks." Rebecca Waters' firm voice left no doubt as to who was running this call. "Is everyone clear on what's needed to make this town hall meeting happen? Any questions?"

"How many residents do you think will show up?" A female voice Lydia didn't recognize.

"The health department estimates fifty or so, Suzanna." Hessley's CEO said it as if she doubted even that many would come.

"Well, that'll be three times more than any other town meeting we've run." A male voice that did sound familiar. Hessley's real estate lawyer. She swallowed, committed to keeping an open mind about this Malvisti.

"You know as well as I do that people don't care about these things, Michael. We run them because they'll care if we don't."

"Sure. And it's equally important that we do everything possible to create the perception that *we* care."

Spoken like a true politician. Like a Malvisti.

"Because we do." He added.

Oh.

Lydia reigned in her negative thoughts. She'd committed to giving this man the benefit of the doubt, right?

Right.

CHAPTER THIRTY

"People are trickling in," Michael handed Tyler an agenda for the town hall meeting.

"Thanks." Ty added the paper to his existing pile on the U-shaped table.

"I don't need one, but thanks, luv." Suzanna sipped from a short glass of water. "I've been working on that agenda for weeks now. Know it by heart."

From his vantage point on the corner of the stage, Michael took a silent inventory of the number of people in the high school auditorium. About a dozen people stood shaking out wet jackets or hats in the middle rows. A few others were already seated front and center. Hessley managers, as well as officials from local and state agencies, occupied the twenty or so swiveled chairs pulled up to the folding tables on the stage. "So far, there are more speakers and police officers here than residents."

"Don't forget the media circus back there." Ty jerked his head toward the right side of the auditorium. Video equipment lined the wall. On a sudden impulse, Michael searched for the young reporter who had accosted Uncle Sal at the groundbreaking last fall. But the only female so far had cropped gray hair, and sat perched behind a camera. Not the right woman.

"The media is here because they want to know about the Pavati Towers Miracle." Suzanna poured herself another glass of water and downed a few gulps. "Rebecca led them to believe we had some answers. The press release was just a teensy bit ambiguous."

That was news to Michael. "Well, do we know what happened at the Towers?"

Ty lifted his shoulders. "None of our other engineers have said anything."

More rain-drenched residents arrived through the upper back doors. All at once, crowds began to pour in through the lower-level entrances, some leaving soaked umbrellas at the door. The seats filled quickly. Maybe more people cared than he thought.

"There's your uncle, luv." Suzanna's chin raised. "He's holding court with the other city council members."

Michael looked in his uncle's direction and back at her. He chewed his lip.

"You look a little distracted." Suzanna's eyes searched his.

He lowered his voice to a whisper. "Rebecca's making me introduce her today. She wants to bank on our," he crooked his fingers in the air, "'good family name' to reassure residents that there's nothing to worry about at Cascata Verde."

"Hey, it's part of our job." Ty punched his arm. "We've got hundreds of millions invested in Cascata Verde. I don't need to remind you that your job also rides on its success. Malvisti or not."

Like he needed a reminder. Right now, with the Green City project underway amidst swirling rumors of legacy waste, the Malvisti reputation hung precariously in the balance. His last name guaranteed that he'd be lumped in with the rest of the family, even if his own kin wanted to exclude him.

One of Hessley's administrative assistants tapped the center-stage microphone. Outside, the downpour intensified, pounding a discordant tune into the metallic roof. Although a few people glanced upwards, most looked expectantly at the speakers on the stage.

Rebecca cast a meaningful look in Michael's direction.

"You're up, man." Ty said.

Michael left his seat at the table and hustled around it to the podium, anxious about what might unfold today.

"Good morning, folks." He adjusted the mic. "I'm Michael Malvisti. It is a privilege to be with you today."

Chris Magnano slipped into the room from an upper side entrance, momentarily interrupting Michael's train of thought. A white paper bag poked out from under the resident's arm. *Another picture?*

He forced himself to focus. "Thank you for coming to this informational meeting. Today we will hear from a number of speakers, including representatives from four governmental agencies, all of whom will address some aspect of health and safety matters in and around Cascata Verde. At the end, there will be an opportunity for you to ask questions."

Muffled coughing echoed from the rear. Nobody clapped, but nobody heckled him, either. "Our first speaker is Rebecca Waters, CEO of Hessley Development. Rebecca has years of experience in developing large-scale, environmentally responsible mixed-use projects. She has overseen Cascata Verde from its beginning. I know that I speak for all of my colleagues at Hessley when I say that I am honored to be working with her in bringing this Green City to life. Please welcome her." He watched his boss stride confidently toward the table as residents clapped enthusiastically.

A deep-throated roll of thunder shook the auditorium from the outside. The rain answered with the tinny sound of pellets striking the curved roof of the school's performance wing.

Michael moved aside to make room for Rebecca as she reached the podium.

He wasn't exactly sure what she would say today. She'd orchestrated every aspect of this meeting. Even her tailored muted-green suit had been carefully chosen during their preparation meeting for its calming effect. Too bad they had no control over the rain.

"Thank you and welcome." She sounded confident, as usual.

Michael returned to his seat behind the table. He flinched when the lights dimmed momentarily.

"I applaud your desire to seek answers and make informed decisions about your community. We operate with a high degree of transparency at Hessley. We are pleased to share our knowledge with you at every step of this venture."

Rebecca recited an abbreviated company history. She told a moving story of how Cascata Verde grew from a drawing-board dream to an environmentally responsible corporate citizen. Along with the governor, she had worked to develop an identity for New York as a leader in green innovation.

Sonorous thunderclaps reverberated outside. This time, heavy raindrops thrummed the building, echoing its applause.

But the audience would not be distracted. People stayed with Rebecca as she spoke. He suspected that the story appealed to these hardworking Western New Yorkers.

"She'd make a great politician, don't you think?" Tyler whispered.

"I don't like politicians." He'd lost respect for public officials ever since Uncle Sal had been elected as a city councilman. He needed only to look around the decrepit and dying city to know his uncle's true intentions. The man served nobody but himself. And Malvisti Industries, which by now was essentially one and the same.

"… EPA and the state public health department have examined the data collected from investigation reports compiled by Tomeo Environmental," Rebecca continued. "They looked at soil, air, and groundwater test results. They also examined complaints of airborne dust from the site remediation and construction phases of the project."

Several people leaned forward in their seats. This is what many came to hear.

"Based on the testing done by Tomeo Environmental, these agencies concluded"—she read from a paper she held high in front of her—"that 'no on-site contaminants or dust releases from Cascata Verde are at levels that would cause adverse health effects.'"

A murmur spread across the room. A city councilman next to Sal began to clap, prompting others to join.

Michael scratched a note to Tyler. *All cleanup goes back to Tomeo, doesn't it?*

And isn't that what Chris Magnano had implied at the groundbreaking?

Ty nudged him to pay attention.

"Further, to prevent any possible future residential contact with potential soil contaminants, we installed a two-foot soil layer over large areas of the western half of the site, where residential, commercial, and park space is almost complete. A conservation easement, in which Cascata Verde and the State of New York have a limited ownership interest, ensures that the soil barrier will remain in place forever."

Michael tuned Rebecca out. He fixed his eyes on a wet spot that had developed in the acoustic ceiling tiles above the side steps. What was he missing? There had been many rumors about past contamination at the Cascata Verde site. He knew there had been a remediation that lasted several years, and he knew that Malvisti Park had been repurposed from its prior life as a privately owned landfill. A Malvisti Industries landfill. But everything he'd heard for the past five years made Cascata Verde's soil seem squeaky clean. Was it even possible to clean up a site that perfectly?

Water seeped from the ceiling. The steady plop-plop of drops created a puddle on the bottom step. A maintenance worker arrived and stuck a pail under the leak. A quick fix. But it did nothing to correct the underlying problem.

Ty wrote back. *Gotta learn more about that company.*

An uneasy feeling welled up inside his stomach. Too much depended on Tomeo, a company that he'd never heard of until recently.

Rebecca read from the bottom of the document. "With the available air-monitoring data and the continued effectiveness of site barriers, exposures at the site are not at levels likely to cause adverse health effects. Moreover, Tomeo Environmental found no statistically significant evidence of radioactive materials at Cascata Verde, including the recreation areas and Malvisti Park."

Rebecca swept the audience with her steady gaze, daring anyone to challenge Tomeo's conclusions. Even the rain slowed in response to her authority.

No one spoke. She had given them a lot of information to process.

"I'm turning the microphone over to local and state government representatives for some further information. First up is Mr. Eugene Walker, from the Department of Environmental Conservation." She looked behind her, gesturing to a stern-faced man, whose shorn gray hair and black-rimmed glasses underscored the gravity of his demeanor.

Who? Michael didn't remember seeing Walker's name on the agenda.

Michael detected a gleam in Rebecca's eye. But she said nothing more. Instead, she sat in her chair and gave the rep her full attention.

"Eugene Walker with DEC here." He set his glasses on the podium. A small Band-Aid on his temple provided the only smooth spot on his otherwise leathery skin. "We have made a discovery that should put to rest any environmental concerns or fears that you may have about the area around the Green City. In fact, after this announcement, some of you might agree with me that Western New York has been reborn."

The audience tittered. Hardened outdoorsmen puffed air out of their cheeks, looks of surprise evident. Eugene Walker did not come across as a man given to exaggeration.

"Some of you older folks may remember how common blue pike were in the '40s and '50s. We used to haul those fish in by the boatload."

Mature-looking people all over the room nodded.

"You may also know that blue pike haven't been spotted in the Niagara River since the mid-'70s. Not a single one in nearly thirty years. The species was declared extinct here in '83."

"That's right, Gene." A man in a fishing hat with deep creases across his face folded his arms. "Shame on us."

"Some folks, like my friend here"—he gestured to the old fisherman—"think the species' disappearance is related to high levels of water pollution. Others believe it had to do with non-native species of shellfish coming into the Niagara River. Fact is, we're not sure why they're gone." Walker searched the faces of the residents. "We only know that it happened."

This issue hit close to the hearts of many Western New Yorkers. Grandpa Joe had often complained about the loss of the popular fish.

"Now and then people think they've caught one," he continued, drawing out every syllable. "Well, folks, we tested every one of those suspect blue pikes. None turned out to be the real thing. They were blue-hued walleyes, which can sometimes be mistaken for the blue pike."

"It's those young fellas." The ancient fisherman drew laughs from the men surrounding him. "Don't say I didn't tell 'em they was wrong!"

Walker ignored the outburst. "Several weeks ago—just after the Pavati Towers Miracle in March—some folks from the fishing club came to my office. Caught themselves a blue pike, they said." Walker pursed his lips together before continuing. "Fact is, we were skeptical. But after we noted the large eyes, the tapered head, and the blue color under the second dorsal fin, we rushed those DNA tests right through."

All joking stopped. The rain ceased its aerial roof assault. Michael sensed that the room's atmosphere shifted, as if everyone knew something significant was about to emerge from Gene Walker's mouth. The old fisherman in the audience raised himself to his feet.

"Today I have the distinct privilege of revealing to you the results."

More people got out of their chairs. One man in the front row crossed his fingers.

Spit it out, Walker. Michael held his breath. He had no idea what the DEC representative had to say, but somehow he knew it would profoundly impact this expectant gathering. Suzanna grabbed his hand under the table. Her sweaty palms suggested a nervous anticipation too.

Eugene Walker looked directly at a young woman hidden beneath a camouflage-design hoodie. "I'm pleased to report that DNA tests have confirmed that the specimen fish *is indeed a blue pike.*"

The teen threw off her hood and screamed, "I knew it as soon as I caught it!" She stood and hugged those nearest to her.

Shouts reverberated across the auditorium. Someone whistled. The political representatives, led by Sal Malvisti, gathered at the base of the stage. They pumped Walker's hand. Frantic reporters typed away on smartphones. The camerawoman with the cropped hair panned the auditorium with her video equipment.

Michael leaned over to Ty. "This revelation will rock the fishing world. Blue pike are a big, big deal. Walker's speech will go viral in minutes."

"She knew." Ty lifted his chin in Rebecca's direction.

Michael followed his gaze. The satisfied set of his boss's arms confirmed Ty's observation. Nothing more from Hessley would be needed today. The public had its proof: Cascata Verde was a special place of restoration. Miracles happened there.

Walker rapped the microphone to regain the crowd's attention. "There's more."

The room fell silent once again, including Uncle Sal and the animated residents crowding the floor.

"We conducted an informal field study of the waters off the shores of Cascata Verde. We fished. We tested." Walker removed the microphone from its holder. "Guess what, folks?"

"What?" screamed a dozen voices.

"There's suddenly a *whole lot* of blue pike swimming through those waters."

Joyful noise drowned out Walker's next words. Men hugged one another. An entire fishing club in matching hats made their way down to the auditorium floor. Questions rang out as people pressed for details.

"Is the blue pike's reappearance related to the glow at Pavati Towers?"

"Is this another miracle?"

"How will the DEC protect the fish this time?"

"Are there natural predators in the lake?"

"Can we fish there again?"

Walker's attention bounced from one questioner to another, until he finally shrugged his shoulders and looked to Rebecca for help. Michael pitied him, knowing that he was out of his depth. When she offered no assistance, Walker's standard response became "We don't rightly know," or "Fact is, we're investigating that."

Eventually, the questions petered out, but not the excitement stemming from the announcement. The clamor tested the limits of the auditorium's acoustics.

Michael turned to Suzanna, who had moved farther down the table. "Meeting's over, I guess."

Suzanna's face lacked color. Her eyes had a peculiar glaze over them, as if she weren't really present. Michael rushed over and squatted next to her.

"Are you okay?" He patted her back. "Do you need an ambulance?"

"Mercy, no." She snapped to attention. "I have a … condition." She rubbed her hands around her swollen belly.

"A baby?"

"Not just one, luv." She cradled the bottom of her stomach. "Two. And they aren't giving me an easy time. I think I'm low on iron."

"That's great news!" He refilled her water glass from a pitcher, spilling some on the white tablecloth. "Not the iron part, but I'm so happy for you. All three of you."

Suzanna stared at the glass. "Do you think the water's okay to drink?" Her eyes crinkled. "I mean, I don't want to glow in the dark like a turtle."

"Ask Ty." Michael motioned for Tyler to come closer. "He's the environmental guy."

Tyler moved to a chair beside her.

"Is the water okay to drink?" She playfully elbowed Ty.

He rested his head on his hands, absently rubbing his temples. "I hope so."

Suzanna dropped her arm to her side. "What do you mean, you *hope so?*" She peered closely at the glass on the table.

"Right before today's meeting, one of our real estate agents had a security officer deliver a package to me. While everyone's attention was on Walker just now, I took a look at what's inside." He puffed his cheeks and blew out his breath. "I've got a few concerns."

"What was in the packet?" Michael looked around for a box or an envelope.

"It wasn't exactly a packet." Ty tapped his briefcase. "More like a crumpled doughnut bag."

Michael broke out into a sweat. The stocky resident had delivered the picture of his grandfather in the exact same way. He hoped that Magnano still lurked here somewhere. They needed to talk. Today.

Ty looked around and lowered his voice. "Inside the bag I found a used napkin and an electric resistivity scan of the closed landfill underneath Malvisti Park. There's an anomaly, or something that doesn't belong there. A circular structure that's about forty feet in diameter. It hadn't shown up on any of our own reports or scans."

Suzanna grabbed Ty's arm. "Does Rebecca know about this?"

"Heck no." Ty leaned back in his chair. "I want to confirm a few things before she sees this bombshell. I mean, maybe the report is old, and the ... whatever it is ... was removed during the conversion from landfill to park. I also want to check with the agent, Lydia Vallone, to see where she got this. Frankly, I need to make sure I didn't miss something big."

"I know where she may have gotten the bag." Michael stood and searched the rows of auditorium seats. Happy people high-fived one another. Someone dangled a lure to a large gathering of men and women. Laughter erupted. But there was no sign of the environmentalist. "Why don't you track her down, Ty. Lydia Vallone will be with the other realtor, Dana DuPays. You won't miss Dana. Platinum blonde."

Tyler hurried off.

Rebecca materialized beside them. "I need Michael a minute."

"Sure." He followed his boss to the far side of the stage.

"I need you to gather some information for me." Rebecca stole a glance to her right. Maybe she didn't want the press to pick up whatever she was about to say. "Visit the church at Cascata Verde. The service starts at ten tomorrow. Find out who's attending and do a head count. Let me know if you think it's cultish or strange in some way."

Michael cleared his throat. "Am I looking for anything in particular?"

"Pastor Amos has hundreds of people attending now. Given all this miracle talk, I'm concerned." She checked her watch. "Let's touch base on Monday when you get back to Florida."

What was happening to his legal career? Doughnut bags. Paranormal investigation. PR control. And now church recon? He missed the predictable days of negotiating and reviewing real estate documents. Those routine tasks made sense. Black-and-white answers existed in the form of detailed contract terms.

"What was that about, luv?" Suzanna whispered after he returned to her chair.

"I have to go to church." He did another visual sweep across the cavernous space. Magnano had to be around here someplace.

"Do you need forgiveness for something?" She looked at him strangely. "That can't be possible. You never do anything wrong. You're Michael Malvisti."

"Rebecca wants me to check out the new church at Cascata Verde." He ignored her teasing. "I'm to attend, mingle, and report."

"I'll go with you. I'm not one for churches, but my flight doesn't leave until late tomorrow night."

"Until my grandfather's funeral, I hadn't stepped foot in a church in years."

"Me either." She massaged her stomach. "Maybe now's a good time to return. I'm staying at The Cascade. Pick me up in the lobby."

"Sure. I'll be there around 9:45."

"See you tomorrow." She gathered her briefcase and lumbered past him. Her long skirt stretched tight across her backside.

Michael hurried down the steps at the end of the stage and made his way up through the thinning crowd interspersed throughout the auditorium seats. A man waved to him from the last row, then exited out the double doors in the back of the auditorium. The orange baseball cap looked familiar. It had to be Magnano.

Michael took the risers two at a time. A lot had been revealed today. But now it was time for full disclosure.

CHAPTER THIRTY-ONE

"There's the man who gave me the money for my minivan!" Lydia shook Dana's arm to get her attention. It was no use. Her friend's eyes were riveted on the well-built man sprinting up another aisle through the auditorium stairs. Michael Malvisti was a looker, all right. But something more important was on Lydia's mind.

Dana turned her attention back to Lydia after he disappeared through the back doors. "What were you saying?"

"Councilman Malvisti." Lydia spun her friend around. "Over there. Down near the stage."

"Oh yes, attorney *Michael Malvisti's* uncle." She gathered her purse and coat, and then smoothed her already-perfect hair. "Let's go thank the guy properly. You owe him that at least. After all, without his land, we wouldn't be selling houses in Cascata Verde."

"Oh no, no, no." Lydia dropped her arm. "He'll realize how much he gave me for the minivan and ask for it back. I gave it away, remember? Plus, my face and eye still look bad." She patted her cheek. Although her Bell's Palsy had mostly resolved itself, her eyebrows appeared uneven after hectic days like this one. The physical ordeal was almost over. But something equally traumatic lurked just around the corner. She was sure of it.

Dana gestured impatiently for Lydia to get in front of her. "However much he gave you doesn't matter to him one whit. He's filthy rich. Now go thank him."

"Fine." Lydia grudgingly stepped in front of Dana.

A masculine hand reached for her arm from the seat aisle in front of her. She stopped, her foot poised on the stair.

"Lydia?" She recognized the friendly voice of Tyler Morales immediately.

Towering over them, he nodded to Dana, firmly enfolding each woman's hand in his own massive ones.

She didn't expect the engineer to be so ... strong.

"Sorry if I scared you. I need just a minute, Lydia. Some answers to questions you had asked."

Lydia silently pleaded with him not to mention the doughnut bag she'd forwarded to him earlier. Dana didn't know about that yet. She shook her head slightly, and Tyler appeared to understand.

"Ms. DuPays, you should check in with Rebecca." He nodded toward the stage. "She may have an update for you on closing dates for the arts enclave."

Once they were alone, Tyler spoke first. "I was disappointed when I opened my bag of doughnuts and didn't find the Boston Cream that I was anticipating."

Lydia smiled. "The doughnut seems to have something other than cream inside and I'm wondering if we know what that could be?"

"No." His dark eyes turned serious as he searched her face "I don't have a clue. But I need to know where you got that ... doughnut." He pulled a business card and pen from his suit pocket. He handed it to her after writing his cell number across the back.

Lydia shifted. She focused on her shoes. This sounded like more involvement. "A friend of mine, Chris Magnano, approached me with the bag. He's extremely concerned about calories and other things that are harmful to a body. I thought you'd be the one to put some fears to rest."

"I'll look into the scan." Ty stuffed the pen back into his pocket. "But contact me right away if he delivers any more goods, okay?"

"Tyler, I love my job. I love working for Hessley. I don't want to lose everything by coming to you with what may or may not be a real concern." She felt sick. "Am I doing the right thing?"

"Of course." The engineer reached out and lightly touched her elbow. "Listen, our boss is a straight shooter. She respects the environment and she's definitely not a hypocrite. She'll look at everything fairly."

Lydia chewed her cheek, unsure of whether to say more. "I'm very ... worried."

"We'll get to the bottom of this." Tyler looked her straight in the eye.

He seemed sincere, so she trusted him to take it from here. At least she could cross the doughnut bag off her worry list.

Heels clicked up the stairs behind them. "Hey." Dana looked at Lydia inquiringly. "Are you ready to head back to the office?"

"I'm ready." Lydia turned back to the engineer and offered a smile. "Thanks, Tyler."

"What was going on there, my friend?" Dana teased after they'd walked out into the rain.

"Nothing you're implying." Lydia had wondered whether Tyler was married, but beyond that nothing struck her other than an appreciation for his straightforward and trustworthy manner.

"Stop staring at me." Lydia feigned annoyance.

"Then tell me what were you talking about?"

"We were discussing the Pavati Tower Miracle. I told him some theories I'd heard."

Another lie. Dana deserved better from her.

She looked up just in time to see Chris Magnano splashing through a puddle as he approached them. He balanced two doughnut bags and a cardboard tray of coffee.

"Helloooo, ladies." Dimples appeared on his cheeks. "I figured you'd both be here."

Dana studied him closely. "You look really different from when we last saw you at the reunion. Your hair is thinning and you've lost a lot of weight." Her brow wrinkled. "Feeling all right?"

"Well, thanks! And here I braved the rain to bring you coffee and doughnuts for the office." He handed Lydia a specific bag, his hand lingering a few moments longer than necessary. He distracted Dana with the drink carrier and the second, smaller bag.

Lydia understood. The contents of the first delivery were meant for her eyes only. Her heart sank.

"I knew that I would run into the two of you here. I saw you on the *Western New York Morning Show* a few weeks back, Dana. That glow was quite an event, huh?"

"Yes." A rare smile lit up her face. "It was exhilarating, enlightening, and energizing."

"That's like $E=MC^3$, or something like that." Chris cracked up.

"Not really." She opened the top of her coffee. "We've gotta run. Calls from buyers should be pouring in after today's confirmation. Take care of yourself, Magnano, and thanks for the treat."

"Thank you, Chris." And no thanks for involving me even more, she wanted to add, but didn't.

"I wish that John would bring me coffee sometime." Dana unlocked her car and slid in with care.

"Wrong beverage. He deals in wine." She stepped across a rivulet of water to get into the passenger's seat. "You've still got a thing for him?"

"Maybe." She looked uncomfortable. "Seems like he'd matured since our high school days. I thought he might call after the reunion last year. But I never heard from him."

The women stayed silent during the short drive back to the office. Once inside, Lydia bolted towards the bathroom and locked the door. She couldn't wait any longer. Whatever was inside the bag would no doubt require something of her. Best to tackle it head-on.

The doughnut bag contained a stapled stack of documents, reduced and printed on half-size paper. The first page appeared to be a summary of a scientific study. Thankfully, she didn't see any electric scans or pictures. It couldn't be too bad.

But it was the study's title that sent a shiver up her spine: *Deer Sampling Study For Land Parcel 332-9898.*

A deer study? Could those be the mutated deer Jeff Stanton had mentioned so long ago, the day Cascata Verde was announced? Weren't those just old wives' tales?

❖

It took over two hours before an opportunity to call Tyler presented itself. When Dana announced that she had to fetch her laptop from the car, Lydia knew she only had a minute or two alone, max.

Her hands shook when she punched in Tyler's cell number from her office phone. This was it. The last time she'd contact Tyler Morales—or anyone else—about secret studies possibly affecting Cascata Verde. She'd jeopardized her job twice in one day. She'd done her duty. Done. Done. Done. She stared at the office door handle.

"The doughnut man has given me some additional goods." Lydia blurted as soon as the engineer picked up. She eyed the door. "It's a study about animals at Cascata Verde, I believe."

"Is it recent?" Tyler sounded surprised.

"I don't think so. I remember a neighbor mentioning radioactive animals a while back. We thought he was crazy. An urban legend or something."

Background noise made it hard for her to hear him. "Listen—"

An amplified voice drowned out his next words.

She ignored the interruption. "Why isn't this common knowledge? It seems like it should be front page news." She flipped a page.

"I don't know, but I'm sure it'll be up on that anti-Hessley website soon." A stern female voice could be heard in the background talking to Tyler.

"Are you there?" Lydia bounced out of her chair. The doorknob moved. She stuffed the papers into her purse.

"Lydia, my plane's about to take off ... I'll send Michael Malvisti by your house tonight to get the papers. You can trust him." The call ended.

Lydia stared at the receiver. She ran her hands through her hair. Michael Malvisti, coming to her home. *The* Michael Malvisti. Her first impulse was to tell Dana, who had just returned from her car. But she knew her friend wouldn't want to hear about environmental concerns of any type. Not yet. In Dana's eyes, environmental issues threatened their livelihood. Worries would only feed more negativity. Plus, this was the last time Lydia would be involved for any reason. No more secrecy. No more lies.

Her eyebrow drooped a little lower. She couldn't shake the feeling that she'd just deceived herself. How could she *not* pass along this type of information? Forget about jobs; lives were at stake.

CHAPTER THIRTY-TWO

Lydia's heart skipped when she heard a knock on her front door a few hours later. She kicked some toys under the couch, her breath still ragged after the frantic clean up. It still hadn't sunk in that Michael Malvisti was coming to see her.

Well, not *her* exactly. He needed the latest document Chris had slipped her.

She opened the door before he could ring the bell and wake the boys. Other than Mr. Mahoney and Robby, they had never seen a man in this house, and she had no idea how to explain one.

Even if it was just her employer's attorney.

"Come on in!" She beamed, happy that she was able to manage a fairly normal smile after a short after-dinner rest on the couch. "Pretend you don't see the mess, the sneakers, or the fact that I'm in my oldest jeans." She looked down at the hole in her knee that had grown larger in the last half-hour.

"Not to worry. Everything looks fine." He smiled as he handed her his overcoat. She recognized the clothing label from the most exclusive men's shop in Buffalo.

"You wouldn't have been able to say that with a straight face an hour ago."

They laughed as they re-introduced themselves. More relaxed now, she led him down the hall to the kitchen. "I put together an antipasto.

You probably haven't had much time to eat with the town hall meeting going on." She poured him some water, and then removed Italian bread from the oven.

"You're right, I'm starving." He pulled out a counter stool and sat.

"I'm still trying to process what we heard today."

"Especially the last part. That revelation about the blue pike kept people there for hours. They wanted to hear every last detail about the testing, the next steps, you name it." He ripped off the end of the warm loaf.

"I had no idea those fish were such a big deal."

"My grandfather used to talk about them all the time. No one could ever figure out why they disappeared from the lakes." He dipped a chunk in olive oil and herbs. "Do you make your own bread?"

"I do. I like to know what's in my boys' food." She pushed the antipasto closer to him.

"Have some cheese and olives."

"This bread tastes a lot like my grandmother's."

"I'll take that as a compliment." The highest, coming from a man brought up in a traditional Italian family. "Two restaurants use Annunziata Malvisti's dough recipe." Lydia opened the freezer and allowed herself a private smile.

"I had no idea."

"For dessert, I've got some homemade *cucidati*. I make them every Easter." She unzipped a plastic bag and took out a dozen of the fig-filled cookies to thaw. She elbowed the freezer door to close it.

"I may never leave." He speared an olive and it disappeared into his mouth. "You'll have to roll me out of here, against my will."

"Trust me, if my boys wake up you'll be running for your life." She hoped they wouldn't awaken after Michael let out a full-throated laugh. "They're a handful."

"Kids don't scare me," he said, causing Lydia's heart to skip a beat. "Long ago, I had a large, noisy extended family."

"Me too." She decided to keep the tone light and leave out the fact that most of her family had died. She switched on the coffeemaker and took out the white bag Chris had given her. After all, that's why Michael Malvisti had come over.

"Ahh … the doughnut man strikes again. I was hoping to run into him at this morning's meeting. I saw him walk in." He removed his suit jacket and hung it on the back of the counter stool.

Lydia tried not to stare at his athletic build. He wasn't as tall or beefy as Tyler, but pretty close. "You've had a delivery before today?"

"More like a pickup." He grabbed a cookie. "How do you know our mutual friend?"

"We went to high school together." She wiped some crumbs off the counter.

"Really?" Michael unrolled the bag. He pulled out the stack of half-size papers. "I pegged him for a middle-aged, modernized version of a hippie. Maybe a tree-hugger. He must be younger than I thought." A twinkle appeared in his eyes. "Or you're older than you look."

Lydia playfully swiped the plate from the counter.

"I'm sorry, I'll stay in line." Laughing outright, he reached over the counter and snatched another *cucidati* right off the plate in her hand. "These are great. Made the right way, with fresh figs."

"Thanks." She held up the coffee decanter. "Decaf?"

"Please."

She poured them each a mug full of the brew and together they moved to the family room. Michael spread out the pages of the study on Lydia's coffee table.

She turned on the gas fireplace while he scanned the document. She had a good opportunity to study him while he read. Movie star good looks, that's what Dana had said more than once. Wavy dark hair … squared chin. Lydia forced herself to look away before he caught her staring.

After about five minutes, Michael sat back on the couch and looked up. Concern darkened his hazel-green eyes. "Tyler told me you're worried about bringing this to our attention. That took a lot of courage."

"I don't feel brave. I'm getting secret information disguised as food from a tree hugger. In non-recyclable paper bags no less. And just to make matters worse," she paused, letting her finger hang in the air. "I've kept it from Dana, my best friend and business partner. You may have guessed that she would not handle it well."

"Believe me, I too have discovered a whole new side of myself in recent weeks. Cloak and dagger stuff, compared to my relatively sedate responsibilities as a lawyer. I haven't even talked to Rebecca Waters about the details yet. I know how you feel."

"I really need my job, Mr. Malvisti." Lydia perched herself on the arm of the couch. "But I also feel uncomfortable having access to this type of information and not sharing it."

"It's Michael." He picked up the first page again. "You're doing the right thing. The truth will come out as we nail down facts. And it should."

Lydia tucked a foot under her leg. "This report is pretty old. Was it kept under wraps since the '80s?"

"I don't know." He skimmed the last page. "You probably know this, but much of the property discussed in this paper was owned by my family."

She nodded. She'd read the anti-Hessley web site, just like the rest of the Hessley employees.

"For the most part, I've been kept out of the family business." He sipped his coffee. "I don't know much about Malvisti Industries' history, but I'm trying to learn more."

"Will you tell me about your career? I mean, you've accomplished so much, and, compared to me, you're still such a *young* man."

Michael's eyes crinkled. "There's not much to know." He loosened his tie and sat back on the couch. He told her about growing up in the area as the son and grandson of a prominent family. He described what it was like to attend private schools, travel to Italy, and spend summers at the country club pool. The family drifted apart, he told her, after his dad moved his branch of the family to Florida.

She could empathize, even though Michael grew up in a world light years apart from her own blue-collar upbringing.

"I miss the old ways of our clan," He got up and snagged two more cookies from the plate on the counter. "We were close then, you know. We spent a lot of time with our grandparents, cousins … just together. Mostly eating." He returned to the couch and dipped one of the *cucidati* in his coffee. "Speaking of which, your cookies also taste similar to my grandmother's. They're fantastic."

"Thank you." Lydia savored the moment. He was quite possibly the best-looking man she'd ever seen. And here he was, sitting in her family room, enjoying her cooking. *The* Michael Malvisti. Her head spun, but she kept her cool. "Our family was close, too. I miss that stability. I miss my dad, uncles, grandparents …" Her voice trailed off as she privately tallied the losses. They were down to five people in her family, and that was including Mr. Mahoney.

"I'm sorry to hear that." He sipped his coffee. "May I ask about the boys' dad?"

"Sure." She studied the floor. "He died several years ago. We were in a car accident. DWI."

"Oh, I'm sorry." He set down his coffee. "I hope that person spends a long time in jail."

"It was my husband who was drunk." Lydia felt her face flush. The shame of it still haunted her.

"I apologize for bringing that up." His neck reddened. "It's none of my business."

"That's okay. Harrison was a baby, and I was pregnant with Travis. Neither of the boys remembers him."

"Seems like you've been through a lot these past few years."

Her heart raced. This man was so ... solid. Sure of himself, but not in a conceited way. She hardly knew him, but she had the irrational desire to throw herself in his arms and cry for a long, long time. Instead, she got up and poured more coffee for them both.

It was all she could do to keep her hands from shaking when she handed his cup back to him.

They talked a little more about families. About the Malvisti name and the sometimes unfavorable responses he'd gotten at the mention of it. He seemed wistful. Nothing like the prideful Councilman Sal Malvisti she knew by reputation. She was pleasantly surprised to discover that he wasn't anything like the rest of them.

"It's got to be eleven-thirty by now." He checked his phone. "Whoa. I need to get going. I've got somewhere to be in the morning, and then a flight back to Tampa."

"I've really enjoyed talking with you."

"Me too." He gathered up the loose pages of the study and shrugged into his suit jacket. He carried his other coat on his arm. He filched another *cucidati*.

Lydia wondered what sort of goodbye was appropriate. After all, they'd discussed both business *and* deeply personal matters.

"Hang on, I've got something for you." She wrapped a paper plate containing some cookies and handed it to him.

"Thank you." He gripped the package. "Thank you for everything."

"You're welcome." She pointed to the plate. "Don't eat them all in one day. They're figs after all."

"But how can I resist?" He laughed.

After he'd walked out, she leaned against the inside of the door. She caught remnants of his expensive-smelling cologne. Snatches of their conversation returned to her. She regretted every negative thought she'd ever had about Michael Malvisti just because he was a member of *that* family.

But tonight didn't change the fact that she was done entangling herself in the environmental woes surrounding the Green City. Chris would have to publicize his own doughnut bag goodies. And Tyler and Michael would have to investigate their own concerns. She'd stick with real estate and her boys.

A light rap startled her. She opened the door. The chilly spring air carried the faint smell of earthworms and fresh dirt.

Michael's square jaw was set. "There's a man getting into the back seat of an SUV across the street. He just yelled some pretty ugly things to the woman standing in the doorway. Do you know them?" He pointed at Mara's house. "I want to make sure she's safe. Looks like your neighbor's concerned too."

Lydia stood on tiptoe to peer over Michael's shoulder. She saw Mr. Mahoney at the end of his driveway watching Mara's house.

The driver did a U-turn and headed down the street toward them. It picked up speed as it passed under a street lamp.

Michael turned and squinted. "It's got government plates."

Even in the dark she recognized the vehicle. Although the bumper had been fixed, it was unmistakably the same truck and driver she'd hit in the church lot.

Lydia bit her lip. She didn't want to be a witness to anything, least of all something political. Or worse, criminal. She'd already done enough. But she couldn't lie. "I ... I think it's your Uncle Sal."

Michael's face froze. "Thanks again, Lydia." He jumped down the front stairs and drove off in a hurry.

No more involvement. Of any kind. Not even for the very good-looking man who'd given her one of the nicest evenings she'd had in a long time.

She had to face facts. It was just her and her boys, and maybe Mr. Mahoney, trying to survive in an out-of-control world.

CHAPTER THIRTY-THREE

Michael eased to a stop outside Cascata Verde's newest marvel, a twenty-room eco-boutique hotel nestled within the vineyard district. Buckets of rain falling from the sky could not detract from the beauty of this stone and cedar building. The slow-turning white turbines in the distance added to the peaceful setting. A rested and contented-looking Suzanna appeared in the front doors held open by two bell captains.

Michael used his handkerchief to wipe rainwater that had splashed across the seat of his rental car. He then loped around to the other side to help his pregnant co-worker into the car.

"I'm wearing the same skirt that I had on yesterday, I know." Suzanna plopped into the passenger's seat. "It's the only thing that fits."

"You look very nice. And don't worry. I'm wearing the same thing as yesterday, too." He slid behind the wheel, trying to ignore the rainwater dripping off his hair. It took ten minutes to drive across the community. He parked on a quiet residential street that emptied into the main square where the church was located. He brought the umbrella to Suzanna's door, nearly bumping into a group of men walking along the sidewalk next to him. Other umbrella-toting men and women braved the weather behind the first group.

"Do you think they're all going to the church?" Michael helped Suzanna stand. He kept the umbrella directly over her head.

"Yeah, Sherlock." Suzanna shot him a playful grin. "They're all carrying Bibles."

She was right. He noticed that most wore jeans or khakis. No one sported a suit like him. Michael felt self-conscious as they entered the front door. A drywall subcontractor recognized him and nodded.

He smiled back.

"Good morning." A casually dressed Pastor Amos shook Michael's hand vigorously. "I was hoping you'd visit sometime. Welcome to our service." He introduced himself to Suzanna.

"Thank you." Michael parked his wet umbrella near the fireplace hearth. "Rebecca Waters asked me to come by and see how things are coming along. I stick out like a sore thumb." Michael indicated his business attire. He helped Suzanna remove her coat.

"We don't care what you look like." Pastor Amos offered a welcoming smile. "We're just glad you're here."

A squat man whose bald head shone with rainwater joined them. A white and red badge sewn to his electrician's uniform said 'Tom.' "Mr. Malvisti, sit with us up front. We're working overtime to finish a few buildings in the commercial district, but we always take a break on Sunday mornings to come here."

"Thanks." Michael and Suzanna followed him, grabbing the last two free seats in the middle of a row of chairs. He felt the weight of many eyes tracking him. Hadn't they ever seen a Malvisti in church?

Unless it was a funeral, he certainly had not.

"What do you think goes on in this place?" Michael whispered to Suzanna as he looked around for some type of printed program. He wiped damp hands on rain-soaked pants.

"I don't do church, remember?" She handed him a tissue.

"Why'd you come today?"

"Moral support, luv." Suzanna patted his knee. "For you. And Rebecca's gone on and on about this Pastor Amos. Nothing negative, but she seems curious about him. I wanted to see for myself what's going on."

"So you're here for the gossip." He returned the knee pat. "Noble."

"Let's stand to praise the Lord on this glorious morning!" Pastor Amos appeared behind a simple, square lectern at the front of the church. Scattered behind him rested an assortment of stools and instruments.

Amos selected an electric guitar and settled himself on the stool closest to the mic on the lectern. A man from the audience took his seat at the drum set, which had been hidden from Michael's sight by the podium.

Michael's pulse beat a little quicker. He'd never heard of drums played in church.

A young guy in torn jeans and a baseball shirt grabbed a bass guitar. He helped a petite woman adjust the height of her bench at a digital piano. The band broke into a contemporary song. Michael stole a glance at Suzanna. She didn't seem nearly as shocked as he felt.

Amos's strong voice carried throughout the room. The slight woman provided vocal harmony as she played the piano.

Suzanna caught Michael looking at her. "You've got that deer-in-the-headlights look," she whispered. "Chill out. Go with it."

The people in front of him raised their arms high in the air. Someone clapped. Others joined in all over the room. Michael buried his hands deep in his front pockets. Feeling conspicuous, he pulled them out and clasped them together in front. Sweat gathered at the nape of his neck. For a brief second, he wondered whether Lydia Vallone went to church, and, if so, whether she was part of this energetic audience. He stole a look around.

He and Suzanna were the only ones not singing. He squeezed his shoulders together, trying to shrink away or disappear altogether.

The next song carried a slow beat. Suzanna did the unthinkable. She opened her mouth and sang, her voice growing in confidence as she learned the words. She steepled her heavily ringed fingers and rested them across her stomach.

Michael was on his own now. The *only* person in the room not participating. His cheeks burned. He considered walking out, feigning a coughing attack. But then he envisioned the service screeching to a halt while people ran to assist him. He tried to regulate his breath and appear as inconspicuous as possible.

After what seemed like an hour, but was probably only twenty minutes, Pastor Amos set down his guitar and pulled the stool closer to the podium. He removed a Bible from somewhere inside. Duct tape striped the disintegrated binding of the book. Sticky notes poked out from the middle. He turned the copy over in hands before opening his mouth, his expression sober.

"I had a sermon planned." The pastor scanned the faces in the front row. "But today, something else is pressing on my heart. It's not something preachers normally talk about, but I believe it's got to be said. Today."

"Do it, Pastor." A man in the back encouraged him.

"Amen," the guitar player answered.

"For most of my adult life, I was active duty military. I've always exercised. Eaten right. I don't have too many bad health habits. But after a recent long run around Cascata Verde, I noticed something that stopped me in my tracks."

The congregation, Michael noticed, sat absolutely still.

"I'm getting older."

Suzanna chuckled. "Me too," she turned and mouthed to Michael.

"The mid-section here is just a little bit softer." Amos slapped his stomach, which appeared to Michael to be rock hard. "I was just a tad bit more out of breath than usual for my ten-mile run. I tried to read a notice posted near the pier and no matter how close I got, I couldn't focus my eyes to read it. To make matters worse, I ran my fingers through my hair in frustration and ... it seemed thinner to me."

Several men nodded knowingly.

"It's happening. I'm aging." He smiled. "Now some of you have the answers. I'll get the emails after this service: 'Try this gel for your hair,' 'eat more antioxidant-rich foods, or 'cut sugar.'"

A man next to Michael grunted. "He's talked to my girlfriend, no doubt."

"And you're all correct. All of those things will probably enrich the quality of my life, and perhaps help me look better and live longer. And we should care for our physical selves, right?" Heads bobbed in agreement.

"But guess what?" He kept his eyes on the bamboo floor. "No matter what I do, I'm still aging. There will come a day when my body will give out and I'll die. The Bible tells us that, although mankind was created perfect and in the image of God, the process of decay is the result of man—people—choosing to disobey God in the Garden of Eden. Because of man's choice, physical death and disease are now part of our existence. So, for now, at least, our bodies are in bondage to that steady march toward the end. But even though we know death is a certainty, we can and *should* take certain steps to stay healthy, right?"

"Sure, Pastor." One of the electricians behind Michael shouted out.

Michael wasn't quite sure where this was going.

"Folks, the rest of Creation—animals, fish, plants, trees, soil—is in that process of decay, too." Pastor Amos caught Michael's eye. "Like mankind, it was created perfect by God. But when man introduced sin into the world, Creation suffered alongside man. The Bible puts it this way in Romans eight, verse twenty:

For the creation was subjected to frustration, not by its own choice, but by the will of the one who subjected it, in hope that the creation itself will be liberated from its bondage to decay and brought into the freedom and glory of the children of God.

The Apostle Paul, the writer of Romans, presents a powerful image of Creation in agony as it waits to be freed from its bondage. He writes that the 'whole creation has been groaning as in the pains of childbirth right up to the present time.'"

Michael had no idea.

"And just as we can't completely reverse the process of aging, we can't completely fix what has been destroyed or used up on this Earth. But that doesn't mean we don't try. We can care for God's Creation, just as we do our physical bodies. In fact, we're commanded to in Genesis." Pastor Amos read a passage about stewardship over the Earth.

Interesting. Michael had never thought about people being directed by God to care for natural resources. As far as he knew, environmentalism was something straight out of the '70s. Something influenced more by the Love Canal disaster than anything in the Bible.

"And someday, my friends, there will be a permanent restoration of Creation, just as our bodies will also someday be made new again."

"Amen!" a woman spoke up from the front row. Others voiced their agreement.

Made sense. But why was this preacher talking about the environment in the first place?

"So, believers, until that day when God restores all of His Creation, how do we respond to a natural world in decay? Do we simply use less plastic? Put out the recycling bin? Eat vegetarian, or refuse to buy fur?"

No one answered. Surely the Bible didn't address any of those things.

"For starters, we use the Earth's resources responsibly. We're called to care for God's Creation, and not harm the Earth unnecessarily. I think most people would agree with that."

"Yeah, Pastor." A man shouted from somewhere in the back.

"But I think there's more, especially for Christians. I believe we're called to participate in God's plan to bring everything—mankind, the Earth, and every part of it—back into a right relationship with Him. It's God's plan to right things that became broken when disobedience entered the picture. He calls it reconciliation. And the Word of God says that he's reconciling to Himself *all things* through Jesus Christ. That includes *all* of His Creation. The environment included. These are some heavy-duty concepts, I know. But I want you to start thinking on a practical level as we start this new series. So, let's start with some basics. If we're called to participate in God's redemptive plan, then what does that mean?"

Pastor Amos scanned the room. A few people filtered in from the foyer entrance to the side of them.

"Let's take it down to the most fundamental level: as Christians, we pursue and practice what Jesus taught. So, it's logical to ask ourselves what *did* he do? He spoke truth—every time, even when to do so upset the civil and religious authorities of the time. He humbled himself, taking the very nature of a human baby, no less. He confronted hypocrites, especially those who considered themselves religious leaders. He exposed deceivers who profited at the expense of the oppressed. He served others, loved others, and sacrificed for others. He restored broken people and things. He never bowed to intimidation. And he always communed with the Father, holding himself accountable to His will.

That's what He did.

Let's strive to interact with the natural world and with each other in the same way. Let's do business with transparency. Let's not lie about the numbers or fudge testing results. Let's not misrepresent our products or their capabilities. When we see an injustice, especially against the natural world, let's act. There's been an oil spill. Or a leaking landfill. Or a pesticide that kills more than weeds. Do we ignore it? Do we throw our hands in the air and say 'oh, it's too big a problem, there's nothing we can do'? Do we just wring our hands in frustration, or do we speak up?"

"We speak up!" An elderly man in front of them turned to look at Suzanna. "Right, young lady?"

She nodded, visibly moved.

"Yes. As Christians, who love the things God loves, we should be at the forefront in preventing, confronting, and responding to environmental degradation. So, along with truth and justice, let's use love, gratitude, vigilance, and accountability as our guides. We confront wrong things in truth, but we're guided by love. We hold people accountable, but we do it with integrity. It might mean that someone goes to jail. Or that someone has to pay financially. After all, as we humans know all too well, there are consequences to the bad choices we make. But there's also forgiveness. Maybe ... just maybe ... by following after Jesus we can help push society toward a sustainable future that reflects the character of God. Wouldn't that be something to see, folks?"

Michael had never heard such teaching. That he was hearing it in a church was especially surprising.

"If God's plan for restoration centers upon his Son, then we should use Jesus as the model in how to respond to wrong things. I've been wrestling with this message for a while now. For the next few Sundays, we're going to dig down and look at what Jesus actually *did* do. So that we can do it too." Amos stepped back up to the lectern. He turned to face the congregation.

Michael breathed in and held it.

He let out his breath slowly, thoughts swirling through his mind. Did this ... lecture really apply to *him?* Was he even a Christian? Except for the sound of Suzanna's soft crying, the congregation sat in silence. She managed a small, reassuring smile when their eyes met.

Michael took her fingers in his, not sure what to do. A man behind her placed his hand upon her shoulder. Others followed suit. He heard quiet words of encouragement as someone prayed over her. Michael felt like an intruder, silently observing an intimate moment of which he wasn't a part.

He didn't belong here. He clutched her hand more for his benefit than for hers.

"Pastor?" Tom jumped to his feet on the other side of Suzanna.

"Yessir?"

"I need to get something off my chest. It can't wait."

The electrician plowed through others seated in the row, excusing himself until he emerged in the center aisle.

Michael froze. What was he doing? Was this normal in this type of church? He searched the faces of others in the row. They didn't seem alarmed, but many trained their eyes on the floor. Maybe they were praying. Maybe they were as embarrassed for the guy as Michael was.

"Won't take but a minute." The man's face reddened. Hands in pockets, he cleared his throat to speak. But at first no words came out.

Michael's heart beat faster. What was happening?

The electrician's chin quivered. A tear rolled down his face. "I'm guilty of taking some copper wire from the worksite here. I resold it and made a huge profit." The worker covered his eyes with both hands.

Pastor Amos clapped his hand on the man's sloped shoulder. "Keep going, Tom. Get it out."

Michael's hands went from damp to clammy. Tingles pricked his arms, his neck, even his toes. How could this man stand in front of his fellow workers, maybe his boss, and call himself out?

"I'll pay it back, I promise." Tom reached into his pocket and pulled out a single bill. "This is a start." Still visibly upset, the worker stepped off the altar. He stood on tip-toe, as if searching for someone.

Michael couldn't look away. They locked eyes and the man nodded. *At him?* Was he going to apologize to Michael now? Michael wondered if the man saw him as a Malvisti, or as a representative of Hessley Development. He was both, of course, but still he had no idea of how to respond.

The contrite man stood near the end of Michael's row. "Pass this to Mr. Malvisti. I need to do this in front of all of you." He handed the bill to a woman five or six chairs away from Suzanna. The bill worked its way down the seats until it was laid in Michael's palm. The money was as damp as Michael's own hands.

"More to come in the next few weeks, sir." Tom returned to his seat and hung his head. Silent sobs shook his bent body as Suzanna gave him a side hug.

Michael stared at the wrinkled bill. A hundred dollars. What was he supposed to do with it? Give it to Rebecca? It was Hessley that had been cheated. Michael felt the eyes of two hundred people boring into his back.

A poignant piano melody filled the space. Suzanna squeezed his hand tight. An out of shape, bearded man in jeans and a sweatshirt galloped to the platform. They both strained to see what was happening.

The man's breaths came in large, unsteady gulps. "Brothers and sisters, I know what I'm doing when it comes to the installation of wind turbines." He turned his head to the side and tried to slow his breathing. "We worked on a flat-fee basis to install equipment here in the Green City." His voice broke. "I'm ... not proud to say this, but I cut some corners. Turbine number six? That was ... my fault."

Suzanna leaned over to Michael. "That's the one that caught on fire!"

Stunned, Michael nodded. A band of heat clamped down on his heart like an invisible vise. Its loud thuds surely overrode the quiet strands of music surrounding them. He let go of Suzanna's hand and wiped his arm across his forehead.

"I'll try to make it right." The man looked up at the rafters and then at Michael. "God, forgive me ... I knew better. Just glad no one got hurt."

Two women dressed in black, one much older than the other, clung to each other as they took hesitant steps toward the raised altar. Together they collapsed on the first step. "Forgive us, Heavenly Father!" they cried in unison. The older one flattened herself across the bamboo floor of the platform. Sandaled feet poked out from below her dark maxi dress. The younger female stayed upright on her knees, with hands raised toward heaven. "We've fallen in love with your Creation, oh God. *It* became our god, not you. And we've led a lot of other women astray with our take on religion." Sobs exploded from her body. She didn't, or couldn't, continue.

Sweat dripped down Michael's back. He was startled to feel something tugging him forward, but he resisted the overwhelming urge to fall to his knees.

Suzanna grabbed Michael's clammy hand. She slid forward, tossing him an apologetic, but determined, look.

He tightened his hold. "What are you doing?"

She hoisted herself upright, patting his hand before releasing it and turning away. "I gotta do this."

Tom and the rest of those seated between her and the aisle half-stood to let her pass. Her chin quivered when she started up the steps, but she squared her shoulders and looked directly at Pastor Amos where he knelt with the two women in black. Both women gazed up at her from the floor.

"I confess that I've used every empty cliché to navigate through life: 'do what makes sense,' 'do what feels good,' 'do what's best for you,' "go with it,' 'do what's best for others.'" Suzanna threw her head back and squeezed her eyes before continuing. "I bought into so many lies. Sometimes those approaches worked, sometimes they didn't. But I'm sick of the uncertainty, Pastor."

Michael kept his eyes riveted on his friend, willing her to get through this. If only he knew what "this" was.

"I've always felt that there was a better way." Smears of mascara darkened her lids. "A way that doesn't change depending on who you're listening to, or what's in vogue at the moment. One that has consistency."

Suzanna had come here to fill the time, for moral support for him; what was she doing?

"Thank you, Lord!" Someone in the congregation shouted. Prayers were sent up from all over the room. The volume rose and fell, creating a rhythmic cadence that made Michael want to sway. Or run.

"Go on," Amos encouraged her. He reached under the lectern and handed Suzanna a water bottle. She opened it absently, but didn't take a sip.

"But now I see why Jesus is *the* Way. He's the embodiment of God's plan to right all of the wrongs in this world. I'm not sure that I know what that all entails, but I want to learn and to follow Him." She smiled through the waterworks that stained her face.

Shouts broke from those still in their seats. Many people filled the aisles or made their way forward. "Praise God!" and "amen" could be heard mixed among the prayers. Michael loosened his tie. He was at a loss to explain what was happening. Judging by the whispered prayers of thanks coming from those around him, he guessed that these outbursts weren't happening every week.

The older woman in black raised herself to a sitting position and grabbed Suzanna's hand.

More amens shot out from the back. Michael turned, surprised to see dozens of teens standing on the ledge outlining the round fireplace in the entrance hall, their heads rising above a sea of expectant faces. More people poured through the front door. *So many people.* When had they arrived? Did they know that something different was taking place here?

When Michael looked back to Suzanna, he saw that a line of congregants had formed near the lectern. Were they all going to confess something?

A distraught, heavy-set woman confessed to adultery. Her best friend's husband. She wept, seeking forgiveness from God.

A tattooed teen revealed that he'd lied about a co-worker to get her fired.

The fervent prayers intensified around Michael. Most people had their hands raised. A few knelt on the floor. Still others streamed up the crowded aisle.

A shaky, older woman owned up to faking a resume entry to secure a job at Cascata Verde.

A tall blonde admitted to inflating her prices for sustainable baked goods sold in the Green City.

A man Michael recognized as a small wind turbine representative told the congregation that he had overstated the wind energy capacity of his products.

Who knew man's limits for finding a way to behave badly?

More than one person directed their confession to Michael, as if he represented the Community itself. Hessley personified. Embarrassed, he held his body rigid until he lost track of the confessions. They poured forth from the young and old alike. Pain and pent-up guilt found an outlet. The burdens carried by these people ... there seemed to be no end. The experience remained a mystery.

But more than that, one thought overrode all others swirling around Michael's mind: *No one here should be seeking forgiveness from a Malvisti.*

CHAPTER THIRTY-FOUR

Near Tampa, Florida

Michael shifted the GT-R into low gear, saddened by the sight of the skeletal man and his emaciated dog dawdling outside the coffee shop. A matched pair. Still waiting to die.

He pulled between the diagonal lines painted on the road. Michael stuck his head out the window. "Can I take you up on that cup of coffee, sir?"

"I can barely hear you over that rumbling machine of yours. You buying me a cup of joe?" A happy smile spread wider than the old man's shoulders. He let out Clary's leash.

Michael shut off the engine, stepped out, and hurried through the potted palm barrier. Clary noisily sniffed Michael's pants and then sought out his hand. She shook her head and sneezed. Even Clary could smell the Western New York gloom he'd brought back with him. "Do you have a few minutes?"

"Well, we have a busy day planned of walking, wandering ... doing a crossword puzzle or two." The old man wound up the leash. Michael thought he looked more gaunt than when they first met. A worn gray sweater with stretched front pockets hung from the old guy's shoulders. The familiar blue polyester shirt collar poked out around his neck.

Clary turned in awkward circles before settling down under a plastic outdoor table. She sniffed Michael's pants again when he took a seat.

"I neglected to get your name when we first met, sir."

"Friends call me Duff." Clary's ears perked up. Her owner pulled a dog treat out of his drooping pocket and tossed it between her paws. Her tail slapped the sidewalk. "I get these organic biscuits next door. She's crazy about them." The way Duff sung the last phrase made Michael unsure whether it was a statement or question.

"Were you born in Niagara Falls ... Duff?" He felt strange addressing the elder man by his first name.

"No, no. Gdansk, Poland. Nineteen and thirty-two."

That explained the lingering accent. Michael nudged a dropped piece of the biscuit back to Clary. "Why did you come to America?"

"Necessity." Duff propped an elbow on the table. "My parents were worried about our safety. And rightly so. All kinds of evil soon crushed our homeland."

"Hmm." Michael thought about the rise of Hitler's regime. Rumors must've reached Poles even in the early '30s.

"We had some relatives leave before we did. They settled in Buffalo, probably because it was a port city like Gdansk."

"Did you come through Ellis Island?"

"Sure did, Mr. Malvisti—"

"Michael, please."

"All right. So a few years after our cousins left, we made our way to Buffalo. I started working at fourteen in the National Gypsum plant in Niagara Falls. Picked up a second job or two hauling waste, working on various construction jobs. Then settled down with my wonderful wife." Duff's voice quavered. He leaned back and signaled the waitress inside the shop.

"Hey Clary-girl." The red-haired server set a stainless steel bowl full of water under the table. It splashed, soaking Michael's leather dress shoe. "Oooh ... I'm so sorry!"

"That's okay, Pam." Duff chuckled. "Mr. Malvisti can take it. He's young and strong. Maybe even single."

Michael shrugged, almost wishing that were the case. Some days with Jillian left him confused. Most days, if truth be told.

The young server blushed. She hurried back into the coffee shop.

"It sounds like you had a happy marriage." Michael looked thoughtfully at Duff. "I'm not sure that I've actually ever seen one."

"A good marriage?" Duff asked. "Yes, but that doesn't mean it was easy. Plenty of hard times, but we came through them together. At least until she died." Duff leaned forward to stroke Clary's head. "It's me and this old girl, now." He looked up at Michael. "How about you, son? Any marriage plans?"

Michael shifted.

"Uh oh, some difficulties with the ladies I see." Duff chuckled again. Clary sat up to lick his knee.

"One difficulty in particular. We've been together for some time, but I'm just not sure if she's the right one. She yo-yos from happy to unhappy most of the time."

"Would she say the same about you?"

"Probably."

"Well then, it seems that some type of decision needs to be made."

"That's the rub." Michael sat back. "I'm not equipped to make these types of relationship decisions. One day I'm frustrated, and the next I can see us staying together. It depends on the day, sometimes the hour."

Unexpectedly, an image of Lydia Vallone bearing a plate of cookies flashed in his mind. Her pretty smile encouraged him to take the plate. He felt his cheeks heat up. Comfort food, nothing more.

Duff's rheumy eyes widened. "Something else you want to say?"

"I'm just not sure about a lot of things, especially when it comes to relationships."

"Lots of people feel that way, son. A fella I knew divorced his wife, married another gal, but never shook the feelings of restlessness or doubt he had with the first wife."

"Sounds familiar."

"You don't have to be tossed about like those ocean waves over there. Or misguided by ridiculous philosophies. There's an anchor for the soul, Mr. Michael, firm and secure. Yes, there is."

"What's that?" He leaned over to pet Clary's head. She nipped at the spot where her back leg used to be.

"His name is Jesus."

Michael looked up quickly, eyebrows raised. "Been hearing a lot about Him lately." He didn't want to tell the old man about the events at the church two days ago. He hadn't yet sorted through what occurred or his own feelings about the service.

"Well then," Duff's eyes twinkled. "It would seem that the Almighty has something to say."

It wouldn't be the first time this week.

They sat in the sunshine for a few minutes more. Again, Lydia came to mind. He thought about mentioning her to Duff, but decided against it. Enough self-disclosure for one day.

"Michael," Duff said, serious now. "Nothing stands if Christ is not the foundation. Not a person, not a family, not a city. And certainly not a marriage. I encourage you to do some business with God before you start making those types of life-changing decisions."

Michael nodded. "Thank you for today." They stood up and shook hands. Clary scrambled up from under the table. "I'm looking forward to seeing you again soon." He anchored a five-dollar bill with Duff's empty coffee mug.

"I'm heading up to Niagara Falls within the week. I hear the fishing just got real good. I've missed those blue pike something awful. Just want to catch one before I'm too old." Duff returned Michael's bill. "This one's on me, son."

Marriage talk nagged at Michael as he crossed the Sunshine Skyway. He thought about Duff and his wife, and wondered whether Jillian would ever pine after him if he died. She'd move on quickly, he decided. Lydia, on the other hand … she'd be a different story. Grandma Ziatta would've liked that girl. And her cooking. He couldn't suppress the smile that crept across his face.

By the time he reached the office, Michael was no closer to an answer on anything. Later he would set aside time to think. Right now, since dozens of messages clamored for his attention, he shifted his attention to work matters, including a text from Rebecca that she was on her way to his office to talk.

How early had she gotten to work? Then again, he wouldn't be surprised if she slept at the office. The woman was married to this company. It wasn't lost on him that building a green city could take over his life, too, if he let it.

CHAPTER THIRTY-FIVE

Michael blew on the hot coffee Rebecca had handed him as she walked in his office. Nice gesture, but something other than kindness motivated it. His boss normally couldn't stand the thought of the stuff. Too many pesticides or fungicides are used on coffee crops, she'd often warned.

She got right to the point. "Tell me about Amos's church. Every detail. Start to finish."

He'd hoped to avoid an interrogation this early in the day, but he needed to at least alert her to the strange turn of events on Sunday. "It was, let's say, different."

"Different from what?" Rebecca parked herself on the corner of his desk.

"From anything that I was used to as a kid. The last time I was in church, priests followed a program, you know?" Michael decided to ease her into it. "The first part of this ... service, I guess, was more like a teaching seminar in a casual atmosphere."

"What did he teach?" Rebecca crossed her legs.

"The Bible." He set down his coffee. "He probably could use a new copy. His is worn out."

"That's it?" Rebecca leaned closer to Michael's side of the desk. "Give me something more to go on here. Too many people are in and out of that place."

"He talked about how Christians should respond to environmental disasters." That was something.

Rebecca frowned.

"After that, things sort of exploded."

"Go on." Rebecca's green eyes narrowed.

"It was as if something had awakened in that building." Michael searched for the words to describe what he'd witnessed. "Lots of people got up and confessed to wrongs they'd committed. You should've heard some of this stuff. I left exhausted after two and half hours."

"Why would they do that?" She stood and faced him. "Give me an example."

How to describe the admissions pouring forth from the pulpit? Rebecca would find out about them sooner or later. It was Hessley, after all, that had been deceived by many of them. He pulled his wallet out of his suit pocket. "Here." He handed her the money Tom had passed to him. "A Hessley contractor confessed to theft. Now he wants to make good."

Rebecca took the folded bill. "Is this a joke?" She turned it over in her hand.

"Don't think so. Seemed genuine."

Suzanna appeared in the doorway. She cradled a steaming cup of herbal tea in her hands. A smile lit up her face. "Did you hear, guys? Something similar happened in churches all over Niagara County yesterday. I saw it on Facebook." She headed toward an empty chair in his office.

Michael hurried around the desk to pull it out for her. Her belly seemed to have popped overnight.

"Explain to me what happened up there. Is it connected to Cascata Verde?" Rebecca pulled out her smartphone.

"I think it's connected to our Creator." The smile covering Suzanna's face was contagious. "I didn't want to go away from that building. Leaving felt like walking out of the presence of God Himself."

Something hardened in Rebecca's demeanor. Rigid fingers poked at her phone. She squared her shoulders as she swiped across the screen. "Something unusual took place at a hospital chapel too. Weak minds. Mass hysteria."

"I don't think so. I'm pretty smart." The smell of red raspberry tea intensified. "The whole experience blew my mind. The understanding I gained, the feeling of peace ... incredible."

Rebecca stood. "Your pregnancy is magnifying things." She bid them a productive day, and walked out of the room with the same square set to her shoulders.

"Did you tell her about the babies?" Accusation flashed in Suzanna's eyes.

"Absolutely not." He got up and shut his office door. "She's no dummy. She's probably noticed that you're wearing the same skirt a lot these days. And, you left lemon candy and Saltines on your desk last week. Dead giveaways."

"How would you know that?"

"My assistant." He sank back into his seat. "She's been onto you for a while now."

She sipped her tea, scrunching up her face at the flavor.

His phone beeped and email alerts indicated four new messages. He ignored them. The church matter consumed him. He needed to know what he'd witnessed. What he felt. Maybe he should've mentioned it to Duff—the guy sure seemed certain about his faith.

"What happened to you at that church, Suzie?" There had to be some logical explanation. "You smiled, cried, sang, and cried some more, all in the space of a few minutes. Was that just pregnancy, or what?"

"I don't think so. I had a breakthrough of some kind. Things made sense to me for once." She placed her hands around her bulging stomach.

Michael had to admit that he too had felt something that morning. The undeniable *presence* of something far greater than any mere human in that building. Michael studied her closely. "Where did you put my free-spirited, don't-put-me-in-a-box friend?"

Suzanna lumbered to her feet. She aimed for the door, opening it wide. When she looked back at him, her smile confirmed that something had changed.

"Just don't get crazy on me with this religion thing, okay?"

But Suzanna wasn't listening. As she walked out, he recognized the tune she hummed as one they sang on Sunday.

If only he had that same certainty.

CHAPTER THIRTY-SIX

December 28, 2003

By the mid-1970s Salvatore and Joe, Jr. knew the landfill business inside and out. It was time for a change of control.

The twins, now married men in their thirties, had their own ideas about how to run Malvisti Industries. The profession had grown complex, they repeatedly told me. New technology would allow us to dispose of double or maybe triple the volume of chemical and radiological waste.

Formal training in engineering, chemistry, and business were necessary to grow the company. My boys had that education. I was in my sixties and lacked a degree, but I wasn't useless.

The changeover was inevitable, but it would have to proceed slowly. And on my terms, of course.

I chose our annual Christmas Eve bash to announce my intentions. My boys would commit to the business in front of a sizeable mix of family and close friends. Public pressure on these young men would raise the stakes and heighten the pressure to excel, which is never a bad thing.

"Gather 'round, folks." I stood in our festive family room and clinked a spoon against the heavy crystal goblet in my hand. "I have an announcement before we leave for midnight mass." Through the small lead-paned windows of our room, I saw thick snowflakes piling up on bare tree limbs. Inside, our home brimmed with slightly tipsy guests and the savory smell of sausage, peppers and onions. The meal would be served late, after the midnight Christmas service. In all, it was the perfect setting for such a momentous announcement.

"Sal, Joe, come stand next to the fire with your old man." I moved over, accidentally brushing up against the twinkling colored lights of our seven-foot Fraser fir. They joined me, standing closer to the fire. "Someone call the women out of the kitchen."

My wife's teenaged niece jumped to her feet and disappeared through a swinging door. Guests hurriedly stubbed out cigarettes or grabbed a handful of Italian cookies before taking a seat on the couches grouped in front of the hearth. Several women emerged from the kitchen. Most stayed close to the door, as did our niece.

"*Buon Natale!*" I held the goblet of wine in the air.

"Merry Christmas!" The sound of people clanking their glasses rippled across the great family room. I heard the oversized logs in the hearth shift, no doubt launching sparks against the iron grate behind us.

I took a step away from the roaring fire after the heat made me sway a bit. My sons followed suit. Sweat beaded on Joe's temple and he looked uncomfortable. Probably too much heat.

"Thanks be to God for the opportunity to celebrate this special holiday with family and friends. In Italy we used to say *durare da Natale a Santo Stefano*, which means roughly 'no time at all.' It refers to the one-day interval between Christmas and the feast of St. Stephen. Folks, my life has raced along at that speed. It's been exhilarating. And endlessly fulfilling. But it's time for some changes."

"Amen," my wife murmured, causing a few women to chuckle. She stood close to the kitchen door, partially hidden by a large *presepe*, our nativity scene. She put an arm around her niece.

"Sal and Joe have worked hard for Malvisti Industries and I have great confidence in their abilities." Servers filtered into the room carrying silver trays laden with glasses of *spumante*. "The sky is the limit for these two. They have degrees. They have experience. They are proven businessmen. It is with great pride that I turn over the majority of both ownership and control of Malvisti Industries to my sons." I looked up at my strapping boys, both of whom had about five inches on me. Sal's eyes shone. He'd been waiting for this moment all his adult life. Joe, Jr., on the other hand, seemed preoccupied with a piece of silver tinsel clinging to his arm.

"Congratulations, men." I tried to catch Joe, Jr.'s eye.

Guests shouted approval. Annunziata came toward us, tears in her eyes.

"Thank you for the honor, Papa." Sal pumped my hand. Then he threw his thick arms around my neck. "I'll make you proud."

"I know you will." I returned his embrace.

I leaned over to Joe, Jr., and the smile on my lips died away. Sweat streamed down his cheeks. His eyes shifted between the ground and my face. My gut urged me to pull him aside and see what was going through his mind. But the announcement had been made. Already, a line of people had formed to shake hands with the new majority owners of Malvisti Industries. Laughter and joyous conversation filled the smoky room.

After that Christmas night, Joe operated in the background, leaving his brother to be the public face of our business and philanthropic efforts. He remained a part of the company, and even supported his brother during each of Sal's successive political runs. But in the late '80s, he moved to Florida with his second wife and Michael, my beloved grandson. It broke my wife's heart when they left.

It crushed my heart more, though I never told Joe or my wife. Real men didn't admit to such things back then. But the fact is, I forced them to move. That's a story for another part of this memoir. I can't bring myself to write about that yet.

My failure to investigate the reason for his uneasiness was a mistake. I should have probed Joe's heart and mind. I should have drawn him aside that very night, that year, or *sometime* in the next two decades. Then I would have learned the real reason for his ambivalence.

The man had a conscience. He just wasn't strong enough to act on it. Or to stand up to me.

CHAPTER THIRTY-SEVEN

Tampa, Florida

Two days passed before Michael had a chance to call Ty about the documents Lydia had given him. His friend's faint voice came on the line after the fifth ring "Yo."

"Hey. What do you know about sick deer studies?"

"Talk English, man." Tyler's voice competed with background sounds.

"Get somewhere quiet." Michael paced the length of his office. He'd made sure the door was shut.

"… trying. Not easy. I'm at a Hessley site in Denver running air quality tests. What's up?"

"I've got that information Lydia Vallone called you about a few days ago. An animal study."

"*Deer studies,* got it. I thought you said '*six-year studies*' and I was worried I had forgotten something. Lay it on me."

"I'm not sure what any of this means, but here goes. In the '80s, a nuclear physicist did a deer sampling study near Malvisti Park. He found abnormalities in seventy-five percent of the sampled deer. You want to know what was in the deer livers?"

"Tell me."

"High amounts of radium and cesium. Nothing we want in a park or a community."

Ty stayed quiet.

"There's more."

"Lemme guess. Your name isn't really Michael Malvisti?"

"Close. I don't know that Tomeo's name is really Tomeo Environmental. I couldn't find a physical address, and so I went where you told me you thought it might be. Nothing there. I looked at the state corporation databases and there was only a recently defunct corporation with that name. No current address available."

"Geez … let's get up to Cascata Verde as soon as we can both swing it, Mikey. We're going to do our own—"

"I can't hear you, Ty. You're being drowned out," Michael tried to keep his voice low. His temp assistant worked for other Hessley execs and none of this needed to be whispered elsewhere. "Get somewhere quieter."

"I'm moving." Rustling noises could be heard.

"Much better."

"Call Lydia and ask her to see what else her friend has for us to review. I'd like to talk to him directly. Should we call that reporter that fired off questions at your uncle at the groundbreaking? She used to be at Channel Four, right?"

Michael's head snapped up when someone rapped on his door.

"Just a minute!" He turned toward the window and spoke into the phone. "I think so."

"She knows something worthwhile. Let's get our arms around this thing before we talk to Rebecca. You dig?"

"Yeah." Michael groaned inwardly. "Next few days are going to be tough with work, but I'll make it happen."

A soft knock this time. "Gotta go, Ty." Michael hung up. Annoyed, he took three long strides to the door and flung it open.

Suzanna's growing midsection filled the door frame. Tears traced her cheeks. She held a wadded tissue under her nose. "The deer are *sick?*"

Michael blinked. "How did you—?" He stopped himself and motioned her inside.

"Super-sharp hearing, luv. Ever since the day I got pregnant."

He paced the length of his office.

"And someone posted it to the Internet."

Michael groaned.

"I'm a mess about the innocent animals, sorry." Suzanna sniffed and pulled a tissue from a hidden pocket in the side of her skirt. "But c'mon Michael! We've got to do the right thing here. If people or creatures are in danger, then it's our responsibility to protect them, isn't it?"

"Of course." He slowed, taking in the calming aqua color of the bay outside his window. Boaters loaded drinks and snacks; crafts of all sizes rocking as people jumped aboard. He snapped back to attention. "But Tyler and I need to firm up some facts. The deer study was done over thirty years ago. The property was remediated or properly closed, and tested again and again. We've gotten the all-clear. I've no reason to doubt the science." He turned and met her steady gaze.

"Did they find radioactive materials at Cascata Verde the first time they tested there?"

Michael grimaced. He wasn't sure.

She pushed her hands up. "Just askin'. I'm leaving now, luv. Don't be upset with me. I just can't stop thinking about Pastor Amos's sermon on Sunday. He stressed that God entrusted us with the care of His Creation. Maybe that was meant for our ears in particular." She opened the door wide and tiptoed out backwards.

Her words hit the mark.

He remembered a decay-chain chart from college physics. Radium is a daughter-product of … uranium. *Uranium?* The urgency of the situation suddenly struck him. He pulled out his phone and scanned the Channel Four website for the name of the young female reporter brave enough to challenge Uncle Sal. He scanned a dozen slick headshots. Not a single one resembled the blonde journalist.

He dialed the real estate office at Cascata Verde. He had an excuse ready in case Dana DuPays answered, but he heard Lydia's youthful voice pick up first. A smile sprang to his lips.

"Are you alone in the office?"

She cleared her throat. "No. Did you need me to look something up for you on the Cruller residential contract I just sent?"

"Yes … very clever." Doughnut varieties had taken on new meaning. "Can you find out whether the Crullers have any additional information that they might wish to share?"

"I'll get right back to you on that, Mr. Malvisti."

He hesitated, knowing he was about to cross an undefined boundary. "I had a really nice time Sunday night."

"I thought the same thing about that matter."

Good. He hadn't imagined the easy conversation they'd shared. "I'll be coming back up to the Falls in the next few days. We'll nail down some specifics."

"Take care."

"You too." He almost added. "Keep safe," but thought it might be premature. After all, they had little in the way of hard facts. A few dated studies, all from before the work on the landfill under Malvisti Park or the remediation of the surrounding properties, didn't amount to much. Yet.

Still, he cared about Lydia and her safety was important to him.

So were the animals.

And … he cared about the safety of the people of Niagara Falls. After all, they were all part of God's Creation, too.

CHAPTER THIRTY-EIGHT

Niagara Falls, New York

Lydia stomach roiled. She couldn't lie to Dana again. She peeked under her lashes, hoping not to catch Dana's eye. How could she explain the two-minute conversation with Michael Malvisti without telling a lie?

Dana stayed busy on the laptop docked at her desk.

Lydia decided to bring up another subject. "I'm thinking of checking out Amos's church next week. The place has been packed. Even on some weekdays, I've heard." Lydia tried to act normal. "Do you want to come with me and the boys next Sunday?"

"No, thanks. I'm meeting with a woman who is going to teach me about herbs. I want to prepare myself for the upcoming home buying blitz."

Lydia waited for an explanation to clarify the connection. She narrowed her eyes, hesitant to press. "Do you want to come over for dinner after you meet with her?"

"Maybe."

"I'll ask Angie's family if they want to join us."

"I'll pass then." Dana's icy eyes flashed when she looked up. She fingered the rose-colored amulet around her neck.

"What do you have against her?"

"Jesus freak, hello?" Dana's sneer marred her otherwise gorgeous face.

"I thought you believed in tolerance for whatever path people choose?"

"Her religion is intolerant, so it's excluded."

Lydia let it go. Their friendship was already on shaky ground.

❖

As she pulled in her driveway, Lydia noticed an oversized light-gray envelope leaning against her front door. She looked up and down the street for retreating taillights, but didn't see a soul. She got out of the car quickly.

"How're things over at Miracle City, missy?"

Lydia jumped. Mr. Mahoney sat on his porch with his arms crossed. The wicker loveseat and its striped cushion had become his late afternoon post, even in the chilly, late-spring weather.

"What do you mean?"

"Cascata Verde. I've been following the articles and letters in the newspaper. They say it's a place of miracles and prosperity—what more could the politicians behind it ask for? Do you get what I'm implying?"

She let out a short laugh. Everything traced back to public corruption for Mr. Mahoney. But she didn't have time today for one of his politically charged rants, as amusing as they usually were. Not when a mysterious envelope sat sentry at her door. "Things are coming along well. Phase II is almost complete. The site looks beautiful ... and the first wave of residents seem happy."

"Huh." For once, Mr. Mahoney seemed to have nothing to say.

"Did you see anyone near my house?"

"Nope." He stretched. "Just woke up from a snooze."

Lydia's front door swung open. The boys ran out in their socks to jump on her, each taking a leg. She glanced back at her neighbor. "I'll catch up with you later, Mr. Mahoney."

He tipped an imaginary hat.

Angie bent over to pick up the envelope. Both boys clung to Lydia's hip, their wet socks stained with mud.

She squeezed through the front door with the boys still attached and took the package from her babysitter. "Let's put that away for later. Did you see who delivered it?"

"No. It must have been someone on foot. I can hear when a car pulls up. I heard you." Angie peeled off the boys' socks. She pretended to race them upstairs to change.

Lydia didn't like the thought of someone so close to her home. Or her children. A security system had become a necessity. She could afford such a luxury ... for now.

❖

For hours, the envelope's very presence had irked her. Just reviewing its contents would suck her in deeper. Now that the boys were in bed she had no excuse but to open it. As she flipped it over, she noticed a small triangular symbol in the corner. A recycled envelope. Chris Magnano would be one of the few people who might care about such a thing.

She stole a quick peek inside. More scientific-looking documents, but no doughnut bag this time. She wished Michael could be here, sitting on the couch next to her, puzzling out the past. She breathed in deeply and let out a long, slow breath. Why did the future seem that much more secure when he was around?

Maybe she should call him. He'd want to know about this new information, wouldn't he? She could leave him a message for the morning. She tapped out his number as she simultaneously dumped out a wad of documents.

"Hello?"

Michael answered instead of voicemail, his voice loud enough to be heard over the thumping music in the background. "I think Mr. Cruller made a delivery before I even had a chance to contact him."

"Interesting. Let me call you back later tonight, Lydia. I'm about to start a fitness class. Is ten too late?"

"Not at all." Something to look forward to.

Lydia busied herself with laundry and tomorrow's lunches. She checked on the boys, then took care of some bills. She nearly jumped out of her skin when the phone rang a little after ten.

"How are you tonight?" Michael said.

Lydia's heart skipped a beat. Outside of work hours, this question felt more personal. She had to remind herself this was her employer's attorney. *The* Michael Malvisti.

"I'm fine, thanks. We've got documents. Lots of them."

"Give me an idea of what's there."

"I haven't yet read them all. I figured nothing would make sense without you." Lydia's cheeks flushed. She hadn't meant to say that out loud.

"Then we're the blind leading the blind."

She laughed and spread out the pile on her coffee table, just as they had done together a few days ago. "Let's see here." She started with a copy of a land contract. "There's information showing that ownership of the property beneath Malvisti Park changed hands for very brief periods of time. I'm looking at a deed conveyance, and then another one back to the original conveyor within a week."

"Huh. I've been looking for those. Go on."

"There's an investigative-type memo documenting quantities of toxic waste. Some addresses around the Falls are listed. The memo concludes that the burial of wastes took place with 'little regard for worker safety.'"

She read further. "This paper is ripped at the bottom corner, but from what I can read it says that site workers were 'likely exposed to elevated levels of radiation.'"

"What's the date of the memo?"

"No date. It was typed on a typewriter, though. Smells old"

"Go on."

"I don't know what 'products of fission' materials are, but they were found at the site 'in significant quantities."

"*Fission*, did you say?"

"Yep." She sighed. With every line, she sank deeper into the region's environmental problems.

"That's the first I've heard of fission products in Niagara Falls. You are sure it says fission and not fusion?"

"I'm sure." She peered at faint scribbles on the memo. "What's the difference?"

"Hang on … I'm looking this up on my phone. Stay with me." Twenty seconds ticked by. "Okay, both are types of nuclear reactions in which enormous amounts of energy are released. Fusion is the process of lighter nuclei coming together to form larger nuclei."

"I got you so far." Kind of.

"But fission is an altogether different process. Fission is the breaking apart of a heavy nucleus, like uranium or plutonium. It says here that products of fission are the fragments left after a heavy atomic nucleus fissions."

A female voice called to Michael in the background.

"I'm on the phone, just a minute."

Lydia heard what sounded like a door being slammed shut. She couldn't help but wonder who was with Michael Malvisti this late at night.

"It says here that some fission products are dangerous, but this is way above my head. What else is there?"

"The last document makes no sense to me. It's written on Gemelle Hauling letterhead and it lists operation costs for equipment. It looks really old."

"Probably a hazardous waste hauling company. Never heard of it."

"Based in Niagara."

"I'll check it out."

"Did you enjoy your class tonight?"

"No." he sighed. "It was a fitness class and I think I was invited to provide comic relief for everyone else."

"Maybe they were laughing with you, not at you."

"Good try, but no. A group of women started doing 'the Malvisti,' a pseudo-stretch they had made up in my honor." She could hear the smile in his voice.

"What would you like me to do with this information?"

"Keep it to yourself. Nobody needs to hear about 'the Malvisti.'"

"I mean the documents and memos." She laughed lightly. A lightness penetrated her spirit, despite the heavy subject matter.

"Put them somewhere safe. Will you call the doughnut man and see where he's getting this stuff? Then call with an update?"

"Absolutely. I'll call Chris tomorrow after work."

"And Lydia? It's probably not a good idea to share this with anyone yet. Even Dana, as much as that pains you, I know."

"Got it." Lydia had the feeling that more than her and Dana's friendship was on the line. Pastor Amos was right. The lens through which every person viewed the world mattered. Even if she knew what her perspective encompassed, would it stand up to a challenge like the one brewing here? Would Dana's? She forced herself back to Michael's advice. "I won't say anything yet. And I'll keep reading and let you know if there's anything else that seems important." Lydia hesitated before adding "good night."

Familiar, but it felt right.

CHAPTER THIRTY-NINE

"**M**y car won't start." Lydia said into the phone. She buttered wheat toast for Travis, while keeping an eye on the local news. "My sitter will be here any minute. Can you swing by and get me?"

A news alert flashed across the small television screen. "Niagara Falls" appeared in the caption.

"Again with the car? Buy. A. New. One. I'll be there in five."

"Hang on. There's breaking news out of the Falls." She squinted at the headlines ticking across the TV. "A body was found in the whirlpool, three miles downstream from the Falls." Lydia set down her knife.

"Just another jumper." Dana sounded annoyed. "We average one a week in the summer, you know. This one got an early start."

Lydia sucked in her breath. "Dana! Oh my gosh ..."

"Travis hurt himself again?" Dana's dry tone seemed meant to send a message.

"It's Chris ... on the news." She stifled a shriek. Her eyes darted to the boys. She didn't want to scare them, but she couldn't rein in her distress either. They looked at her with curious expressions, unsure how to react.

"Chris Magnano?" Dana beeped her horn in the background. "What's happening?"

Lydia covered her mouth and spoke directly into the phone. "They're saying 'a man identified as Christopher Magnano, local technical writer and environmental activist, was found inside a barrel floating in the lower Niagara River.' She moved closer to the TV. Bile rose from her stomach when a picture of a battered wooden object wrapped in yellow caution tape appeared. "Oh!"

Dana must have removed her earpiece because her voice suddenly rang clear over the phone. "Do they know what happened?"

"They suspect foul play. Fishermen found him wrapped in a plastic barrier material inside the barrel. They're guessing it went over the Falls. The barrel was nearly destroyed. Oh ... poor Chris!"

Angie walked through the front door. Lydia motioned for her to look at the kitchen TV screen. "My friend," she mouthed silently.

"I just pulled in behind your babysitter." Dana's voice hardened. "Come out and let's get to the office. We can talk about it in the car."

Tears streamed down Lydia's face. Angie's eyes widened. She covered her mouth with her hands.

Dana beeped from the driveway.

A few seconds later, Dana poked her head inside the front door. "My car's running, let's leave and talk about it on the way." She stepped out without acknowledging Angie, or the boys.

Lydia looked at her sons. Her stomach turned. This horrific situation had to be related to Chris's digging around, gathering information. Could anything be tied to her? People would only have seen Chris giving her coffee and doughnut bags.

And perhaps the envelope from yesterday.

It had to be Chris who left the envelope. Who else would have shared information about toxic contamination with her? Chris alone had a knack for slipping in and out of places unnoticed. Until last night. Should she tell the police?

Another beep.

"Should I leave the house?" Lydia searched Angie's eyes for confirmation that she was doing the right thing.

"I don't exactly know what's going on." Angie's face contorted in anguish. "But are you worried that someone targeted your friend?"

"A little." Lydia threw on her coat as she thought about what to say. "Listen, stay inside with the doors locked. Keep the boys home from school today. I'm not so sure it's unrelated to me or ... even you. I don't want to take any chances."

Angie squeezed Lydia's arm. "Be careful. Lyd ... what if that envelope yesterday was meant for me? I submitted a few articles to that Internet site, and ... I don't know. It could be something designed to scare people off."

Lydia used the back of her hand to wipe a tear. "We'll figure it out. I'll keep you posted." She kissed the boys and bolted out the front before Dana could beep a third time.

"I'm shaken to the core," Lydia wrestled her briefcase and purse into Dana's small hybrid.

"Well, it's unfortunate, and he was a nice guy, but let's not let it consume our lives." Dana backed out in a hurry. "We'll send flowers."

Lydia stared at her friend's profile. "Nothing fazes you." She bit back tears. "Except eagles and bushes. And chakras."

Dana shrugged. Lips pursed, she sped down the street.

Lydia shifted her focus to the modest houses outside the passenger window. Everything looked relatively normal in the neighborhood, a place where a living, breathing Chris had perhaps crossed her path only last night. She pulled a tissue from her purse and dabbed under her eyes.

Dana sighed loudly. "C'mon, Lyd. I mean, what can we do? He was a nice guy, we knew him, and we can't change what happened to him. We can't get shaken up by things we can't control. Besides, I don't think Chris had any family left. He's probably better off."

Lydia dug her nails into her hand to avoid saying something she'd regret. She held her body rigid until they cleared security at Cascata Verde.

"I've got several showings this morning," Dana said, her voice placating. "Are you up for answering phones and meeting with the Paxtons at eleven for their walk-through?"

"What if I died?" Lydia threw one hand up. "Would that move you in any way?"

"Of course. I'm not a zombie." Dana pulled into the same spot where Chris had waited for Lydia after the broker's open in February. "What's with you lately?"

Lydia blinked back more tears. She couldn't say. She didn't quite know herself.

❖

"It gets worse." Michael spoke in a low voice.

"Worse than Chris's death?" Lydia couldn't take any more distress. "Do I really need to hear this?"

"You need to." Michael sounded genuinely worried. "I called the TV station to talk to the young reporter who confronted my uncle during the groundbreaking last fall. I wanted to know where she'd gotten her information."

"She seemed pretty sure of her facts."

"She's no longer there. They said she moved to San Antonio, where she had worked before moving to Western New York."

"Did you try to track her down?"

"The girl's dead."

Cold fear squeezed Lydia's heart until she thought she would crumple in a ball. Her hands shook. On the other end of the line, Michael Malvisti went silent.

He cleared his throat before speaking. "There was a suspicion of suicide, but her parents deny that anything was wrong. Plus, she was found in a dumpster. They just filed a lawsuit against her life insurance company."

She didn't trust her voice to say anything coherent. Her quaking body caused her teeth to chatter.

"You there?"

"Yeah. I'm processing." Lydia held the phone closer to her ear. She wheeled over to look out the office window.

"Here's what I want you to do." Michael's voice took on an urgent tone. "Unless the police talk to you, do not talk to anyone, under any circumstances, about anything. Ty and I are coming up as soon as he gets back from a business trip. We've got some things to check out. Then we're going to present everything to Rebecca when she returns from some business in the Middle East and let her make the big decisions."

"Can this be connected to me somehow?" She stretched the office phone cord to the bathroom door and locked it. She lowered her voice to a whisper. "What about the envelope left at my house?"

"Don't take any chances. Stay temporarily in one of the unoccupied condos on the property." He tapped a couple of computer keys. "Two are scheduled for a certificate of occupancy this week. Have Dana stay in the other one. Otherwise, she'll wonder what's going on. Tell her we want you both to experience life at Cascata Verde so that you can better sell the concept to buyers."

"Okay." Specific action made her feel better. The fact that she didn't have to think of it lifted part of the burden from her shoulders.

"I'll make the arrangements. Until then, why not stay with your mom tonight?"

"Okay." Despite her distress, a slight smile played at the ends of her mouth. Michael Malvisti was in take-charge mode. No man since her father had ever expressed this level of concern for her safety. It felt good.

"One other thing. Tape the envelope under the vanity in the office bathroom. I'll pick it up when I get there. Ty and I will look at the papers together."

"Will do."

But what would happen if Dana found them first?

CHAPTER FORTY

As soon as she pulled in the driveway later that afternoon, Lydia spotted Mara Stanton shivering on her porch. The woman's thin face was partially obscured by a cap. Lydia suspected that her neighbor's shaking was the result of more than just the slight chill in the air.

"Angie wouldn't let me in." She met Lydia at the top step. "Strict orders from you."

"You can't be too careful these days." Lydia silently thanked Angie for her good judgment.

"Don't I know it," Mara looked over her shoulder and across towards her house. She seemed agitated. "May I come in for a quick second? I'm here as a friend, not a journalist."

"Sure."

The boys hugged Lydia, begging to go outside. "Give me a minute, guys."

Angie took them into the kitchen.

"I can't stay." She kept her coat on, but opened the first few buttons and reached inside. She pulled out a yellow folder. "I just wanted to give you some papers."

As if her stomach weren't upset enough. Documents, envelopes, doughnut bags ... all complications to her already overwhelming life.

She hadn't even begun to process Chris' brutal death. Tears stung her eyes.

"Oh, I'm sorry." Mara opened the folder and set it on the dining room table. "I didn't mean to make you cry."

"It's okay. I'm upset over the loss of a friend." She wiped under her eyes. At least these documents didn't come in a doughnut bag. Lydia caught a glimpse of spidery handwriting down the side of a hand-drawn diagram.

A receipt with blocky writing fell to the floor. Mara's bony fingers snatched it up. She waved it in the air. "My father and my grandfather worked for various waste hauling companies over the years. They had saved what I thought were interesting scraps of historical significance. There are some old diagrams of properties in the area, as well as odd lists of items perhaps buried there. I've since learned that they might be relevant to Cascata Verde."

"How so?" She fought to keep her voice under control.

"They appear to be related to the former Malvisti landfills. Some of those landfills were repurposed for parts of Cascata Verde, remember? Malvisti Park?"

"Oh ..." Lydia covered her face. "I can't take any more rumors about the Green City."

Mara touched Lydia's shoulder. "But you work there. You deserve to know everything that could potentially affect you, right? Do with these what you will."

"I'm not sure how to handle anything at this point." Lydia took the papers from Mara. She flipped through the first five pages. "How did you know these were connected to the Malvistis?"

"I tried to donate these papers to the library. The librarian told me to check with some of the industry owners identified on these documents. So I started asking around." Mara looked out the dining room window. She pulled her cap lower. "Next thing I know, Councilman Sal Malvisti himself shows up on my doorstep at eleven o'clock at night. He offered to buy them."

"Why was that a problem? Why not just sell?"

"He offered me a quarter-million dollars for everything."

Lydia's mouth fell open.

"I thought about it for a day." Mara seemed embarrassed. "But, I'm no fool. That offer tipped me off that something more was going on here. I needed to think about things."

"I'll say."

She leaned close to Lydia's ear. Lydia held her breath. "Today he upped his offer to four hundred thousand."

"Oh." Lydia puffed her cheeks, letting her breath draw out while she thought about the enormous sum of money. "If this information is so explosive, why not give it to your news station?"

"There's a personal aspect to this story. Nothing I want known publicly."

Lydia reached behind her and tightened the window blinds. For all she knew, the Malvistis could be tracking Mara's whereabouts this very minute.

"My father and my grandfather both worked for a subsidiary of Malvisti Industries." Mara's eyes reddened, a film of tears ready to spill. "They died too young—I never even met my dad. I was born after he and his father died within days of one another. And the circumstances of their deaths were very similar. A sudden, unexplained heart attack, the doctors said. Something wasn't right."

"Doesn't sound like it." Lydia shuddered. So much loss.

"My papa and grandpa knew something." Mara pressed her thin lips together. "Something the Malvisti family doesn't want disclosed."

"Like what?" Lydia asked, but wasn't sure she wanted to know the answer.

"It had to do with the land. Do you recall the discussion we had a few years ago in the street?" Mara gestured at the covered window. "Remember I thought that Gregg Blass's news station was going after something specific when they hounded you with questions?"

"Yes. But back then you were dismissive of environmental problems."

"And of my ex-husband."

Lydia nodded. Mara spoke the truth.

"Well, I knew better. Even then. My mother told me a few things before she died. I thought they were just family stories. You know ... nothing factual, just suspicions. She told me to leave this area. To move as far away as possible."

"Why didn't you?" Lydia touched her arm.

"I liked my life here. We had just moved into our first house. I had nice neighbors. My husband had a good job and my career as a journalist had just taken off. My son had friends at school." Mara pressed her slender hand just above a perfectly arched eyebrow. "Why would I wreck that life because of hunches or rumors that I couldn't prove? I mean, what could my mother have known anyway?"

"That revelation must've been hard to keep inside all these years."

"I told one person." Mara's eyes held regret. "My son."

Lydia realized she didn't even know Mara's son's name. "How did he react?"

"Not well. And I don't blame him. He never got to meet his grandpa, either. I've included some documents my son just gave me in that pile." Mara cleared her throat. "He told me to give them to you. And also to trust you."

Lydia froze. "Do I know him? Why—"

"Please don't ask any questions." Mara secured her cap tighter. "I'm leaving to start over somewhere else—they say your sixties are the new thirties, right? My house is sold. I just wanted to say goodbye and ask that you do the right thing with these." Mara turned to leave. "Maybe giving these to you is my good deed that will get me through the pearly gates someday. God knows that I wish I had done something sooner." She stepped out onto the porch.

"Mara." Lydia whispered after her. "Why me? You know the dangers more than anyone. I'm all my boys have. This information could rock this city and I don't know if I ... we ... can handle the fallout."

Images of Chris' barrel materialized in her mind. *Caution*, the yellow tape wrapped around it had warned.

"Lydia, it's because you want a normal life so much that you will do the right thing." Mara smiled weakly. She shoved the empty folder into her coat and buttoned it all the way to the top. "The way we live here is not normal. Fear and sickness should not be a part of our daily existence. But I don't have it in me to fight this. Maybe you do."

"I'll do my best. Let me know if there is anything you need." Lydia leaned over and hugged her. "Good luck with everything."

"Thank you. And listen, I'm back to my maiden name now, Palowski. It's all a rewind of sorts. I hope that someday things turn out all right for you."

She hurried down the steps.

This was definitely a new Mara. This was her neighbor stripped of the nice house and hard-working husband. The real woman behind the false front she put up for the television cameras. Lydia hoped that Mara's son, whoever he was, stayed in the picture. And remained alive.

She locked the door.

"Mom." Harrison emerged from the kitchen and hugged her. "I don't feel so good."

"Okay, lie down on the couch. Ms. Angie will help you. I need a minute to make a quick work call, and then we'll check your temp." She dialed Michael as Harrison curled up on the floor.

"Awwww ... we're sick of the house." Travis plopped on the floor next to her. He wrapped his arms around her legs and squeezed. "I want OUTSIDE. I need to practice my swingshot."

Lydia allowed herself a brief smile at her son's mispronunciation.

Michael's voice mail picked up.

She disentangled herself from Travis's grip and hid in the bathroom. Hands trembling, she dialed again. Her mouth twitched on the right side. She attributed it to frayed nerves and a lack of sleep.

"C'mon boys, let's give your mom a minute." Angie groaned as she lifted Harrison and helped him to the couch.

This time Michael's voice mail picked up immediately. "I have some pertinent information on the Land family contract. Call me at your *earliest* convenience." She hung up and looked in the mirror above the vanity, mildly surprised at the troubled-looking woman reflected there.

Thankfully, Angie didn't press her for details before she left for the day. But nobody could miss the apprehension visible in her babysitter's eyes.

❖

"Are we going away?" Travis watched as she packed some basics for the move to the condo.

"Just for a little while. We're going to stay in one of the brand new places at Cascata Verde. I want to get a feel for what it's like to live on the property."

"Yes! We're moving there, aren't we?" Travis skipped upstairs before she could answer. She heard him spread the news to Harrison. Harrison didn't answer. He must have fallen asleep.

❖

Lydia tried Michael again a little while later. No answer.

A wind gust from the fireplace ruffled Mara's loose papers on the table. How many lives, she wondered, would be affected by the publication of these documents? She avoided looking at them as she trekked to and from the laundry room off the kitchen.

But the pile wouldn't be ignored. It ruffled some more. The Gemelle receipt floated to the floor. Responsibility required something of her. Now.

Anxiety set in, making it hard to catch her breath.

She needed Michael. She needed to share the burden of this knowledge, even if only electronically. She stopped packing and fanned the papers out on the floor. It took fifteen text pictures to send everything to him. She hoped he'd pay close attention to the close-up of the diagram on Gemelle Hauling letterhead. The scribbled names in the margin were largely readable. Maybe he could use them to get more information.

She felt a little better.

Lydia checked the door locks. Why hadn't she gotten the security system installed already? She studied the street from the dining room window. Two streetlights were out. Monk let loose a deep "woof." His next agitated bark came out like a howl. The thought of that old bag of bones moving to breathe, let alone yowl, sent goose bumps up her spine.

She should get a dog. And an alarm system. Maybe learn to use a gun.

But would a weapon have helped Chris? Her stomach recoiled again at the violence of his death.

She stayed at the window, shuddering when a shadow passed through the circle of light from Mr. Mahoney's porch fixture.

A swaying tree branch, nothing more. She lifted the window blinds to get a better look.

Monk let loose a full-throated series of howls. Another neighborhood dog joined in with a chorus of staccato-like barks.

Her mouth went dry.

A taller shadow crossed the floodlight. The goose bumps were not going away.

GET OUT. She felt the warning in the deepest part of her spirit. A third pet added an insistent, full-throated bark to Monk's baying. She took the steps two at a time, grabbing the half-packed bag on the way. "Harrison!"

More dogs agreed that something wasn't right in the neighborhood.

"What's going on?" Harrison rubbed his eyes. His hair stuck up on one side of his head.

"We need to leave. I don't want you to be scared, but we need to hurry. Help me get your brother out of bed." She located her purse, and felt around the outside pocket for her car keys.

A dull thud shook the second floor. It came from the back side of the house.

"Let's go, baby." She moved swiftly to Travis' room and used one arm to gather him and the slingshot he clutched. She swung the overnight bag over her shoulder, and then scooped up Harrison from the top of the stairs. She would lift the house from its very foundation to protect her children.

Oily smoke greeted her at the bottom landing.

Why didn't the fire alarm go off?

"I smell a fire!" Harrison coughed behind her, then took a deep gulp of air and coughed again.

"Hold your breath. We're going right out the front."

She opened the door, not caring what waited outside. Twenty feet to the safety of the car. She bolted.

Both boys cried out as she pushed them through the van's slider door. The rough treatment jolted Travis awake. He sought out his brother.

Lydia's hand shook violently as she shifted into reverse. "Hang on my loves." They lurched down the short driveway. "We'll buckle up when we get closer to the main road!"

"Mommy, seatbelt!"

"There's times we break the rules, Trav."

"Smoke on our roof!" Harrison choked on his words, abandoning his attempt to buckle his brother's belt. Sirens could be heard over Monk's insistent howl.

"I know, baby, the firemen are on their way." She locked the car doors.

"Someone wrote on our garage!" Harrison tried to read the words aloud. "First … the … Alar …"

Lydia slammed her breaks at the end of her driveway. Her heart skipped a beat.

"First the alarmist."

"Teenagers playing a mean joke," she managed to say while surveying the street. "I can hear the emergency trucks on the main road. We'll let them do their job while we go to Dana's house."

Waves of resentment against her late husband flooded her mind. *Do you see what we're going through? Do you see me being the only nurturer, breadwinner… protector?*

She knew what he'd say. "It was you who endangered them. You caused the trouble." Blame always was the steady factor in their short marriage.

Lydia felt every painful stab of being a single mother.

Harrison wheezed. A sickening thought struck her. She'd left his asthma inhaler in the house. As she weighed her options, she spotted Mr. Mahoney against the door frame of his open garage door, stooping to grab Monk by the collar. The dog turned in circles, still howling.

Even in the minimal light, Mr. Mahoney's face registered anguish. He burst into tears when he saw them.

She backed out, and pulled across the apron of Mr. Mahoney's driveway. "We're all okay." She swallowed, her throat dry from the smoke. "We're all out. I'm heading to the hospital to get Harrison checked out. I'll call you, okay?"

Smoke filtered out of a garage vent. The flames had spread, destroying her refuge. Taking what little semblance of their lives was left.

Mr. Mahoney put his hands around his mouth. "I'll tell the police what I saw."

She nodded and drove the long way around the block to avoid the oncoming emergency vehicles. Neighbors appeared on the street, some in bathrobes.

She checked Mara's house as she accelerated past. Although the house looked empty and dark, a nearby floodlight made it easy to see the threatening message scrawled all over Mara's white garage door.

The inscription chilled her bones. *Oh, God, what have I gotten us into?* She pushed the vehicle as fast as she could safely drive it around the corner, praying that Harrison hadn't read the warning on Mara's door. Praying that Harrison could breathe. She cut through the church parking lot, barely registering the weekly message: 'God will make wrong things right. Amos 5.'

Wrong. Everything about this city was wrong. Where were all the good people, the decent ones who stood up for what's right?

Bitterness overcame her. The good people get sick and die. They leave. They keep a low profile.

Sometimes they get murdered.

Lydia had no idea which of those options described her future. She knew only that keeping quiet was no longer a choice. All she had ever wanted was a normal, healthy, low-key family existence. She glanced in the rearview mirror at Harrison. His constant struggle with asthma, fevers, and fatigue forced her to agree with Mara on one point. Living in fear wasn't right. But being free from worry required something more from her.

It was time for this alarmist to step up.

CHAPTER FORTY-ONE

December 29, 2003

I n the late 1980s, God began to take me to task for thinking that Joseph Malvisti reigned over Niagara Falls. I wrestled with that concept for years. Now I get it: God is in control, not me. But I didn't fully understand it until a week or so ago. Right about the time I started this memoir.

I see now that my divine lessons started early. In a public, and rather humiliating, way.

Our landfills along the upper Niagara River reached capacity in 1984. My sons spearheaded the decommissioning and remediation process. A few years later, we donated the transformed property to the City of Niagara Falls for a riverfront park. Nothing permanent would be built on it, of course. Even I wasn't willing to take that chance. But even as we purchased swings, a tall slide, and a whirler, I wondered whether using the park for recreation was a good idea. When the city added walking paths, decorative lights, and a parking lot, I pushed my concerns to the back of my mind. Progress of any kind must be supported. Our region's downward slide had showed no signs of slowing.

I began to look for confirmation that we had made the right decision. People had been fishing along the shoreline near the landfills for many years. They seemed fine. Why not make it official? Other than vague warnings about some sick fish in the Niagara River, no one from the city had ever expressed any concern about the property or the surrounding parcels of land.

Besides, a new park would be a welcome distraction from a series of black eyes marring the area. Niagara Falls had by now become synonymous with Love Canal, an environmental disaster of epic proportions. On top of that, several manufacturing and chemical factories had moved south, taking skilled and unskilled workers with them. Our population dwindled. Of those who remained, almost half received some form of financial assistance from the government. My gift of a park would give the land back to the people, even if it was only symbolic. While we could never erase the underlying problems in the area, it sure made me feel better.

I'll admit it. The land wasn't perfect. But there was hardly any property in Niagara Falls that hadn't been impacted by some chemical or another. That was just the nature of our region.

"Wake up." Annunziata swatted my back. I had overslept.

"What time is it?" I rubbed my head, trying to escape the confusion that held me. I noticed my arm felt stiff.

"Eight-thirty. Forecast calls for rain. I laid out your galoshes." She opened the drapes and sighed. "Let's hope the mayor keeps her park dedication speech short. Cut yours in half." I heard that last bit in Italian.

I rubbed my shoulder. A tingling sensation spread downward. I licked my dry lips. "Water, please."

My wife plunked down a large glass on my bedside table. I drank, but didn't feel any relief.

I dressed as fast as I could. Two police officers on motorcycles waited outside to escort us to the park. We raced ahead of a ragged cloud front all the way. I was relieved to see my sons and their families waiting for us in the half-full parking lot.

"Grandpa?" Michael grasped my hand. "Can me 'n Danny be the first kids down the slide?"

"Of course." A fine mist began to fall.

"I'm gonna beat you." Danny shoved his cousin out of the way and sprinted to the playground. He thundered up the wrong side of the slide and ripped the red ribbon across its top. His mother's heels clicked on the asphalt as she took off after him. Danny needed a good swat on the behind. I would've administered it myself, but I felt weak and short of breath.

As it was, it took all my energy to walk to the intersection of two pathways, near the play area. My breath came in shallow huffs. No one seemed to notice.

The mayor took her position at the podium. My grandsons had calmed down, or at least Michael had, and together we stood next to her. On the wet grass behind me stood my wife, and Sal and Joe, Jr., and their wives. All the people I loved in the world. About two hundred residents had come out, which was more than we had estimated. This city didn't celebrate things like it used to. Not milestones, new buildings (well, there weren't many), or political victories. And certainly not the dedication of a park. Apathy paralyzed the residents.

The mayor kept her remarks brief. Drizzle turned to steady rain. Umbrellas popped open just as the park lights twinkled on.

My turn.

I thanked the residents for being there, and wished them decades of fun on the playground. I sipped the water someone had placed on a shelf in the podium. My face suddenly felt like wet rubber. Despite the cool air, rivulets of sweat stung my eyes. It was time to end my speech. I wondered how quickly I could get to the car.

The mayor covered the microphone. "Are you okay?"

"Yes," I lied.

She turned to the crowd. "It is with great pleasure that I present the key to the City of Niagara Falls to Joseph S. Malvisti!" She dangled a large golden skeleton key in the air before turning to me with a great flourish. Whistles pierced my fogged ears.

"Congratulations! We are proud to call you a city father."

I reached for the key. Or at least I tried to. I couldn't control my left arm.

The key fell. It clanged off the podium and landed in a foamy puddle in front of my sons. Sal looked hesitant to touch it.

The small crowd uttered a collective gasp. Annunziata cupped her hand to her mouth. Joe, Jr. shot toward me, followed closely by Sal.

Their faces were the last thing I remember seeing before darkness fell around me.

❖

A sense of control is a curious thing. One minute, you're secure in your ability to direct your time, talent, or resources to carry out the plans in your heart. You believe that most things, given the right amount of money, can be fixed. You can buy, build, or invent whatever it is you need. It's a heady feeling.

A minute or a lifetime later, you want to kick yourself for thinking you had an ounce of control over anything. Control isn't real. It's simply a state of mind. And a foolish one at that.

Look at the daredevil Lussier. He conceived a plan to use a big rubber ball to conquer the Horseshoe Falls, and then withdrew his life's savings to bring it to fruition. For thirty years thereafter he boasted of plans for a second trip over the Horseshoe Falls, and later a run at the American Falls. Except that his savings were gone. He had spent it and most of his life chasing dreams. His were the manmade plans of his own heart; not those of the Creator.

Don't you know, my friends? God's purposes always prevail.

Always.

I just wish it hadn't taken me a lifetime to figure that out.

CHAPTER FORTY-TWO

Near Tampa, Florida

After witnessing a stunning early morning sky from the boat, Michael drove alone to his condo to shower before work. Jillian wouldn't be up and functioning for a few more hours. He pulled up in time to see his neighbor Paulie ringing his doorbell.

Michael thumbed the condo next door. "You live there, remember? Confused again after too much fun last night?"

"You're the one who's out of it, bro." His neighbor tossed him a bright blue case containing an iPhone. "Found this on the sidewalk this morning. Figured you wouldn't get too far without it."

"That's Jillian's." Michael checked the screen. "Thanks, man."

"It buzzed up a storm. Heard it from the mailbox."

Once Paulie left, Michael couldn't help himself. He had to check the phone. After entering the code, he almost wished he hadn't looked. Ten missed calls from an area code he recognized. Niagara Falls.

He dialed the number.

"Tomeo Environmental."

Michael clicked off. *What?*

❖

Twenty minutes later, he found himself driving straight to the seaside village where he'd met Duff earlier in the week. He needed the old man's opinion. Should he have checked Jillian's phone? Should he confront her? He pulled up to the coffee shop right around the time they'd met a few days before.

No sign of the old man or his dog. Maybe they'd already left for their trip to the Falls.

He popped his head into the coffee shop and, for once, hoped that Pam was working. The redhead would know if Duff had been in. She wasn't there, but a middle-aged woman with graying hair he had never seen before cashed out an elderly couple. Coffee stains dotted her tan uniform. Apparently, clumsiness was an occupational requirement in this place.

"What's his last name?" The waitress drew a rag from a bucket of brown water to wipe the counter. "Never met anyone named Duff, sorry sir."

"He's the one with the three-legged dog that comes here a few mornings a week. You'd remember them." Michael answered, realizing that he didn't even know Duff's surname.

"I might've seen them last week, sir, but I haven't been here for a few days."

To kill some time, Michael ducked into the adjacent store to buy Clary one of the organic dog biscuits she liked. He returned to his car, leaning against the door to wait. The quietness of his cell phone made him realize that he'd turned it off at the boat and had forgotten to turn it back on. He pressed the power button, startled when text after text appeared on the screen. A pop up screen notified him that his messages were 97% full.

Between the discovery on Jillian's phone this morning and the barrage of messages now, any peace he'd drawn from the vibrant sunrise had long since evaporated.

He skimmed the list. His assistant had tried to reach him last night. Suzanna had called. Lydia had sent picture messages. He opened them first, knowing that she would only contact him with important news.

The first picture showed a list of heavy equipment charges and service receipts. They meant nothing to Michael. He zoomed in on one of the slips of paper. The handwriting on it was mostly illegible, but he caught the date: 1950. Intriguing.

The next text revealed a diagram on Gemelle Hauling stationery. He still didn't know anything about the company, but he recalled reading it on documents Lydia had gotten from Chris. The picture on his phone showed a technical drawing for the burial of a large object. Its exact depth and placement seemed critical, judging by the level of detail. Eight names had been scrawled along the margins. Most were Polish surnames. Workers?

Michael looked at his watch. Maybe he should head to work. He and Ty had a lot to discuss.

He heard the old man and his dog before seeing them. Clary let out a small bark, while her tail wagged back and forth. Michael produced the dog treat and rubbed behind her ears.

"Got time for a quick cup?" Michael shook hands with Duff.

"Sure do, son."

"How have you been?"

"A bit low. Missing my wife something awful. This weekend is our wedding anniversary."

"I'm sorry." Michael held open the restaurant door for the frail pair. "What was your wife's name, Duff?"

"Kazimiera Ania Krzystyyna." Duff settled himself in a chair next to the front window table. Clary rested her head on her paws next to him.

Pam rushed into the café, explaining to nobody in particular that she had forgotten she was scheduled to work. Both men waved hello.

"Ania was a blessing from God to me. That's what her name means."

"Well, that's a Polish name, all right." Michael was pretty sure he'd correctly guessed her ethnic background.

"That's nothing. My given name is Przemyslaw Krzystyyna."

Michael's eyes widened in mock surprise. "I thought your name's Duff?"

"It is. People have called me Duff for years. Nobody could pronounce my birth name, not even old Kostek at the corner Polish grocery. And he was straight off the boat."

"So where'd Duff come from?"

He chuckled. "That's a good story. The guys at my night job used to rib me because I'd show up with a ring of white gypsum on my backside." Duff started as Pam nearly slipped on spilled coffee.

Michael cocked his head. "I don't get it."

"I worked days at a gypsum plant. We were so busy after the war that there was no time for a proper meal in the lunchroom. Plus, I once saw a rat as big as a cat in that building." Duff demonstrated, placing his hands shoulder width apart.

"That's just wrong."

"Yessir. So I ate in the dusty refining area. You couldn't avoid the white ring on the seat of your pants. The name just stuck. Literally."

"What was your night job?"

"I drove the backhoe and some other heavy equipment for Gemelle Hauling."

Michael swallowed. Gemelle again. And another unpronounceable Polish name to add to the list of others scrawled on the papers Lydia had sent. A thousand questions surfaced.

"Would you mind writing your last name for me on this napkin?" Names of certain ethnicities often sounded different than they looked. Polish was one of them. But the Gemelle Hauling connection felt too coincidental.

"Sure." Duff borrowed Pam's pen and wrote out his name in uncertain, loopy letters. The fine point pen tore up the napkin, making it difficult to read.

He flipped it around towards Michael.

Michael felt like he'd been punched in the stomach.

"Why'd you have me do that?" Duff absently stroked Clary's head.

Michael studied the name for a second and then pulled up the text picture on his phone. "I'll show you."

"Krzystyyna." Michael struggled through the difficult name. "Are you related to the person listed in the margins of this diagram?" Michael enlarged the picture as Duff got out his reading glasses.

"I can't read that, son."

"It's a picture of the plans for some type of installation. It appears to be from Gemelle Hauling and it's quite possibly old. There are names listed here on the side ... I'm thinking it's a work crew. One says Przemek Krzystyyna? You related to him?"

"That's me." Duff tipped his head. "Short version of my first name."

"Oh ... wow." Michael thought carefully about his next question. He was missing something, a connection just beyond the reach of his logical, linear mind. "How long did you work for Gemelle Hauling?"

"Just three or four years." He held a mug up to Pam. Clary yelped after the young server stepped on her tail.

"Sorry, Clary-girl."

"Thanks." Duff turned back to Michael. He took off his readers. "I was promoted to supervisor at the gypsum plant and no longer needed the second job."

"Do you know what years you worked there?"

"Well, I still considered myself a newlywed and I wanted to be home with my wife ..." A gleam appeared in his eye. "... so, it was probably about '51 or '52 when I stopped working for Gemelle. I was still a young man."

"Do you mind if I ask you about these other names? This document is important for some research. If it's ok, I'll attempt to read them aloud."

"Wiezzz ..."

"Wieczorczuk," Duff corrected. "Pavel, if I recall."

"Do you know him?'

"Used to. He died young. Cancer. Left a wife and two young ones."

Michael tried to sound out the next name. He squinted, trying to decipher any recognizable letter pattern, and then gave up. "There should be a rule against this many consonants in one name."

"Write those names down here." Duff handed him the bill. Clary licked Duff's pant leg from below the table. "Mind your business, you." He tickled her ear.

Michael used the borrowed pen to list the names. Out of the corner of his eye, he could swear Clary was smiling at Duff.

"You know," Duff raised one wiry eyebrow, "that job was the last time our hauling crew worked together."

"Why's that?" Michael double-checked the spelling on each of the listed names. He made a few corrections.

"I don't know. Now that I think about it, one fella died that day. We stopped work for a few hours. I felt bad, but the job needed to get done right away. A few others kicked the bucket within months after that project. Very sick." Duff's accent made the word sound like "seek."

"Sick?"

"Yessir."

"That's too bad."

"Two of those names should be the same. A father-son team. Died of heart attacks, they'd said. All that Polish sausage." Duff looked out the window. "The Palowskis. I haven't thought about that family in years."

Chills pricked Michael's spine. He showed Duff his re-written version of the remainder of the names. "Are you the only one alive on this list?"

The old man's eyebrows drew together. He held the list far from his eyes. Then he put on his glasses again. "I'm not sure, but I wouldn't be surprised. We're old men now."

Michael folded the paper neatly and shoved it in his pocket. "But still, it sounds like several of these workers died young. It makes me a little suspicious, you know? Maybe you should be careful?"

"Those events happened more than a half-century ago! It was a different time. Nothing's happened to me yet, so why now?" Duff leaned forward in his chair.

"Why do you think nothing has happened to you, Duff, but everyone else is long dead?"

"I'm not a threat to anyone. Supervisors told us to clap our trap, and we did." He shrugged. "Or at least I did. Lives depended on our staying quiet."

"What do you mean?"

"That's how it was back then. This burial project related to equipment used just after the war ended. Niagara County stayed in high gear because the Cold War was on. We were very much involved in the defense of this great nation, especially as our relationship with Russia went south. These were important jobs, and they paid well. It was really not our business to question what we were told to do. We just did it." He leaned back.

Michael's phone vibrated. Another text marked "urgent."

"Excuse me just for a second." He touched his phone. "This could be related to what we're talking about."

Suzanna. Exciting news, she wrote. She'd had another ultrasound, but this time they learned she would deliver a girl and boy. Jemma and Thomas, due at the end of the summer.

Jemma and Thomas?

Connections are obvious in hindsight. But this link came together in a painstaking fashion, one half-thought at a time. He looked up at Duff, hardly daring to breathe.

"Thomas means twin, right?"

"I believe so. Thomas, Tomeo, all of those "T" names often refer to twins. They're always popping up in my crossword puzzles."

Michael's mind whirled.

"What about Jemma, Gem?" Michael felt certain the name would mean the same. Suzanna loved a good play on words.

"Gemini. The constellation associated with the twins Castor and Pollux. Just saw that in a last week's *New York Times* crossword."

Michael wasn't sure how or why he knew it, but he realized he'd known it all along. Twins owned Tomeo Environmental and Gemelle Hauling. More accurately, Uncle Sal and his father owned the shadowy entities. No wonder he'd been kept out of the loop. Malvisti Industries had its fingers in the process of hauling, burying, testing, and ... green city developing. They'd covered the toxic waste industry from A to Z.

Michael's stomach lurched. Through a labyrinth of family trusts, he himself probably owned a portion of those companies.

One more question needed an answer. He lowered his voice and leaned close to Duff. "What did your crew bury?"

He whipped off his glasses with surprising agility for an old man. "I'll tell ya, but then I'll have to kill ya." A smile played around his lips. "We sank a pressure vessel. Never seen anything like it. Huge. Round. For storage, I'd heard."

"What was stored in it?"

Duff shrugged. "We never asked." His mouth turned down, revealing long, thin age lines around his chin.

Michael used both hands to rub his eyes. He tried to think. He needed answers to questions that should have been asked decades ago. Today, more than ever. "Why not, Duff? Why didn't anyone ask?"

"We kept it under our hat. Like I said a minute ago, we believed the wartime propaganda plastered all over the factories." Clary shifted. Duff stared at her, the smile gone from his lips. "Careless talk costs lives."

And loose lips sank ships. Michael had heard them all before from Grandpa Joe.

After today's revelations about who owns Tomeo and Gemelle, Michael's life was not just unanchored. It was sinking fast.

CHAPTER FORTY-THREE

Michael pulled into his spot in Hessley's parking garage, unable to shake the sense of foreboding he'd developed after this morning's coffee with Duff. Next to him, Ty sat in his new sports car, waiting for Michael just as they had arranged. Only Tyler could interpret the technical details in the documents Lydia had texted.

Michael's cell lit up. He motioned his friend to wait.

"Thank God you're all right!" The rushed voice on the other end resembled Lydia's.

"Lydia?"

"I tried to get ahold of you last night. So much is happening." She stifled a cry. "Someone torched my home last night."

"What?" Michael's throat tightened.

"We're all okay." A single sob escaped. "The house is a loss, though. Pretty much everything's gone."

"Were you home? How did it start? How are the boys?" She couldn't answer fast enough to suit him.

"I know it was deliberate. A message spray painted across my garage confirmed it: 'FIRST THE ALARMIST.'"

"I don't know what to think." He squeezed his temples, his mind already crammed with information so monumental that it was dizzying.

"I do. I think it has to do with the documents I texted to you last night." She cried into the phone.

"Take your time. I'm here."

"Just please tell me that you didn't erase them. I know someone wants those papers."

"I've got every text. The documents are mostly readable. I was just about to look at them with Tyler."

"The originals disappeared in the fire. My back window was broken before the firemen arrived. Someone must have slipped in and took them while we escaped out the front."

"Man ... where are you now?" He signaled to Ty that he'd be another minute. "And you didn't say how the boys are doing."

"They're okay. We're at the hospital, though." Another soft sob. She described what had happened with Harrison and how the hospital had kept him overnight for observation.

"I made the arrangements for the two condos at the property."

"Thank you. My boys aren't sure what to think about it, but they're taking their cue from me. I'm calm on the outside. Petrified everywhere else."

"I'm sorry I'm not there to help you."

"You've helped us plenty." She paused, as if uncertain whether she should continue. "I'm meeting with Pastor Amos at the Green City church on Monday for some moral support. He came over to the hospital for a bit last night. He's been great."

"You know him?" Once again, Michael wondered whether she had been in the church last Sunday.

"Oh yeah, someday I'll have to tell you that story."

"I can't wait. Do you have anyone else to help you?"

"My neighbor and a few friends. I'll see how my mom is feeling. We'll figure it out."

Protectiveness for her and the boys overcame him. "I'll be up there in two days. How about if we meet at the real estate office in the late afternoon? I'll help you get things sorted out. In the meanwhile, stay on the property and stick with the pastor. We're going to get to the bottom of this mess."

❖

Michael scrambled out of the GT-R and climbed into Ty's new Camaro. "Nice." He adjusted the seat and shut the door.

"You look uneasy. What's up?"

"I'm worried. Furious." Michael chewed his lip. "You're going to have to keep me from hurting someone today."

"Who?"

"There's a list." Michael leaned forward, balling his fists. "Let's start with Jillian. She's been very attentive to me these past few months. Last night, she made dinner and brought it to the boat—"

"Stop right there. She's up to something, man." Ty shook his finger. "That girl don't cook for nothin'."

"Exactly! And she keeps asking about my work, what I do every time I'm in Niagara Falls. Then, she suggested we take dive lessons together, and on and on." Michael cocked his head to the side. "I wanted to give her the benefit of the doubt. It was kinda nice to have that attention from her again."

"So what's the problem?" Ty tucked his keys into his pants pocket. "And this is way too much detail, bro."

"This morning my neighbor found Jillian's cell on the sidewalk in front of my condo. She must've dropped it on the way to the boat. I'm not proud to admit this, but I looked at her calls and the Buffalo-Niagara area code popped up a bunch of times."

"She's cheatin'?"

"I'm not sure." Michael shook his head. "But I called one number. It was Tomeo Environmental."

"Why in the heck would she be talking to Tomeo?"

"I think she's talking to my Uncle Sal."

"Okayyy." Ty's brow creased. "So why in the heck would she be talkin' to Sal Malvisti there? He doesn't work at Tomeo."

"Because I figured out this morning that he might own it. Either individually or Malvisti Industries itself owns Tomeo Environmental."

Ty swore under his breath. "Dude ... do you know what that means?"

"It means we've got problems we don't even know about yet." Michael yanked his phone out of his pocket.

"I know one huge problem. If Malvisti Industries owns the environmental testing company, then that means that it's been doing its own monitoring, analysis, and remediation! That's like the fox guarding the henhouse." Ty pressed his hand to his forehead.

"That's only the beginning."

"We've got a disaster on our hands. We've made representations to the EPA. We've issued press releases ... we've held public meetings and told people that all testing was done by an independent company!" Ty rubbed his face. Sweat stains appeared under the arms of his blue dress shirt. "Do you think that Rebecca knows?"

"I doubt it." Michael hung his head. "She never would have invested in property that had such a tangled history. There's something much bigger going on here."

"The implications are huge. Your family ... man."

"Oh, I'm well aware. It casts a big shadow over all of Cascata Verde. We need to contact Rebecca in Israel and tell her."

"And the legal staff." Ty added.

"Don't I know it." Raul would hire an army of lawyers and experts. That resourceful man did nothing in small measure.

"The board's gonna flip out."

"Probably." Michael opened his phone, running his finger along the screen.

"Hey." Ty grabbed Michael's arm. "I know we've got a big conflict of interest here. But let's not overreact. This makes no sense. Tomeo's testing shows that the land underlying Cascata Verde is fine. So, it *could* actually be clean, or ... Tomeo could've tested it and lied about the results. The point is that we don't know."

"But you can confirm a few things, right? Can't you fly some sampling equipment to Buffalo?" Michael swept across a few more screens.

"Yep. I've already got some testing equipment stored in a construction trailer there."

"Good." Michael turned the phone toward Ty. "I've got pictures of documents that might help. Lydia sent them to me last night, just before someone burned down her house." Michael handed the device over.

"Really?" Ty looked up from the pictures. "Everyone okay?"

"Physically, yes."

"Do ya like her?" Ty zoomed in on something. His eyes widened.

"I'm—"

Ty's mouth fell open. "*Dude.*" He blinked once or twice before looking up at Michael. "These are samples taken from several spots around Cascata Verde and Malvisti Park." Ty did a double-take. His eyes bulged. "*Rare trans-organics?*"

"I need English. What's going on?"

"I ... I don't know." Ty huffed out a breath. "None of this makes sense. Tomeo has tested those sites over and over, but I don't recall ever seeing some of these materials on the pre-remediation list."

"What materials were there?" Michael dreaded the response.

"Let's see, in the vineyard we had a wide assortment of volatile and semi-volatile chemicals." Ty's eyebrow raised. "... benzenes, carbon tetrachloride."

"Sounds bad." Toxic grapes. He groaned. Casks of them.

"Not *that* unusual for the area." Ty kept reading.

"That's disturbing."

"Oh, ho, ho ... but look here, Michael. Uranium-238, uranium-235, uranium-234, thorium-230, radium-226, radon-222, and plutonium." He cursed again and looked up. "Uh oh."

"Those last ones are all radioactive, right?" Michael asked.

"Yes. All radionuclides." Ty put the phone down. "I haven't seen plutonium at any of our development sites. Ever." Tyler returned to the screen, peering closer.

"How much is there?"

"I can't tell. I'm looking at the concentrations found at certain spots right now. It's a wonder there weren't spontaneous fires bustin' out all over that park."

"Where would the radioactive material come from?"

"You got me." Tyler enlarged a document. "Plutonium doesn't occur naturally, except in trace amounts. These are *very* high concentrations."

"Well, where do very high concentrations come from?" Michael shifted in his seat. "C'mon, give me something. I'm in the dark here, man."

"It can come from certain experiments. Like where atoms are smashed together. But those activities wouldn't yield the quantity that's listed here either. This amount of plutonium would only come from a nuclear reactor. Or ..." Ty squeezed his eyes shut.

"Or what?"

"The detonation of an atomic bomb."

"Come on, man. Are you kidding me? There's never been a reactor in Niagara Falls. And we'd know if an atomic bomb was detonated, right?"

"True." Ty enlarged the document even more. "This list goes on and on. There's inorganic chemicals like antimony, arsenic, beryllium, cadmium, chromium, copper, lead, magnesium, mercury, cyanide, selenium, barium, and more."

"Bad?"

"Bad." Ty confirmed Michael's worst fears. "Look, we already knew a lot of toxic chemicals were buried there once upon a time. Heck, I think the city itself was designated a federal Superfund site at one time."

Michael's head throbbed. He leaned back against the headrest, a thought coming to mind. "Is plutonium a fission product?"

"Yeah, how'd you know that?"

"I looked it up when Lydia told me about some other papers."

"Can't wait to see those. Look, I'm pretty confident that Cascata Verde went through a thorough cleanup. We've been told that over and over. I saw the post-remediation sample results." Ty looked up quickly and then back at the screen. "Wait a minute."

"What?" Michael rubbed his right temple, letting his head fall toward Ty.

"Brace yourself, man … these test sample results are dated two months ago. I've never seen these. Are these for real?"

"I don't know. I'm just as lost as you."

Ty cocked an eyebrow and handed the phone back to Michael. "Where'd Lydia get these papers?"

"She didn't say."

"This information changes the type of equipment I'll need. An old-fashioned Geiger counter wouldn't pick up many of these compounds. That piece of equipment just tests for gamma emitters. Some of these radionuclides are primarily alpha emitters, meaning a whole different set of tools, sampling, and testing is needed."

"Okay, let's think this through." Michael tucked the phone into his suit pocket. "Can we wait a few days or so before we call Rebecca … or anyone else? We need to be sure."

Ty stared straight ahead, his brow furrowed. "I've never known you to bend the rules, Mikey."

"I want to nail down some specifics before we cause widespread panic."

"Okay. Sure." Ty tapped the steering wheel. "Either way, my career is over. This shouldn't have happened on my watch."

"We got something wrong, that's for sure. More than our jobs are on the line. This is bigger than either of us."

"True that."

"Rebecca lands in Toronto in two days, and then plans to drive to Buffalo." Michael opened the car door. "I had already emailed her that you and I were heading back up the Falls, and that we need to talk."

"Okay. I'm cool with that. It's not a lie."

"Get some field-testing equipment. Use the company card. Buy whatever you need and I'll take the heat. I'm not going into the office today. I've got two places to go that can't wait."

Ty looked at him curiously. "Care to elaborate?"

He stepped out and poked his head back into the new car. "Some business with Jillian and then a family member. I'll tell you about it later. Pray for me."

"Since when do you pray?"

"Since I've got stuff to pray about."

"Good luck, man. Let's just make sure we're on the same flight to Buffalo. Shoot for tomorrow morning."

CHAPTER FORTY-FOUR

Despite the bad news delivered by Ty, Michael felt like a free man as he pulled onto Route 17 towards Apollo Beach. He was getting to the bottom of things. Taking action. He longed to put the car through its paces. See what she could do on the open road. He settled for gunning the engine a few times. No time for a ticket today.

Jillian had already packed her clothes by the time he'd pulled into the driveway. She didn't seem too upset, and, if Michael was honest with himself, neither was he. Her talks with Sal were harmless, she'd said. Uncle Sal had simply befriended her.

Did she think he was that stupid?

Michael titled the Charger in her name and she rolled out of his life forever. If only the next encounter would go as smoothly.

❖

Dad had been expecting him, even if his mother looked baffled. The old man looked pale.

"Michael," Joe said dully.

"Dad."

"What's going on? Aren't you supposed to be at work?"

"I need some confirmation. You and Uncle Sal own Tomeo Environmental, don't you?" Michael tried to keep his voice calm. He climbed the sculpted front steps. Stone cold, just like the house that had never been home to him. His mom disappeared up the foyer stairway.

"I don't know what you are talking about." His father's ears reddened.

"Why didn't you tell me? You two own Gemelle Hauling, too." Michael kept walking into the house, his eyes focused on his father. "Or at least Malvisti Industries does, right?'

"You sound like a conspiracy theorist. Keep your focus on your business and stay out of mine." His father slammed the front door shut behind them.

"You've wanted me to stay out of your way for a long time, haven't you?" Michael walked into the enormous tile-floored kitchen and took a seat at an ornate iron table. "Or maybe stay out of your life altogether. You've made it abundantly clear that you're disappointed in me."

"I'm not," his dad inhaled. His eyes watered after taking a second breath before continuing. "I'm disappointed in the choices you've made. You were always a straightforward, honest kid. But you don't understand a thing about the businesses we've built, or why things had to be done a certain way."

"Then tell me."

"Here's all you need to know. We saved people. We employed people. We helped our nation. You don't know squat about anything, but you're sure quick to tear down a lifetime of good works." Joe's breath came at irregular intervals. "Stop this. You'll destroy the Malvisti name. Maybe that'll satisfy you."

"You are trying to justify things that can't be justified. Those rationalizations about jobs and patriotism don't fly anymore. Maybe during World War Two it was a different story. A certain amount of community sacrifice was expected. But we know more now, Dad. People's lives are on the line. The health of our land is at stake."

"See, this is what I'm talking about. Stop making moral judgments." His father pointed his finger. "We knew you'd never be able to see the bigger picture."

"Who's we?"

A loud scoff. "Your grandfather. Me. Sal. We knew you could never have been a part of the business. It would've required you to make ... messy choices that required a certain amount of fortitude."

Michael's mouth hung open. *Grandpa Joe had deliberately kept him out of the business.*

"Face it. Sometimes difficult decisions must be made for the greater good." A ragged breath this time. "Those choices might not fit into your somewhat naïve view of what it means to be a good person, or a good corporate citizen. But they were necessary choices."

"You don't get it, do you?" Michael nearly choked on his disbelief. The pieces came together. Every disjointed thought he'd had over the years suddenly coalesced. Things he'd believed about his family simply weren't true.

"Just go." His father stood. He leaned on the table, still trying to catch his breath.

Michael shook his head. "I've realized something."

"I don't want to hear it."

"I'm telling you anyway."

His father turned away. He folded his arms, trying in vain to catch his breath. Michael half-expected him to cover his ears.

"You need to hear this. It's not about building an empire or making money, whatever the cost." Michael stood. "And it's not about proving what you as a man can accomplish."

"Really now." His voice calmed, and he wiped his palms on his khaki pants. "What's it about, my son? Now you're going to tell me the secret of life?"

"I'm listening to you trying to justify a way of life that has been built around glorifying the Malvisti name. You've elevated that *name* above the well-being of people. Above that of even our Creator."

"Is that what this is about?" Joe whipped around and narrowed his eyes. "You've converted to some freak religion, and now you're out to destroy your family? Maybe rack up some brownie points with some invisible god? That god will disappoint you as surely as I have you."

His father took a step to leave, then stopped.

Michael felt a twinge of compassion for his father. Michael always had faith in his abilities and hard work. They were not unlike one another in some ways.

"Dad—"

Joe's head swiveled. "Stop! Your life has amounted to a whole lot of nothing. You played the Marine, wasted time in law school, and now you sit behind a desk reading papers all day." He tone deepened. "Long before you were born, Malvisti Industries helped this country survive. Where would Niagara Falls be without our know-how? Our money?"

"I'm beginning to see that our lives should be about building a business, a life, or a family anchored on God. It's about—"

"Enough!" The color drained from his father's face. He felt behind him for his chair and sank into it. "You have a choice to make, my boy. You can stand by your family and the good that we've done for Western New York. Or, you can destroy all of us, including yourself. You won't escape this, either."

The last bit sounded like a threat. Michael's mind searched for the right response.

"Your grandfather would be ashamed of you if he were still alive."

Michael recoiled at the barb. "Grandpa respected honesty and hard work, Dad." He searched his heart for the principles his grandfather had always talked about. Respect. Power. The importance of your family name. "No, sir. He wouldn't have been ashamed of me. But something got corrupted along the way. That's what he'd be ashamed about."

"Go ahead and say what you want to say, boy. Some*one* got corrupted." Joe coughed. A sheen of sweat covered his face. "Isn't that what you're hell-bent to prove?"

Carmella appeared in the archway to the kitchen. She clutched a small wooden chest. Her mouth twisted as she looked from Michael to her husband.

His father waved her away.

She set the box on the floor, but remained in place.

Michael tried to moderate his tone, despite the turmoil raging in his mind. "What's wrong with you, Dad? You don't look so good."

"Nothing."

"You sure?"

"Yes."

"Look, I'm not out to prove anything against you. I just want to understand what happened to our family and our business. Where did things go so wrong? I've got nothing of substance from this family to build on. Nothing I've been taught holds true."

Carmella began to cry. The sound of her sobs softened something in Michael.

"Dad." Michael paused. "Please look at me."

His father complied.

Michael kept his tone respectful. "You've got a choice to make, too. Will you stand by the Malvisti name, no matter the cost, or will you take responsibility for the things that you and Uncle Sal have done? If you pick the family business, I won't be a part of that anymore."

"You never were."

"I'll keep in touch." Michael kissed his mother on her wet cheek. "Let me know later how he's feeling. And I want to discuss something else with you next week." He needed to talk to her—outside his father's presence—about the seeds of faith that seemed to be growing inside him. He also wanted to know what secrets lived in the box. Twice she had brought it out. It hadn't been lost on him. But now was not the time.

She nodded, her gaze fixed on the box.

Michael walked out to the driveway. Fear and excitement coursed through his body. Overcome, he fell to his knees next to the GT-R. "God, I need some direction. My family's ideas of respect and honor and power are so distorted ... I don't think they line up with your plan for this world. Please forgive me for not understanding that sooner. I want to be a part of your plan. Give me what I need for whatever lies ahead."

Michael knelt a few minutes more. His body quaked. He now knew why Suzanna had cried at Pastor Amos's service. If what he'd heard from Pastor Amos and Suzanna was true, then he was part of God's family now. Home wouldn't be found in this cold, remote residence. It wouldn't be found in the Malvisti legacy. But the family of God felt right. An anchor for his soul.

Surely God's legacy couldn't be corrupted like that of the Malvistis.

The hot pavement felt good on his hands as he pushed himself up. There was a sharpness to the scenery that Michael had not experienced before today. He felt happy to feel the heat of the sun on his face. Happy to see a blue Florida sky. He couldn't wait to talk to Duff, Suzanna, and Pastor Amos about his decision. He'd try to talk to Ty on the plane.

And Lydia? Someday soon he'd share this with her, too.

As he backed out of the driveway, his eyes were drawn to the second-floor window. His father stood framed by white sheers, his eyes fixed on Michael, and a cordless phone attached to his ear.

Michael was sure Uncle Sal was on the other of the line. The companies comprising Malvisti Industries would likely go into protection mode, a massive corporate shell game of hide-the-ball.

Joe had made his choice.

Then again, he'd probably decided where to cast his allegiance ages ago, long before Michael had even been born.

CHAPTER FORTY-FIVE

December 30, 2003

By 1990, I didn't recognize my beloved city anymore.

Pollution, crime, and neglect had taken their collective toll. Thriving neighborhoods of just a few decades ago now appeared desolate. Manufacturing had moved south, taking people and jobs with them, and leaving those left behind to shoulder a heavy tax burden. Even tourists were not spared our misery. They arrived to find crumbling concrete eyesores instead of the historic buildings that once enhanced our city. But perhaps most depressingly, Joseph S. Malvisti Stadium lay in ruins. They told me addicts inhabited its dugouts.

A general malaise had settled over the area. Sure, it was better than the smog. But our city was meant for more than this dismal existence.

Around Thanksgiving of that year, my old friend Sammy had agreed to meet me at a downtown diner that a group of us industrialists used to frequent. Our numbers had been bigger then.

"How the heck have you been, old man?" Sammy removed his scarf and fedora and sat opposite me in the vinyl booth. Although he'd shrunk an inch since I'd last seen him the year before, he still had a full head of silvery-white hair.

"Been better." And I meant it.

An aging waitress brought coffee, even without our ordering. Perhaps she'd remembered us from back in the day. I smiled and thanked her.

"You're welcome, Mr. Malvisti."

"You don't sound too good." Sammy turned his coffee cup upright. "Thanks, Alice."

"I never fully recovered from that heart attack." I sat back and shrugged. "Don't feel like myself."

"I was there that day, Joe. That was sure something. You scared everyone." He chuckled. "You know it's serious when someone drops the keys to a city."

"Baah. Enough about that episode." I shifted in my seat, catching my pant leg on duct tape being used to cover a hole in the vinyl. I smoothed the frayed adhesive, grateful for the distraction. "How about you?"

"Not so good either." He dumped three sugars into his coffee. His chin quivered as he stirred absently. "You know, my granddaughter's sick."

"With what?"

"Brain tumor." Sammy leaned forward. "The docs told us its terminal."

"Ahh." I fumbled for the right words, my stomach sick. Sammy always mentioned his sweet Katy when our group used to gather here. "Kids aren't supposed to get that. How old is she now, twenty? Twenty-two?"

"Twenty-two."

"How could she have gotten a tumor?" A twinge flashed in the innermost part of my heart. I tamped it down. Her situation had nothing to do with me.

"They say it's common around these parts." Sammy tossed his spoon aside. He covered his eyes, then pressed his hand flat against his forehead. As if the problems in his own head were the issue. I'd never seen Sam Carlosi cry, not even after his wife died ten years ago. I sure hoped he wouldn't start now. After a few seconds, his stooped shoulders sagged even more.

I reached across the table and patted his forearm until he looked up. I handed him some napkins.

"Katy told me there are four others from her high school class."

My throat constricted as I waited for him to elaborate. But he just blew his nose, and then added more sugar to his coffee.

"Four other what?"

"Kids. Sick with cancer."

My mind raced. *Was it possible?*

"Could this have something to do with the landfills, Joe?" Sammy looked into his mug, probably searching for words that had been on his mind for some time. "I mean, we've always suspected there's some chemistry buried around the high school. We know there's some at Malvisti Park. Do you think there's a connection to the kids?"

"No," I responded automatically. "There's not. Whatever's buried at the park would've stayed in the barrels, or leached downgradient, towards the river. The school is in the opposite direction. I'm not worried."

I reminded myself for the next few weeks that I wasn't bothered. Not at all.

But I was fooling myself.

A month later, my anxiety exploded into full scale alarm. I had arrived about thirty minutes early for my grandsons' basketball game at the high school. Checking for black ice, I sat in the driver's seat and used my boots to dig under the snow. My legs were still weak from my heart attack several years before and I didn't want to fall. Would I ever regain my strength? My dignity?

My gaze shifted to the scene of my humiliation, just across the street. Bare shrubs and miniature pines stretched across the vast park, all the way to the river on the far side. Snow drifts rolled across the playground, as if erasing the memory of what happened there. A colorful and lovely tree bloomed next to what remained visible of the slide.

I took off my glasses and rubbed my eyes.

I needed a closer look.

It took several minutes for me to make my way toward the road. Spectators had made a mess of parking in the semi-plowed aisles. I stopped short of the curb and squinted. Sure enough, a twenty-foot red maple challenged me in all its leafy glory. My eyes had not deceived me.

Impossible.

Had spring arrived and I'd missed it?

No. The tree was mistaken, not I. It had been tricked into believing warm weather had arrived.

I had heard of such phenomena occurring at industrial sites, including Love Canal. Ten years before, in the middle of a blustery snow-storm, scientists discovered two mature weeping willows in full bloom. Mystified, the research crew determined that chemicals around the base of the trees had raised the soil temperature, signaling the trees to blossom. Was that what was happening in Malvisti Park? On *my* former property?

I felt gooseflesh prick my arm, despite my thick woolen coat and gloves. What if Sammy was right and toxins had migrated toward the school? I had an even deeper concern, plunging me further into despair. My mind flashed to the General's delivery after the end of the War. Only a handful of us knew about the hulking object interred in the middle of Malvisti Park. I'd vowed to keep it hidden. National security demanded it. After all, some secrets are just part of our shared sacrifice in the name of freedom. But what if it was causing a problem all these years later? What if … ?

Sweat trickled down my back.

I loved my grandsons, even more than my own children. I turned back toward the high school, assessing the situation with a heavy heart. Was I willing to risk the lives of these fine young men? My boys? Not a chance. Especially not after talking with Sammy.

I entered the gym and slipped into the second bleacher up from the floor. My grandsons each gave me a nod as they returned to the sidelines after the pre-game warm up. I tried to relax, inhaling deeply. My breath came in even measures, but my heart rate had noticeably increased. Worry flickered across my chest. This could be it, the Big One.

And I was at peace with that possibility.

So it was settled, then. I would either die here ... or I would handle things the Malvisti way and figure out a plan to fix this city. Someone had to. The current city leaders, excluding my son Sal, had probably never heard of the saying about power and responsibility. Couldn't these politicians see that we lived in and among a failure of responsibility? Someone had failed to lead. Someone had failed to tell citizens the truth.

Honestly, in that precise moment, fear seized my body. I suddenly couldn't speak or move my quivering limbs. The truth was as stark as the hard wooden bench upon which I sat.

That someone was me.

And Sammy, Vito, and a half-dozen other industrial leaders from a bygone era.

The basketball game had started, but I couldn't stop thinking about the past. The waste business had for years operated on primitive technology. The old, uninformed approach had worked ... until it didn't anymore. Toxins persist in the environment and in the organs of living things, causing irreversible damage. Who knew?

But there came a point when we did know—and didn't act on it. We didn't need to. No one called us to account.

Beads of water ran down my neck. A tingling sensation pricked my shoulders. This was no repeat heart attack. I was certain of that. Something else had seized hold of my mind and body. I experienced a revelation that nearly dropped me to my knees!

I could fix this.

Step one involved getting my family out of Niagara County. I would never admit it out loud, but my memoir won't be complete until I get this off my chest. It's true: I took care of my family before anyone else. Like I said before, you need to hear about my mistakes. All of them.

Joe, Jr., my daughter-in-law Carmella, and Michael moved within weeks of the tree incident. They bought a peaceful home, nestled in the lush palms of Florida. They would be safe there. Michael would continue to grow into the man I envisioned him to be: handsome, confident, uncompromising. And healthy. For his own good, I refused to allow him to be a part of our family business. He was better off going to law school. The boy had a strong sense of right and wrong.

Sal presented a tougher challenge. Politics had worked its way into the very fiber of his being. He enjoyed the recognition and the power. He would never agree to move his family. His son, my grandson Danny, was stuck as a result. I prayed that Danny would escape the health problems that Sammy's granddaughter and Vito's wife had experienced.

My second step was to focus on the city itself. At first I had little hope. Everyone knew it was in dire shape. If the number of people going over the Falls without a barrel were any indication, brokenness characterized our hometown. Things were too far gone already, weren't they?

But the ideas flowed that day on the gym bleacher. I realized that technology may have just caught up with man's needs.

I'd read that scientists had developed new sources of wind and solar energy, while others advanced novel theories for bio-remediating contaminated water or soil. Apparently, "green chemistry" had become a new buzzword on college campuses. Environmentally minded thinking had begun to take root all over the world. Why not incorporate the newest technologies here? These modern processes and techniques seemed foolproof. Not even the deceitful heart of man could screw up green innovation, right?

Perhaps it could even restore broken things—like the trust and optimism of a once-grand city.

Here was a concept that I could get behind.

I walked out of the gym that very minute. There would be other games. Already, a fresh wind transformed me. I entered that building a fearful, weak old man. I left a man energized by a new, lifesaving mission.

As soon as I could, I contacted two brilliant female graduate students already making their mark in the design of smart buildings in Europe and green technology in Israel. Why not expand their concepts further? Why not build something here that could help fix the problems that plagued Niagara Falls? My money could open up a myriad of possibilities for these two young women. For this city.

And I had plenty of it.

It wasn't lost on me that these ideas might result in even greater prominence for our family. I thought it might also relieve some of the guilt.

I tried not to think too much about the motivation. My city needed a deliverer. She needed me.

And I was confident I could fix this mess.

CHAPTER FORTY-SIX

Niagara Falls, New York

The house was largely intact but had been severely damaged from smoke and water. The roof had a large hole where the firefighters must have tried to vent the fast-spreading fire.

Lydia picked her way through the damp debris all over the first level. Through the kitchen floor vent, she heard two muffled voices in the basement. Fire investigators, she thought, as she plodded down the wet carpeted stairs. A bright work light had been placed on the bottom step.

"Oh, hello!" A short, balding man in denim overalls called out to her. He turned quickly towards the circuit breaker and flipped a switch. "You scared us there, lady."

"I'm the owner, Lydia Vallone. Do we know what caused the fire?" She directed her question to the much taller second man, who wore an official-looking uniform. His gray hair was pulled back in a low ponytail. He held a handful of tools. She realized uneasily that she was alone with two strangers in a shadow-filled basement.

"No, ma'am." The man in uniform pitched some of the tools into a duffel bag at his feet. "This one'll be complicated."

"Why is that? I smelled an oily odor when it started."

"We're working on a few possibilities, ma'am." The man dressed in plain clothes moved closer to her. He smiled at her, revealing short, even teeth. "Try and be real quiet and patient."

Lydia backed up one step. What did that mean?

She put her hand on the stairway railing. "Have you talked with Conrad Mahoney next door? He said that he had information for you."

The uniformed man fiddled with his flashlight. "We'll get to him. Don't worry."

"I'll have him call you." Lydia took another step up the basement stairs. "Can you give me your business cards?"

"Uhhh ... I don't have one on me," the man in denim patted a pocket. "Knew it would be messy business today."

"Me neither," the taller one said, without even checking. He moved closer to her. Unsmiling eyes sized her up.

The hairs on her arms prickled, like a sudden draft infiltrating a warm room. Time to go. She wasn't sure where. The only place of safety she'd known had been this house. Lydia sprinted up the remaining stairs. She moved through the dank house, nearly tripping when heavy footfalls hit the stairs behind her.

"Lady!" The voice of the large man called after her.

Lydia halted at the open front door. She could see Mr. Mahoney's porch from here. She could run if necessary, but needed to hear what this man had to say.

"You need to shut your trap." The shout came from the basement doorway. "You hearin' me?"

Lydia ran all the way to her car. She stabbed her key into the ignition, barely waiting for the van to start before she threw it in reverse. Wildly, blindly, she backed out of the driveway and nearly dropped the transmission by shifting into drive too fast.

This was crazy.

She braked at the stop sign and checked the rearview mirror. Took a deep breath.

A bee flew into the front seat with her. She lowered the window even more, allowing it to escape. She followed its jagged path until it disappeared against the backdrop of the modest homes of her neighborhood. The old ache for wholeness returned. Out there lived normal husbands and wives. Healthy children. Complete families. She didn't blame the bee for not wanting to stay.

❖

"You've been through a lot this week." Pastor Amos cleared room for Lydia to sit in the office visitor chair. His eyes watered, but thankfully he didn't say anything about the cloying smoke smell that hung from her hair and clothes.

"The understatement of the year." She opened a window and leaned against the sill. "I'm counting on the sophisticated shower system at my borrowed condo to get rid of this smell. Then I'll throw out these clothes." The acrid odor at her burned-out house had been so strong she could still taste it.

"How are the boys? Travis was holding up well when I was there two nights ago, but Harrison's cough sounded kind of rough."

"I know. He's breathing better now, but his doctors are scratching their heads over some of his test results. We need to follow up with a hematologist and a lung specialist."

"Let me know what I can do."

"Thank you. I can't believe how well they're doing emotionally. Especially since they can't count on anything anymore. They've lost so much. Their dad, their uncle. Their house … even the nearness of our neighbor, Mr. Mahoney … their sense of security. Harrison read the message spray-painted on our garage. Now he's afraid of teenagers."

Pastor Amos shook his head sympathetically. "Why would someone do that to you?"

"I think it has to do with some papers I've been given. They suggest there are some environmental problems here at the Green City." She sighed. "You know, my neighbor left town because of this information. Someone sprayed "leave" across her garage, but she had already moved.

And I'm pretty sure my friend was killed because of this stuff. I'm a wreck."

"I'm very sorry to hear that." Amos handed her a box of tissues. "Was it the guy they found at the Falls?"

"Yeah. His name was Chris, and he was a great person."

"Maybe you should go to the police."

"Not yet. I don't trust many people in this city. But can I ask you something?"

"Of course."

"Why would God let these horrible things happen in my life?" She threw the tissue in the trash. "Why did my brother die? Why was my home burned down? Why did my dad die before he was able to enjoy his grandchildren? And my mom ... she might as well be gone, too. She's just lost. The list goes on and on. I mean, did my kids deserve to lose their dad?"

Amos looked down at his hands. "I can't know the answer to those questions specifically. I'm so sorry. But I do know a few things to be absolutely true."

She looked up. "Tell me."

"God gave us the freedom to choose His Way or our own way. Some of those situations you listed are the result of people making the choice to go their own way. Some of those choices were evil, and caused the sickness or death of someone else."

"My friend Angie said something along those lines." She dabbed under her eyes with a clean tissue.

"Look, someone made the choice to burn down your home. Someone made the choice to defile our environment and possibly cause our cancer rates to soar. Maybe that's connected to your father and brother? I don't know the situation with the father of your children—"

"Another bad choice. He chose to drink and drive. We were all nearly killed."

"But know this, Lydia. God will make wrong things right. He sees the wrong that man does and he won't tolerate it."

"I saw that on a church sign the night of the fire."

"It comes from the Book of Amos." He smiled. "There will be a consequence—either on Earth or later—to sinful choices. His Word says: "But let justice roll on like a river, righteousness like a never-failing stream!"

"Well, if He cares about me or justice at all, He'll send a whole lot of people from Niagara Falls to jail."

"That's certainly a possibility. I encourage you to read the Word of God, Lydia. You'll learn about God's character. You'll see that He has a plan for you. And you'll see that you can trust Him—with everything. Your hopes, fears, and concerns. Even your cry for justice. He won't disappoint."

CHAPTER FORTY-SEVEN

Lydia slipped on her jacket and left the church. Her mind churned with the words she'd just heard. She wondered whether it was harder to let her cares flow out of her arms, as Dana taught her to do, or to give them over to God.

Scores of residents walked up and down tree-lined Riverview Boulevard. Fishing poles rested on the shoulder of more than a few fathers. Excited children jumped from one end of the sidewalk to the other. Moms carried backpacks no doubt loaded with lunch and treats. Normal families with normal lives. With the exception of the immobile turbines, everything in the Green City appeared *so* normal.

Hopefully, that was the case underground too.

She wound her way down the sloped path towards the fishing pier. Her sneaker slipped a few times on the gravel, but she caught herself quickly. A feeling of panic rose up as she remembered being in this very spot and almost losing Travis.

Lydia stopped in her tracks as feelings of every kind assaulted her.

Fear, resentment, apprehension. And all of it undergirded by paralyzing grief. But in the midst of that chaos, somewhere in between the discovery of the fish with tumors and the torching of her home, she had forgotten one emotion.

Shame.

Shame for keeping silent about a multitude of problems that plagued her community.

She—and many, many others—knew that there was a problem in the river and on the land. They all had caught enough mutant fish to know that something was very wrong. Even Mr. Mahoney himself had caught some of the disfigured fish from this same fishing spot. He personally had delivered fish with worrisome tumors to the local DEC office. But he didn't follow up and press for answers. Or write letters to the paper. And, despite his continual diatribes against politicians, he didn't even vote.

And then there was Michael.

He had said to keep quiet, that all would be made known in time. But Michael was in over his head. His safety, whether he wanted to admit it or not, was probably at stake too. Would it matter that he was the grandson of the powerful Joseph Salvatore Malvisti? She didn't think so. Too much was on the line for its living members. For its legacy, and for that of Councilman Sal Malvisti. Michael was a marked man.

You didn't need to be a scientist to see that there was a problem in Niagara Falls. Creation itself had screamed its warning. Fish species had died out. Tumors proliferated. Trees bloomed or shed out of sync with the seasons. People were sick in numbers too high to discount.

Wasn't her family proof enough?

So where were the Internet viral videos? The grassroots protests? Where were the leaked documents that could have mobilized a new generation of Earth-worshipping free thinkers into action?

Well... some of them were in her possession.

Sure, she had quietly shared them with Michael and Tyler. But not with anyone else. So far, she wasn't doing much more than Mr. Mahoney had. She'd acted no differently than the complacent residents she had resented all her life. She had become one of them. The quiet people. The ones who kept their mouths shut because to stick one's neck out was dangerous. It would upset the apple cart or devalue the neighborhood. You can't fight City Hall, she'd heard. Better to lay low.

But not anymore.

She tapped out a text to Rebecca Waters. Lydia had no idea where Rebecca stood; she could be one of the bad guys for all Lydia knew, but at least things would come to a head. And besides, something told her to trust Hessley's formidable CEO. *Let's meet as soon as you can.* Pressing "send" felt like an accomplishment. It was action.

After Rebecca, Lydia would talk to Michael and together they would take it further. The Internet or the news, if necessary.

A text from Angie's number beeped through. *"It's Andre. Angie arrested while protesting. I warned her!! ur kids with me. All ok. Working on bail now."*

Disbelief raced through her. She'd complained about people taking no action, but why had Angie taken things *that* far? What would Angie's son say when he saw her in jail?

Lydia realized that speaking up was going to cost her in ways that she couldn't even begin to fathom. Her friendship with Dana, or at least what was left of it, would be the first casualty. After that, her financial security. Possibly their physical safety. Certainly their future. How would she know what to do?

And where did God's justice fit in all this?

Confusion set her nerves on overload. Her numb legs propelled her forward, further down the pier. She was on autopilot now. Twice she failed to step aside and allow a family to pass her. She hoped that she had the will to stop herself before she walked right off the edge. Right into the swift current.

She wouldn't be the first.

An elderly man sitting on a low stool blocked her way at the far end of the structure. He was busy loading old-fashioned fishing gear into a metal tackle box. An ancient, light-colored dog napped next to him, its body curled around a white bucket. Maybe Lydia could just lie down next to the dog for a while.

Maybe she'd lost her mind.

She stared into the old man's pail, half expecting to see a tumor-covered creature struggling to breathe.

Instead, she beheld the most beautiful, silvery-blue fish she'd ever seen. Its large eyes took in the new environment while it flicked blue-tinged fins.

"One fine, fine fish, eh?" the old man said proudly.

She stepped back at its hefty size. "A walleye?"

The man looked up at her curiously. "You fish?"

"No sir, not since I was a girl. I used to fish at the creek near Love Canal, right where the water had a pretty, rainbow sheen and never froze." She wanted to add that the object of fishing then was to catch the bullhead with the biggest tumor. But her cynical tone had already been unfair to this kind-looking stranger. She considered apologizing, especially after seeing a darkness shadow the man's rheumy eyes.

"This one here's a blue pike." He used his foot to push the bucket closer to her. "Hope restored, if you ask me."

Lydia squatted to take a closer look. Her hand trembled as she reached out to stroke the nearly two-foot long miracle. "Can I watch you catch another one?"

"Wish you could, but we caught one and now we're quitting," He nodded curtly to the dog. She seemed to nod back. The dog shifted her weight and resumed her nap facing the other direction. "In fact, we're quitting for good."

"Why is that?"

"Because I've thought long and hard about this day, catching the elusive blue pike and all. I enjoyed it, especially on this nice day in this beautiful new community. But it wasn't as satisfying as I thought."

"Why not?"

"It's temporary joy." He gently emptied the contents of the pail into the water. The stunned fish hesitated before it swam away. "I've lived a long time, my dear. But for all the time I have left I'm going to focus on lasting things. Things that satisfy the soul." The man looked towards a circle of clouds that ringed the area. For a second, he seemed transfixed by the gray and pink rays of color that danced along the top tier. The dog popped her head up to look in the same direction, then lay back down, seemingly unimpressed.

"Lasting things, huh? I'm not sure anything lasts." Lydia searched the old man's lined face. She had so many questions. Maybe someone who had lived a long life could provide some answers.

"Love can last, right? And peace too—at least the kind that comes through Jesus Christ. He's the author of peace, my dear."

"I don't mean to be testy, but how do you know that?" Lydia persisted, hoping that she wouldn't offend the man with her prying. But she had to know ... and he seemed so certain.

"God's Word says it. I believe it. God has been incredibly faithful to me. I feel his perfect peace every day. I know it to be true, right here," he said, placing his hand across his chest. His knuckles were thick and arthritic, curving in ways that fingers shouldn't. "Let me tell you our story, dear one."

He told her of living a good life, but one without the blessing of children. How his wife became his world; her happiness his only focus. But then he shared what happened when he lost her, and realized that God still had a plan for his life.

"Thank you for telling me that. I'm glad you've found answers, at least."

"Now that our fishing career is over, me and Clary-girl here have decided to be joyous in living and bold in our faith, things I've wrestled with for a long time."

She nodded. Her gaze followed a migrating flock of songbirds. They settled contentedly in budding bushes all up and down the river.

"You've got some things on your mind?"

"Yes." She sighed as she knelt forward to stroke the dog's head. "Too many."

"Anything you want to share? Clary here thinks I'm a good listener."

"Then I'll throw you a curveball. I want to have that peace you mentioned." She rested her face in her hands and her eyes on a pair of great blue herons picking at darting dragonflies. Two babies trailed behind them. Lydia could no longer hold back her tears. Another perfect family.

"Now, now, dear." He patted her shoulder. "Friends call me Duff. Tell me what's going on."

Lydia ignored her cell phone beeping. She reached into her pocket and lowered the ringer. "Your faith is authentic. I want that, but I don't think that God cares for me like he does you. I've had so many disappointments. Can you help me with those doubts?"

And he did. They talked for some time, and every so often one or the other stopped to look up at the motionless turbines upriver. The machines stood as silent sentries arrayed against the thick wall of clouds moving in from Lake Erie. The way that the light illuminated the top of the circle of clouds filled her with awe.

Occasionally, noisy mallard ducks passed under the pier. Although Clary's ear twitched each time, she made no move to get up.

After a while, Lydia knelt while Duff held her hand, leading her in prayer. Their conversation changed her life, of that she was sure.

So did Rebecca's text message on her phone. *Let's meet at the Tower 3 helipad. Bring the kids. How soon can you get there?*

She thanked Duff and kissed his cheek.

Then she ran, filled with something that resembled peace. Maybe even joy.

CHAPTER FORTY-EIGHT

Michael and Ty maneuvered a luggage cart to the airline's small office at the Buffalo airport. A half-dozen bags and boxes lay stacked in front of the closed door.

"I'm in over my head, Mikey. Here, load this heavy one first. Lead-lined."

"Have you ever dealt with plutonium before?"

"Uh, no." Ty stopped loading the cart and cocked his eyebrow at Michael. "Not many people have."

"What's this instrument?" Michael pulled a bright yellow rectangular device out of a beat-up box. "It looks like something left over from World War Two."

Ty laughed. "She's a Cold War relic, actually. That's Vickie, my vintage civil defense Geiger counter. I think she has instincts. She always leads me to the right place, like a divining rod for water."

"Weird." Michael said, studying the equipment. "It doesn't sound very scientific. I thought you said that plutonium doesn't give off radioactivity that can be detected by one of these?"

"It does in very small amounts, but cesium, a fission product of uranium that forms in reactors, emits gamma particles. It's often found alongside plutonium. This will help me get a better picture of what's at the site. Plus, I have some hand-held radiation survey meters."

"Vickie sounds like our best shot at getting the answers we need." Michael laid the instrument on the cart.

"Be careful with the white one there, Mikey. I have others, but that one is the smallest and I'm saving it for a particular sample location."

"I see it's got a radioactive symbol on it. Did you bring a hazmat suit?"

"Yep. Level B, with breathing apparatus. Best I could do on a few hours' notice. It's not gas or vapor-tight, but it will provide some protection."

"If those documents are accurate, and there's plutonium and other radioactive material at the site, how do you think they got there?"

"Could be a poor disposal job, although that would be surprising if we're talking about that much plutonium. It would've had to come from another reactor site." Ty secured the equipment, and double-checked the number of boxes. He was all business today.

"Go on."

"Could be that there's a nuclear reactor under there." Ty's eyes crinkled at the corners. "Hey, I know it's a ridiculous idea, but who knows? The government could have been using plutonium for some secret purpose."

"I may know someone with a clue." Michael kicked some boxes into a straight stack. "Do you remember Duff and Clary?"

"Yeah, the dog with no legs."

"Three legs."

"How would that old guy have any idea?" Ty looked doubtful.

Michael took out his phone and showed him the picture of Duff's name on the Gemelle Hauling diagram. "He told me they were burying a large pressure vessel in the early '50s. Maybe it's the anomaly that showed up on the electric imaging scan Lydia gave you?"

"A reactor pressure vessel?" Ty paused. "I'm not sure that any manufacturer was making them that soon after the war. Maybe just after? Nowadays those spheres are strong and thick enough to handle energy generation in the field. Temporary nuclear energy, on demand."

Michael watched him think. "Are you joking around here or what?"

"Maybe not. Listen, we're going to get to the bottom of this. I just need to test and collect some soil samples to satisfy myself that we're not blowing this out of proportion."

"Let's do what we need to be certain."

❖

"Does Tyler really need to wear that suit, Michael?" Pastor Amos looked out the front door of the church. "I saw people clear out of the park after he arrived."

"Maybe they're leaving because it's getting dark." Michael opened the double doors to watch Ty at work. A massive red maple, right near the fountain in the center of the park, served as his starting point. Moving fast, he worked his way south to the next location, closer to the river.

"He put a sign near his equipment that says 'routine testing.' That should help."

Amos looked at him skeptically. "Is there reason to be concerned? I've been hearing some rumors. One of the guys at church hooked a crazy-looking fish."

"We'll know a lot more in the next few days." Michael hadn't heard about the fish, but it sure sounded familiar.

Ty struggled in the distance with a heavy box. "Do you think he needs some help?"

"Nah." Michael closed the double doors. "He told me to stay away completely. My job was to help carry equipment and pull some items out of a construction trailer. That's just as well, because I wanted to talk with you if you have a minute."

"Shoot. I've got all evening," Amos pulled two chairs near the circular fireplace. He sat in one, resting his feet up on the stone hearth, while his hands rested on his stomach.

"I made a decision, Pastor." Michael sat in the free chair.

"To do what?"

"To believe in God." Michael looked over to see if what he'd said registered. "To put Him in charge."

Amos sprang out of his chair so fast it almost fell over. He grasped Michael's shoulder. "That's awesome, brother!"

Michael's heart leapt. He truly felt like he'd joined a different family. "I'm still unsure of a lot of things. Believe me, I talked Ty's ear off the whole way here. But, I'm trusting Him to help me learn. I'm a believer."

"Suzanna emailed me that she's been praying for you every day since Sunday. She thought that you would overanalyze things and hold off making a decision until all the proof was in."

"She knows me well." Michael ran his hands through his thick hair. "My father thinks I'm an idiot. But I'm starting to see a side of him that I'm not too sure about either. My family spent many years growing the business, pursuing influence, and making money. I don't think there's anything wrong with making money, but it's the underlying motive that bothers me."

"What's that?" Amos squared the seat and sat back down.

"To build up the Malvisti name."

"And you stayed out of it? The business, I mean."

"Yeah, and it wasn't by choice. But I thought that by working hard like my Grandpa Joe, and by playing by the rules, I could build my own name, with none of the negative associations that Malvisti Industries now has attached to it." Michael paused. "I'm starting to realize that my grandfather made some choices that aren't lining up with my idolized view of him. I worshipped that man."

Grandpa Joe, Michael realized, had revered the General in much the same way. Maybe his grandfather's warped sense of patriotism had blinded him to the real impact of his choices.

"Lots of guys think like you once did." Amos took his seat.

"I'm sorry to get so deep on you, Pastor. Aside from Ty, I haven't talked about this with anyone yet. But God's been showing me so much. I started reading the Bible last night and I didn't want to stop."

"That's one of the things I love about God." Amos bounced out of his chair again. "He provides a blueprint for loving, working, parenting, and worshipping."

"Like a manual for life." Michael got up and leaned against the heavy door. "I like that."

"Maybe more like a foundation. And everything that's anchored on that foundation—the Rock that is Christ—stands firm, even in the midst of a flood. Even a flood of toxins."

"That makes a lot of sense."

Michael took in Amos's erect bearing and high-and-tight haircut. "Were you ever active duty? On the ground, I mean?"

"Before I was a chaplain, and before my helicopter was shot down, I served in the Navy. Special Forces. Three years."

"Force Recon. Nearly three."

"Marine, eh? Well, I'm looking forward to learning right alongside you, brother. I've got some books to help you get started." Amos jogged towards his office. "Check on your guy out there, and I'll be right back."

Michael opened the front door. He stood on the top step, hoping to catch a glimpse of Ty's white hazmat suit through the trees.

No sign of his friend.

The second and third sampling locations, including some equipment, were still visible in the waning daylight. But Ty's suit didn't stand out. No one was there.

Adrenaline unexpectedly coursed through Michael's body. He felt the urge to move.

Go to him. Now.

Michael whipped around. He was alone in the small church foyer. But it seemed that a deep, commanding voice had come from someone very close, and it sure wasn't Amos's. Michael looked back outside, scanning the sprawling park for signs of movement. But the pressing feeling continued.

Then the words '*go, go, go, go*' roared in his head, unbidden.

CHAPTER FORTY-NINE

Michael cupped his hands and shouted toward the back of the church. "Pastor, I think Ty's in trouble. I've got a bad feeling something's wrong!"

He heard Amos slam a drawer. Seconds later the man emerged, struggling into a long-sleeved shirt. "I felt it too. I'm armed. You?" He buttoned the middle holes.

"Not at the moment. Scared the ex." They pushed through the front door and descended the church steps two at a time.

Both men broke into a quick jog when they reached the curved bike path that circled Malvisti Park. To their right, near the fountain, a flash of bright yellow caught Michael's eye. "Swing by there, that's Vickie."

"Who?" Amos slowed.

"More like what." Michael looked around for Ty before he picked up the metal equipment. "Ty's Geiger counter."

"Turn it on." Amos locked his arms behind his neck. "See what she says."

Michael switched a black knob. Random, intermittent clicks turned into a steady staccato pulse. A needled meter zoomed to the highest measurement.

"That can't be good. Let's head toward the water." Amos pointed southward.

Michael returned the knob to the "off" position and took off at a jog, with Amos on his heels. The river's distinctive odor hit Michael's nostrils hard. He guessed they were a half-mile away.

A strange sound echoed across the distant water. It sounded like a wounded dog, but had an eerie overtone. Seconds later they heard a succession of dull thuds. Rounding the corner, the bright white hazmat suit made it easy to identify Ty.

So did the screaming.

A bulky figure wearing a ski mask used two hands to deliver rapid-fire blows across Ty's head and arms. "Ty!" Michael's stomach twisted. He gulped heavy air and pumped his legs even harder.

Ty sank to his knees, hoisting one arm to protect his head. His other arm cradled something, but Michael couldn't make it out from this distance.

Pastor Amos had already started to pull away.

"Go, go, go man!" Michael urged Amos on ahead. The pastor was bigger and faster by far.

The assailant continued to pummel Ty's shoulders and arms. Crimson stains materialized along Ty's hooded neckline.

"Tyler!" This assault had to stop. Michael ignored the searing cramps stabbing up his side. He nearly stumbled on a branch that he'd only noticed after Amos jumped it. "We're coming!"

Ty stopped defending himself. Still clutching something, he inched backwards onto the pier.

"Watch the edge!" Amos poured on the power and pulled further ahead.

"He can't see!" Tears stung Michael's eyes. "The hood— it's ... it's twisted around his head!" Michael used every muscle to stay upright. He was coming apart, forgetting how to run, talk, breathe. He looked nothing like the soldier he was trained to be.

The aggressor's next swing missed. He struck the pier's metal railing instead. The reverberation struck dread in Michael. Rebar ... or a metal pipe. This guy was out to kill.

Amos drew his weapon and released the safety as he ran.

Another whack.

Keep your head covered ... do something, Ty! Oh God ... Michael suddenly realized why Ty couldn't keep his free arm in a defensive position. His friend's gloved hand and fingers must have been broken and useless. No doubt his arm had fractured too. Only the thick material of Ty's hazmat suit provided any protection now.

The blows did not stop. One connected squarely with Ty's body. The next missed, and the deafening crack of metal striking metal hurt Michael's ears, but it did nothing to drown out Ty's agonized cries.

They were so close. Maybe a hundred yards more.

Ty's body convulsed. But he continued to crawl backwards. *God, protect him, please!* Only the pier's lowest railing separated him from the fast-moving water below the structure.

Amos drew within fifty yards of firing range. "Drop the pipe or I'll shoot!"

The attacker ignored him.

Amos fired a warning shot. The report ricocheted across the water. "Drop the pipe! Put your hands in the air!"

Amos's demands were met with another vicious blow to Ty's shoulder. Suddenly the attacker turned and put himself between the gun and Ty.

"I don't want to hit Tyler!" Amos's anguish added to Michael's own.

Blood dripped from what remained of Ty's glove. With his head hung low, he used the respite to inch further out on the pier.

"You're dead!" Michael screamed at the assailant. His fingers itched to encircle the thug's neck and jerk it hard. And he wouldn't stop there. He'd do what every other Malvisti man would do: force the man to scream for mercy, then answer with a knee to the guy's face.

Amos reached the pier.

Ty drew himself up to rest on his heels. He swayed, and then pitched sideways into the lower railing. Somehow he righted himself. With a groan, he hurled the white sample box into the river and slumped over into a motionless heap. Ty must've had a plan all along.

The attacker didn't hesitate. He whipped the pipe low across the wood slats toward Amos and then climbed the pier's top railing.

The agile pastor jumped the skidding pole.

He's not going in that water, is he?

Amos grabbed the thug's neck. But the man swung his heavy boots over the top rail and used his heft to slip out of Amos's grasp. A splashing sound followed his plunge into the river.

Michael nearly flipped over the railing himself. His breath came in ragged gasps. "Shoot him, before he goes under!" He picked up the pipe and hurled it into the river. It washed away harmlessly in the fast current, just like the thug who had just bought a one-way ticket over the brink of the American Falls.

Amos crouched low beside Ty. All three men labored to breathe.

"Forget him, Michael. Ty needs us now." Breathing heavily, he holstered the pistol and began to pray over Ty.

With hands so shaky they were nearly as useless as Ty's, Michael tried to remove the battered remains of Ty's plastic helmet.

Sirens blared. "Go meet them at the top of the path." Amos checked for a pulse.

Michael hesitated, until he saw the amount of blood that seeped through the hazmat suit. He begged God to heal Ty, and then realized he had no real idea of how to pray.

Tears blurred his vision. The emergency lights blinded him as he waved his arms frantically at the ambulance.

"Mr. Malvisti." A shaken-looking Cascata Verde security officer reached him first. "Someone heard a shot. We got here as quick as we could. What's going on?"

Michael told him the barest details.

The officer paused to radio the dispatcher for a life flight.

"Can we get a second helicopter over to the brink of the Falls? The attacker's out there, somewhere. He had no intention of dying today."

The man nodded, speaking into his radio and turning to wave the first responders down to the pier.

The medical helicopter arrived and put down on a level section not too far from the pier. Crew members spilled out and got to work securing Ty to a gurney.

Once on board, Amos quietly explained to the doctors what they'd witnessed. Even with that advance knowledge, nothing prepared them for the gruesome condition in which they found Ty. The suit's face shield had splintered, and pieces of PVC grade plastic were sticking in Ty's bloodied left eye. His nose had shifted to the left side of his face, while his jaw stuck out on the opposite side at a sickening angle. His face resembled bloody pulp. Ty was unrecognizable.

Michael wanted to hold Ty's hand for support, but stopped himself when he saw the extent to which Ty's fingers and arm had been shattered.

"Stay with us, Ty!"

Judging by their grim faces, neither the lead female doctor nor the EMTs expected Ty to survive.

CHAPTER FIFTY

"Tyler's in a coma." The doctor's firm, businesslike voice was not unkind. She stuck her hands in her coat pockets, avoiding all eye contact with Michael. "The body can take only so much pain. We're doing our best, Mr. Malvisti."

Michael's adrenaline rush ebbed, leaving him shaky and exhausted. He held his head in his hands, wishing he could do more for Ty.

The ventilator's rhythmic rise and fall provided the only evidence that something remained to save. Bandages covered his friend's body. Straps immobilized Ty's splinted arms. A team of critical care providers moved around the intensive care unit, while two local police officers stood sentry at his door.

Questions turned in his brain. That thug went after Ty specifically. His friend was onto something.

Didn't he say at the airport that he'd had a particular box for a specific spot?

Michael stepped out. He motioned for Amos, who was waiting in the hallway, to follow him. They slipped inside a cramped waiting room. Its two chairs and small television were as stark as the options before them. For Michael, one choice stood out.

"We need to go back to the river. Right back to where Tyler launched those samples." Michael kept his voice low as he walked the length of the tiny space. "That box Ty dumped over the railing was important enough for someone to kill another human being. That scumbag used a sharpened pipe, for Pete's sake."

Amos's thick shoulder muscles tightened.

Michael continued to pace. "He meant to kill. There's no question."

"I agree with you there." Amos tilted his ear to the cracked door.

"That sample box is the one Ty reserved for a special location in Malvisti Park. He knew more than he let on. He knew exactly where to look." Michael stopped to face Amos. "We need to get our hands on that container."

"What was it made of?"

"It's a lead-lined acrylic box. Not too big, but heavy. I lifted it at the airport. 'Bout ten pounds or so."

"It wouldn't have gotten too far, even in that current." Amos folded his arms. "What are you proposing?"

"Let's go in after it. It'll be easy to locate. It's white with a pretty noticeable radioactive symbol on the front."

"Do you dive?" Amos furrowed his brows. "I know you had some underwater training with Force Recon, but that may not be enough for what we need here."

"Yes, yes. I'm a technical diver—wreck, cave, Trimix. I recently completed my cave certification with Albert Triffin in Florida." Michael lowered his voice. "I know what your training as a SEAL would've involved, Pastor. And I heard that you volunteer with the fire department as a public safety diver. Between us, we can do this."

Amos looked at the white tiled floor, kicking away a used tissue.

"Well?" Michael stooped to catch Amos's eye.

Amos looked up sharply. "Here's the thing. This is the Niagara River we're talking about. It's not a cave, it's not a lake, and it's certainly not a place for an inexperienced technical diver. The current is swift. With all the rain we had this spring, it's about 3-4 knots, minimum. There might even still be ice floating downstream."

"The ice boom was lifted weeks ago. It's pretty clear."

"Still—"

"Look, I'm competent in every other kind of diving, and I have some swiftwater experience." Michael felt like a kid pleading with his father to drive.

"There's another complicating factor. Pavati has rearranged the shoreline upstream from the pier to build its massive water intake corridors. It's not only fast, but the current's unpredictable now. It's dangerous down there, brother."

"I'm ready." Michael opened the door and leaned out to see whether anyone was listening. An officer looked in his direction and nodded. He nodded back, then pulled his head in to the room. "You don't happen to have equipment lying around, do you?"

"Yep." Amos spoke deliberately. "Two of everything, of course. And, we can borrow a thing or two from the fire department."

"If we have time." Michael zipped his jacket.

The pastor closed the door. "Meaning what?"

"We're going in that river tonight."

CHAPTER FIFTY-ONE

Michael looked past the well-lit Pavati Tower complex, letting his eyes follow the arched line of wind turbines that stretched for two or three miles upstream. None of the wind machines rotated. He marched to the end of the massive pier, hoping for a better view. Of what, he wasn't sure.

Something seemed off.

Amos shot Michael a quick look. "What's the matter?"

"I can't put my finger on it. It feels different down here tonight." Michael walked to the edge and looked underneath, where solar lights had been installed. The river appeared calm, even at their location a few miles above the Falls. He looked up and studied the darkening sky. The dense cloudbank gave off helpful light, but otherwise hadn't moved in days.

It just seemed too ... quiet.

"The turbines aren't movin' because there's no wind." Amos set down two large bags of equipment and hastily uncoiled some rope.

"You nailed it." Michael put his hands on his hips. He felt slightly better, but still unnerved. "It's weird. There's always a ten- to fifteen-mile per hour wind near the river. Do you think the stillness has to do with the cloudbank?"

"Don't know." Pastor Amos lifted his chin. "Have you ever seen a mass like that here?"

"Nope. It's like being wrapped in a giant cotton cocoon. The river sounds muffled, but I can hear higher pitches, even your voice, really well."

"Yeah." Amos unzipped one of the nylon bags. "Time to get focused on the dive, brother. Worry about the cloud formation later."

The bulk of their time that evening had been spent in preparation for the night operation. They agreed on the point where they had last seen the container. Using that location as a reference, Pastor Amos mapped out the parameters of the search pattern, leaving nothing to chance.

Michael admired the man. His measurements were accurate, and his calculations correct. If he had to find a flaw in the Pastor's dive prep, it was that he checked everything over seven or eight times. Michael was all for safety, but time was of the essence here.

He was ready to go.

"You were right about the tethered arc search pattern being our best bet." Michael laid out his drysuit. "The pier gives us a stable platform. You can oversee the dive from there ... and jump in if necessary."

"Yep." Amos clapped Michael on the shoulder, squeezing hard. "That's why the less experienced diver goes in first."

It didn't matter to Michael. He was in good hands. Michael shrugged into his SCUBA gear, whistling softly at the sophisticated technology of the borrowed equipment.

From his dive bag, he caught the soft blue light of an incoming call on his cell phone. Amos saw it too.

"Better get it." Amos snatched it from the bag and tossed it to Michael. "Might be an update."

"Michael here." He fumbled with his suit clasps.

"Mr. Malvisti."

The ER doctor's steady voice stopped Michael short.

"I've got some difficult news."

"Not Ty?" Michael sucked in his breath.

"I'm sorry. He passed away about ten minutes ago."

Michael fell to his knees, his lungs expelling every last particle of air. "What ... was he ever conscious before he ... died?"

"No." The doctor seemed genuinely upset. "We did everything we could. Again, I'm very sorry for your loss."

Michael hung up. The circle of clouds extended even lower. He thought he might suffocate.

"I'm sorry, Michael." The oppressive air absorbed Amos's voice. Either that, or Michael was about to pass out.

Michael staggered to his feet. Perspiration broke out along his forehead.

"We don't have to do this."

"No ... no." Michael fought down the urge to throw up. "More than ever ... we have to."

"Then we'll make it happen. Let's check you under this light," Amos stepped up the pace. He tested Michael's harness straps.

Time to focus. Michael fought for control over his emotions, thankful for Amos's expertise.

"Your air bars look good. Your weight belt is buckled securely—"

Michael checked a clip. He could do this, right?

"Here are some gloves." The older man offered a small smile. "You'll need some protection for your hands."

"Thanks."

"This is your search line," Amos said, handing Michael a carabiner clip with a heavy gauge rope attached. "Secure it to one of your chest D-rings; I'll be at the other end. This is your connection to me." He waited for Michael to acknowledge the information. The import of every statement intensified. Death could be right around the corner. Or just below the pier.

"Let's talk about line signals."

Michael slipped on his mask, letting it rest on his forehead. "Name it."

"One pull on the rope means that you are about to ascend, or that I think you should ascend."

"Got it." Michael adjusted the secondary regulator around his neck.

"Two pulls means that it's time to change direction."

"And three?"

"Danger. You're in trouble and I need to reel you in." Amos reversed his own mask on the top of his head.

Amos used a neoprene strap to secure a dual LED dive light to Michael's wrist. The device left Michael's hands free to search or signal. He started the once-over process again.

"I've got it. Now let me assess *your* equipment."

Everything checked out. The guy was a pro.

He slipped on the thick gloves.

"I'm going to let out the search line about seven feet at a time." Amos pointed downstream. "Remember, you're going to sweep from the area closest to the shore back toward the center of the river. You'll have a few feet of overlap on each leg."

"Got it." Michael felt the familiar pre-dive rush of adrenaline. This time, though, there was no sense of excitement. This dive wasn't for his pleasure or entertainment. It wasn't an exercise to satisfy his curiosity. And it certainly wasn't for training.

This dive, he was convinced, would reveal long-hidden secrets. Michael rested his gloved hands on his knees, intending to say a short prayer. But the unexpected sight of Ty's blood on the pier from earlier in the day sent him in a different direction. A lump formed in his throat.

Ty's sacrifice would not be in vain. "Pray over me, Pastor."

The men grasped one another by the arms, asking God for success and safety.

Michael climbed onto the top railing and swung his feet over, just like Ty's attacker had done earlier that day. The moonlight sparkled on the water as it washed under his fins. Good light. Negligible waves. God does answer prayer.

He secured his mask and gave Amos a thumbs-up sign.

"Are you ready to dive tonight?" Even in the darkness Michael could see the hard-edged soldier surfacing in Amos's countenance. His eyes locked on to Michael's own.

Michael responded to the customary inquiry with an emphatic "I'm ready." He felt confident and prepared. The entire enterprise shouldn't take more than half an hour.

But all divers learn to expect the unexpected.

Michael leapt off the railing and plunged into the mighty Niagara River, his heart racing as fast as the strong current. He could do this.

The surreal underwater landscape did not remotely resemble Florida. He'd half expected to see sunlit, aquamarine waters. Maybe a reef encircled by darting fish. But here it was darker and cooler than he expected beneath the surface. His visibility stretched four to five feet, even with the dual LED dive light. He oriented himself, and then began a rapid descent.

Almost immediately, he caught a sizeable fish in the beam of his dive light, its large mouth working lazily as it swam across his path. He had been warned about the size of the sturgeon in these waters. Still, it seemed impossibly large for a river fish.

Michael checked his dive computer. Sixteen feet. Fifteen. Seconds later, he leveled off as his light picked up the cluttered river bottom. He scanned the watery landscape, taken aback by the amount of white and brown zebra mussel shells littering the ground.

Earlier, after they'd left the hospital, Amos informed him that this non-native mollusk species had entered these waters from the ballast of ocean vessels. These filter-feeders had since spread and multiplied, threatening fish, birds, and boating. They certainly weren't here the last time he was in this river. Then, he was an inexperienced diver doing his first drift dive many miles upstream from the pier's location. Amateur pleasure diving. Nothing like tonight.

The razor sharp shells had accumulated like snowdrifts around the base of the occasional boulder. Amos had been right to suggest gloves to avoid slicing his fingers.

Tufts of green river grass poked out between the shells. Here and there, larger patches of river grass had taken root, with old glass bottles, dishes, and random items interspersed throughout. A car hubcap looked out of place, even amidst the other human-generated debris.

The line slackened so that Michael could begin his first sweeping arc. He swam close to the bottom, searching for any square-shaped object worthy of investigation. He spotted green and blue colored glass bottles, old but still largely intact. The cool freshwater of the Great Lakes helped to preserve historical artifacts, some of great significance.

Michael felt a two-pull signal. Time to turn around.

No success on the first leg.

On the return sweep, he noticed an array of tools associated with the construction of the Cascata Verde's pier. The objects looked serviceable. It was unusual to see a riverbed littered with such a variety of items. This North-flowing river was unique in other ways too. He started to pick up on the fact that, unlike the typical V-shaped valley, this river was incised in a flattened "V." Western New York everywhere bore the scars of its glacial history.

A curious bass swam next to him. Michael marveled at its size and nearness, but quickly refocused. He checked his equipment, watching his bubbles dissipate quickly in the fast current. He moved between fifteen and nineteen feet below the surface, depending on his location within the search pattern.

He saw nothing that resembled a small container.

A metal cooler caught his attention. He reached out to sweep the top. The familiar red, black, and white Genesee Beer logo materialized. Not his target.

Another good-sized bass crossed in front of him.

His disappointment escalated after two more passes brought no luck. He stuck with the pattern and worked his way further downstream.

The next leg of his sweep brought him toward the center of the river. More fish. Lots of blue pike. More bottles. More boulders. The landscape did not change, foot after foot.

The powerful light beam suddenly picked up a square white object on his left, just a few feet ahead. Michael did a double-take. Zebra mussel shells had piled up so high on the upstream side of the box that it resembled a ski ramp. He must have missed it on the shore-bound leg of his search.

With some difficulty, Michael nosed himself into the current to investigate. The thought crossed his mind that if the search rope hadn't been attached so securely, holding on to the rope would be the equivalent of underwater rock climbing.

His pulse sped up as he reached down.

A storage container. As he looked closer, it had three short legs. Spots of rust were visible through the white paint along the sides. Wrong box. He dislodged it out of frustration, kicking up a small cloud of silt and empty shells that quickly dissipated in the current.

A glimpse of bright white in the turbulence underneath caught his eye. A smaller box and a bunch more shells had lodged in between the three rusty legs. Debris must have built up around the larger storage container, hiding it from view on the first pass.

Michael brushed away the empty shells and gently pulled the smaller box out of the silt. His heart jumped. Even upside down its newness looked promising. He forced himself to concentrate on taking even breaths from his regulator to conserve air.

The weight and size were approximately those of Ty's sample container. He peered through his mask and turned it over, looking for the radioactive warning symbol on the other side.

Michael could hardly believe his eyes. He wanted to shout out to the fish slowly circling near him. The red, internationally known symbol stood out in the murky water. This definitely was the same container Ty had singled out at the airport.

When he was alive.

Ty. His stomach turned over. He could hardly believe his boisterous and loyal friend was gone. Absently, he tugged on the rope and then located his second carabiner in an attempt to secure the box to his harness.

Without warning, a hulking object barreled headlong into him. It clung to his equipment with frightening force. The impact sent both Michael and the unidentified object into an uncontrolled roll. Pain exploded across his shoulder, causing him to release the sample box into the cloudy water before he could clip it. Through the silt kicked up by the collision, Michael was able to see an arm attached to a flashlight. This was no object.

He'd been bombed by another diver.

The unexpected visitor wasn't letting up; the person clung to Michael's back and tanks with a vise-like hold. It felt like the grip of Death itself.

Images ricocheted across his brain. Scenes from his dive training, Tyler's broken fingers, even Lydia Vallone's sweet face.

This could end badly.

At least he felt ready to meet his Creator. It was just much sooner than he'd expected.

CHAPTER FIFTY-TWO

Lydia wrenched open the metal door leading to the roof. Wind from the Eurocopter AS 350B-2's spinning rotors forced her to brace herself in the threshold. The powerful craft touched down on the "H" in the center of the circle-shaped helipad. Red lights ringed the large space. The helicopter generated enough noise to drown out her boys' excited shrieks. But it wasn't enough to quell her unease.

"Follow me." She bent low to the boys' ears.

Travis' mouth moved in response, but she couldn't make out a single word. They made their way to a marked safety area until the rotors wound down, and then slowed to a stop. She wished the ringing in her ears would do the same.

Lydia shifted her bag, and placed a hand on each boy's shoulder. Although dust clung to her contacts, she was still able to discern the name of the bird, "Gem IV."

Rebecca Waters, dressed in a black cape, opened the door. "Welcome and duck real low!" Hessley's CEO crouched down, even though the sagging blades rested well above her head.

Lydia urged Travis and Harrison forward. "Boys, this is Ms. Waters, my boss. Rebecca, this is Harrison and my younger son, Travis."

"Nice to meet you, men. You're in for a treat." Still crouching, she motioned them toward her and helped them climb in. "We've got to go over a few rules first."

"Yes ma'am." They clambered up into the gray cabin. Four seats in a row faced the front of the chopper. The pilot occupied one of the two chairs up front.

Travis bolted towards the far window seat. Lydia climbed into the space next to him, and Harrison sat between Lydia and Rebecca. The women secured the boys' shoulder and lap belts.

"First rule: whether the rotors are spinning or not, we duck low whenever we get in or out."

Lydia nodded, nudging the boys to respond promptly. She needed them to be on their best behavior. Everything needed to go right tonight.

"We never go behind the helicopter. Always approach it from the side or front. If dust blinds your eyes, Lydia, stay put and squat lower. We'll come get you. I don't want you feeling around for the door."

"Got it." The boarding briefing added to her anxiety, especially when Rebecca pointed out the emergency flotation gear.

Rebecca grabbed their purses and bags and tossed them in the rear of the aircraft. The pilot turned around and passed out wireless headsets. Only the women put them on.

"Ladies and gentlemen, are we strapped and ready?" The pilot's voice boomed in Lydia's mike and earphone set.

"Yes, Marco." Rebecca's tight response suggested she was ready to get moving.

The Eurocopter's engine roared to full power. Wind from the rotors created a dusty uproar, nearly flattening the building's green roof garden.

But as they rose higher, the scene struck Lydia as especially tranquil. Soft light emanated from the stationary cloudbank still encircling the region. Blue solar lights twinkled on all over the community. Below them, the blades of the wind turbines made no movement. She sat back and allowed herself to enjoy the ride, grateful that no high wind conditions would complicate things. Before today, she never would've had the guts to do this.

"This patch of clouds forms a perfect circle." Marco's voice thundered through Lydia's headphones. "It's unreal and ... a little unnerving."

Rebecca ignored the pilot, instead directing her attention to Lydia. "Have you seen the Falls from the air?" She adjusted her headset.

Lydia's heart lurched. "No."

"Marco, swing over the Falls, would you? The lights are due on in a few minutes."

"I'll get permission, Ms. Waters, but if those clouds move, we're settin' down for the night."

Again, she ignored him. "Boys, you're about to have a whole new perspective on your hometown." Rebecca reached across Harrison and Lydia and tapped Travis' knee. "I want you to tell me your favorite part before we go home, okay?"

"Sure." Travis swung his feet and looked out the window.

Harrison stifled a yawn.

The pilot swung the machine in an arc. "The rules changed recently, ladies. We've got to follow a designated route over the Falls. We'll go about 1,900 feet over the Canadian Falls and then loop back towards the Niagara Gorge."

She looked where the pilot indicated and immediately wished she hadn't. Roiling waves raced below them to the brink of the American and Horseshoe Falls. They disappeared briefly behind a curtain of white mist before emerging as a cascade that exploded on the rocks below. She shuddered when she remembered how close she and Travis had come to plunging over that same crest.

White lights from the Canadian side floodlit the entire breadth of the Falls.

From above, the most prominent feature became the sharp outline of a deep basin, filled with billowing mist and house-sized boulders. Lydia swallowed. "I've lived here my whole life and I've never seen such a view. Boys, look how the river is divided by Goat Island to make the different sets of Falls." Lydia grabbed hold of Harrison's hand and pointed out the pilot's side of the chopper. Harrison rolled his head away from the window, blinked a long blink, and then another, before falling asleep facing her.

"How can you sleep now, Harry? This is the coolest thing ever." Travis tried to reach across Lydia and shake his brother's arm. "Wake up."

"Let him be, Trav. He's tired." No matter the cost, tomorrow she would find him the best medical care in the area.

The pilot looked as if he was heading to the Canadian side, toward the freestanding glass-walled Minolta tower, but then changed direction before leveling off and heading back toward Pavati headquarters on the upper river.

Lydia jerked off her headset and motioned for Rebecca to bend forward. "Can we talk freely?" She pointed towards the pilot's chair.

"Of course. The helicopter was borrowed, but the pilot is a contractor from Ohio. He's fine."

Lydia spoke over Harrison's sleeping form. She may as well get to the point. There was no good time to bring up bad news of this magnitude.

"I'm worried that we've got a major contamination problem at Cascata Verde. I've been given some documents that don't make sense. You need to see them right away."

Rebecca's eyes hardened.

Marco's voice crackled through the headset on her lap. Lydia hastily slipped her headphones over her head. Rebecca followed suit.

" ... the clouds have thickened. I don't like it."

"Is your visibility impaired?" Rebecca looked confused as she looked out the window. The circle of clouds hadn't moved. The night remained clear, other than the ring.

"No ... this cloud formation is just so odd." He exhaled. "I feel disoriented."

The women looked at each other and then at the boys. Dire scenarios played out in Lydia's mind, even as she looked around the cabin for the flotation devices she saw earlier. The helicopter vibrated as the pilot made another turn near the crest of the American Falls. Mist obscured their view. Rising air currents swirled around the machine until they reached a wild section of the upper Niagara River, just above the cascade. At least they wouldn't die on the rocky talus below the American Falls. Unless they went over ....

The pilot's voice cut in and out. " ... difficulty breathing ... might pass out."

Rebecca covered the mic on her headphones. "Panic attack?" Her eyes darted all over the chopper's cabin.

So this was it. The last of the Vallones would die here, over one of the seven natural wonders of the world. Lydia's heart constricted in her chest. She grabbed both boys' hands.

Travis tore his eyes away from the window and flashed a smile. "This is the best day of my entire life."

All five years of it. Lydia prayed that God would allow them a hundred more.

In a flash, the words of every one of Dana's self-help mantras came to her. Maybe the pilot needed centering. He needed to breathe. She spoke firmly into the headpiece. "Marco, open your air vents and let the air cool your face."

She saw him fiddle with the controls. "Now, try to still your heartbeat by breathing deeply and regularly."

"Okay." They heard deep and even breaths through the headpiece.

"Good. I'm guessing you've never passed out before. We all know you're well trained in emergency procedures." She shot a glance at her boss for encouragement.

Rebecca lifted her eyebrows and nodded.

"See, you're doing fine, Marco. Keep breathing. You can do this. We trust you."

"I need to put down ..."

"You're doing great." She peered over Travis' mop of hair. Only the white foamy tips of waves could be seen against the dark ribbon of the river.

"Not attempting the helipad." They heard a deep breath. "There's an area near Malvisti Park that's pretty open."

As they drew close, she could see a mass of emergency lights lighting up one section of Cascata Verde. Someone must have picked up their radio transmissions. Or Marco had signaled his distress.

Harrison remained dozing, oblivious to the danger. Maybe it was better that way.

What was it that Angie and Pastor Amos had tried to drill into her mind? Trust. Trust God for what she couldn't control. Trust that whatever God has for her and her children, that He will be sufficient to see them through.

Okay, God. Our lives are in your hands. Do with us what you will. Unless it involves crashing into that river and going over the Falls. She squeezed her eyes shut and prayed all the harder.

CHAPTER FIFTY-THREE

The bulky figure swung his arm around the front of Michael's face, ripping off his tethered face mask. Michael struggled to get out of the diver's grasp, knowing full well what would come next. His air supply was about to be interrupted.

Sure enough, the diver dislodged Michael's regulator from his mouth. It was bad enough that he couldn't see more than a foot in front of him.

Now he couldn't breathe.

His training kicked in. He located his secondary regulator from a cord around his neck. He inserted it quickly and tried to draw two breaths. No air came through. The other diver must have twisted the air pressure valve on Michael's oxygen tank, cutting off his air from that source, too.

Two can play this game.

Michael deftly reached behind him and snatched off the other diver's mask and regulator. Panicking, the figure released Michael and flailed around for his own floating mouthpiece. Michael grabbed hold of the diver's harness, wrenching him around so that he could access the assailant's air tank. Michael twisted the air valve, satisfaction filling him. The diver thrashed in the water, but held fast with one hand to the tether rope.

Facing the attacker, Michael pointed his fins straight up and kicked the diver's body away. At least he was able to put some distance between them.

His lungs burned. Michael needed air. Now.

He'd done this drill a hundred times in training exercises. Albert Triffin's words echoed in his mind: *stay calm, think, act.* Michael used the pony air tank strapped to his side, grateful for the air that instantly filled his lungs. He turned on the tank valve behind his head and transitioned back to his primary regulator. One crisis averted.

Michael relocated his target. The box had come to rest just a foot or so away. He grabbed the second carabiner and secured the box to his harness, all the while watching the other diver succumb to panic. An amateur.

Even in the dim light, Michael could see the person floundering, unable to locate his air tank valve. He was unfamiliar with the equipment. And he was alone. Only a fool would have attempted this dive without a partner.

The hair on Michael's arms suddenly stood on end. There was an unmistakable flash of light near the diver's wrist. He trained his beam on the diver, stunned to see the blue-green glow of a familiar dive watch.

Danny Malvisti.

Anger blazed from within as Michael struggled to stay in control. Flashes of Ty's vicious beating blinded Michael, tearing at him. His cousin was after the box, even if he had to kill to get it. Every fiber of Michael's being wanted to hasten Danny's death. He cried out, nearly expelling the regulator from his own mouth.

Danny rolled toward Michael, and then went limp. Danny's portable rope pouch was tangled in his harness, for now keeping him from being swept away in the current. He'd be swept over the Falls when the rope unraveled. He'd deserve it.

Danny's body waved languidly on the end of the tether. He'd slipped into unconsciousness. The ordeal would be over soon.

All of it. The family secrecy, the murders, and probably more destruction. With Danny gone, Niagara Falls would be a safer place.

Michael wondered, what was at the other end of that rope? Whatever it was, Amos could undoubtedly handle himself.

A second ticked by. And then another. Michael was suddenly torn, gripped by a feeling that he couldn't explain. Could he watch his cousin drown and live with that image for the rest of his life? Shouldn't Danny face justice for his crimes?

Another, more disturbing, thought sprang to Michael's mind. Wouldn't Michael be just like the rest of the Malvistis if he let Danny die? Kill when it's expedient. That's what Malvistis do, right?

An unworthy life rested in his hands.

Michael prayed without words. He sought direction. He listened. The answer came in the form of a feeling, starting as a nudge, and growing into an insistent shove forward, just like at the church this morning when Ty was in trouble. Over and over he felt the words spur him to action. Life and death was not up to him. Justice wasn't meted out by him. But action by him was required.

Michael worked his way over to the swaying, flaccid form of his cousin. The sight sickened him. He inflated his own buoyancy compensator, accounting for Danny's weight and the ten-pound sample container. Working quickly, Michael secured Danny's body to his gear, and then flicked off his own weight belt. He inflated Danny's BC as they surfaced.

Michael groaned when his head broke through the water. They were in the full rush of the immense Niagara River. At least forty-five feet downstream from the Pier.

And only a mile from the sign marking the Point of No Return. He could almost feel the thunder of the Falls in the distance.

He flipped up his mask, searching for Amos's muscular form.

The pier lights revealed a masked head and torso poking out of the rushing water. One hand gripped the bottom rung of a sturdy rope ladder. The other held a portable rope pouch. It was Amos, with a knife between his teeth.

"Amos!" Michael turned onto his back to pull Danny into a safe position. "Stay at the pier and pull me in. Unconscious diver!"

Amos scrambled up the rope ladder, ripped off his mask, and took hold of Michael's tether rope. Although it was less than a minute, time seemed to stretch interminably before Amos could pull two men and a box against the current. Amos tied off the rope, while Michael willed his stiff arms and legs to help lift the unconscious diver. But it was no use. His body was too cold, his mind too stunned.

"At least two-eighty in dead weight," Amos croaked. He boosted Danny's bulky form over the railing, and then hauled himself over the bar. Gently, Amos laid Danny's inert body on the wooden boards and began CPR.

Michael's legs quaked. He reeled in the sample container for which two people had paid a high price, and struggled up the remaining ladder rungs. He squeezed through the metal railing, crumpling in a heap on the pier. Shivering, he watched Amos puff air into Danny's slack mouth. "I called the EMTs." Amos announced between breaths.

"How'd you know to call?"

"I was monitoring your rope in the current ..." Amos blew more air into Danny's lungs.

Blue lips barely moved as the air flowed out.

He used two fists to pump Danny's heart. "... on your last leg ... a second dive light switched on near the pier."

More breaths. More compressions.

"I put on my night-vision goggles," Amos gulped for air. "but all I could see was a dull light moving with the current. You didn't respond after I pulled on the rope. You didn't surface right away, either."

"How'd he find me?"

"I think he tied himself off on a pylon under the pier and used your taut rope like a zip line to your location. And to the box."

Amos listened to the unconscious man's chest.

Michael could only stare mutely. Danny must've been watching them all day. Sirens drew close, their wailing sounds distorted by the water, or maybe by the stationary cloud formation. A helicopter whirred over them. It set down on the grass only a hundred yards away.

"What happened down there? Who is this?" Amos looked exhausted. He continued to administer aid.

"My cousin." Michael unsnapped his air tank and peeled off his equipment. He rolled on his back, wishing desperately he could help Amos. His numb arms were useless. "Doing what our family does best. Destruction, death."

"You didn't do that."

Michael let that sink in.

"No, I didn't. But it was close." He shifted to his stomach and crawled closer to his pastor, gathering the container under his arm. Amos's stamina amazed Michael.

For the second time that day, first responders skidded to a stop near the pier entrance. The professionals unloaded a gurney, shouting directions to one another.

"What about the box?" Amos looked over his shoulder.

"I'm not handing it over to them." Michael followed his stare. Police officers and EMTs advanced toward the pier. "Uncle Sal's got his fingers in every department of this Godforsaken city."

A vibration in the floor boards caused him to look up. Someone jumped onto the pier ahead of the first responders.

"I'll take those samples off your hands, gentlemen." A woman. With an authoritative and familiar voice. Michael shielded his eyes from the glare of the pier lights, but couldn't discern who walked toward them.

The woman's form was hidden by a dark cape and a beret perched low over her eyes.

"Who are you?"

Her perfume wafted toward Michael. He would've known that expensive scent anywhere.

"Give me the box, Michael." Rebecca pulled her arm from within the cape. "Hurry." She looked over her shoulder at the arriving EMTs. Heavier footfalls hit the pier boards.

Michael wrestled with conflicting emotions. Rebecca had the most to lose by the revelation of test results from this container. Too many lives had been ruined to retrieve it. Did he *really* trust her? Hasn't she worked with Uncle Sal for six or seven years now?

Decision time. Again. It was too much.

"*Hurry.*"

Michael took a chance, furtively passing her the sample container just as a fire captain reached them.

"We're hurrying, ma'am." The fire captain focused on Danny's still and seemingly lifeless body. "Step aside, please."

Rebecca's face softened when she caught Amos's eye in between administering breaths. Her voice lowered, but was no less insistent. "I've got a helicopter in need of a pilot, Pastor Amos. I remember what you told me about your past training and service. Come with me quickly."

He stood and held his hands over his head, his rib cage rapidly expanding.

She turned back to Michael. "Stay here with the officers and tell them what happened. The pastor and I have an emergency."

"We need to talk." Michael looked meaningfully at the box in her arm. "Can I meet you somewhere?"

"Ty needs you." Rebecca patted Michael on the shoulder. "Things will be okay. I think I know what you did here tonight."

"He's dead." Michael flinched at the finality of his words. "Ty, I mean. Dead at the hands of my family."

A soft whimper escaped from his boss. He'd made the right choice to trust her.

Amos nodded to the first responder and hustled Rebecca off the pier. Helplessness pressed in on Michael as he watched them disappear into the helicopter.

Blue and red emergency lights illuminated the rescue scene. Residents of Cascata Verde gathered all along the river pathway. A few shouted offers of help.

"We've got a pulse!" The EMT jerked his chin to Michael. "Do you know this man?"

"My cousin." Michael looked away. "Danny Malvisti."

"Councilman Malvisti's son?"

"Yeah."

The EMTs doubled their efforts. Shouts for speed grew insistent. Even the cloudbank held an urgent red hue.

Michael's stomach churned. Danny might survive his ordeal after all? The EMTs strapped his cousin on a gurney, just as they had earlier in the day with Ty. The irony wasn't lost on him. The assailant survives and the victim dies. Where was the justice in this world?

Michael narrowed his eyes, blurring the lights into formless streaks of color. The eerie lightshow would have chilled most people. But, for him, the effect commemorated an achievement. Tonight, in this innovative eco-city built next to an ancient river, Michael Malvisti escaped his family's dark legacy.

He fell to his knees and cried. For Tyler. For his family. For their lost green city, nestled within the limits of a town on a rapid downward spiral. Tears continued to fall, supplied by a hidden spring of pain deep within his soul. He wept until the reserve had emptied itself.

Then he thanked God for deliverance through murky waters.

CHAPTER FIFTY-FOUR

December 31, 2003

Tonight, I'm dictating to Tonya, my nurse. Carmella normally handles these duties, but she's taking a break. I want to talk, and I'm about out of time.

We got off to a rough start. It took two nurses to get me out of bed and situate my wheelchair in front of the window. When Tonya raised the aluminum blinds for me, bits of dust cascaded down on us.

I blinked. She sneezed and then apologized for getting dust in my eyes.

No matter, I told her. My eyes are useless. The sight I require originates in the mind. Maybe the heart.

I see only shadows now, but I'm inspired by the sweeping view that I know exists outside this window. Last week, from my room, I could still make out the city streets and the mist plume from the Falls. Now I must settle for a memory of our region's wintry landscape.

Things are still bleak. For me, and for our treasured city.

Some of it is the result of the cold season, the natural order of things. The tree-lined gorge is bare on both sides of the border. Gray rock strata is visible until spring renews the shrubs crowding each layer. Nothing grows now. The deep water pushing through the near-frozen chasm represents the only sign of forward movement. Of progress.

But more is going on here than meets the eye. As I write, pieces of limestone rock break off from the crest of the Falls, undermined by the eroding shale layer beneath it. In a hundred million years, Niagara Falls won't have this tremendous spectacle to claim as its own. The daredevils will have to move on. My friend says that the city of Niagara Falls won't even exist that far into the future.

She's wrong.

Niagara Falls will rise again, with or without the Falls. With or without me.

I've put in motion some forward-thinking plans of my own. For many years now, I've worked with a visionary architect and a developer. Together, we've conceived a plan for the world's first green city. I can picture it as if I've been there. Smart buildings. Outdoor spaces. A sparkling river that rushes by this city-of-the-future. Maybe even a vineyard to please an old immigrant like me. My vision represents the best in urban living that a human can design.

Who says man can't think his way out of despair?

Innovation is the answer.

My green city is your savior, my friends. Support it. Expect a recovery. Prepare to be cleansed, from your soul to your fingertips.

❖

In the meantime, for it will be a while before this gift comes to fruition, tainted water flows over the retreating crest line, flushing away some of the destruction that man has caused. That I've caused. Washing and purifying, sins and deeds ... I wonder, can a corrupt thing heal itself? I hadn't considered that until just now.

I'm certain of this: I need a miracle healing. Nothing will rinse away the sickness that will soon claim my body. I'm an old, old man. But I seek a new, unblemished soul, the real "me" that reflects my good intentions for this city, but leaves out the wrongheaded means I used to accomplish my ends.

I've become convinced the future city will redeem me and my family. It's the culmination of a lifetime of good deeds and bad choices, but surely its progress will outweigh the devastation I've wreaked upon this land. I'm filled with a sense of restoration, and a belief that the magnificence of Niagara will be renewed.

It feels a lot like hope.

CHAPTER FIFTY-FIVE

Near Washington, D.C.

Lydia blinked her eyes, forcing herself out of a groggy, fitful sleep. She'd been half-awake all night in order to keep an eye on Travis and Harrison as they slept next to her on a curved chrome bench. The state-of-the-art government lab had been equipped for all types of analytical emergencies, but nobody had thought to include cushioned seats for those waiting on the results.

Dr. Reginald Waters strode across the facility's sleek lobby carrying a handful of papers. A day's worth of stubbly gray growth couldn't mask the set of his jaw. The news must not be good. The dignified scientist folded Rebecca in a warm embrace. "I'm sorry, my girl."

Lydia blinked at the intimate greeting. Pastor Amos, more alert than anyone, did a double-take.

"There's nothing good to report." Dr. Waters shuffled a few pieces of paper and then laid the straightened pile on the reception desk. He cleared some pictures and personal items out of the way and sat on the corner of the desk.

"Let's hear it, Dad." Rebecca leaned over to examine the results.

Dad? Lydia hadn't made the connection between their identical last names. Pastor Amos seemed visibly relieved.

"We've got high concentrations of plutonium, a fission by-product, and other radionuclides. And, as expected in this part of Niagara Falls, a whole lot of chemistry." Dr. Waters allowed his words to sink in.

411

Rebecca tapped the first page of the report. "Let's start with the plutonium."

"Although rare, it's not necessarily dangerous until you breathe it in or ingest it somehow. Even then the body will usually excrete the particles before too long. But keep in mind that these particles can migrate from this particular land area through rain, underwater streams, or by birds and small animals. It's toxic."

"How do the birds factor in?" Rebecca frowned.

"They might eat worms carrying the particles."

Rebecca's cheek twitched. "What else?"

"These test results show extremely high concentrations of these rare radioactive particles. They're probably leaking from something on site." He gathered the papers and gently placed them in Rebecca's hand. "There's more to the report, but I thought you'd want to read it yourself. I know you're in a hurry."

She closed her eyes briefly.

"I'll have to notify people, my dear."

"Yes. Of course," Rebecca replied, acting as if they had already discussed that possibility.

Dr. Waters squeezed his daughter's arm and gave a thin smile. "Tread carefully, but get residents out of there as soon as possible."

If Lydia ignored the words just spoken, the cool and collected pair could've been talking about any minor family issue.

"Thank you." Rebecca's chin lifted. The businesswoman in her returned. "You've gone above and beyond for us. Please extend our appreciation to your entire staff." She hoisted her purse to her shoulder, already moving on to the next step.

Dr. Waters followed his daughter with his eyes. Concern mixed with fatherly pride shone from them.

A pang of grief struck Lydia in her chest. If only she had a living, breathing dad to help her figure out what to do.

Amos hefted Harrison to his shoulder. Lydia smiled her gratitude as she picked Travis up from the couch. The weight of his slack body buckled her ankle. She should've handled Harrison. Although older, he was a heck of a lot lighter than Travis.

After a helicopter transfer, flown by a fresh pilot, which caused Lydia's heart to beat faster, they boarded the private plane on which they had arrived from Buffalo. A flight attendant with a shock of pink hair had boarded before them. She handed each of the adults a mini pillow and a soft green blanket.

Rebecca slid into the seat next to Amos and called Raul from her smartphone. Lydia gathered that the attorney would join them in Buffalo.

On the opposite side, Lydia secured Travis and Harrison's belts and spread blankets over both boys. She slid into the seat behind them. The attendant dimmed the cabin lights.

At first, only the sounds of the boys in deep sleep filled the narrow cabin. Their breathing was soon drowned out by the whine of the plane's jet engines as it prepared to take off.

Lydia didn't dare speak. After the bomb that had just been dropped on them by Dr. Waters, Rebecca would surely need time to sort through things. Lydia spread her own blanket over her lap and rested her cheek on a pillow.

But despite the fatigue that enveloped Lydia's limbs, her eyes wouldn't stay shut. She wondered what Michael was going to say about all this. They'd already exchanged a few texts about Tyler, but she didn't want to burden him with more bad news any sooner than necessary. Plus, he'd said that he had something else to discuss with her, but couldn't talk right then.

"What brought you to Niagara Falls, Pastor?" Rebecca yawned, acting unfazed by the night's events.

If Pastor Amos was surprised by her calm demeanor, he didn't show it. "I read an article about the Coast Guard station on the lower Niagara

River. Something about the Niagara Frontier got ahold of me, and, well, over the years, I developed a strong affinity for the area and its residents."

"You had no other connection?" Skepticism crept into her tone.

"None."

"Did you? Before Cascata Verde, I mean?"

"Not exactly."

"Well, there you go. But I knew that God was at work in Niagara County and that I was supposed to be here."

Lydia listened with closed eyes, hoping that her eavesdropping wasn't too obvious.

Pastor Amos told Rebecca that after a helicopter accident, he'd spent six months in an overseas military hospital. He described how God used every agonizing hour to draw him closer to Him. After he recovered, he rejoined the military as a chaplain.

"Then what?"

"While stationed in Italy, I kept up online with all the happenings in Niagara Falls. I rejoiced when there was good news, and prayed when the news was not so good. I felt an unexplainable connection to the area, like I was supposed to be here. Pretty soon, I got the confirmation I needed."

Lydia's ear crackled and filled with pressure. She swallowed and then lifted her head to hear better.

"… a stocky chaplain with a thick head of hair walked into my base office in Italy. 'Captain,' he says, 'I'm Lieutenant Antonio Guardi, CHC, USN, sir. I'm joining the unit in light of your retirement.'"

"'Where's home, Lieutenant?' I asked him."

"Niagara Falls, New York, sir." Amos laughed. "Lieutenant Guardi said this with great pride, let me tell you."

"That's an amazing coincidence." Rebecca's voice had perked up.

"I could only stare at him for several seconds. I'd never met anyone from Niagara Falls. Coincidence? No. Not at all. God's fingerprints were all over this duty change."

The engine noise shifted. Lydia felt the plane slow.

Lydia couldn't help interjecting. "Did you tell Father Guardi that you had been praying for his hometown?" She wanted to get the details before they set down in Buffalo. She felt her face flush.

"Yes. Absolutely."

"What did he say?" The pink-haired flight attendant asked him as she handed Rebecca an open juice carton. Everyone but the sleeping boys had been hooked by the story.

"He said 'Captain, I've got an empty two-bedroom home sitting right smack in the middle of the city, about one hundred yards from the edge of the Niagara Gorge. I'll rent it to you, cheap.' Then he took out a set of keys, removed one rimmed in red plastic, and tossed it on my desk."

Lydia reached around the seat and stroked Travis's curly hair while he slept. She looked at Amos in the dim light, willing him to finish the story.

"Twenty-four hours later I found myself walking along the Niagara River … praying that God would use me in any way He saw fit." Pastor Amos put a finger across his lip. He cleared his throat. "That's the day I met you, Lydia, and little Travis at the river."

The day she'd almost lost her boy. Lydia wiped a sudden wash of tears with her finger. The flight attendant handed her a napkin. "Thank you."

"That gut-wrenching rescue was further confirmation that I belonged here." Amos turned to Rebecca. "This was home."

"Serendipity." But not even Rebecca seemed convinced by her own words.

Pastor Amos shook his head. He leaned over and flashed a smile at Lydia before responding to Rebecca. "God has a plan for your life and mine. It's a plan to draw us closer to Him, so that He can fill us up until we are overflowing. He's even got a plan for Cascata Verde. We're seeing bits and pieces of it unfold, but the big picture may not be clear for some time. If ever."

Rebecca turned her head away from him, her gaze seemingly locked on the miles of brightening clouds surrounding the plane.

"I ..." She seemed unwilling to continue.

"People will disappoint you, Rebecca. Every time. You've been deceived all along with this project. That's clear."

A sniff came from her boss's direction.

"But God never disappoints."

Soft cries filled the small space. Lydia didn't want to intrude, but in the dawning light she thought she saw Pastor Amos put a comforting arm around their formidable boss. Lydia averted her eyes, unwilling to witness yet another unmistakable sign of the serious circumstances that threatened them all.

The pilot made a full turn eastward, into the sunrise. As a new day broke over their beloved city, Lydia wished that she knew what awaited them on the ground. More loss and heartache, certainly. A public outcry? Evacuation? Probably a lawsuit, or two or three?

Or, if Pastor Amos was right, the unfolding of God's plan.

CHAPTER FIFTY-SIX

Niagara Falls, New York

After a cat nap, during which she dreamed she lived by a crystal clear, blue-green river, Lydia awoke to the nightmare of living in a borrowed condo built on top of a toxic mess. Questions haunted her with every step to the real estate office—what was buried below this sidewalk? What's underneath the church? Next to the office? Was radiation weakening her bones right now?

Poisons would assault her and the boys as long as she lived and worked in Cascata Verde. She had to get her family out of the Green City. Just as soon as she figured out where to go. Where to work.

She'd give anything for her dad to be here. Or for her mom to be whole again. They'd know what to do.

The office atmosphere felt as toxic as the community itself. Lydia leaned against Dana's desk as they both watched Rebecca in action. Two mobile devices kept their boss in control of Hessley's Florida headquarters. She lined up conference calls with their legal team. Ordered three Hessley engineers to get on a plane and be there by two o'clock. And her clipped tone left no room for discussion. As Rebecca worked, Lydia's anxiety escalated.

At one point, Raul stopped taking notes, and simply locked his wheelchair in place. He sat with his hands folded in his lap, just watching her.

The worst part for Lydia was that only three of the four people in the room knew that Cascata Verde's doom was inevitable. Neither Rebecca nor Raul made any effort to enlighten Dana.

The truth was that no one knew what would happen today. Last night's wild helicopter ride and unexpected flight to Washington were nothing compared to the fear, anger, and rage that would be unleashed from the families who had moved to Cascata Verde from all over the country. They had a right to be mad, just like the residents of Niagara Falls, itself. Too many people had been exposed over the years and the health effects were just the beginning. How many marriages had suffered? How many jobs had been lost? How many dreams had been shattered because people were consumed with simply trying to stay alive?

She had to believe that God knew the way out of this situation, because she sure didn't.

Rebecca pulled her briefcase onto a chair. "We've got a lot more to do today. Let's start with this media release. We're calling an urgent press conference for tonight at six. Take a stab at the language for it, Dana, but avoid revealing too many details." Rebecca scooped papers from Lydia's printer. She tossed the first several to Raul. "Read these."

Dana played with her necklace. "What's the press conference about?"

"An announcement about Cascata Verde. Be sure to notify the residents and Cascata Verde workers, staff, and anyone who has a connection with this community. Work with the Florida PR folks and get this release proofed and out the door by noon."

Dana nodded.

Rebecca's demeanor mirrored the clouds that still hovered around the city: solid, fixed, unflappable. She looked the part too. Unlike Lydia's own worse-for-the-wear appearance, Rebecca's hair and make-up team had eliminated any physical trace of the long night. No wrinkles marked her light-gray suit.

Dana pushed off the desk to get to work. She had no idea that their dreams for this development, and for their lives, were about to crumble. The green city couldn't save them after all.

"Lydia," Rebecca seemed to eye her with a new respect. "Work with maintenance and our staff at headquarters and get the church piazza set up for a press conference. If the weather holds, I'll stand on its front steps to give my statement."

"I'm on it." Lydia hurried to the other side of her desk.

"I called the Mayor, the city council, and members of the legislature." Rebecca sat down opposite Lydia's desk, her face suddenly strained. "Have either of you heard from Michael Malvisti?"

Lydia's heart lurched. For nearly a week she hadn't been able to say his name out loud. To hear it spoken so casually was a shock. "He sent me a text last night."

Both women looked at her in surprise.

"To you?" Dana's tone cooled.

Lydia cleared her throat. "He wanted me to know that he couldn't be in the office today as planned because of Tyler Morales' death yesterday. He's making arrangements with Tyler's family." She tried to control her breathing and act normal. She had nothing to be embarrassed about. Nothing significant to hide. But then, why was her heart ready to burst out of her chest?

She left out the end of the message, where Michael said that he had something to discuss. She'd turned over the possibilities all morning.

"Ladies," Rebecca packed up her belongings and grabbed her purse. She indicated to Raul that it was time to leave. "Once you've made these calls, go home and change into your best suits. Have the stylists at the eco-boutique do your hair and make-up. They're expecting you. We need to be *on* today." She stopped talking and squeezed her hand shut in midair. "And make sure Suzanna Frederick is dressed appropriately. No hippie look today."

They nodded dumbly as Rebecca and Raul left the office. Neither moved until the sound of Rebecca's clicking heels on the sidewalk grew faint.

"You're holding out on me." Dana turned her body toward Lydia. "You already know what this big press conference is about, don't you?" She tapped her pencil on a metallic herb diffuser.

"You're right." Lydia glanced at the clock on the wall. Dana deserved the full story, but there was no time. "I'll explain everything once we get it arranged, okay?"

"Give me the gist." Dana turned her pendant over and over, finally wiping her hands on her suit pants. "Everyone's on edge today and I don't know why."

"Some environmental issues have come to light—"

"Are you kidding me?" She stamped over to Lydia's desk. "You're behind this, aren't you?" She kicked its wooden front leg, causing Lydia's ultra-thin monitor to rock. Lydia stabilized it, and then backed away.

So much for being centered.

"You're at it again, aren't you?" Dana threw her pencil to the floor. "You can't leave well enough alone. I think you intentionally screw things up so that you can play the victim!"

"Dana!" Lydia fumbled for words. "I would never—"

"Stop!" Dana placed both hands in the air. "You're not ruining this opportunity for me. This eco-city is all I have, don't you get it?"

"Let me—"

"No!" Dana's chest heaved. She stalked back to her desk, accidently knocking over a handful of clear quartz she kept in a bowl. "You are negative energy personified, and you're sapping the life out of my body. Look at me—I'm so out of balance that I can't even walk straight!" She squeezed her eyes shut as she touched her knuckles to her lips. After a few seconds, she settled into the chair, color slowly returning to her face.

Lydia adjusted the screen and returned the pencil to its holder. She gave up trying to explain. A few months ago, there was uncertainty about the green city's foundation. But now the facts were uglier than anything the online eco-extremists could conjure up. She dialed Hessley's headquarters, hoping that the quaver in her voice would stop before someone answered.

An incoming call lit up the second line. Dana snatched her office phone and thumped the button. Anger hardened her face.

A Hessley staff member picked up Lydia's call. Lydia introduced herself and started to state why she was calling, but stopped short when she heard Dana say "Good morning, Mr. Malvisti."

Which one?

Dana flicked her eyes toward Lydia and faked a smile. "You need Ms. Vallone?"

The hair on Lydia's arms prickled. She ignored the attempts at introductions emanating from her own receiver. *"Ms. Vallone?"*

Dana held her attention now. Depending on which Mr. Malvisti was on the line, it was the difference between help and harm, life and death. Maybe even love and hate.

Dana paused. "Let me give you her home address, Mr. Malvisti. She moved to Cascata Verde a few days ago." Dana purposefully avoided Lydia's imploring looks.

"Ms. Vallone?" The Hessley employee's voice shot through Lydia's receiver.

Dana giggled into her phone. "She'll be there in about an hour or so. Take care." She hung up.

"Hello? Ms. Vallone ... you there?"

"Uh ... just a sec." Lydia put her hand over the speaker. She stretched the cord as close to Dana's desk as it would reach. "Was it Michael?"

But Michael knew she had moved.

"No." Dana offered nothing more.

"Ms. Vallone?"

"Who then?" Lydia whispered. Her internal alarms triggered, striving with the callers for attention.

"The Councilman." Dana grabbed her purse and walked out the office door.

"*Ms. Vallone!*" The disembodied voice shouted from the line. "*Are you there?*"

Lydia dropped the phone. Icy fingers of fear probed her body. *We're next. The alarmist and her kids.*

She rushed out the door, nearly catching her heels on the threshold. The sweat soaking her back cooled in the morning chill. The drop in temperature stopped Lydia in her tracks. The feeling reminded her of the dream that had roused her from sleep just this morning. Her mind's eye saw acres and miles of water. Floods of refreshment. Liquid had seeped through buildings, around trees, through her toes. But the impossibly dazzling substance had purpose.

Life flowed through that water.

The sun glinting off the copper spires of the church made her think. She'd responded in fear to every challenge in her life. How had she responded to cancer? Now physical symptoms of any kind sent her into a tailspin of worry. Single parenthood? She idealized so-called normal families, and despaired that hers would never meet that model. Physical harm? She had that covered, too. She stayed home as much as possible.

Hadn't she made a commitment to trust God? Yes.

Then she needed to act like it. No more cowering under the covers, no more fretting about messing up.

She would respond to today's challenges in faith.

CHAPTER FIFTY-SEVEN

Lydia rapped on Mr. Mahoney's front door. "It's me. Lydia." She mashed the doorbell, frustrated by the slow sing-song chime.

"Quit the racket! I know who you are, missy!" Her former neighbor unlatched three locks and opened the door a few inches. "Ach. Hold tight, one more." He slammed the door shut. The scrape of a chain lock against metal raked her spent nerves.

"Please hurry." She rocked on her heels, trying to avoid looking at the charred hole in the roof of her home thirty feet away. She locked her gaze on a yellow and black butterfly instead. Although the creature was as silent as the burned out wreckage she had called home, it was much easier on the eyes.

"Well, c'mon in. Don't waste all day making up your mind." The softening in his eyes at the sight of her belied his harsh tone and grizzled appearance.

"Can't." Lydia looked over her shoulder. She'd come straight from picking up the boys from Andre. "Travis and Harrison are with me."

"What's the trouble? My boys all right?" He craned his hairy neck out the front door to look for himself.

"They're fine." A white moth chased the butterfly. The insects dipped and flitted as if nothing mattered in the world. "But we need your help again. Can you come with me to Cascata Verde?"

"What happened to that one normal day you promised me?" He felt around the pocket of his gray workpants for his keys, grabbed a Yankees hat and wooden cane from just inside the door, and stepped out to the porch. "Let's go."

Just like that. Mr. Mahoney was as reliable a friend as they come. Words of thanks caught in her throat. "I ... I'll explain on the way." She hooked her arm in his flannelled one and helped him down the porch steps. Monarch butterflies alighted on the flowering bushes outlining his porch. A pretty day, if you ignored the loss of a career, house, sense of safety ... and the green city.

"You driving?"

"Yessir." Lydia kept her tone gentle. They both knew his reflexes had slowed. He offered no argument.

The boys waited with the passenger door wide open. They hugged the old man, crowding him as he used his cane to slide backside-first into the company hybrid Lydia'd borrowed. He pulled a stiff leg on board. The other followed, but not before the boys bombarded him with questions.

"Didja see our house on fire?" Harrison patted his shoulder with affection.

"The windows are boarded up!" Travis flicked his ever-present slingshot in the direction of their empty former refuge. "See it?"

"C'mon, shut those doors now. All kinds of pests trying to come along for the ride." He swatted at a bee that found its way into the vehicle. Two others buzzed in the inside corner of the windshield. "Pay no attention to that house there. It'll be fixed up fine. We'll be buddies again before too long. I'm workin' on getting some BB guns for you boys."

Lydia didn't have the heart to tell him she'd never go back.

"There's an important press conference today at Cascata Verde, Mr. Mahoney. Will you stay with the boys inside the church? Angie spent the night at the jail, which I'll explain later, but she's getting out soon and will meet us there to help. I brought marbles and books to keep the boys busy."

His eyes cut sharply in her direction. "You don't just need a sitter, I know that much. Should I read more into this? Something with the politicians?"

"Yes." She buckled her seatbelt and started the car.

He scowled. "Nothin' but nothin's gonna happen to those boys on my watch."

"I know." She cast a smile in his direction. That's exactly why she came here. Who else would've thought to tie a rope around a child fishing at the river? "This is the last favor I'll ask of you, I promise."

He looked skeptical, grumbling under his breath. "You still owe me one normal, worry-free day, missy."

"I do." Still smiling, she directed the hybrid toward Cascata Verde. This time she returned with reinforcements. One old man. Two kids. Three bees. And an awesome, all-powerful, all-knowing God.

❖

For the first few minutes of the drive, the boys rolled down the windows and seemed to be content watching the passing scenery. Mr. Mahoney seemed pensive. Even the upper river minded its own business and flowed noiselessly toward the Falls. Barely a ripple marred the waterway's glassy surface. Her eyes registered the tall cottonwood trees lining the road. White puffs containing thousands of seeds sailed through the air. The torrent resembled snow in some places, even piling up in drifts near the curb and against buildings.

The trees held another surprise. Red-winged black birds lined the cotton-laden branches. Their chorus of "oka-lees" competed with blunt honking noises. High in the air, Canada geese flapped in formation, returning north for the season. The region teemed with signs of spring. There was vibrancy to the air that hadn't been there in a long, long time.

"Gorgeous day, isn't it?"

Mr. Mahoney didn't respond. She'd caught him sleeping. The boys, too, seemed on the verge of a nap. Being alone with her thoughts wasn't appealing. It was as good a time as any to start preparing for the logistics of the press conference—

A black and white blur streaked across the road in front of the hybrid. She slammed on her breaks. "Uh-oh!"

Mr. Mahoney cried out. He held his free hand over his heart. "Tryin' to give me a heart attack, missy?"

"An animal. I'm so sorry." She felt terrible.

"Just a raccoon, Mom." Harrison turned to Travis. "Why's it out during the day?"

The animal scurried across the road, but continued to run in the same direction as they were driving.

Lydia's pulse returned to normal. "Everything's all right, guys. Just relax."

A pack of skunks hurried across the road.

"Look out!" Mr. Mahoney gripped the door handle. "Stay the course, hit 'em if necessary."

Her heart jumped in her throat. She slowed to avoid hitting the two creatures trailing at the end of the pack. The boys screamed. With inches to spare, the animals cleared the front bumper.

She pulled to the side to catch her breath. Odd. They followed the same path as the raccoon.

"No tellin' what's going on today." Mr. Mahoney's bushy brows furrowed.

"Have you ever seen this much wildlife out here?"

"Not in years." Mr. Mahoney took off his cap and scratched the back of his head.

"Maybe they're all going to the Green City meeting!" Travis offered.

They all laughed. Lydia accelerated with care, scrutinizing the clumps of trees lining the riverbank. Swarms of sandflies bounced off the windshield. She pressed a button and wet spray fanned out, removing living and dead bugs.

"Watch for the deer!" Travis shouted from the back. "A mama and her two babies ... just like us!" He punched Harrison in his excitement.

She eased to a stop once more. The rusty-brown doe tweaked her graceful ears back and forth. Her trusting eyes gazed at them before she nudged her skittish family along the shoulder. From the shrubs next to her, a pair of orange-breasted robins took to the air, startling the two fawns.

"My eyes must be bad." Mr. Mahoney leaned forward in his seat. "But I'm pretty darn sure there's a bunch more coons following that mama deer."

"Wow!" Travis repeated the word over and over.

"What's that dark cloud up there, Mr. Mahoney?" Harrison strained against his seatbelt to show their neighbor.

Despite her curiosity, Lydia forced herself to keep her eyes on the road.

"That's no cloud, son." Mr. Mahoney shifted forward.

"What is it?" Harrison's voice wavered.

"Birds." Her neighbor opened his window. "Starlings, by the looks of it."

Shadows passed over the hybrid. More birds. "What do you make of it?"

"Don't know." He rubbed his eyebrows with his thumb and forefinger. "Sign of a strong eco-system, that's for sure."

She took it extra slow the rest of the way to Cascata Verde.

Lydia placed her thumb on the newly installed security pad. Officer Biondi zoomed out of the booth carrying an envelope. He nodded to Mr. Mahoney. "See that red-tailed hawk up there, boys? She just caught a mouse."

While they twisted in their seats to look, he tossed a legal-sized gray envelope into Lydia's lap. "Left here for you. Didn't see who dropped it."

Lydia stiffened. Wax sealed the top. Someone had handwritten her name across the front. The precise writing didn't look familiar. She shoved it in her briefcase behind Mr. Mahoney's seat. "We didn't think we'd make it here alive. Creatures everywhere."

"Lots of people reporting unusual sights today." The officer leaned on her door. "One guy almost ran over a handful of redbelly snakes on his way in here. Scared him half to death."

"Cool!" One of the boys shouted from the back seat.

"Really?" She only half-paid attention to the guard. The envelope rattled her thoughts. Who would send it? Chris was gone, Mara had moved. And Dana would never have communicated with her in this way.

"Everything ok, Ms. Vallone?" The security guard bent low. "You look white as a ghost."

"Just shaken from the drive," she croaked.

"You guys be sure to head home early tonight."

"Nite."

Biondi hesitated before heading back toward the security installation. Either he was afraid of the squirrels perched atop the roof of the security hut, or he had something more to say.

"Ms. Vallone, I'm not sure what to make of those clouds around here." He gestured towards the soft bank. "They almost have a weird glow, don't they? Reminds me of that Pavati Tower Miracle."

"Lots of things have a weird glow in these parts, Officer."

The man's laughter faded as she drove into the heart of the Green City.

CHAPTER FIFTY-EIGHT

Lydia thought that the Cascata Verde church looked like the site of a rock concert three hours before showtime. Hessley employees dressed in green and blue hemp/cotton golf shirts struggled with sound equipment and wires. A woman scowled after an unsuccessful microphone check.

Two men dropped a sign containing the Hessley logo just as she and Mr. Mahoney walked by with the boys. Rattled, they steered the boys through the chaos to Pastor Amos's office in the back.

At least the pastor's office was quiet and tidy, just as Lydia imagined it.

Angie slipped in behind them and hugged the boys. "It's getting crazy out there, girl!"

"I'm so glad to see you, Ang." Lydia embraced her friend. "We can talk about the arrest later. I might know a good lawyer."

"Look at all those birds, Ms. Angie!" Harrison pulled her over to the corner window. The sea-green river sparkled in the distance, its banks alive with great blue herons and double-crested cormorants.

"Thank you both for doing this." Lydia placed a hand on Angie's arm and called across the room to Mr. Mahoney. "I wish I could tell you what to expect today, but I don't know."

"No worries." Angie patted Lydia's arm. "Remember, we know who's in charge."

"Who?" Mr. Mahoney's eyebrows knitted together.

Before she could answer, Amos's computer powered down. "Did you touch it, Trav?" Lydia searched for the on/off switch. This arrangement might not work after all.

"Nope." The boy lifted his shoulders.

She believed him after Harrison nodded his agreement. "Listen, I've got to go. The press conference starts shortly. Be good. Mr. Mahoney and Ms. Angie are in charge."

"Thought so, missy." Mr. Mahoney leaned against the doorframe. The boys were in good hands. She planted a quick kiss on his whiskered cheek and left.

❖

Lydia prayed as she returned to the church sanctuary. God, give me the words, the attitude, the peace that you've promised. Soften Dana's heart towards you. Soften it towards me. Keep us safe.

Despite her prayer, the unease in the room was palpable. Dana stood on a chair in the center of it all, impatiently directing workers on different tasks.

"What can I do?" She stood beneath Dana's towering presence. Her friend looked striking in an off-white, scoop-neck dress. Probably bamboo.

"Nothing. There's no electricity here or anywhere else in this city. The techs are checking to see if it's county-wide."

"Can we rig something?"

Dana ignored the question. She shouted instructions to a worker before looking back at Lydia. "Why did you bring Angie?"

"She's helping Mr. Mahoney with the kids." Lydia chewed her fingernail. Dana more than anyone should know why she didn't want to leave them alone. "Why did you tell Sal Malvisti where we live? He's dangerous, and I don't trust those people."

"No worse than your Jesus-freak friend in there."

"What are you talking about?" So much for a softened heart.

"She's part of that fanatical anti-Hessley group." Dana spit the words. "For all I know, you're secretly part of it too. Maybe you'll get arrested next."

"No ... no, what are you saying?" Lydia couldn't find the right words to respond. Someone jostled her. The room noise grew louder. "She's not against Hessley."

"Not buying it." Dana raised her eyebrow. "Call Rebecca. Let her know what's going on with the power."

Maybe it was best to do as Dana asked. There'd be time to talk after the press conference. She pulled out her phone and pressed the power button, but no amount of clicking would restore power to the device. "Does anyone have power or cell service?"

Everyone within earshot checked. All shook their heads.

"It's county-wide folks." Michael Malvisti's appearance caused even more of a stir.

Lydia wasn't sure if the commotion was the result of what he announced, or the result of his position with Hessley. She only knew the reason for the uptick in her heartbeat.

"Do we do this press conference without power?" He addressed everyone in the room.

A chorus of "nos" rang out.

"I disagree. Let's do it." Dana jumped off the last rung of the ladder. "We may not have a microphone, but it seems important to Rebecca that this take place today. Maintenance will find a generator."

"Okay. Let's get to it." Michael turned to Lydia and guided her by the elbow outside the church. "I need to talk to you."

Questions raced through her mind. The familiarity with which he touched her arm spoke volumes. "I'm so sorry about Tyler. I know you were great friends."

He appeared too choked up to speak. He held the door for her and nodded.

Lydia wasn't prepared for the mass of moving people that greeted her outside the church door. Citizens streamed in from every sector of Cascata Verde. She knew the energized crowd would need facts. In just the past two days, a man had been beaten to death, and another nearly died after jumping off the pier. This community of unexplained miracles had turned into crime city.

Mayor O'Donahue shook hands with residents. Off to the side, she saw the group she'd seen a few times before, holding hands—and still praying. In the midst of the throng, she immediately recognized Councilman Sal Malvisti, and another man who looked just like him. Maybe a member of the councilman's ever-present entourage? Another Malvisti? She swallowed.

She chose to focus on the Malvisti man beside her. "How are you holding up?"

They found two chairs tucked along a curve in the stone patio. From here, she could keep an eye on the councilman and the front door of the church.

"I'm wrung out." He leveled his gaze at his uncle. "My family was behind the attack on Ty."

Lydia felt the blood drain from her face. No one was safe with Sal Malvisti walking the earth. "I'm so sorry."

"And it's very hard to tell you this, but I'm pretty sure my cousin, Danny, torched your house." Michael's face screwed up. She could tell he was on the verge of tears. "He may also have murdered Chris."

"Oh—"

He drew a breath.

"Is that what you had to tell me?"

He exhaled slowly. "There's more. So much more. I need to back up to a few days ago. I've ... made some changes in my life. Became a believer in Christ, and I'm looking at everything differently now. Especially my family." Michael seemed to flush as he looked at her for a reaction.

Lydia's mind reeled. "I don't know which thing to address first. Let's back up."

"To the part about your house?" He looked directly at her.

"No, no, no. We can talk about that later. Get back to the part about finding God." She touched his arm. "Tell me why that was important for you to mention."

He gave a wan smile. "I've thought long and hard about it, Lydia. I've helped build this incredible Green City from the ground up, only to have it destroyed by lies. It's like a monument to everything bad in human nature. Or all that's wrong about the Malvisti family. I don't know why I didn't see this before, but all my Grandpa Joe's notions about respect and power were wrong. Completely wrong. I'm like this city—I had no foundation that holds firm. Until recently."

"I sound like a broken record, but I'm so, so sorry." Lydia swiped at a tear under her eyelashes. "About everything."

"You?" His voice cracked. "Please. My family's hurt you and every other person in this city in ways we're just beginning to see."

"It's not your fault."

"Feels like it." He shook his head slowly. "I'm watching my life, my career, and my skewed perception of my family legacy get rocked from every direction."

She studied his face. A torrent of emotions played across his handsome features. He looked over her shoulder at something beyond the stone terrace that must've caught his eye.

She turned in time to catch a cluster of hovering blue dragonflies. Lavender smells wafted up from the area behind their chairs. She closed her eyes and inhaled deeply, savoring the rich handiwork of God. Her career and any hope of financial or physical security had unraveled before her eyes, but still she felt strong and alive. The insects' hum resonated with a re-awakening deep within her soul.

"Where do you stand with God, Lydia?"

"Well, there's quite a story there. Hang on." She turned in her chair to scan the growing audience. "See that man over there? The elderly guy with the pretty dog? He sat with me on the pier yesterday and talked with me about life and faith. Changed my life."

"Duff and Clary?" Michael's eyes widened as he waved to them.

Clary's ears perked up. Duff flashed a mischievous smile as he waved back.

Now it was her turn to be curious. "You know them?"

"Oh yeah, but that's a story for later." He shook his head. "I can see God orchestrating so much in my life. I'm speechless."

She nearly slipped her hand in his, but checked herself.

He opened his palm. The invitation plain. "I want to see you, Lydia."

Her heart skipped. "I'd like that."

"We can take it slow, I know that there are children involved, and I know that—" He stopped talking as Dana and Rebecca made their presence known. Raul locked his chair in place.

"It's time to start." Rebecca nudged Lydia's briefcase with her open-toe shoe. "Can you move this out of the way?"

The envelope! She pulled her bag out from under her chair and felt around inside the zippered pocket section. Arms folded, Dana glared when Lydia pulled out the packet and handed it to Michael. "I almost forgot. This was delivered to me on my way in. I haven't read what's inside, but I'd rather you look at it first."

He scanned the first few pages. His face tightened.

"Look at that later, Michael. We have enough concerns here, starting with the fact that we don't have a mic." Rebecca turned on her stiletto heel and walked to the podium. The crowd quieted, even as the chirps and twitters of birds, insects, and squirrels seemed to grow louder. A woodpecker's insistent knocking on wood echoed throughout the square.

"Ladies and gentlemen," Rebecca's voice exploded across the piazza. She cast a surprised look toward Raul.

He shrugged. "Keep talking as long as they can hear you."

Confused, Lydia looked around for some type of amplifier. She didn't see one.

"Let's get started, folks. I assume you can hear me in the back?"

Scattered yeses could be heard.

"Today I have news for the Cascata Verde community that is difficult to deliver." People exchanged glances. "Nonetheless, my responsibility to the community is to be open and honest about the process of bringing this city to life."

Reporters forced to use pens and paper pressed close. The audience grew restless.

"Part of the preparation for this green city involved scientific studies and reports. The studies were done by an environmental company, Tomeo. All of those studies confirmed that our green city had been properly remediated and was safe for living, working, and recreating."

Lydia cringed. She did not envy Rebecca and the weight of responsibility on her shoulders.

"We've just learned, however, that Tomeo falsified the data for those studies."

A collective gasp rose.

"We—"

A juvenile bald eagle alighted on the podium. It tucked away its black and white mottled feathers, nosing its dark beak toward Rebecca. She took a step backward, her mouth open. A hush fell over the audience. A minute later, the parent flew by, let loose a high-pitched whistle, and then perched at the top of the tallest church spire. Chirps and tweets from other birds filled the air, their songs joining a downy woodpecker's whinnying call. Deep honks and piercing caws echoed across the distant river.

Hundreds of winged creatures swooped and darted, many coming to rest along the church's elegant roofline.

Lydia held her body rigid, only relaxing after Michael grabbed her hand.

"God's Creation has showed up to witness this day," he whispered, for her ears only.

She shivered. "My son, Travis, told us the same thing on our drive in, but what are they here to see?"

"Restoration, Lydia." His gaze swept the entirety of the piazza. "I can feel it."

CHAPTER FIFTY-NINE

Rebecca seemed frozen in place. Her head hung low, and it seemed as though she was trying to collect herself.

Residents shouted questions at her. "What's here?"

"Are we in danger?"

"Will there be an evacuation?"

A voice from within prompted Michael to stand. After yesterday, he knew better than to ignore that voice. He dropped Lydia's hand and inched towards the edge of his seat so as not to scare the eaglet. He reached his boss in two long strides and asked if she wanted him to take over. She shook her head. "I need a minute more."

"Folks," she continued, "at some point today, there will be answers to all of your questions. But I need to address something else, first. I'm not a religious person. But over the course of the past few days, I have had the feeling that this difficult situation arose in this community for a reason. There's a bigger plan here, bigger than you or me. Maybe it has to do with the fact that our largest tenant is in the bioremediation business. It fixes contaminated soils and waterways." Rebecca paused to let that statement sink in. "Maybe this contamination needed to come to light so that it could be remediated the right way. With truth and accountability as our guide. I think the answers will soon become clear."

Low-key applause arose from pockets in the crowd.

"The original vision for our city was to build a monument to all that man could accomplish while leaving the smallest footprint on this earth. It was an enormous display of talent and know-how. I wanted to honor people, animals." She straightened. "I believe we were meant to live in harmony with one another."

The mayor shouted his encouragement. Like Michael, he must have sensed that, in sharing feelings, Rebecca Waters swam in uncharted territory.

"I got some things backwards."

Pastor Amos jumped up onto the platform. Cries of 'Pastor Amos!' rang out from the crowd.

Amos broke out into a smile.

"I've done everything in reverse order. I built a city to worship created things, and not one dedicated to worshipping the Creator. And I'm very sorry for that."

Rebecca's slim shoulders began to shake. Pastor Amos put an arm around her.

Michael kissed her on the cheek. "Let me handle the rest. I've got some information you don't."

CHAPTER SIXTY

"Ladies and gentlemen." Michael felt his voice resonate across the crowded piazza. Newcomers continued to file in. "I'm Michael, and yes, I'm a member of the Malvisti family and a Hessley employee. Ms. Waters did not have a chance to read some new information delivered to us today. It came straight to Lydia Vallone, a woman who has lost her home, her security, and so much more, to uncover what's happened here. But I've read it, and I think it needs to be shared with you."

The sea of expectant faces waiting for him to continue humbled him.

And one of those faces, he realized, belonged to his father.

He stepped up the pace, knowing that time was important. Although he couldn't see Uncle Sal, he knew the man would tear out his vocal cords to stop him if he were able. And he knew he'd have only minutes before his dad skulked out of the crowd and made tracks for Florida. Everyone, including his father and uncle, needed to hear some hard truths about the Malvisti family.

"Tomeo Environmental, the company that for many years conducted the environmental studies, remediation, and testing here, is indirectly owned by Malvisti Industries. As you probably know, the Malvisti family sold or donated the land upon which this amazing green city was built. Tomeo and Malvisti Industries told the world that this land was safe. It wasn't."

439

Cries of alarm escaped the audience.

"I have in my hand pictures documenting the misdeeds of some members of my family. The photographer included detailed soil and air test lab reports to back up the pictures. These results appear legitimate."

People moved towards the church steps. Or maybe toward the spot where Sal Malvisti was last visible.

He hurried.

"These lab reports match sampling results that a Hessley employee obtained yesterday. That employee, my friend Tyler Morales, was brutally attacked while collecting those samples. He died last night as a result of his terrible injuries."

Michael understood the uncertainty playing across many faces in the crowd, some of whom he recognized from Pastor Amos' church. Before them was a Hessley employee with a prominent name. He had everything to lose by exposing his well-to-do family. Most men in his position would keep their mouths shut and lawyer up. But they didn't know that Michael Malvisti had a new boss with new rules.

Before he could continue, a light-haired man bounded up the church stairs. He stooped to examine the eaglet, and then held up an envelope identical to the one held by Michael.

"John Palowski, sir. I took those pictures."

Michael shook his hand. That name was all over the envelope's contents.

John turned towards the residents. "I'm here today for one reason, everyone. I want to see wrong things made right. I want to see justice carried out."

Tears filled Michael's eyes. But something closer to terror clouded those of the officials in the front row. Uncle Sal had disappeared.

"Ms. Waters," John stepped back to include her in his line of vision, "I will assist you in any and every way possible. As the viticulturist for Cascata Verde, I've been testing this land for the past several years. It took a while, but as construction progressed, I eventually figured out that something unusual was leaking at the site. I supplied the information in this envelope. Here's another copy."

A sweet-smelling breeze stirred, gently swaying the package. Nearby flags flapped, causing metal grommets to strike metal poles. The noise brought a certain solemnity to John's promise, Michael imagined. And the new scent in the air? Something else altogether.

❖

Lydia knew John-what's-his-name from school, but where had she recently heard the Palowski surname? Maybe the list of Polish workers on the Gemelle diagram?

Dana's gasp interrupted her. But the connection came together for Lydia a split second later. She'd heard the Palowski name while standing on her porch talking to a scared television reporter. "Mara Stanton's family. You must be Mara's son!" The guy who'd never met his grandfather or great grandfather.

"Yes, that's right."

"Obviously you left the envelope for me this morning, and you sent things to me through your mother ... but did you recently leave another one on my doorstep?"

"No, Lydia." He shook his head sadly. "That was our friend Chris Magnano. We'd worked together quite a bit in the last year. I'm sick about what happened to him."

"I don't get it. You were all working behind my back?" Dana's blue-gray eyes turned icy hot. "To take down Cascata Verde?"

"I can explain." Lydia stood.

Dana shooed her away. "I don't want to hear it from you."

The breeze became more insistent. Lydia noticed the birds had quieted. Adults in the crowd looked as distressed as she felt. She closed her eyes and breathed deeply. The faint smell of ripened fruit filled her senses.

"I can almost taste it." Suzanna joined them on the church patio. "Niagara Falls has never smelled so ... delicious!"

"It's a steady waft of air." Lydia licked her finger and stuck it in the air. "And it's blowing straight down."

"That's impossible," Dana snapped. She craned her neck to observe the turbines, perhaps hoping to find some type of explanation. For the first time in days, the stately machines turned steadily, oblivious to the nearby commotion.

Duff motioned to Lydia from the front of the crowd. She cupped her ear.

"Ask that fella John Palowski what's buried in Malvisti Park."

John had heard him and answered immediately. "It's an experimental nuclear reactor. The first of its kind, and part of a Cold War weaponizing program. Workers like my grandpa buried it. The regular guys had no idea what they were handling. Some of those people died of radiation sickness or cancer, and others were simply eliminated. They were casualties of the Cold War."

"So, we've all been exposed to radiation?" Suzanna gripped her pregnant belly, her face crumpling in fear.

Lydia patted Suzanna's back. "We don't know everything, yet."

Someone cried out. "Is Malvisti Park radioactive?"

"I'm disgusted." Dana covered her face. A sob escaped between her fingers. "All of this incredible design work—all of these natural resources—going to waste?"

But Lydia's thoughts suddenly went in a different direction. One that shook her to the very foundation of her soul. She'd lived all of her life near this site. This was probably why most of her family died of cancer. Why her son was sick.

This was why their city was dying.

❖

"Your dad's coming up here, Michael." Rebecca's voice softened, but still it reverberated across the piazza. Residents were hanging on every word. "I had asked your parents to come today."

"You talked to my mom and dad?" Michael sucked in his breath.

"Yes." She shifted feet, but held his gaze. "I knew your Grandfather Joe, too. He supported me ... I should say, us, because he tasked me and my former colleague with developing innovations in water technology and bio-remediation. Together we conceived the idea for Cascata—"

"No more!" Michael fell to his knees. How many lives, including his own, had been manipulated by Joseph Malvisti?

"He had good intentions, a good heart, Michael." Her tone was not unkind. Rebecca stretched her arm and cupped the back of his head. "You remind me of him in so many ways."

"Good intentions?" Michael didn't believe what he heard. "Did you know what secrets he'd kept? He's destroyed you, this city, every person who ever crossed his path!"

"He wasn't a saint." She looked over at the bench where Sal Malvisti had been. "And people will pay for some of the choices made over the past several decades." Her voice dropped off.

Joseph Malvisti, Jr. limped up the stairs. Michael rose to meet him.

His father avoided his gaze. But his steady voice carried across the piazza long before he reached the podium where the young raptor still perched. "I ask for a few minutes of your time, folks."

Michael wanted to ask his dad if he was sure about this. But he didn't. He needed to hear what his dad had to say more than any resident in the audience.

"I'm Joe Malvisti. Many of you look at me as a son of privilege. And rightly so. My position, wealth, and name all worked together to provide opportunities that most people never have. Unlike most of you, I could have helped this city during its slow decline. I could've spoken up about the dark side of our family business and other industrial concerns.

But I didn't.

I ran away instead. I choked off the words that my conscience wanted to shout from the highest mountaintops."

Michael squeezed the tears from his eyes. He'd never expected to hear these words from his father. Of course, he'd never expected to stand eye-to-eye with an eaglet, either.

"Fleeing bought me a load of guilt," his father continued. "Self-reproach colored my existence, robbing me of all joy. I see gray every-where—in the lush surroundings of my home in Florida, even in the worthy life of my only child." He inclined his head toward Michael. "I withdrew from just about everyone."

"Dad ..." Michael choked up.

"The shackles of shame have kept me entangled in a small world. I bear the most responsibility for this mess, you see. I had the education. I knew the limits of technology. I've shared seventy-plus years with my brother Salvatore. I should've had enough of a conscience for the both of us. But a conscience amounts to nothing if the person is too cowardly to act on it."

Rebecca and Amos flanked Michael. First the string of confessions at Amos's church. Then the revelations over the past few days. Now his father. He wasn't sure he could take any more.

"This week, my wife forced me to read my father's long-hidden let-ters to this city. They're his memoir, really. She's kept them in a box on her dresser for more than two decades, wrongly believing I'd be curious enough to remove the carved lid and look inside. I'm going to release his memoir to you. Sure, it's one immigrant's history of Niagara Falls. But it's more your story than mine now."

Michael regretted not investigating the contents of that wooden box when he'd had the chance. Then again, his father might never have read them if Michael had gotten to them first.

"He admits to a lot of bad decisions. You'll see that he humbles him-self, in a way. I might not have honored my father as I should, but can say with confidence that he was a hard-working, self-made man who truly loved this city. He would help out strangers and always make sure you had a good meal or a place to stay. No matter what you think of our family, even you might agree that the man had a good heart."

The benevolent man described by his father was the grandfather Michael knew and loved. But others today saw a man who lacked any concern for the health of thousands of people. Mixed emotions tore at Michael. How much more could be revealed today?

"Joseph Salvatore Malvisti left this life with many regrets. Now that he's gone, I don't want you to be misled about a matter of eternal significance. For my father missed something when he wrote that memoir. He died clinging to the last vestiges of pride. Papa offered himself—a mere man—as your savior. He wasn't perfect. Neither am I. We're human, and we sometimes make bad choices. But my father's poor decisions conflicted with God's Word. New technology can't erase the defilement here, folks. We can't fix this. Just like in matters of the soul, man's efforts to redeem or restore always fall short."

Pastor Amos wiped away tears. Michael's own soul was about to bust wide open.

"But I learned something recently. It's through the perfection of Christ that God reconciles to Himself imperfect people and things, including our environment. Jesus the Redeemer doesn't fall short. He can right this wrong."

"Amen to that." Amos clapped Joe on the shoulder. "Go on, brother."

"Today I'm reconciled with God. And even though I'm a sick man, physically, I'm ready to break out of my suffocating world and take real action. There's much to do. Complacency can no longer be tolerated in this town. Sure, Niagara Falls has been laid low. But it's time to rebuild on a proper foundation. One that's dependent on truth, accountability, gratitude, and ... perhaps even forgiveness."

Someone clapped. Michael and dozens of others joined in, although he was still processing what his father said. And did he just hear his father say he was sick?

Soon, thousands of people put their hands together.

"Thank you."

He embraced Michael until shouts of alarm erupted from the piazza a few seconds later.

"Watch out!" A man in a baseball hat shouted to the audience. "Water's heading this way!"

"The river's flooding!" another person cried.

High-pitched screams pierced the air. People scrambled to stand on benches and lawn chairs. Craned necks searched the riverbank. Some broke through the crowd to get a better look or searched for higher ground. Terrified adults pulled eerily calm children along by the arm, urging them to hurry. Like the children, none of the birds, animals, or deer seemed alarmed. If anything, the birds resumed their cacophony of calls as if nothing were amiss.

Michael wasn't sure what to do first. But as he watched Lydia disappear through the church doors, he knew that something life-changing was upon them.

CHAPTER SIXTY-ONE

Mr. Mahoney's white pallor scared Lydia. "Don't be afraid of the water," she sputtered. "We'll get out of here before it reaches the church."

"It's not that, missy." Mr. Mahoney pointed behind the door. "It's him."

She turned to her right, knowing intuitively who was there. But instead of seeing Sal Malvisti's face, she was greeted by the black barrel of a gun.

A sense of calm radiated through her bones. She didn't flinch. "What do you want?'

"I don't want to hurt you, or anyone else in this office." The councilman's voice seemed unsteady. "But I want my nephew to come with me out the back emergency door. We've got a matter of justice to work out between us. Get him now. I'll take out the old man if you tell anyone what's happening here." He jerked his silver-haired head toward Mr. Mahoney and Angie. "And maybe the girl."

"Thank you, God," she heard Angie say.

Lydia willed her boys to stay quiet while she processed what to do. Sweat trickled down the councilman's face. His bloodshot eyes darted from her to the opposite corner where the other two adults stood in front of her sons. No way would she leave any of them behind with this madman.

Over the noise of the commotion outside, Lydia heard footsteps across the sanctuary.

"C'mon, Lydia." Michael's rich voice reached them before he did. "Get everyone rounded up in there and let's clear out."

Sal yanked her suit jacket, pulling her toward him. He grabbed a fistful of her hair, forcing her to her knees. She heard a cry from one of the boys, then heard Angie shush them both, telling them it was going to be okay.

"Lydia?" Michael entered the office. His eyes widened. "What do you think you're doing, Uncle Sal?"

"You're coming with me, Michael."

She heard a metallic click. The councilman must've released the safety on the gun. "Cooperate and this will end well for them."

Lydia's eyes locked on to Michael's. Despite his calm demeanor, something fierce burned there.

His gaze shifted above Lydia's head. "I'll go with you. Let her go."

Michael's father hobbled into the crowded office. Again, she was awed by the striking resemblance to his brother, the councilman. "Michael's not going anywhere. It's over, Sal. Everyone knows what we've done. I made sure of that."

The councilman didn't release her hair, which had become ensnared in his sweaty palm. He let out a short laugh. "There's more, Joe, much more. And if you were smart, you'd get out of here and disappear like you did all those years ago. This time, though, Michael's coming with me."

His lookalike's face turned ashen. "We agreed to leave my boy out of this."

"Things changed when he hurt Danny. A son for a son."

Lydia saw movement from the corner of the room. Although she couldn't move her head, she thought she saw Travis wriggle away from Angie.

What was he doing?

"You're a desperate man, Sal." Joe moved forward. "Put the gun down."

She chewed her lip to avoid shouting and drawing attention to Travis. In a practiced motion, her son crouched low, sighted his slingshot, and let something fly.

No! She ducked, ripping loose a fistful of hair, just before a dull thwack could be heard over her head.

The councilman cried out. A marble dropped on the floor next to her and rolled under Pastor Amos's desk. She thought she saw a trace of blood in its wake.

Michael and Mr. Mahoney moved toward Sal with surprising speed. She crawled away just before Mr. Mahoney's cane found its target in the councilman's side. "I always knew you politicians were no good!"

"Mom!" Travis took her hands and tried to pull her out of the fray. Angie and Harrison joined him and Lydia found herself swept across the floor to safety.

"Thank you, God!" Angie repeated to herself over and over.

When she looked back, Michael was kneeling on top of the councilman, who was face down on the floor with his arms pinned behind his back. Blood trailed down the older man's damp face. Lydia wasn't sure whether he was conscious or not, but she didn't care. Her family was safe, for now. Color had returned to Mr. Mahoney's face.

And Michael was here.

She took a deep breath and sat up.

Angie riffled through Pastor Amos's desk drawer and produced a length of bright yellow rope. She tossed it to Michael, who used it to bind up the councilman's arms.

"I'm Joe." The man who resembled Sal Malvisti offered his hand to Lydia. "Michael's father. Your little one did a good job over there. Let's get moving—we've got some water heading our way."

Lydia accepted the help and stood, smiling her thanks. "This is surreal." She put a hand on Harrison and Travis' head. "I can't believe what a great shot you are, Travis. Thank you, my love."

"Been practicin'." He turned to Mr. Mahoney and gave a thumbs-up.

"And thank you, Mr. Mahoney." She kissed his cheek. "That one normal day we always talk about? It will come, bear with me."

"No, it'll never happen. But that's okay. I'm here for you and my boys." Mr. Mahoney poked at the councilman once more. He turned to Travis and Harrison. "I know this is a little scary. But you both acted like fine, brave men."

"We're fine." Harrison looked at Lydia and shrugged. "We'll be all right."

"Let's get out of here, fast!" Lydia peeked out the window. All she could see was water. "Oh, wow ... lets hurry."

"Don't worry about the flood, Mom. It's not gonna hurt us." Travis looked at her as if she were overreacting. "It's part of a plan."

"Yeah, Mom. It's a good thing."

What did they know?

On second thought, the boys did guess correctly where the animals they saw on the way to Cascata Verde were heading.

By the time they squeezed out onto the stone porch and passed off the hand-tied councilman to two stern-faced state troopers, quiet had descended over the piazza. Hundreds of people stood openmouthed, most looking down at the luminous, crystal-clear water submerging their ankles.

❖

Michael needed to see the source for himself. He cupped the back of Lydia's head and pressed his forehead close to hers. "Wait here for a sec."

He motioned for John Palowski to follow him, and together they jumped down the steps, and ran around the building. The vertical wind blew stronger outside the shelter of the church overhang. Shivers coursed through his body.

The claims were true. A shallow expanse of river water had reached the higher elevation of the piazza. It lapped against buildings, and swirled around objects in gentle eddies. Ripples etched steadily outward, all the while seeming to defy the laws of nature.

"Are the Pavati filter installations flooding?" John asked.

"Possibly." Michael wondered if they had become plugged, causing a massive rerouting of the Niagara River. "It seems to have stopped, though."

Both men returned to the front of the church.

"It's gotta have something to do with the wind." Michael spun in a slow circle, looking for any explanation.

A full-grown eagle joined the baby perched on the podium. Pastor Amos stretched a tentative hand and stroked its neck, shaking his head in apparent wonder.

The strength in the raptor's talons would be sufficient to gouge out an eye or two, Michael knew.

"Hold up here, guys. These creatures know something we don't."

Michael caught Amos's meaning. Was this God's hand at work?

CHAPTER SIXTY-TWO

Lydia set Travis down on the top step, mesmerized by the hint of turquoise swirling through the dark water. The blue-gray hue had intensified until it resembled a polished sapphire. Its ethereal reflection bathed everything—and everyone—in an impossibly fantastic light.

She had seen the river look this beautiful somewhere else.

The dreams.

Thousands of people and animals stood rooted to their spots in the softly lapping water. Panic that had struck people dumb only minutes earlier had given way to a collective fascination.

Lydia was sure Michael was experiencing the same thoughts.

"You can't analyze this one, Mike." Pastor Amos put his hand on Michael's shoulder. "I know you're a fact man. But how do you explain this? I mean, this eagle is as tame as can be."

"I'm in awe, Pastor. Everything looks and sounds more vibrant. My senses are on overload."

"Smells good, too." Travis breathed an exaggerated breath.

A rumbling sound emanated from Malvisti Park, close to the stately maple tree at its center. Tiny waves danced across the thin sheet of water that covered the grass and concrete pathways.

Lydia wasn't sure if she *heard* the sound or simply felt it reverberate through her body. The decibel level was so low that it seemed to originate deep within the bowels of the earth and gain intensity as it rolled toward the surface.

She was almost too stunned by the noise to realize that the vertical wind had stopped.

Michael grabbed her free hand, their arms resting on Harrison and Travis's shoulders. A faint whirlpool seemed to rotate near the maple. She squeezed tighter after a large sucking sound gave way to a circular depression that immediately filled with water.

The crowd retreated from the area around the maple tree. Nervous cries echoed across the piazza. The top of what appeared to be a large metal sphere worked its way to the surface. Judging from the size of the visible portion, she guessed it was probably the size of a small house.

Men and women alike reacted with alarm.

"A septic tank?" A man dressed in work clothes shouted. "Those pop out of the ground all the time."

"... more like a bomb?" a woman shouted. But even she didn't move.

The massive, dark object held them in its pull. Hundreds of capped pipes stuck out of the sphere at random points. It resembled a metallic sun, devoid of life and light.

The emergence of the cold sunburst created a small ripple in the water that gathered momentum and spread out in ever-increasing rings.

Lydia had seen this object before. Or, at least its rough silhouette on the scans that Chris had dropped on her.

She shivered. The black and white scan could never have conveyed the foreboding vibe emanating from the sphere. It felt unnaturally sinister, and wholly manmade. Like something corrupt that the Earth just had to spit out. Seconds later, first the roof, and then the cab, of a rusty, deteriorated backhoe sprang to the surface next to the mysterious sphere. It bobbed and the hulking objects clinked together. Emblazoned across the side of the backhoe were the words "Gemelle Hauling, Inc., a division of Malvisti Bros. Enterprises."

❖

Michael nudged his father to force Uncle Sal's body around. Let the man witness what the Malvisti family had inflicted on the people of this city.

He heard a small cry escape his uncle's lips.

A young woman broke away from her male companion. She waded closer to the machines. "Something's inside the backhoe!"

A man followed, grabbing the girl's shoulder to stop her. "Stay back." He shouted for others to come forward and help.

Michael motioned to a police officer to join him. Dread filled him as he slogged through the shallow water. The officer shined a flashlight into the narrow, rusted compartment. Wet, straw-like hair poked out from under a faded cap. Mud-stained denim overalls hung over a skeleton.

Michael wondered, briefly, if the bones belonged the one of the Polish workers who'd buried this object many years ago. Whoever he was, he'd been there for a very long time.

CHAPTER SIXTY-THREE

The shock of the sad discovery began to wear off.

"Do you feel it?" Lydia knelt in the water next to her children and Mr. Mahoney.

"What?"

"Peace." She cupped the water to her lips, inhaling deeply. "Peace like a river."

Others were noticing it, too. It flowed through the crowd as people stood in the water. Lydia's toes and feet tingled. She felt a massaging sensation encircle her lower legs. Health and well-being flowed upwards, through her torso, and out her arms and fingertips. A renewed vigor burst forth from her soul.

"Yes!" The boys plunged their hands in the shallow water, splashing tentatively at first. Soon they'd soaked each other, and their neighbor, laughing.

"My joints don't ache." An elderly woman flexed her fingers.

"Clary!" Duff exclaimed. Duff was on his knees in the water, hugging Clary around her neck. "My knees don't creak!"

"Mom, it's a present from God!" Travis gathered water in his small hands, then dumped it on his head.

"We knew that inside the church." Harrison's chin was set, as if challenging her to disagree.

Lydia looked at him curiously. "How did you know?"

He simply pointed to his chest. Or maybe his heart.

She flicked some water at Angie. "Do you think kids can be more in tune with God's plan than adults?"

"Wouldn't be the first time." Angie gathered both boys in a hug.

Rebecca leaned over to Amos. "Is this what you meant by God having a plan?"

He nodded. To Lydia's surprise, Pastor Amos reached out and swallowed Rebecca in an embrace. She didn't let go.

Even Dana's features softened, especially after she glanced at John, who had tears flowing freely down his face.

In the stillness of this awesome revelation, before the emergency vehicles arrived and the people fully realized the scope of what was happening, Lydia knew that Niagara Falls was somehow saved. She didn't know if science or God, or both, had accomplished it, but she knew it to be true. She knew it in her heart. Just like her boys had known.

❖

Snatches of conversation reached Michael's ears. Pavati's bioremediation facility must've overflowed, some said. A hundred year flood had occurred. Another miracle took place.

He was certain of the latter.

Michael used his hand to shield his eyes from the setting sun. The surge had infused water into every inch of the homes, buildings, and parks of Cascata Verde, and had spread as far as his eyes could see. The Pavati towers rose from the shallow water like glass and stone monoliths, but held strong. Michael smiled when he saw that the graceful wind turbines had resumed their tranquil turning. Aside from one boy's slingshot, they were likely the only machines functioning properly in the Green City.

From a distance, he could see that the vineyards had a renewed beauty about them. Super-sized green grape flowers graced the leaves, even though May was still early for blooms. Closer in, shiny new leaves flitted on the branches of the trees surrounding the Piazza. Nature's rules, as men understood them, did not apply today.

If this was just a glimpse of God's restored Creation, he could only imagine what God had in store for them in the future.

His gaze swept the area where the river should have been, had it stayed within its boundaries. Its green-blue-tinted water seamlessly connected with the shallow deluge that had swept across Cascata Verde. Birds buzzed the surface just as fish arced out of the water. A handful of deer lapped up the liquid, edging near people as if they were no more threatening than a tree.

The river sparkled. Never had he seen any body of water so arresting, so inviting. What an incredible contrast to the dark, swirling waters of last night's rescue dive. Just hours before, the fast-moving current and the darkness of his own heart had challenged him. But he had emerged from the waters triumphant. Today those same waters washed everything clean. He, too, felt restored.

As Michael looked out at the chaotic and wonderful scene before him, he was certain of only a few things. That God is real. That Christians should love the things God loves, especially Creation. And that he and his friends— maybe even his father— would be at the forefront in preventing, confronting, and responding to environmental defilement. No complacency here. God had entrusted him to build truly green cities, founded on the solid Rock that is Christ.

And he felt something else deep within his soul. He was falling hard for a brave woman named Lydia and her two children. Michael searched her and the boys out, eager to share this moment with them. He found her leaning over the side of Raul's wheelchair, holding the attorney's hand. Rebecca held his other one. Behind him stood a group of residents five deep, each with their hands upon the shoulders of the person in front of them. And each praying mightily. The dignified man's chin hung on his chest. Michael reached them in time to see tears streaming down Raul's face.

"I saw it!" Rebecca rested her head on his. "You're not imagining things!"

"I saw it too." Lydia's voice shook. "Your foot moved! Try it again."

The women stepped back. The group that had been praying gathered around the wheelchair to watch. Raul bit his lip, gripping the sides of his chair.

His toe moved up and down. Rebecca led a chorus of cheers from the group.

Amos sank to his knees, pulling Michael down with him. "Pour out your favor, Father God. Restore this region. Heal our people. Let the Revival begin, Lord!"

ABOUT THE AUTHOR

Christen Civiletto is an attorney, author, and adjunct law school professor.

She's passionate about exploring the intersection of faith, environmental justice, and the law, and has devoted tireless efforts to helping others appreciate such a connection. She enjoys staying up on current events, reading great fiction, hiking in South Carolina, and spending quality time with family and friends.

Christen experienced a wake-up call after wondering why she and so many other residents in her hometown of Niagara Falls, New York, were dealing with cancer or other terrible diseases. She began to research the area's environmental history, and her findings led to the writing of *Green City Savior*—an environmentally themed suspense novel set in Niagara Falls. Ultimately, Christen's research resulted in the recent filing of a series of lawsuits stemming from the historic Love Canal disaster.

Christen previously authored *Full Disclosure: The New Lawyer's Must-Read Career Guide* (ALM 2001), a practical mentoring guide for first through fourth year lawyers. She co-authored *The Practice of Law School: Getting In and Making The Most of Your Legal Education* (ALM 2003). Her articles have appeared in national print and online publications, including *The National Law Journal*, NYLawyer.com, and law.com.

She resides in Western New York with her husband and four children.

Please visit **christenciviletto.com** for more information or to visit her author's blog.

Reading Group Guide

1. Christians often view environmental issues through the lens of stewardship of the Earth's resources, as commanded in Genesis 1:26-28. What does stewardship require, at a minimum? Conservation or resourcefulness? Do you think Christians should work to prevent, confront, or respond to environmental degradation?

2. Green City Savior explores the justifications given for environmental defilement during WWII and the Cold War-era. Massive amounts of chemical and radiological wastes were haphazardly dumped, buried, or stored during those years. The excuses were numerous: National security demanded it. The needs of the nation took precedence. People were expected to sacrifice in the name of patriotism. But, now that we understand the devastating impact of some of those choices, the question must be asked: when, if ever, is there a justification for sin? What circumstances would support wrong choices? Why should we now revisit those long-ago choices? Joseph Malvisti thinks it'll help us make better choices for the future. Do you agree?

3. Do you believe that the natural world will be restored? If so, will that restoration take place on the earth or in some heavenly realm?

4. Michael Malvisti begins to believe that his family's notions of respect and power are misguided. Are there family values that

you've internalized that don't necessarily line up with the Word of God?

5. Dana DuPays loved all things green. Can people make an idol out of environmentalism? How so?

6. How can society's move toward a sustainable future can reflect the character of God?

7. Do you believe that miracles still happen? What about healing through modern medicine or technological breakthroughs like a bionic arm—are those miracles?

8. Have you considered your role in God's redemptive mission to reconcile to Himself all things—defiled creation, corrupt people, or flawed green innovation—through Christ?

9. Some early Jewish apocalyptic literature describes the renewal and perfection of Creation in vivid terms – abundant fruitfulness, numerous trees, oversized grapes. Why might Niagara Falls provide a good backdrop for a glimpse of restored Creation?

10. Green technology is a fast-breaking area of invention rife with overblown claims or flawed designs. In the book, readers may identify the similarities between today's eco-technology and the speedy development of the nuclear age, another time when solutions were implemented before scientists fully appreciated the risks. Would you agree that although mistakes will be made as we make technological advances, sin cannot be tolerated? Why or why not? How do we balance the benefits of technology against the potential for harm?

11. The Green City can be a metaphor for the best that humans can design. Why did it fall short? Why couldn't it save this declining city?

12. Is there anything that can stand if Christ is not the Chief Cornerstone? A life? A family? A city?

13. The characters in the book, including those claiming faith, all wrestle with *how* they should respond to widespread environmental devastation. Some ignored it. Some fled from it. Some stood up to it. Some did nothing more than blame others. Who got it right? Did anyone take it too far?

14. The Falls themselves are an agent of cleansing (symbolizing the washing away of sins) and erosion (symbolizing decay as the Falls recede backward). How is it possible for one media to both benefit and harm mankind? Is this in any way analogous to the Word of God?

15. Environmental issues affect all people, regardless of race, religion, or nationality. Shouldn't Christian novelists be writing fiction that influences or shapes the way people think about the care of Creation? What about innovations in technology?

16. Writers like Whitney R. Cross have long referred to Western New York as the "Burned-over District," an area shaped in the 1800s by waves of religious revivals. These revivals were characterized by mass confessions, physical healings, and large numbers of people acknowledging Christ as Savior. Do you believe that revival today is possible? Is God still in the miracle business?

What might you expect to see during a revival? Would you be skeptical about those claiming to be healed as a result?

17. Do you think that God will eventually rights the wrongs of this world? If so, what about people who never are healed physically? What about children who die of their illnesses? What if those illnesses were likely caused by someone else's wrongful choices—will those wrongs ever be addressed?

18. Have you ever blamed God for wrongs that, in reality, are attributable to an injustice committed by someone else? On the flipside, have you ever taken credit for the wrongs that are made right, instead of acknowledging God as the originator of that justice?

CPSIA information can be obtained at www.ICGtesting.com
Printed in the USA
LVOW11s1920150715

446367LV00012B/221/P

9 780986 116308